Dragon

THE HALLOWEEN BOYS BOOK TWO

KAT BLACKTHORNE

Cover by Shanoff Designs

Editing by V.B. Edits

Proofreading by Krys

Lore Consulting by Eric Titus Albion

Chapter Art by Turning Pages Designs

Formatting by Kat Blackthorne

Song lyrics by Kat Blackthorne, edited and performed by Orcus Auditory

Author's Note

Dear Gothic Romance Lover,

You hold in your paws a story about demons, vampires, dragons, werewolves, the devil, death and all the passion and adventures they share as a budding polyamorous unit. Within those characters are stories of trauma, loss, identity, and deep love and acceptance. It is my hope that you find comfort in these pages. With that said, this is a dark and twisted tale. Our monsters all have their particular tastes and proclivities. Content warnings include but are not limited to: sleep play, red substance play, *several* graphic love scenes, graphic violence, monsters and imagery some may find disturbing, fictional occultism, witchcraft, rituals, and biting… lots of biting.

There are many more, so be sure you check them under the book on the author website before proceeding. This is not a Dracula retelling, though it is loosely inspired by vampire lore and old Hollywood horror. This is not historical fiction or a true representation of each occult theme explored. This is a villainous, monster story where the bad guys get the girl. Ready your sails because you're about to venture into vampire territory. I hope Onyx steals your heart.

Xo,

Kat

For all the melancholy girls… you are exquisite.

&

For everyone who wants their vampires less glittery and more bitey.

Vibes

Dragon's Playlist

Onyx's Cassette Tape

Dragon's Mood Board

Death's Love Song

BY ONYX HART

Verse
    Bella, belladonna I am dying
    for your taste
    Would you ever let me taste you?
    Can I burn my soul to keep you warm?

Chorus
    I offer her my fire and my blood.
    She is my flame I am her cinder ash
    The melody I've been seeking
    Is sweet death in her red kiss

Verse
    Bella, belladonna
    How long will you let me suffer
    Your current of lonesome pulls me under
    My cursed stairwell in the woods invites
    Our gruesome paradise

Bridge
    I step off your plank, through your door,

Screaming in your forbidden forest
Bleeding dry my onyx heart
In offering to love's death song

Chorus
I offer her my fire and my blood.
She is my flame, I am her cinder ash
The melody I've been seeking
Is sweet death in her red kiss

(Whispers fade out)
Bella, my belladonna
Deadly Nightshade, Wolf's Bane
Devil's cherry
Beautiful Death
Sweet poison
Death's Love Song . . .

LISTEN TO ONYX SING AND PLAY THIS SONG ON THE AUDIOBOOK.

CHAPTER 1

Onyx

NO JUSTICE FOR OLD MEN

> There may be a great fire in our hearts, yet no one ever comes to warm himself at it, and the passers-by see only a wisp of smoke.
> *Vincent Van Gogh*

The opposite of love isn't hate; it's death. Your dreams dying, resolutions and loyalties writhing on the floor. On the other side of the door of love is a funeral for who you thought you were. A mirror revealing who you hoped to be as a distorted and idealistic farce. And if it's romantic love we're talking about? God help you, it's a funeral for two. The opposite of love, the ending, the goodbye to who you hoped you'd be together.

I'd witnessed a lot of death and very little love in my two hundred years of existence. Normal beings would seek out the latter. Unfortunately for me, normal was far too boring. I chased after death, taunted it, played with it, finding it in the oddest of hiding places. I pushed its rules and barriers, seeing how close to the line I could dance. And then, sometimes, I'd coax death out from hiding and revel in the satisfaction of meeting it face to face. God, how I loved a good murder. But death was Blythe now, too, wasn't it? A reaper. My mate was a reaper. My

Claimed, as the demons would call it. My blood simmered in knowing agreement.

The spindly blond human tapped her heel. What was her name again? I forgot my clients' names often. Who cared? The woman wrung her sweaty palms as the sadist entered the room. The heavy weight of her anxiety tightened my shoulders. For such a small mortal, her emotions were so loud they were deafening. Sometimes I could block out the feelings of others, but lately, it was damn near impossible. Most vampires only felt others' emotions during sex, but I was cursed to feel them constantly. "This will be over quickly. It's open and shut," I assured her. Her tired hazel eyes found mine, and she nodded calmly, though I sensed her heartbeat pick up as he neared.

Cemeteries, haunted houses, hospitals, morgues—none of them felt as strongly of death as a courthouse did.

Opposing counsel—didn't know his name either—sauntered over. I didn't stand, only asked, "We good?"

We'd met in chambers with the judge yesterday. It was an open-and-shut domestic violence situation. The girl had photo evidence, abusive text messages, and an email confession from the fucker. I'd convinced them all to reach a deal where the human scum did hard time and fucked all the way off so this woman could live her life without his interference. The attorney tapped the table, and my client jumped. "We're more than good, Hart," he said a little too happily.

I raised an eyebrow. Bored. Already bored.

I glanced over at his jackass woman-beater client. And they called me the monster. I may have had the blood of hundreds on my hands, but I had never hurt a woman. And I'd sure as hell never defended anyone who had. My clients were those in need. It was the only reason, I suspected, that Ash Grove, my haunted holding place, had allowed me to venture just outside its borders for all those years. Though now that the curse was broken, I could go wherever I wanted. I knew who I wanted to find, but I had no fucking clue how to find them. And all I could think about was Blythe. It was why I'd gone back to work. Law was a distraction. A safe distraction.

Mr. Domestic Abuse Charge met my gaze and smiled. The fucker smiled. Ah, my teeth felt heavy in that moment. My fangs wanted to rip into him. He looked like a screamer. How I could make him cry in agony … *No, not doing that.* Laws, rules, and due process would suffice. He could rot away in prison.

The judge entered the room, and my client bit her nails. "I'm not going to have to testify today, right?" Blondie whispered.

"No, this is just sentencing. Easy, quick—"

The judge rumbled, "Mr. Hart, disrespectful as ever. You may consult with your client outside my court time."

My answering dazzling and pointed grin made Judge Middleton swallow. I felt his flash of fear. At least there were some sort of survival instincts buried under his robe. I remembered this judge's name because he was on my watch list. More and more abusers were filing charges first so that their attorneys could request the Honorable Judge Middleton. Why? Because he was crooked, that's why. Not today, though. Not under my watch—

"Well, this is a simple case, folks," the Judge barked.

I leaned back in my seat, still hearing the fast beating of my client's heart. I casually moved a knee over to touch hers. With a small breath, I sent her peace. Her pulse slowed immediately. If my curse was feeling others' emotions, my blessing was the ability to change them. A gift from the other half of my bloodline: Dragon.

I tuned out the judge's legal speak. *Section blah, blah of laws yadda, yadda* … "In conclusion, there is nothing left to discuss—case dismissed." The gavel clanked. My client gasped and put a hand to her mouth. *What the actual fuck?*

My chair loudly scraped the floor as I stood. "Your honor, no. Absolutely not," I challenged. It wasn't professional, but what the hell did I care? "You're mistaken. We submitted evidence, and he admitted to at least one count of domestic violence and alluded to the others—"

The attorney clapped his client on the back as they snickered, now sitting firmly in their seats to watch this judge hand me my ass.

"Mr. Hart, again, if you had been paying attention. I can see why your clients don't pay you. Because you don't earn your wage. The evidence was inconclusive. We don't know whether those photographs were altered. And with how crafty Ms. Willis seems to be, she likely sent the email confession herself from Mr. Sher's address. There simply isn't enough here for a conviction, and frankly, I'm not eager to ruin a man's life today. Though you always seem to be more than willing to bring down honorable men who've made a few mistakes, Mr. Hart. I suggest you advise your client on how to be honest in a court of law."

Ms. Willis sat frozen. Stunned, still under the influence of my touch. "You're implying she went through all of this," I gestured around the room, "for what? Just to ruin a man's life? Ah, yes, the villainous temptress, the life-ruiner, *femme fatale* angle. Mr. Sher is living in his mother's basement and can't hold a job for longer than a month. It looks like he's doing just fine at ruining his own pathetic life. Oh, you know, on top of being a violent menace to society."

Judge Middleton's face went red. "Your behavior is the height of unprofessionalism, Mr. Hart. And frankly, I'm tired of seeing you in here, week after week, with little lying housewives. Coaching them in how to pretend to be pitiful just to end a man's career and garner attention and sympathy—"

I moved around my table and took two steps forward. *A big fucking no in court world.* The bailiff was at my side with several labored footfalls, and the judge took a step back. The police officer took my elbow. "Come on, Onyx. Take a walk."

"Hey, Sal," I said lowly. "I think you want to take an early lunch and clear the waiting area, don't you?"

The man's jaw loosened. "Sounds good to me." He turned on his heel and left, my abilities convincing him it was his own idea. Humans never saw me coming. Unfortunately, the effects of my abilities waned over time, so I couldn't realistically use them to win in court. Though I'd considered it.

"Man, you're embarrassing yourself," the opposing counsel complained.

When I turned around, I saw it all happen. Things humans missed. I beheld the scum smirk at her. Like he deserved to even look in her direction. She sank low in her chair, trying to appear smaller, as he cracked his knuckles. Threatening her. Threatening her right here in front of a judge and two attorneys. I could only imagine what he was like behind closed doors. What horrors he instilled to make a woman fearful in daylight in a house of justice. *Justice.* But these corrupt motherfuckers weren't just in the presence of an attorney, were they? I was more—much more.

"I will have you banned from this court for your display, Onyx Hart," the judge boomed.

The opposing counsel—what was his name?—laughed before giving his client a high-five.

It was getting harder. These past few weeks, something inside me had shifted. The curse was broken. I was free. Free to find my family, to seek out my vampire father and learn of my dragon mother. Yet somehow, being close to Blythe Pearl stopped me ... knowing she was mine, but I couldn't have her. At least not yet, because my friend thought she belonged to only him. The combination of finding my soul's mate and the curse being lifted had me pulsing with energy. So much energy and ... rage.

My knuckles turned white at my sides. Wolf, Ghost, and I could hunt this motherfucker down later. We could string him up and drain his blood and—

"Next time, I'll make sure you don't live long enough to take fucking photos," Mr. Sher whispered in her direction.

The judge heard and quirked a small grin.

Oh, that was fucking it.

I faced Blondie. "You might want to close your eyes."

She paled slightly, but her pulse was steady. I walked over to my briefcase and pulled out my cassette player and propped it on the desk, pressing play. The slimy lawyer stood and stretched. "Well, my work is done—"

"Knockin' On Heaven's Door" by Guns N' Roses rumbled through the speakers. I'd be done before the song ended, but damn, the acoustics in this room were elite.

In a flash of movement, I appeared behind the attorney. Before he'd even lowered his arms and realized what had happened, I snapped his soft little neck.

Judge Middleton didn't have time to scream before I was upon him. That was unfortunate because I loved making people scream. I caught his eyes widen and his face blanch before I dislocated his head from his shoulders. He lolled forward, hitting the Judge's chair he didn't deserve to sit in. Now he never would again.

The wife beater fell backward, his seat clattering to the hardwood floor. He scurried to stand. I glanced over at Blondie who, to my surprise, was watching with rapt attention. "You want to watch?" I asked, gesturing toward the rat who thought he could flee. She nodded, holding her elbows. "All right, then."

I caught Mr. Sher by the back of his collar and dragged him backward. "Please, no," he begged. "I won't tell anyone what you are if you just let me go. My parents have money, lots of money. I can—"

I shoved him to the floor in front of my client's table. She swallowed, and her hands trembled as she stared down at her abuser.

"You won't tell anyone what I am, huh? What am I?" I asked, kneeling next to him.

"You're—You're something … evil." He panted, glancing from me to his ex-wife. "Heather, tell him to stop."

I raised an eyebrow at her, curious to find that even under my calming control, she felt less nervous now than she did when she'd come into court today. Heather shook her head, her eyes flicking back up to mine. Few things were sexier than a woman with bloodlust. Too bad I was already dick-whipped by my best friend's girl.

Mr. Sher began sobbing. He looked to the ground, shaking on his knees. I grabbed his short blond hair and yanked his head up. "You're right, I am something evil. And you? You're something worse." I jerked his chin up again as he wailed like the coward he was. Blood from his attorney expanded atop the glossy hardwood floors. Maybe I snapped his neck a little too hard … A puddle of red stalked toward us. "But her?" I continued, forcing his gaze to his victim. "She's not like us. That woman has the heart of a dove, and you beat her, you raped her, you tried to break her …" I glanced up at Heather, her jaw tight. "But he didn't break you, Blondie, did he?"

Her gaze met mine in surprise. Slowly, she shook her head. "Do it. I'm ready," she replied evenly.

"No, don't—"

With a spark of rage, I tore my fangs into his throat, feeling hot blood splatter my face. His limp, useless body slumped onto the floor in a splash of another man's blood. It wasn't the most gratifying way to kill, but the pop of dislocating a head and fang-cutting a throat was still pretty fun.

I shrugged, wiping my chin with the sleeve of my blazer. "Normally I'd draw it out longer, but we should probably get you out of here. The courthouse staff is back from lunch in five minutes."

Heather shakily grabbed her purse, and her heels clipped as she walked around the table, carefully avoiding stepping in the blood. "I don't know what to say," she whispered, looking around at the carnage. "Wh-what are you?"

I caressed her shoulder gently, erasing the effects of my previous touch. Horror invaded her system—and likewise mine—and she began shaking again.

"I'm just a half-bored, half-lifeless ... nothing. I'm a nothing." I sighed. "Get out of here. Go far, far away and start over. You can have a new life, Heather. I'll take care of this. You were never here, got it? If anyone asks, I told you that your presence wasn't required at this hearing."

After a moment, her terror eased enough that her knees unlocked, and she took careful steps backward. She was afraid to turn her back to me, afraid to move too quickly. The primal nature in all humans recognized a predator when it saw it. This woman feared me, as she should. When her back hit the tall courtroom door, she pulled it open, stopping halfway out. "Thank you," she whispered. And then she was gone.

I packed my briefcase and ran a blood-stained hand through my hair. This wasn't how the Halloween Boys operated. We had a system, a code, for our killings. We found worthy targets and worked together. It was enough to satiate our desires ... or it used to be enough, at least.

Blythe had wrecked everything by fixing everything. She'd freed all the lost souls in Ash Grove while capturing mine. What I felt for her I hadn't experienced since Minnie. And I'd lost her, just like I was losing Blythe. Every morning we had breakfast in the diner, and I'd have to limit myself to coy flirting. I'd watch while Ames-Fucking-Ghost wrapped his arm around her. I had to smell his scent all over her, radiating from her supple thighs. Blythe was mate to all of us—me, Ghost, Wolf. And somehow Devil was involved, too, though we hadn't seen him since Halloween night. But the fucking archdemon was acting as if she were only his, and Wolf and I could deal. Wolfgang had been patient, advising me to let him cool off and come down off his rabid demon-claiming bullshit. But I'd waited hundreds of years for a mate … and watching her with only him was some sort of torture. I couldn't have Blythe. I had no idea where to look for my parents. And I'd just slaughtered a courtroom. My careful grip on control was steadily slipping. I surveyed the carnage with a long exhale. The courthouse was still closed for lunch, so there was only one solid option.

Something inside me danced, delighted, excited. It was the way I always felt among embers. I walked to the door and turned to the bodies on the ground. After a sharp intake of breath, I exhaled my fire, setting the room ablaze in green flame. "See you in Hell, fuckers."

My dragon genes sent waves of gratification through my bones. God, I fucking loved fire. The room went ablaze in my own brand of green. Such an old, historic building would be leveled within the hour. Alarms trilled behind me, and the fragrance of smoke wafted past as I exited the building. By the time I reached my car, fire trucks were speeding past. But they were too late. I'd left my mark and rattled the bars of my cage. What did it matter? I was a hybrid nobody with a past as full of ash and sorrow as the courthouse I'd left in ruin.

CHAPTER 2

Blythe

BEYOND

As I sat cross-legged on the ground, leaning against a gravestone, a translucent figure floated past. And another and another.

My life used to make sense in all its trauma and earthly woes. My mortal existence was a predictable domino effect of a shitty childhood, a psychotic stepfather, and living life on the run. I never thought I'd miss the simplicity of predictable human dread. Now all I could think about was how little I knew about this world, my new world. The world that, prior to October, I thought was make-believe—ghost stories and fairy tales. But now I embodied the creature that lore depicted as a hooded, shadowy figure holding a scythe. A reaper—death itself. Whatever that meant. And I was in love with an archdemon. While everything finally made sense within my heart, my brain was still scrambling to catch up. To make a place for myself among this new world of monsters and magic. The only place I found peace was in the cemetery.

"I miss my friends," Maud complained. Her gravestone was so time-worn it had been overtaken by moss and dirt. I'd cleaned it up to the best of my ability, but only a shallow *M* remained.

"If you let me, I could help you move on, and you'd probably see them again," I replied, picking at the dry grass. "You still haven't told me why you decided to hold on and not leave with the other trapped spirits on Halloween."

Maud crossed her arms and slumped against a tree. "Do you know for certain that I'd see my family again? Can you tell me what lies beyond?"

It was an honest question from a very old ghost. "No … I don't know." *Some reaper.* I didn't even know where they reaped to. "But it has to be better than sulking around here forever."

Something soft and warm rubbed against my leg. "Moody Maud, I thought you were going to make me a coat," Cat purred.

Maud nodded, drifting closer. "I don't know how to knit a sweater for a cat, but I'll try."

Cat licked her paw as the apparition floated past, distracted by her task. "I know you want to help, but some ghosts are stubborn and confused. Who knows what goes on in their heads, but they're holding on to this world for some reason."

I scratched under the black cat's chin. "I'm a shitty reaper, aren't I?"

Cat chuckled, licking a paw and cleaning her whiskers. "No, you're just new. You need the thing the ghosts have had too much of—time."

"And she'll have as much time as she needs," a deep voice interjected. "Because reapers are immortal." Ames, my archdemon, my Ghost. The sound of his voice sent shockwaves of heat and calm through me. He was always both for me. Part hell's smoke and part bouquets of bats. And I was completely enamored with every part of him.

"How are the Damned?" I asked, noting the way the orange light of the rising sun glinted off his taut, ink-colored muscles. His demon form was huge and menacing and irresistibly sexy. I yelped as velvety blue smoke encompassed me, hooking under my arms and ass, floating me up to his eye-level. "The honey taste of your arousal is a much more interesting topic."

My core heated at his gruff timbre and the deep blue of his eyes.

Cat yowled as she sashayed away. "Get a room."

Smoke pressed against my back like a warm blanket, inching me closer to my archdemon's lips. His long, dark fingers delicately tucked a tuft of hair behind my ear as he whispered, "Let me have her taxidermized. She'd look excellent on Onyx's mantel."

Raven cawed from somewhere above me, always watching. I giggled, shoving at his chest. The smoke gave way like a swing, and I rode the ropes to the ground. "We aren't stuffing any familiars."

By the time I'd grabbed my bag, Ghost was Ames and was changing into the clothes he had stashed in a tomb. All the Halloween Boys, I'd learned, had wardrobes hidden around the town. It was both adorable and concerning how they anticipated trouble, or rather, maybe they brought the trouble.

"Cat may be a flea-ridden busybody, but she does have a point about one thing," Ames said, taking my hand. "We should get a room of our own."

I bit my lip as we fell into a walk down the stony and moss-covered path of Ash Grove Cemetery. It was buried in the woods and solitary, especially in the mornings. I'd spent most days of the last two months sitting against gravestones, meeting the souls who stayed behind and listening to Cat's gossip while Raven hunted mice. Maybe I felt at home among the hollow ground, and maybe that was another clue to me being a reaper. A reaper. A title I knew nothing about other than I was someone … something … infamous and legendary. While that may have been true, I still only felt like Blythe Pearl. A twenty-something year old nerd who still slept with stuffed animals. I loved my new world of immortals and monsters … but I wasn't sure how I fit into it.

"I like staying at Onyx's farm. It's cozy."

Ames snorted, pulling the helmet off his bike. God, it wasn't fair how sexy he was. Both as man and demon. His jet-black hair brushed back and blue eyes gleaming with a quiet fury.

He towered over me as he tugged my helmet over my head. "It's crowded. And I don't like knowing that the guys are in the other room jacking off while we fuck."

My cheeks heated. I'd tried to be quiet, but I knew they heard. A werewolf and a vampire-dragon hybrid definitely heard way more than

I wanted to even acknowledge. Despite my embarrassment, something deep inside me needed Onyx and Wolfgang nearby. When they weren't around, it felt like a puzzle piece out of place. I'd hoped that staying on the farm together after Halloween would help to settle the dust kicked up from the drama of Hallows Fest. Maybe I also secretly hoped it would give me a chance to get to know the Halloween Boys better, too. All of them together. Not just Ghost and me. We were a unit, a family, and maybe … more. But the guys seemed wary of me for some reason. Were they freaked out about what I was? That would be hypocritical, considering I'd accepted them from the get-go. However, I was … you know … *death*. I couldn't be sure, or even get a moment to ask, with Ghost's domineering presence.

"Honey mixed with … What are you worried about?" Ames clicked and tightened my helmet. His gaze searched mine beneath furrowed brows.

"I'm meeting Yesenia. I've bailed on her a lot lately. I just hope she's not mad at me." It was true, but not the whole reason I was currently worried. My archdemon's ability to taste my emotions was sexy in all its intrusiveness. But it also made it almost impossible to gather my thoughts on my own before needing to express them. I found myself monitoring my emotions so as not to concern him. He'd been so protective these past few months.

We might not have known what being a reaper entailed, but we did know it was powerful, and it had already attracted the attention of beings we didn't want to mess with. Would whatever force that turned and sent Ellie May, the baphomet, come searching when she didn't return? If word got out to even more immortals beyond that … The amount of chaos it could attract was too daunting for me to think about for too long. The guys had made it their mission to keep me safe and explain away the curse lifting as a gift from the witches.

I supposed attributing such a thing was Ghost's thank you to the crone, Marcelene, for saving his life. Though the details of how that came to be still hadn't been shared with me fully. Somehow the Halloween Boys wanted to insert themselves into everything about me, all while keeping things about themselves close to their chests. The double standard had begun to grate on me.

"She'll understand," Ames assured as I got on his bike behind him. "Shall we go fast?"

My mouth dried slightly, but I nodded. "Yeah … fast."

CHAPTER 3

Onyx

GROUND CONTROL

> It's a compulsive need to wreck everything. You might notice there's a pattern of stripping down and building back up again throughout my life. I guess that's how some of us conduct our lives.
> *David Bowie*

Life is dull. Music makes it less so. After washing my face with a wet wipe meant to clean my instruments and ripping off my suit jacket, leaving only my undershirt, I palmed my guitar and stomped through the withering grass. She hadn't shown for breakfast. We always had breakfast, or at least coffee. She was meeting with Yesenia, but I'd assumed we'd have coffee and crosswords first. But when she wasn't at my breakfast table, or the diner, I went into court irritated.

He snuck her out early to stand me up, didn't he? The ice in my lungs wasn't from the frosty January day. My fire was swirling inside my chest like a coiled viper waiting to strike. Even my morning kills and incinerating a courthouse hadn't impeded the appetite of the growing green beast within. I probably should have driven home, or hell, to another town, but I went somewhere else instead. The only place I'd have a shot of finding any sort of peace. But where I'd hoped for a quiet sanctuary, the bustle of shifters and children laughing rang through the air.

At least it smelled like fire. Then again, Fenrir always smelled like campfire and meat and goddamn idyllic happiness. I made my way toward the warmth when my foot snagged on something. I swore, dropping my guitar and wiping out in the dirt.

The patter of paws approached, and when I looked up, a wolf pup transformed into a little boy. "Hey, Onyx, you're dirty."

With a huff, I picked myself up and wiped my knees. "Hello, Callum, you're naked."

The boy giggled. "I've got clothes over there. Whoa, is this your guitar? Sweet!" He picked it up, and it covered him completely.

"Why the fuck are there holes everywhere?" I rubbed the back of my neck. My human body needed a workout. And a massage. And a stiff drink.

"It's a Laverna Day. Duh. Hey, can I show my friends? I'll be really careful." He wiggled his eyebrows.

Laverna Day. I'd forgotten. "Knock yourself out. But dammit dude, put some clothes on first."

"Will do!" he shouted, bare-ass sprinting toward the tiny homes in the distance.

My lips curved slightly despite myself.

A deep voice rumbled behind me. "Kids and pups. Got to love 'em. Though I'm pretty sure Callum and his buddies will damage your guitar."

I turned to see my friend stalking out of the forest carrying a pile of logs. The guy's body put mine to shame with his broad and muscular frame. The long hair was nice, too. Everything about Wolfgang was nice. The exact opposite of me. I was hot as hell, don't get me wrong, but in a completely different way than the werewolf. Where I was pale, he was bronze. Where I was sharp, he was chiseled to perfection.

"Glad to see at least one clothed wolf here."

"Are you?" He quirked an eyebrow before pulling me in for a hug. "Want to"—he pulled back. *Here it comes*—"Whose blood is on you?"

I looked toward the milky winter sky in exasperation. "You know I'm not good with names."

"Ash, too," he sniffed. "You killed … brutally. And burned something … old wood. Onyx, what the fuck happened?"

"Can you at least buy me dinner before making me admit to murder?"

Wolfgang's tight jaw shone with disapproval before he picked up his logs. "Come on, watch out for holes. They're everywhere."

I dodged several as I followed him. "Some luna is really trying to stack the odds over here, huh?"

He was annoyed at the smell of blood, but he still grinned. "It's tradition. But yeah, whoever she is, she's making it a little too easy."

Must be nice to have traditions. To have kin that stretched back generations. Wolfgang had elders who'd watched him grow up. They were older than freaking sin, but they'd always been there for him. The pack at Fenrir was united and strong. Each came from some place different and had varied bloodlines, but they'd all found each other and stayed. I wondered what my extended family was like. I'd combed every recess of my consciousness to try to recall something, anything. Surely knowledge of a dragon mother and vampire father would be at the forefront of some string of memory within me, but nothing. Only the foggy memory of a woman with long blond hair and green eyes like mine, and a father, tall and brooding … sending me away. *Why*?

"I've got my own fire going behind my house. We'll have some privacy there."

Wolfgang always spoke to clear my silence. If I got too in my head, he'd say something, anything, and the mood would lighten. For a while I thought it was just a werewolf thing, and then after a decade or so, I realized that, no, it's a Wolfgang Jack thing.

I took a seat next to the embers behind his ridiculously small dwelling. "You call this a fire?"

"Oh, not good enough for Dragon, is it? Want to make it pink or purple or whatever Blythe's favorite color is?"

I smirked lightheartedly before blowing green flame onto the bundle of sticks. A healthy inferno erupted, warming the space around us instantly. "Her favorite color is black."

"What happened?"

"Blythe wanted to roast marshmallows on her stepdad's corpse, so I asked her favorite color and made the fire black—"

Pain struck my bicep at Wolf's punch. "Cut the shit, man. Who'd you kill?"

I rubbed my arm before leaning back on the log. "No one important."

"Didn't you have court today?"

I didn't answer. Instead, I only stared into the flame.

"There's a reason we have this system, Onyx," he scolded in that oh-so-knowing tone.

"What is that reason?" I challenged.

"We all want to kill. You, me, Ghost. Presumably Devil, but who the fuck knows where he is? The point is, we do it together. It keeps the humans from suspecting anything outside of the typical psychopath. And it keeps us from … losing it. You know that."

I scoffed. "What the fuck does it matter? I could slaughter this town, you know—*again*—and in ten years, no one would remember. Hell, five years. *Don't scare the humans.* Give me a break."

"Those are the rules," he replied resolutely, tossing a rock into the blaze.

"Those are Ghost's rules. Or Devil's rules. Or whomever. Did you ever ask why we listen to those assholes? Who the hell put them in charge of our lives?"

"What's gotten into you? Why are you so pissed off?"

The swirl in my ribs intensified. I wanted to kill him for asking such a stupid question. I wouldn't hurt my friend, but *fuck*, I wanted to kill him.

"Here." He passed me a flask, *thank god*. "That was dumb of me. I know why."

I snatched it and downed a burning mouthful of bourbon. "According to the witches, I have a mate, but *plot twist*—I'm not allowed to have her, thanks to him. I'll get through it. Not the first time a demon's stolen my girl."

"This isn't like what happened with Minnie. Don't talk like that. Ghost is our friend, our brother. And this situation is … you know it's complicated with all of us being mated to her."

I sat up, gripping the flask so hard I was sure it would bend the metal. "How are you being so diplomatic about this? Aren't your wolfy hormones fucking raging right now that another being is hoarding your mate? Our mate?"

Wolf looked at the ground as a few beats of silence passed. "I wanted to argue that the crone was wrong in her assessment. But we were all there. We all saw her in our mind's eye. We all went to her when she needed us. I know Blythe's my mate, … and I know she's yours and Ghost's, too."

I raised an eyebrow and took another gulp, the alcohol warm now from my burning hands. "Yeah, and?"

"And nothing." He shrugged. "I can wait. For her, I can wait. And for you … I have to make sure you're okay before anything else."

Shaking my head, I passed the liquor back. "You're just so goddamn sweet, aren't you?"

"Shut the fuck up," he growled, knocking back a drink. "And ease up on Ghost. You're both fucking with the vibe."

"Ghost is being a self-centered prick. You won't be so high and mighty when your alpha male kicks in and you're knotting her in the dirt every night."

"Alpha sol," he corrected. "Wolves who identify as female are lunas, and the ones who identify as male are sols. Nonbinary are stellas."

I nodded but caught his gaze and raised an eyebrow. He sighed. "The women are alphas. There hasn't been a male alpha in centuries. Yes, the elders think I could be … special … but even if that were the case, it doesn't mean I'm going to turn into one of those sex-crazed maniac werewolves just dying to mount their mate and breed."

"Uh-huh." I clicked my tongue. "Sure, sure." I stood with a stretch, my anger waning slightly due to Wolf and Fenrir's energy. "Well, I guess I've got to chase down some pups and teach them how to play rock 'n' roll." I made it a good twenty yards, far enough away that I could run if needed, before turning over my shoulder and adding. "Oh, and to answer your question—I murdered a judge, an attorney, and his client. And, uh, I burned down a historic courthouse."

CHAPTER 4

Blythe

THERE'S NO PLACE LIKE HOME

The motorcycle came to a thunderous halt outside Magia Eclectics. Ames handed me my backpack as I shoved off my helmet.

"Kiss?" I requested sweetly.

"Ditch Yesenia, and I'll do more than kiss you." He grabbed the corners of my jacket and pulled me flush to his chest. Our lips touched in a sort of heat and electricity I'd come to crave.

"Your tongue tastes like honey when we kiss," I whispered into his mouth.

He tilted his forehead to mine. "I still haven't figured out how you can taste me tasting you … like that. But we should try out other flavors to be sure."

A laugh rattled my shoulders. "What do I taste like angry?"

"Cinnamon, usually."

"And when I'm afraid?"

Darkness flashed across his blue gaze, and he stood from his perch on the side of his bike. My heart fluttered at his height. His human size didn't hold a candle to his demon form, but I could sometimes see the archdemon lurking behind his stare. It thrilled me more than anything I'd ever experienced, and I knew I loved them both—the man and the monster.

He leaned down, his hot breath tickling my ear. "That's my favorite flavor of all, Blythe Pearl. I'd love to sample that later and show you just how much I enjoy your delicious terror."

I sucked in a cold breath of wintry air that did nothing to cool the heat dropping to my core. "But you don't scare me anymore."

"I'd like to test that theory," he replied. "I bet I could."

I raised an eyebrow in challenge. "You're on."

He chuckled sinisterly. "You just made a very bad deal with a very bad archdemon." He caressed my cheek with his thumb. "Never make agreements with any immortal other than me. It'll always come back to bite you."

Raising onto my tiptoes, I nipped his full bottom lip. "Not if I bite first. Yesenia is waiting, and you're late for work."

A bird cawed from the wrought-iron lamppost above us. Ames looked up. "You got her from here, right?"

Raven squawked and nodded before gliding down onto my shoulder. I nuzzled my cheek against his cool, velvety feathers.

"He's been awfully quiet lately," Ames said, crossing his arms and surveying my familiar.

I stroked my bird's chest. "I suppose there isn't much for him to do right now since I'm so heavily guarded by the Halloween Boys at all hours of the day and night. But he speaks when he wants to."

Raven made a vibrating noise of approval in his throat, almost like a purr, and I giggled. Even my stone-cold demon cracked half a smile.

"Have fun. I'll pick you up around five."

"Yes, Demon-Daddy."

The growl behind me wasn't from his bike as I quickly scurried into Magia. The *very ironic* plastic reaper let out its mechanical, "*Wah, ha, ha,*" announcing my presence. It was the only remnant left over in the shop from the Halloween décor. I wondered if the witches left it up just to taunt me. The aroma of maple syrup was thick among the shelves of crystal balls and tarot cards. Between the shop items, pinecones, cypress branches, and holly had replaced the orange pumpkins of October. It was fine, but my heart preferred orange and black to red and green any day.

"Come on upstairs!" Yesenia shouted. "I'm elbow deep in pancake batter."

Raven hopped off my shoulder, careful not to nick me with his talons, and flew up the stairs ahead of me. I tentatively glanced around, as if Marcelene or another Crone from the Moon Halo Coven were waiting to pounce. But the shop was empty, thankfully. The witches had pieced together my abilities after the events of Halloween. As if surviving an encounter with a baphomet wasn't enough, I'd somehow summoned the Halloween Boys to my side that night as well. Though Ames was reluctant to give me many details of what transpired in the hours after I'd been taken, I knew the Moon Halo Coven assisted the Halloween Boys that night.

The witches were aware that I'd broken Ash Grove's curse and freed the trapped souls. My reaper status was obvious to them now. Which wasn't a good thing. The fewer people who knew, the better. Especially being that I'd already attracted attention before even knowing what I was. But lucky for me, since most of the immortals who patrolled Hallows Fest weren't locals, they hadn't come to the same conclusions as the witches. At least, we hoped not. I'd been avoiding the coven, including my friend, not wanting to be subjected to their questioning or further tests like they'd performed three months prior. But I couldn't avoid life forever, wrapped up in the farm-bubble of Onyx's property. I'd only ventured out for breakfasts at the diner with Onyx and casual trips to Fenrir with Wolfgang. I loved Ash Grove and my friends, and it was time to do … something, anything. After running for so long, I'd finally found my home, my very own town. And if being a part of my new home meant making peace with some ornery crones, then so be it.

"Welcome home, girl," Yesenia said, wiping her hands on a dish towel. My heart swelled with both love and guilt as she wrapped me in a hug. "I kept everything the same up here in case you ever called wanting your room back. I'm sure being mated with three dudes gets old fast. I only have one husband, and ugh! The snoring, the stinky socks—"

"It's so good to see you," I gave a nervous chuckle, "but I'm only with Ames. I just like being around the other guys, too. They're all sort of a package deal."

Yesenia clicked her tongue and threw her hair over her shoulder. "Only with Ames, huh? That's not what I heard. At least that's not what was revealed when you went through your horrid Halloween ordeal ..." Shooting me a sly wink, she transferred a giant stack of pancakes to the table. "But it's okay if you don't want to tell me. I'm just nosy."

I shuddered in remembrance of the baphomet and its ghastly face. Taking a seat, I noted Raven perched by the window, happily observing the street below. "There's nothing to tell. Even if"—I forked a few fluffy pancakes onto my plate—"say there *was* interest there between Wolf, Onyx, and me, I'm not sure Ames would go for it."

"I'm not sure he gets a say in the matter. From what I've heard, at least. But I wouldn't be so sure."

"Okay, now you have to tell me what you've heard."

She slid a cup of orange juice in my direction, and I thanked her. "No way. I'm not about to get the Halloween Boys all pissed off at me. Sorry, but I'm not interested in getting my house vandalized every Halloween for a hundred years. Or, you know, being dragged to Hell or whatever it is they do to their enemies."

I took a drink, not entirely sure whether the last part was an exaggeration or a fact. A cough erupted from my chest at the unexpected tang of my beverage. "Vodka? It's ten in the morning."

The witch shrugged. "I needed something stronger than coffee."

There I was blabbering on about myself, and I hadn't even stopped to ask about Yesenia. I really was a crappy friend. Then again, I'd spent my adult life on the run. There was never time to truly make friends, and now that I could, I was already messing it up. "What's going on?"

She tapped her purple fingernails against the lacy tablecloth. "Look, I'm just going to be honest. It sucks being in the middle of this, but I thought it would be easiest coming from me ..."

My rehearsed excuses played through my mind. I knew what I would say to their demands to poke and prod me like a science experiment or if they wanted to test out my reaper abilities. My thoughts drifted to a few nights prior, when I was playing cards with Onyx at the breakfast table. It was midnight, and I couldn't sleep after making plans to meet with Yesenia. I was worried about this exact scenario. The one where my closest girlfriend tried to wrangle me into some witch coven plot. He'd walked me through all of his lawyer speak. I'd learned that night that a lot of being an attorney was just using several big words, all together, to say a whole lot of nothing. Nevertheless, I felt prepared for that moment. Until Yesenia said something unexpected. Something I hadn't prepared for in the slightest.

"My abuela and the coven ... they want you to leave Ash Grove. Forever."

CHAPTER 5

Onyx

WHERE THERE'S DRAGON SMOKE THERE'S FIRE

I'd hoped for a child once. There were years on the farm when I didn't know what I was. That I was this part beast, part blood-sucking monster. My childhood was spent thinking I was normal. Why wouldn't I believe that? I grew up as part of a small family in Ash Grove in the early eighteen hundreds. My body aged like a boy, and I never craved a human's essence or blew fire. My abilities didn't arrive until after our curse. Or rather, my proclivities were awakened.

That moment of realization slammed into me like a freight train. My body shifted, eyes glowing green, fangs forming within green fire, and turning into … the dragon. While Ames and Wolfgang carried the weight of their *loss* of memory that night, I carried the weight of *regaining* mine. Though, alongside them, I also couldn't recall the exact events that took place. But in my mind, I was sure I was responsible.

The town was slaughtered in a pile of ash. Ash from a fire-breathing monster, most likely. But worse than what my body endured was the turmoil unleashed in my mind. The strong feeling of abandonment and loss racked through me. A vision of a baby's hand, my hand, holding on to my mother's long blond braid. My father's pale, broad face and widow's peak of jet-black hair. My parents had forsaken me and wiped my memory of them, of what I was, and made me believe I was a normal human in Ash Grove. *Why*? That was the resounding question that pierced my tattered soul. Why did they leave me? And for hundreds of years, I stayed trapped in Ash Grove, unable to look for them, to seek answers. Now the curse was lifted, and I should have been sprinting toward the truth. Instead, I sat on a patch of grass, teaching a werewolf pup a riff from a Def Leppard song.

The werewolves, Wolfgang Jack specifically, had been a balm for my charred heart. After I'd lost everything, Wolf had brought me into his community, his pack, and made me feel accepted. I was afraid of the true monster I would have become without his saving. So I'd help with the pups and building homes and pulling weeds so that they'd all know that I appreciated them. I knew I wasn't a werewolf, but sometimes I wished I could be. I wished I could be any one thing. Not some mismatch of evil parts.

"Whoa, that sounded like a real song! I did it!" the kid shouted. I cracked a small smile. He wasn't half bad.

"Just don't tell your mothers that I'm the one who taught you when you're keeping them up all night practicing."

Callum looked up, tongue hanging out the side of his mouth in concentration as he gripped the neck and thrummed the strings. "Wait, what do you mean? I don't have a guitar."

I stood, the kid's happiness sinking into my chest. Absorbing emotions wasn't so bad when they were cheerful ones. Another reason I liked hanging out at Fenrir. "You do now. Don't make a big deal of it. I'll come around a couple of times a week to make sure you're playing the real shit. Queen, Fleetwood Mac, David Bowie…"

Callum's laughter drowned me out. "Thanks, Dragon." He beamed, bouncing off toward the others around the big bonfire.

A large hand clapped around my shoulder. Wolf's emotions were always steady, like a gentle summer rain. I always knew he was near from the distinct feel of him. "That was nice of you. I'm not sure it makes up for executing a courtroom, though."

"I'll throw in drums next time, then."

The werewolf crossed his tattooed arms. "Ames won't be pleased you killed without consulting us. And in public. It's messy, and you're not typically so careless."

I scoffed. "Fuck him. I'm over his power trip. And I'm over caring, too."

Wolfgang let out an exasperated exhale as he swept his hair up into a bun. "Let's get to work."

"On what?"

"I'm on dinner duty tonight, and you're helping." He wrapped an arm around my shoulder as we walked toward the kitchens. "I don't feel like firing up the grill, but luckily, my best guy is a walking barbecue."

I chuckled despite myself as we wove through the residents, young and old, toward what I was sure was a giant pile of raw meat awaiting my flames. Another worthy burning of the day, because I didn't regret ripping apart the men I'd killed earlier. The courthouse was a smoking pile of sticks and debris, and I didn't regret that either. What did anything matter, anyway? The world could fucking burn for all I cared.

AFTER STACKING SMOKED ribs and beef liver on paper plates, I shouted after my friend. "Who gets served first?"

He was on his way toward the songs happening around the main bonfire. The sun was dipping below the tree line, washing Fenrir in violet. Icy air cooled my lungs and temper as I helped cook the community meal. I liked cooking. I liked doing simple things like baking, tending to livestock, working in the garden. It was why I lived on a working farm, along with the fact that there was always something to keep me busy. Caring for chickens and mending fences went far in pulling me out of my twisted thoughts.

"The elders first, then the caregivers. The pups will come and serve the rest."

I nodded. Wolf etiquette had a particular and mysterious set of rules, and they didn't share their secrets with just anyone. Though I feigned nonchalance, I knew in my depths that being included and accepted among them was an honor. Somehow, I'd earned enough of their favor that they let me hang around. Maybe they weren't such good judges of character after all.

Wolfgang disappeared with his plates as I headed toward the row of elders around the fire. A dozen of the elder werewolves sat on hay bales, wrapped in furs, speaking among themselves. I approached the eldest luna; her thick gray hair fell in waist-length braids down her back. A vision of a powerful silver wolf pressed to the forefront of my mind. The wolf changed into a half woman, half beast before rippling into an enormous canine-shaped shadow.

The fire behind my ribs was silenced, either in respect or fear, knowing the images in my mind were either sent from her or something the dragon part of me was picking up on. Awkwardness weighed on my shoulders as I passed her the food. "Enjoy the dragon-smoked ribs." I grinned and went to move on but stalled when her amber eyes met mine. The hue of her irises changed to a glowing yellow as her wrinkled hand wrapped around my wrist. I didn't pull away, though it was more of an effort not to instinctually manipulate her emotions. With skin-to-skin contact, I could make anyone feel anything I wanted them to. Though I wouldn't dare try it on an elder werewolf. The sensation of jaws around my neck was only desirable with Wolf because he wouldn't tear my head off.

"Is everything all right—"

Her voice echoed with old wisdom. "The freedom you seek is found in the heart. Your namesake, Onyx Hart, you are the Dragon."

The words didn't make sense and neither did the stir of fire that levitated to my throat. I felt a presence and the emotion of awe bow next to me. The elder luna pulled her gaze from mine, and the glow of yellow dimmed to its regular amber as she assessed Wolfgang, who kneeled before her. She reached out and pet his hair, like one would any dog, and he looked up with a smile.

"This guy bothering you, Cailleach?"

"Snow is coming. I am bringing it soon. You and your mates should leave on your journey before Friday. You will be gone a long time and much will have changed when you return. The power to set things right lies with you and your pack," she said plainly, picking up a rack of ribs. Taking a bite, she nodded. "Dragon fire is a wondrous treat. It is a gift. You honor us, Dragon. I hope I have repaid you that gift now."

Wolfgang stood, assessing me quickly with a look of concern. Unease settled into my consciousness, and it wasn't the product of absorbing the pack's emotions. This was all my own. I had no clue what the elder meant or if it mattered, but it didn't *feel* great. After Wolf served the remaining elders and directed the pups in their cleanup duties, he pulled me aside.

Trees trembled in a frigid wind as we walked quietly to my friend's small dwelling. His house was on the outskirts of Fenrir, tucked into a pocket of firs and evergreens. It was rustic and commanding, a lot like him.

"Do I even want to know what that was all about?" I dared to ask.

After a moment, he took a seat on his porch. In his silence, I blew fire into the iron lanterns around us. We didn't need the light or the warmth, being that our immortal bodies were always heated and could see plainly in the dark, but the blaze comforted me. Fire had become one of my greatest companions over the years. I knew it, could ask things of it. To me, it was as much of a familiar as Blythe's bird or Ghost's surly cat.

After a moment, my friend shook his head, as if clearing his thoughts. "Cailleach is a goddess to us. She's so ancient I'm not even sure how old she is. Way older than we are."

"Is she a witch?"

Wolf snorted. "No, but many elders develop what could be interpreted as crone magic. Though, from what I've heard, she could sure as hell give Marcelene a run for her money if she wanted to. Some legends say Cailleach can control the weather, which she seemed to confirm. But I'm not sure what her prophecy about you meant."

"That was a prophecy? I got a wolf prophecy?"

"Yeah, I've never seen it happen before, but I've heard of it. Most wolves who receive one end up..." He trailed off, staring into the woods. "It doesn't matter. There are a million ways to interpret magic."

I replied sarcastically. "Sounds promising. She must be wrong, though, because we aren't planning to go anywhere."

Wolf ran a hand through his long stubble. "Not ready to look for your family yet?" he asked carefully. If he'd asked earlier, I probably would have exploded. But I'd finally found my thoughts silenced, or distracted, from my plight.

"No clue where to start."

He put a reassuring palm on my knee. "I have an idea, but you're not going to like it."

CHAPTER 6

Blythe

THE WATCHING

Imperfection is beauty, madness is genius and it's better to be absolutely ridiculous than absolutely boring.
Marilyn Monroe

Several hours and pitchers of orange juice and vodka passed as I tried to make sense of the witches' reasoning. I was dizzy from hurt and alcohol and the pitying gaze of my friend. Or who I thought was my friend. We'd finished eating, and I'd wanted to leave, but Yesenia begged me to stay and talk it over with her. The sun was setting, but none of our conversation had eased my confusion. "So you agree with the coven?" I asked, stroking Raven's back for comfort. "You think I should leave Ash Grove forever?"

Yesenia sighed and put her head in her hands. We'd moved to the sofa. "It's not that simple. Like I've really been trying to explain—I can see both sides. I like you, Blythe. I think you've had a hard life, and you've finally landed somewhere just as weird as you, no offense."

"None taken."

"But at the same time … you're not an ordinary girl, are you? You're a reaper. You're arguably the most powerful being in the world, on par with a devil, and some say even more powerful. The kind of things you'll attract are darker than you could imagine."

My mouth went dry. "The Halloween Boys can protect the town. They always have. And we're keeping what I am quiet—"

"Your guys are strong, yes. But they overestimate their abilities and underestimate their opponents. There's a lot of interest in Ash Grove. There always has been. Why do you think we're the hub for Hallows Fest? Why do the werewolves live in Fenrir in our mountains? Why does an entire coven stay here? This place is special, and that's a big reason to keep it safe. But with you here drawing even more attention? Ash Grove was almost destroyed two hundred years ago because demons got involved. The Halloween Boys did what they did, and a devil cursed the town. The curse is lifted, but now we have a reaper. And I think the witches see that whole situation playing out again. That's what we want to avoid, Blythe. It's not about you personally. It's about what you are and what you could attract to Ash Grove."

My fingers went numb, and my throat tightened. This town was my home. The people, along with my guys, were my family. And now my family was kicking me out. I'd have to leave again. Run again. It was as if my stepfather had never died. This was just another blank letter in the mail, telling me to run far away while all the evils chased after me. I'd never have a home, would I?

I fought back tears as I stood. "I guess you're right. I don't want anyone to get hurt because of me."

Yesenia rose to her feet and pulled me into her arms. Her thick brown hair smelled like clove and vanilla. It reminded me of October, and that memory made me want to cry. My soul wanted to go back to October, back to Halloween, back to that feeling of home. Because now, how could Ash Grove be my home? Ash Grove didn't want me anymore because I was this toxic, deadly, mystical thing.

"Give me some time," Yesenia said, wiping a tear from her cheek. "If I can find some sort of loophole or a protection spell strong enough, maybe I can get the crones to change their minds. In the meantime ..."

I nodded, not allowing the hope of her sentiment to settle in me. "I'll get out of here."

Raven rumbled in his throat and ruffled his feathers. My head pounded from the sob that threatened to break free, so instead of lingering any longer, I grabbed my bag and headed toward the door.

"I'm sorry, Blythe. I'm so sorry—"

The door closed behind me as I bounded down the stairs with hot tears streaking my cheeks. Raven's talons gripped my shoulder tightly in support before his beak nudged the side of my face.

"This was my home. I thought I'd finally found home," I said in a broken whisper.

My familiar's eyes twinkled in the moonlight, but he didn't speak. I'd wondered if his power had waned since Halloween. He'd told me once the crows' powers were strongest then. Regardless, just his presence was a comfort. I stopped and realized it was dark out. Long past five, when Ames was supposed to pick me up. I checked my phone and saw no missed calls, and through the shop window, there was no sign of his motorcycle. Maybe he'd worked late, but it was still odd he hadn't texted.

God, how was I going to tell him that I had to leave? He'd go absolutely berserk. The sound of laughter pulled my attention to the arched doorway leading down to the cave below the shop. Witches were down there snickering while forcing me out of my home, my town. Anger gritted my teeth as I turned on my heel. Ames could wait a little longer. Raven hopped off and flew ahead of me, and I followed the sound of his wings flapping down the twisted pathway flanked by stone. A faint blue glow became brighter as we reached the moon pool. It rippled and swirled as I remembered the time I'd submitted to the witches' tests and customs to figure out who or what I was. I'd always done everything they'd asked of me. And now they'd asked me to leave.

I balled my fists at my sides and stomped toward the long, underground hallway when a churlish voice startled me. "The Reaper."

I stopped and turned to face the voice as Raven landed on my shoulder. "My name is Blythe," I replied to the long-robed witch with a shaved head and multiple facial piercings.

"My apologies. I just wasn't sure if I'd ever get to meet you. I've never met a reaper before." She glided forward. "I'm Elora, High Priestess."

"I'd like to speak with the crones."

"They aren't available," she said curtly. "But I'll let them know you stopped by."

I let out a breath of annoyance. "That's not good enough. If your coven wants to force me out of my home, you at least owe me the decency of telling me yourselves instead of forcing Yesenia to do it. Or are you too afraid?"

Elora crossed her arms, her gaze flicking between Raven and me. "Sweetheart, not much scares the Moon Halo Coven."

"But I do, don't I?" The room went silent. Only the ripples of the pool filled the space.

"I'm not leaving this cave without talking to someone. And if I don't leave, you know who is going to come after me, and there's no telling what an archdemon will do when he finds his love missing." I hated pulling the boyfriend card, but what other power play did I have? I was allegedly the most powerful being in the world but had no idea what those powers were or how to wield them. I couldn't pretend I did, either, because the witches knew. The witches knew everything, it seemed.

The high priestess narrowed her gaze. "Follow me."

We reached a room at the end of the corridor, and I stepped inside the faint purple glow. Three witches I didn't recognize sat around a round table draped with black lace. They stared at us suspiciously as Elora pulled out my chair.

"Piper, Agatha, and Delphine," she gestured from left to right, "this is Blythe. The *love* of Ghost the Archdemon."

I threw Elora a menacing glance as she sat smugly next to me. Blythe, the Reaper would have made me feel a little more badass, but I did use his name to gain this meeting, so the jab was warranted, if not rude.

"It's nice to meet you," Piper replied with a soft voice. Her red hair bobbed at her shoulders. "I take it you spoke with Yesenia."

"Yes, where are the crones? Where's Marcelene?"

"They're detained elsewhere," Agatha replied, crossing her arms. "What is this about? Why did you bring her here?"

Elora sighed. "We can handle this, my dears. Contrary to belief, we do not need our crone mothers for every issue that arises. In this case, a *little ghost* who doesn't want to fuck off and haunt elsewhere."

Raven cawed in annoyance, drawing the wary gazes of the witches around the table. They seemed more afraid of my bird than they were of me. *Some reaper.*

"Again, I'm reminded of why my friends, the Halloween Boys, don't like you all. But I'm not here to play mean girls. I'm here to see whether there's a way out of this. I don't think you understand—"

"You are the one who doesn't understand," Delphine spat, her curly blond hair poking out from beneath the hood of her robe. "You already brought in a legion of demons and a baphomet with an unknown master. And you have hell's very own gang more than willing to tear this town apart if someone so much as glances at you wrong. You, Blythe Pearl, are the danger."

"And that's not even taking into account her powers. The little that is known about reapers isn't good," Elora chimed in.

"There has to be some way," I argued, but the fight was fading from my tone. They were right. I was a ticking bomb mixed with shark bait. My path only led to chaos and destruction, either by me or by the Halloween Boys defending me.

As Elora, Agatha, and Delphine stared daggers at me, I found a kinder gaze in Piper. The smattering of freckles across her face was as lovely as her pale green eyes.

She asked quietly, "Your friends have been trapped here for two hundred years. Is there not someplace they'd like to go? One would think that after being frozen in one spot for so long, they'd be itching to leave."

"There is, but we don't know where to start." I considered how much I should tell them, but knowing the Moon Halo Coven, they likely already knew. "We'd like to find Dragon's parents."

The other witches looked to Piper, and she grinned as if she knew something I didn't. "Perhaps I can help with that. Would finding them encourage your departure?"

My heart sank. They'd really do anything to get rid of me. I nodded slowly. We'd planned to journey anywhere we needed to find Onyx's family. If I located them, we could leave, and the guys wouldn't need to know about the witches throwing me out. Maybe we could stay somewhere else for a while before figuring out a way to come back. Because I couldn't forever abandon Ash Grove.

"Let us join hands," Piper instructed. "And close your eyes as I search."

"What are you doing?" I asked, reluctantly taking Elora's hand and then Piper's.

Elora answered. "More than she should. Looking into minds is a great risk. Piper, my love, you don't have to do this."

The redheaded witch sent Elora a kind smile. "I've got this, my love."

Delphine closed her eyes. "I'm sure this will be quick, High Priestess. Let your girlfriend stretch her magic a bit. Then we can carry on knowing we protected the town from death itself."

The casual jab struck me right in the heart. The coven truly believed me to be a danger.

"Maybe I don't know the full scope of my abilities, but I'd never do anything to harm anyone. I love Ash Grove."

When no one responded, I closed my eyes with a sigh. Piper's hand went cold as ice as she spoke lowly. "We have to be careful looking outward into minds … more powerful beings could sense the intrusion and … see us, own us."

The hair on the back of my neck stood. A breeze floated through the room, and I felt the press of Raven's talons tighten on my shoulder. "I've found a vampire male … in the city in the sky … the city of the beautiful lady of nightshade …" Piper gripped my palm harder then. I peeked open an eye to see her face pale and her neck strained. I loosened my hold on her hand, about to suggest we stop, when a scream shattered through the room.

Delphine's eyes were closed, but her body shook as she shrieked. I looked at Elora in panic, but her eyes remained closed, unaffected, as if she didn't hear what was happening.

Raven cawed as I tugged on Piper's hand. "Piper, that's enough, you can stop—"

Her eyes shot open, but they weren't the lovely and lively shade of jade from earlier. Her irises were gone, flooded in white. "A blood oath must be sworn in the house of Drakon … you must go there and find him … the people there … the screaming, she's screaming—" Piper's body began convulsing alongside Delphine. Raven cawed and flapped his wings.

"Stop!" I shouted, terror shrouding my thoughts.

"Someone, two of them—no, four—are watching you. So many eyes on you, Blythe. They're watching, waiting … oh, such evil … darkness… Sisters, it is so dark here. So many eyes, horrible eyes. They'll find you."

I didn't know what to do. The room had turned so cold our breaths were coming in white puffs. I pulled at Elora and Piper, but neither awoke. My gaze met Raven's, and with a flap of his wings, he launched into the air. He cawed, and the dark room went flush in bright, golden light. A huge bang, like the snap of some large, invisible rope, radiated into the space. The light dimmed back to the soft purple hue from earlier. The witches finally loosened their grips as smoke swirled around the room. I stood, my chair falling behind me, as the fog settled and I beheld the scene before me.

Delphine was rubbing her temples and Agatha was coughing. The other two witches were on the ground. Elora held Piper in her arms, rocking back and forth. I covered my gasp as I noticed the crimson dripping from her ear and into her red hair.

My gut twisted at Elora's pleas. "Piper, come back to me, darling. Piper, I'm here. Follow my voice."

"Is she—"

Elora's gaze like fire shot to mine. "If she dies, you die. I don't care what you are or who your protectors are. I will behead you in the middle of the town square, Blythe."

"I'm so sorry. Please, let me help—"

Something invisible gripped my throat, stopping the words in a gurgle of breath. The hold stretched down to my ribs, squeezing like a boa constrictor. Raven squawked and swooped at the high priestess, but the pressure didn't stop. I tried to call out, but I was swiftly losing air. Raven abandoned his attempt to deter the witch and instead sank his talons into my sweater and yanked me toward the door, encouraging me to run. My knees finally unbuckled, and though my head was fuzzy, I began to move. The farther I stumbled down the hall, the more the invisible tie around me loosened. Ames would surely be outside waiting for me. The witches' ward could keep him out, but they couldn't stop me from going to him. Gasping for air, I crawled like an animal up the stairs and out the front door of Magia, into the dead of night. When I stood, instead of falling into my archdemon's arms, I was met with someone else.

I ran right into a dark, cloaked figure who hunched outside the door. He'd been waiting for me.

CHAPTER 7

Onyx

WOLF'S BANE

My friend had long retreated to his bed while I sat outside tending to a flame that should have died out hours ago. Fenrir was silent, aside from the occasional near imperceptible patter of wolf paws in the forest beyond. The night patrol was on duty, relentlessly protecting their pack. There were a million places my mind could have gone. I could have wondered where the woman went today after I slaughtered the men around her. Did she go home and pack? I'd like to imagine she stopped for a drink first. Perhaps she was at a bar somewhere right now, internally toasting the wretched bastards in Hell. I didn't dwell there, though. I didn't relish in how good it felt to rip out an esophagus with my teeth. Though a part of me would forever replay the look of fear that corrupt judge gave me before I killed him, it wasn't what kept me awake and around the burning logs.

She didn't come to breakfast.

We never exactly set a plan. It wasn't like she officially stood me up. But breakfasts were our thing. Sometimes Ames and Wolf would join, sometimes not. But either way, it was her and me. I'd fiddle with my crossword puzzle, the clues keeping me sharp on popular culture and vernacular. She'd order waffles and tell me about the dreams she had the previous night. Each morning I'd hope that she dreamed of me.

Part of me wanted to go back to the farm, knowing she'd be there. Another part of me wanted to avoid the farm, knowing she'd be there. She was attracted to me. I'd felt that from the moment I met her. But the overwhelming feeling I felt from her was both curiosity and ... loneliness. *Why are you lonely, Blythe? How could you be lonely? What are we not giving you?* It fucking plagued me. Wolfgang's stance was the most mature. He was right when he said we all had plenty of time to sort her and us out. But what was plenty of time when sitting across a greasy diner table staring at your mate?

Ghost expected us to kneel to his command. My only option was to pine for her in silence until she decided to take me on as hers. We could all be together—her, Wolf, Ghost, and me. But could I wait hundreds of years for that pairing to snap into place? It seemed I had no choice. That all made sense in my mind, yet whatever hole I had where a soul should be cried like a wounded animal. It felt like losing Minnie all over. Yet Blythe wasn't Minnie, and Ghost wasn't a rabid demon.

I suppressed the urge to text Blythe and tell her good night. I always told her good night at the farm. Good night, and then I'd wait at the breakfast table in case she couldn't sleep. I'd lie and say I was reading, but really, I'd sit there all night, ready to make her chamomile tea if she needed it. Then wish her good morning at breakfast before Ames whisked her away to have her wherever he pleased. Those small interactions were all I could have with Blythe right now. It was all that was afforded me.

Pocketing my phone, I stood and stalked up Wolf's patio stairs. The rage was building again, mixed with a need to fight something or fuck something. *Which would it be tonight, Dragon?* The werewolf lay sprawled on his bed of furs on the floor. He slept naked because of his high body temperature. Only a thin beige deer pelt lay atop his groin, while his thick arms stretched above his head. My mouth watered instantly. There was something about watching people sleep—they were so helpless, so content, and so blissfully ... empty.

I exhaled a ragged breath. To walk into a room with another being and not have to carry the weight of their emotions … it instantly got me hard. I wanted to fuck him without waking him. It was fucking wrong and went against all my rules of consent. Or at least it felt like it did. I'd never do it to someone who didn't enthusiastically want me, someone I had no rapport with. Wolfgang and I meant a great deal to each other. I'd been with both him and Ghost countless times through the years. Though my bond with Wolf was something I could never fade in and out of like my sexual relationship with Ghost. There was no fading away from Wolfgang Jack, and I knew he felt the same toward me.

I knew, too, that a part of him heard me. The werewolf could smell me standing above him then. Could hear me unbutton my jeans and step out of my boxers. My scent would wash over him as I tugged off my shirt and stood before him, my erection springing free in the space between us. He knew, yet he remained in his slumber. If I'd been a ghoul or unknown demon, I'd have been dead before my feet hit his patio. Wolfgang saw me, smelled me, loved me. And I him as well.

I dropped to my knees and palmed my aching cock. As I watched the rise and fall of his thick chest, I rubbed my shaft in time with his heavy breath. He smelled like earth in its purest form. Wolfgang was spring, while I was dead and barren winter. Carefully, I parted his legs and crawled between them. I made to toss aside his blanket when it moved, sliding aside his cock as it grew. A grin warmed my face. I knew he could sense me. But I was so, so thankful he remained asleep. Hooking a hand under his knee, I brought it up. I pressed my nose to his thigh and inhaled deeply before licking it softly. I took his length in my other hand, feeling it pulse at my touch.

No emotions invaded my brain, so I knew he was lost in a dream. A dream with me now. The warmth of him, the swatch of dark, coarse hair over his legs. My fangs yearned in need. Without thought, I bit his inner thigh with stealthy precision. His shoulders jerked once upon impact, but he didn't awaken. I moaned softly as the smooth taste of his blood poured into my mouth. I drank it, letting it coat my throat, willing it to stay on my taste buds for as long as possible. I pulled off before placing another bite right next to it. Again, I drank as I stroked him.

When I'd had my fill of his blood, his essence danced inside me, bringing about a euphoric and sex-crazed haze. Vampires thrived on the sexual practice of fucking with blood. We went nuts for it. It altered our minds like drugs or alcohol but in a way that bordered on blissful delirium. Many vampires were sex addicts, living for the chase of their next fuck, needing their lover's desire. It's why so many did indeed crave the consent of all parties. The blood wasn't as good, the delirium didn't hit right, if someone was afraid or uninterested. But Wolfgang was never afraid, and he was always interested in me. His blood was delicious, and alongside that, a werewolf's blood carried healing properties too numerous to list.

I took in one final mouthful of his blood but didn't swallow. Instead, I moved to his cock. Dipping over his rounded tip, I sucked him in, letting excess blood spill down his shaft. He grunted, eyes closed, as a lazy hand found its way into my hair. *Please, stay asleep.*

I paused, and when he didn't move, I continued. My lips traveled down his length and back. I lapped at every bead of precum mixed with crimson, sucking it off his balls and licking my way back up again. His cock twitched, and his breathing increased. I held him steady with my grip before lightly pulling back my lips, grazing his cock with my fangs. Both of his hands then grabbed my head, forcing me down deeper. I didn't resist, allowing his cock to push down my throat as he roared a breathy release. His cum flowed down my throat as I devoured him. When I pulled off, wiping my mouth with my wrist, his eyes opened slightly. He didn't say a word, only moved over on the floor and rubbed the furs at his side. Licking my lips, I crawled next to him, and he threw a lazy arm over me. Within seconds, sleep claimed him in an even deeper embrace than before.

And for that night, I'd indulge in rest as well. My fire still raging, but my mind's furious thoughts dimmed at last. With the taste of his blood and cum still thick on my tongue, I slept alongside my werewolf.

CHAPTER 8
Blythe
DEADLY NIGHTSHADE

> I loved her not for the way she danced with my angels, but for the way the sound of her name could silence my demons
>
> *Christopher Poindexter*

I'd seen vampires, demons, werewolves, and more in my time in Ash Grove. They were scary.

But a rickety old man in flowing priest garb standing in the middle of the street? Horror-movie-level creepy.

I clutched a hand to my chest, catching my breath when he spoke.

"Dr. Cove has requested you wait for him at Lamb's Blood Church. His residence is in the attic." He didn't need to add that last part. I knew. I'd been there many times, screaming on my demon's tongue, watching Onyx and Wolf touch each other in the sanctuary while I rode Ghost. But the priest didn't need to know that.

"You must be Father Joseph," I said, extending my hand. When he didn't accept the handshake, I awkwardly rubbed my elbow. "I'll walk over. Thanks for letting me know."

I hadn't even finished thanking him when his hazy gaze turned, and he began slowly waddling away. Where he was going in the middle of the night, I didn't want to know. But why would Ames send him instead of texting me? I checked my phone again. No messages. I called, and it went straight to voice mail. Raven ruffled his feathers from where he perched on a streetlamp above me. My familiar only tilted his head. He was as confused as I was. I thrummed my thumbs over the screen of my phone and hovered over my contacts. I only had four saved numbers, and I stared at the last two.

Onyx Hart and *Wolfgang Jack.*

I wanted to call them, or text, but it was late, and I was being stupid. Cold air pressed against my back, seemingly emanating from Magia Eclectics, as if the shop itself was shoving me down the street. Maybe it was. *That* was a thought I didn't want to linger on. My skin prickled in goose bumps under my jacket as I made my way toward Lamb's Blood.

The square was empty, dreary, and vacant. I missed the pumpkins, the hay bales, and all the tacky Halloween decorations that had littered the town three months prior. January was a month of nothingness. Why couldn't Halloween last all year? The only sound was the steady thrum of Raven's wings above me. My paranoia wanted to look over my shoulder with every step to see if I was being followed. What if I'd somehow been the reason Piper was injured? The high priestess's threat sank in my gut. Another witch who hated me, another reason they'd want me gone … and the things the redheaded witch had said about me being watched … My Halloween attacker had a master. The legion of demons that inhabited my stepfather's corpse had the same master, I guessed, but I couldn't be sure. Was he one of the ones watching me? Hunting me?

My pace quickened, and I jogged up the stone stairs of the fore-boding church. "You can stay out here. I know you love the cold." I forced a smile up at Raven, who'd perched on his favorite branch. He squawked his response as I slipped behind the heavy scarlet door. My exhale was shaky as I stepped into the musty foyer. Why Ames loved this nightmarish place, I had no idea, but at least I was safe.

The Moon Halo Coven would never dare provoke my archdemon. Part of me loved the power and security I had with him. But another smaller part felt … weak. I had abilities, too. I was powerful and strong. I'd freed a town from a heavy curse and brought relief to the stunted ghosts. Yet I was still afraid to provoke a witch or walk alone down an empty street. How could I learn to be a reaper when reapers didn't exist? Or if they did, they were few and far between. I flipped the light switch, but the lights didn't turn on. "Ames?" I called into the darkness. Pale lamplight from outside shone through the stained glass, casting what in the daylight would have been a lovely red glow leading into the church sanctuary. At night, however, it looked like a ruby pathway to Hell. As I reached the spiral staircase leading to Ames's attic apartment, something moved at the corner of my vision.

Or maybe I imagined it? Mid-step, I froze in fear as something clinked in the hollow church sanctuary. "Ames?" I called again, even my eerie echo not enough to liven the dusty space. I set my bag on the bottom step and quietly leaned in the ornate archway, looking down the row of mahogany pews to the looming pipe organ. Maybe I'd wait in here for him. As I took a few steps forward, the banging of the heavy doors shutting behind me startled me, sending my heart into my throat. Whipping around, I pushed on the door. Locked. "Who's here?" I asked, trembling. What if the being after me was the same one who'd taken hold of Piper only hours prior? What if she had been trying to warn me that he was here? A low grumble of a laugh pulled my attention. I looked frantically for the source of the sound before realizing something horrifying. It was coming from above me.

I willed my legs to move down the aisle and hallway, peering into the balcony seats. Only red light streaks from Jesus's stained-glass blood striped the dark wood.

The deep chuckle startled me again, only this time, it was closer. From the corner of the altar, the presence floated in the air. It dangled high enough to touch the curve of the church steeple. A long, muscular demon form shrouded in fog.

"Who are you?" I asked, trying to steady my knees and will faux bravery into my tone. "They'll kill you, whoever you are. The Halloween Boys will end you."

I took a step back as the fog lowered the massive body. As it did, he replied, "You know who I am. But if you didn't, you're absolutely right. We'd kill something for terrifying you as profoundly as I have now."

I recognized that voice, but it didn't stop my heart from racing. The knowledge didn't ring true in my brain. My body still felt as if it were in immense danger. And truly, I always was. He reached the ground but vanished in a cloud of smoke. Hell's smoke, as I knew it was.

His voice came from behind me, then, ancient and pricking the hairs on the back of my neck to stand. "I haven't tasted your fear this strong in so long, little ghost. I want to fuck you like this. Let me feel my demon cock buried inside you as you scream for help."

My breathing hitched as he grabbed me from behind. Suddenly, I was hoisted into the air. I screamed, knowing he had me, but I was terrified of heights. I gripped his massive, inky-black forearm, feeling the bones protrude like even his skeleton attempted to flee from him and failed.

"What are you doing?" was all I could manage when he stopped in the rafters. He sat me on a narrow wooden ceiling beam, and I struggled for balance as he floated backward. I took in the full scale of him then. All his archdemon glory was fit for Lamb's Blood Church. It contained both his size and his eminence. It was as if he'd jumped from one of the renaissance paintings in the hallway. The one where the men threw spears and angels aided them as they fought an onslaught of demons. Though, those demons were small and gangly. Ghost was a legend of nightmares all by himself. His icy-blue hollowed eyes surveyed me from his broad and black skull-like face.

"I'm afraid of heights," I whined, looking down to the pews below. They seemed so far away from the dusty church beams.

"I know," he purred. "I taste your fear, little ghost. But you dared me to scare you. You should have known I wouldn't pass up that delicious opportunity." He came closer, floating on hell's smoke, and rested each palm on the ceiling above my head. My attention pulled from his face to the line of his pectoral muscles. The heat of him, his smoky pine and bergamot scent, sent a thrill straight to my core. I was terrified by a myriad of things that evening—the witches, the priest, the evil ones following me, and now the church and its shaky rafters. But I couldn't bring myself to fear my archdemon. I loved him. But I also knew that somewhere deep inside him, he craved my fear like I craved his love. A cursed and dark part of him needed it, and I'd give it to him. I'd give him anything. So I decided to play along.

I wiggled on the beam. "Please don't hurt me. I'll do anything you say."

Ghost's mouth twitched in a surprised but pleased grin. "You'll do anything I say whether you want to or not."

My arousal bled into my fear, and I looked into his eyes, knowing what I'd find.

He groaned. "So that turns you on? You're just a wicked little demon's plaything, aren't you?"

My pulse pounded and my knees brushed against him as he loomed over me.

"Yes," I whispered. Then I remembered my game. "I mean no. No. I won't let you take my virtue." It was hard not to giggle at that. He'd already taken my virtue a hundred times, on gravestones, in attics, bat caves, and more … He growled low in his throat, and before I could react, his smoke curved around me like a clawed hand, turning me and draping me over the side of the rafter. I gasped, seeing the stone floor so far below. His smoke cushioned underneath me like a quilt, preventing the splinters that would have greeted me. As always, his love for me lurked even behind his darkest corners. He flipped my plaid skirt over my ass before ripping off my drenched panties.

"I'm going to taste you like this, eat you like this. Perhaps I'll find your virtue … here?"

I yelped, feeling the warmth and wetness of his long, forked tongue circle my asshole. It glided, then, down my sex, mixing with my arousal. This angle was high and scary and so exposed. I pushed up on my elbows and tried to turn over, but a large hand on my back pushed me down. "You'll take it like this," he hissed, letting out his demon tone. My heart skipped, and my breaths shortened.

"No," I argued, "it's too high up—" I cried out as his long tongue shot inside my entrance. It didn't stop until it reached my cervix and I felt that deep press of him as far inside me as he could go, tasting me deeper than anything else ever could. He groaned, his tongue moving inside me, writhing like a snake.

"Keep telling me no, little ghost. I like it."

I swallowed, feeling corrupt at the smile that curved my lips. I wiggled my hips and kicked my legs, my heels making contact with his hard abdomen. "No. Stop. You can't do this. Let me go." It came out in a breathy whimper of need. My body betrayed my words. My wetness drenched my inner thighs, mixing with his saliva. The feel of his forked tongue inside me … it curved sharply, hitting that spot deep within. I cried out as an orgasm tore through me.

He lapped at my pussy eagerly as I came. Then he pulled out, the sounds of our slickness wet and indecent along the echoes of a place made for worship. But this was our worship. This was how we worshipped each other, so why not in a church?

"That didn't taste like you want me to stop." He spread my ass cheeks then, pushing the tip of his tongue inside. I cried out in surprise, wiggling and trying to break free. But it was useless. His smoke was as hard as rope. And though I knew that somewhere inside me, I had the power to break free of his chains if I wanted to, I didn't want to. "I like this," he murmured, pushing his tongue an inch deeper. "But I'll save more of it for later. Right now, I need to fuck you."

Yes, please do. "No, please don't."

The smoke dissipated slightly from around my chest, and I jerked forward. I screamed at the drop, imagining the pain of hitting the pews, the broken bones. But it caught me again, placing the tops of my thighs on the beam as my front hung upside down, my bareness on full display.

"Oh, that was a nice scream. Do it again," he growled, and the smoke dissolved again, making me feel as if I'd plummet to my demise once more. The scream and fear were organic as my legs slipped free. But he caught me again and brought me back into position.

"No—" I begged, but it was too late.

On a growl that pulsed through the entire sanctuary, I felt his cock align with my entrance and slam inside. Crying out, I felt tears prick the corners of my eyes. Would I ever get used to the stretch? Each time, I was like a virgin all over again. I never got used to Ghost's massive size in his demon form. But I loved it—the pain, the pleasure, all of it, all of him. He slid in as far as he could go, and we both moaned. His sharp fingers dug into my soft sides as he pulled my ass to meet his thrust.

"You're going to take all of me, aren't you, little ghost?"

Yes. "No!"

He chuckled darkly, thrusting in so hard I saw stars. His pace picked up, harder and faster, as I dangled over the beam, taking him from behind. I was tighter this way, and he was so incredibly large. I looked over my shoulder, the air catching in my throat as I met his dark stare.

"That's it. Watch me fuck you. Watch me paint your pussy in my black seed."

A whimper escaped my throat as I obeyed. I watched as his enormous girth pulled out and pounded back in, over and over. I felt the build increase as my cunt tightened even more around him. Ghost grunted and pushed in deeper than before, pulsing deep within me. Our release was a melody through the hollow and sacred room, a pipe organ cry into the night, as my demon fucked me on top of his church rafters. The warmth of his cum spilled into me, and he stilled, pushing it all in with his hard cock. I looked over again, watching it drip out the sides of my sex, blackening me.

"I love your terrified cunt," he said darkly. Pulling out, he flipped me around to face him. His mouth met mine, and I wrapped my arms around his neck.

"I love your black cum," I whispered against his mouth. I did. "And your forked tongue."

He smiled against my kiss, scooping me into his arms as we lowered to the ground. "Good," he held me tight, "because they're yours for all of eternity."

I giggled. "That's a long time."

He nodded, carrying me up the stairs to his room, where he laid me tenderly on his bed, still Ghost, my archdemon.

"Eternity used to be a long time. I dreamed of death for decades. But now that I've found you, Blythe, my Death, my reaper, eternity will never be enough."

CHAPTER 9

Ghost

ACCOMMODATIONS AND DECLARATIONS

> Beloved, let us love one another, for love is from God, and whoever loves has been born of God and knows God. Anyone who does not love does not know God, because God is love.
>
> *The Bible, 1 John 4:7*

I wanted her again but refrained, willing my body back into its human form. She slept peacefully after her shower, while I stayed awake, watching her sleep. It was difficult not to be paranoid after the events of Halloween. I'd let a legion and a goddamn baphomet into my town. I'd let them almost kill her. It was so easy for them; I was distracted and weak. Never again. I'd never allow her to be taken again. Creatures ancient and unholy hunted her as she slumbered in my bed. Something out there, something powerful enough to command a legion and create baphomets from human girls, pursued my Claimed. It was an effort not to shift and roar at the thought. To track it down and rip its limbs from its form. But I couldn't tell her that. I couldn't worry her. She knew something lurked beyond our reach, but she knew she was safe with me, and that would have to be enough for now.

Safety also found Blythe in the vampire-dragon hybrid and the werewolf. Their current obsession with her would add an extra layer of security, one I was thankful for, despite how they exasperated me with their antics. Onyx and his obnoxious, arrogant charisma, and Wolfgang with his puppy dog eyes and muscle flexing. They wanted her, and I knew she wanted them, too. My raw archdemon instinct wanted to grab her in the night and flee. Take her far away and keep her forever. But that was the demon, the darkness. That wasn't love. That wasn't the love she taught me, the love she deserved. Abducting her wasn't what James Cove would do, was it? The human, the man, the person Blythe reminded me was inside me somewhere. She was more, and she would transform me into more, too. I couldn't be ignorant again and let my evil blind me to who she was and what a commodity she could be to anyone who got their hands on her.

Blythe wasn't just a beautiful human woman. She was a reaper—death itself. And her power was so fucking strong it was invisible. No one could size her up. Most beings couldn't even see or sense her. The crones with all their twisted magic couldn't even detect her all those months ago. Blythe's abilities were earth shattering. This creature hunting her knew that ... and it knew of me, too. And if this creature knew of me, he knew I'd be a fucking idiot and try to lock her in a cage and hide her away so he couldn't get her. So that's what I couldn't do. She deserved better. She deserved better from me. And Blythe sure as hell deserved better than Onyx and Wolf.

I watched her steady breathing until morning, only leaving to fetch coffee and scones. When she awoke, she reached for me, begging me to climb back into bed with her. I tucked her into my arms, relishing the feel of her soft skin against me.

Propping up on her elbows, she said, "What is it with us and churches?"

"I think I'm changing your mind about them."

She giggled softly as I admired the bronze glow of her hair in the morning light of our church attic.

"You know, I was a little surprised you let Wolf and Onyx watch us here a few months ago. You, um ... are pretty possessive."

"I am. But I'm also accommodating to you, my little ghost. And the guys and I, well … you've perhaps pieced together that we've meant different things to each other over the years."

Her eyebrows rose. "Like, you've been together in a romantic sense?"

"Off and on. It always comes back around to Onyx and Wolf, though, which is fine with me. Hundreds of years is a long time, and they have a special connection."

She looked down, her worry tasting like lemon. Perhaps I'd been too rough with her. By wanting to protect her, I'd made her feel objectified —or worse, controlled. I couldn't deny my archdemon had claimed her as our own, but how could I force her into a cage for only my liking? Especially when I admitted that my own doors weren't closed to Onyx and Wolf. Hell, I had let them watch her fuck me only three months prior, and I knew they listened to us at night. I could never be with another woman—Blythe was it for me—but if she would receive genuine love from my brotherhood, why wouldn't that be favorable? She deserved every ounce of love that existed on this earth.

"I know you like them," I said after a moment.

"And that hurts you, doesn't it?" She squeezed my hand. "I never want to hurt you." She was such a gorgeous, tender soul who didn't want to harm a demon. Most wouldn't bother considering the impact of stepping on an ant. That's all I was in the grand scheme of good and evil —an insect. But Blythe Pearl was remarkable.

"I want you to have anything and everything in this life that you want, little ghost. You may explore what you'd like, and you certainly don't need my permission to do so, but I appreciate your concern. That is not my issue with the Halloween Boys currently."

The taste of her surprise curved my lips. "Why are you mad at them?"

"Onyx and Wolf are immature. They don't know what it means to be mated, and I'm fearful of what I would do to either or both of them if they hurt you in any way—physically or mentally. Onyx wants to … I can't tell you the things I know he wants to do to you, and I swear to all that exists if I see one mark on your perfect skin …" I ignored her honey, which invaded my mouth at that statement. "And they've been disrespectful to me this entire fucking time. Onyx especially. He needs to get his mind right before he lays a finger on my Claimed." I took her chin in my grip and investigated her tender gaze. "Ultimately, it's your choice to make in what you want from them. I support your every craving. You've been through a lot, Blythe. With your stepfather, discovering monsters and this realm of evils, learning that you're a reaper … I do feel quite protective of you right now."

Her chest heaved with an exhale, as if she'd been carrying this potential conversation with her for a long while. Guilt clawed at me that I hadn't spoken with her sooner.

"The witches said something about us all being mated—"

"Fuck the witches," I interrupted. "We make our own rules. We don't abide by their shitty magic and haughty customs. You pursue what it is you want. If that is a love with all of us, then that is what I want for you. But don't do it because of some old hag's declaration. Love should never be an obligation. If we all become mated to you, that will be because of you and us, and no one else, got it?"

The Moon Halo Coven may have come to my aid on Halloween, and there was no mistake that the boys and I had found her in magic only available to claimed soulmates. But this wasn't a bond that was going to play by their guidelines. I wouldn't allow Blythe to be sucked into their dysfunctional cult shit.

She nodded, noticing my agitation, and tucked herself under my arm.

Exhaling, I tangled my fingers in her hair. "We have a lot of time, little ghost."

We had all the time until the world ended in hellfire. The guys could wait until she was ready. Neither Onyx nor Wolf would be pressuring her as long as I was around. Whatever happened going forward would be on Blythe's terms, not theirs, and I'd damn well make sure of it.

CHAPTER 10

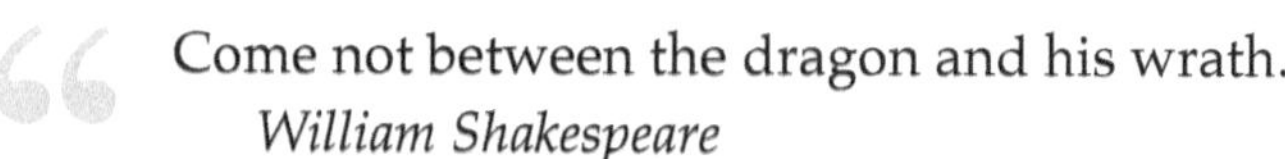

MORNING MEALS

> Come not between the dragon and his wrath.
> *William Shakespeare*

Ames Cove, looking like an angel of night behind thick-rimmed black glasses, kissed me goodbye on the porch steps of the church.

He asked, "Are you sure you don't want to come talk to your ghosts?"

"I'll check on them later. I'm going to get breakfast with Onyx." The mention of the name had his jaw tightening. His blatant tension had me as baffled as ever. He'd been so open that morning and accepting of the possible pursuit of an unconventional romance between us all. He'd let Onyx and Wolf watch us have sex. We all shared an intimacy that was unmatched. The witches even claimed we were mates.

And apparently, Ghost was understanding of my potential exploration of that. So why did he tense at his friend Onyx's name? I sighed. He was bewildering, as usual, and I didn't know what to do. If only I could have been gifted the ability to taste their feelings or read their emotions. Instead, they all read me like an open book while leaving themselves locked shut.

My connection to the guys, Ash Grove, all of it, was bursting at the seams of my consciousness. After he snapped about the witches' input, how could I tell him what had happened the night before? How they'd said someone was watching, or about what happened to Piper? I didn't know what he'd do, but I knew he'd kill for me in an instant. And if he knew the coven was kicking me out of his town … I had to figure out another plan, a plan that would keep everyone safe from … me.

I painted on a smile. "Have fun torturing the damned, my love."

He growled low in his throat and tugged me close. "Why do I love hearing you say that?"

A giggle left my throat as I pushed away. "Because you're depraved."

With a smirk, he mounted his bike. "Only on my best days." With a sexy wink, he took off.

Raven stretched his wings on his maple branch. I held out my arm. "Come on, I'll get you a pancake."

I SAT at our booth for an hour. Pulling out my phone, I brought up Onyx's name in my texts but couldn't bring myself to send him a message. Maybe he had court today, like he did yesterday. Instead, I typed a message to Yesenia. "Is Piper okay? I'm so sorry."

When no reply came, I shoved my phone into my coat pocket and pulled out a cash tip for Doris, even though Onyx had forever paid my tab.

"You're all alone today." She smiled, refilling my coffee.

"Yeah, I guess Onyx is at the courthouse this morning."

Doris pursed her lips. "I doubt that, hun."

I paused mid-sip. "Why? He only misses breakfast if he has an important case."

"Because the courthouse burned down yesterday. It's all over the news. At least one judge, an attorney, and a civilian dead." She shook her head and gave me a sideways glance. "Might want to check on Mr. Hart and make sure he's all right—or rather," she patted my arm, "just steer clear of him for a while."

Panic and confusion swirled inside me. But I wasn't going to steer clear of him, even if it seemed like he was avoiding me and skipping our daily meetup. I knew where I needed to be.

"Can I get this coffee to go?"

My foot sank into a shallow hole in the ground, and I yelped. Mid-trip, a strong hand caught my forearm.

"Thanks," I said sheepishly to my rescuer. I'd somehow managed not to spill my paper cup of coffee. "How'd you get over here so fast? I didn't even see you."

Wolfgang shrugged his broad shoulders. "I'm fast. What are you up to, little one? Taking a day off from the dead to hang with the beasts?"

"I'm looking for Onyx. Have you seen him?"

"You're not here to see me?" He grinned, well, wolfishly, and my heart pattered a strong beat in response.

"You know I always like seeing you, too. It's just that Onyx didn't show up for breakfast, and I heard … I just heard some stuff. I wanted to make sure he's okay."

"He's in a mood; I won't lie. You might want to give him some space. In the meantime, it's Laverna, and I'm sure a luna would be happy to show you around."

My mind spun. "Why is he in a mood? Wait, what's Laverna?"

Wolf extended his muscular, tattooed arm. It was an effort to look past it and not gawk at him. "The land is ready for planting."

"Oh, like crops?"

"Not quite." He put his arm around my shoulder, making me feel warm and tiny in his embrace. "Laverna is our spring festival of …" He hesitated, giving me a slight glance. "Well, you know, fertility."

I'd seen *all* of Wolfgang, and he'd seen *all* of me, yet sometimes he acted so bashfully. His behavior was at odds with the massive, burly protector he portrayed. It was also really sexy. "Sounds fun, and I'd love to hear about it, but I'm really concerned about Onyx. Did you know the courthouse burned down yesterday?"

Wolfgang cleared his throat. "You don't say?"

I shoved off his heavy arm. "You know something, don't you?"

"I have no idea what you're talking about. Hungry? I baked pecan bars using my grandpa's recipe."

I shook my head in exasperation, knowing I'd never get anywhere with Wolf covering for his friend.

"Is he avoiding me?" I asked skeptically.

"My grandfather? Nah, he died a long time ago."

An irritated laugh shook me as I pushed him in the chest. "You're impossible." I scanned Fenrir and the few cars that dotted the perimeter. "His car is here. I'm going to find him." As I marched across the field, I heard the werewolf's labored sigh.

"He's in the woods behind my house. You'll hear him." As I made to stomp away, Wolfgang grabbed my wrist, and my whole body warmed. "Do you know what we do in Fenrir when a baby is born?"

Confusion furrowed my brow at the abrupt change of subject. "What?"

The werewolf looked out over his community fondly before meeting my gaze. "We build them a fire and bundle the parents and pup in mounds of heated blankets. We bring them hot soups and teas. Warmth is life-giving, and cold is death. Vampires are like ice; some say even their hearts are frozen solid. And dragons are flame, life-breathing forces of earth and wind. Onyx is both beings. He has two opposite worlds warring inside him. Life and death, fire and ice, battle within his thoughts, and from moment to moment, we have no hint of which is winning. Tread lightly with the hybrid when it seems he's gone icy. He needs our compassion to thaw him out."

My chest tightened as I took in Wolf's masculine features. It seemed impossible that someone as selfless and kind as Wolfgang existed, but there he was, a steady mountain of calm, day after day. I reached up and tucked a stray wave of chestnut hair behind his ear, and he smiled.

"I'm here to help you take care of him now," I assured. "I'll be careful."

I pulled away and waved my thanks as I kept walking, dodging holes until I reached my destination. Wolf didn't appear to be following me as I curved between the wide oak trees behind his small cabin. Winter had taken all of autumn's leaves and left them dead on the ground. My mind recalled the candles that lit the forest and the murmur of magic from Hallows Fest, and my heart ached. Now, with the witches kicking me out, I'd possibly never see Ash Grove at Halloween again. I swallowed the thought down, not ready to sort through it yet. At that moment, my strongest desire was to make sure Onyx was okay. One of my Halloween Boys needed me, and I'd be there for him, even if he didn't want anything to do with me.

The melody hit my ears right as I was beginning to question what Wolfgang meant when he said I'd *hear* Onyx. I quietly tiptoed toward the soulful acoustics, weaving through mossy trees. From where he sat against a rock, he wasn't facing me, but his fingers and knuckles were visible as they plucked his guitar strings. I caught the glint of his thick silver rings, the veins on his thick hands, and the expert precision of his playing. The music was familiar but different, sort of like Onyx.

It was a combination of every vintage rock ballad I'd ever loved, and yet something wholly unique and its own. Something about the crestfallen atmosphere the music conveyed pulled at my heart. I took a soft step forward, not wanting to disturb him, when he spoke.

"Didn't anyone ever tell you not to sneak up on vampires?"

I'd just opened my mouth to speak when a blur shot across my vision. My mind hadn't registered that Onyx was no longer leaning against the rock when he grabbed me from behind. His hand covered my mouth, muffling my scream, as his hot breath brushed against my lobe. "I bite."

My heart raced while that heady sensation of fear and longing sank between my legs.

"Go ahead and bite me, then, if that's what you want to do." The words were strained against his ice-cold palm. *Vampires are ice*, Wolf had said.

I felt his smile against my neck, and I jerked away on instinct. Was he really going to bite me?

"How do you manage to say the worst things to the most horrific monsters, Blythe Pearl?"

I sucked in a breath and wiggled out of his hold. He allowed it and reclined against a mossy oak, crossing his arms. His beauty struck me like a blow to the gut. His black hair meeting at the point of a widow's peak, the emerald gleam in his too-bright predatory stare, and the lily hue of his skin. Onyx didn't look real. He looked like a piece of art come to life. He smirked in that infuriatingly cocky way of his, like he knew exactly what I was thinking.

"Can you read minds?" I asked.

"No, can you?"

"No."

We stood in silence, only the rustle of a few brown leaves floating down breaking the stillness of the forest. "Are you okay? You weren't at breakfast, and I heard—"

"You weren't at breakfast yesterday." He sounded casual, but there was an edge to his tone. Was he angry with me?

"You had court …"

"So? We always meet at the diner first thing."

He *was* mad. "Well, obviously not because you stood me up this morning."

"Why are you here, Blythe?"

The curtness of his question stung, but I continued. "I heard the courthouse burned down … people died."

Onyx kicked at a pebble. "Oh really? That's unfortunate."

I felt like an idiot for not piecing it together sooner. My mouth dropped. "You did it, didn't you?"

"Did your great master archdemon send you to gather intel? Because I'm already bored with this conversation. You interrupted my song-writing."

I huffed in annoyance. "I don't have a master, and Wolfgang was right—you *are* in a mood."

He waved me off and brushed past. "Unless you have insight on how I can tighten up my acoustic set, I'm afraid I'm too busy for this, B."

I watched him return to his guitar and fought back my emotion. "I don't know what I did to you, or anyone else in this town, to make you hate me, but here." I unhooked my heavy necklace, my gift from the Willow Spirit. I bit my lip in remembrance of how they'd sacrificed themselves for me when all they wanted was a game of hide and seek. And in their wake, they'd gifted me a pendant. One that Yesenia confirmed was indeed a powerful token.

The spirit said that while wearing it, I'd find myself on the right path. It was the most powerful thing I had to offer a being as strong as Onyx. I tossed it into a pile of maple leaves, and it landed with a crunch. "Take it. The Willow Spirit gave it to me before I got them killed. Its magic will lead you to your family. And it's silver. It'll match your other jewelry, so you can't complain about mixed metals or whatever you want to fuss over right now."

The melody halted as I walked away. When Wolfgang's house was in view, Onyx appeared merely a foot in front of me. I startled, putting a hand to my chest. "Jesus, Onyx. Don't do that."

Ignoring me, he dangled the precious stone from its chain. "Why'd you give me this?"

"Because," I sighed, avoiding his intense green gaze, "you were always there to give me things when I needed them. Breakfast, a T-shirt, a … friend. At least I thought we were friends."

"We are," he replied without hesitation. He took a step forward, and I froze, feeling my heart speed up again. "Thank you, but it won't work."

"Great," I sighed. "Then forget it." I made to push past him, but he grabbed my arm, stopping me in my tracks.

"Unless …"

"Unless what?"

He may have been a vampire, and a dragon, but his smile was pure feline as he leaned in and whispered. "You wear it and come with me."

CHAPTER 11

Onyx

THE PHANTOM CIRCUS

George Carlin

I tried to avoid her; I really did. But she came looking for me and gave me her little magic necklace that probably didn't do shit. What was I supposed to do, pass up the opportunity to spend time with her? The train rumbled and shook as we sat on hay bales. Blythe looked wistfully out the side of the open cart. She asked if I could read minds—and I couldn't. What I could do was worse. Her loneliness had shifted into something else; not quite fear, but a faraway feeling. It sat on my head until it was pounding. I wanted to squeeze her perfect little neck and demand she tell me why she was feeling that way. How could we help her? What did she need?

At that moment, it seemed she needed to help me. Sure, I'd let her think she was. We could go on this futile search for my family. What the hell could this godforsaken vampire coven tell us? Only a whole host of bullshit.

Wolf stood, and the train car shook under his weight as we all approached the open door. "Our stop is up here. I'll carry you on my back."

I snorted. "Aw, thanks, big guy."

Wolf kicked my boot as Blythe giggled. The sound was the melody I'd been searching for. *Fuck me.* It didn't help that her tits looked really fucking good in her low-cut sweater. My naughty little librarian.

"I'm talking to Blythe, asshole. You can jump off on your own."

I feigned a pout and chewed on a long stick of salty straw. "I don't want to get my shoes dirty. I haven't been to the circus since ... the sixties."

Blythe exhaled. "I forget sometimes that you guys are so old. You act like such typical boys."

Wolf pressed a hand to his heart. "Ouch, I'm offended. I'll try not to *accidentally* drop you for that one. Now, hold on."

She smiled a lot around Wolf. More than she did with Ames or me. Wolfgang was sunshine and freshly cut grass. I was frosty midnight and dead earth. My jealousy was salt in the wound of her freshly sexed scent. Ghost had to mark her every fucking chance he got. She reeked of demon cum. I could fix that ...

"Come on, sad boy!" She giggled, holding on to Wolf's thick neck. Before I could respond, he'd leaped out of the car.

My lips curved in response as I followed them into the brisk twilight. We landed on a grassy knoll.

"Yeah, I smell a bunch of circus freaks and vampires. They're just down this hill." Wolfgang took Blythe's hand to help her down. I should have thought of that first.

I groaned, avoiding muddying my vintage Doc Marten black leather boots. "Remind me why you've teamed up to force me to talk to Vincent."

Blythe looked over with her sympathetic doe eyes. "Wolfgang made a good point. Vincent is a coven leader and really freaking old. If anyone has a lead on who your father is and where he might be, it would be him. Plus, I'm wearing the Willow Spirit's necklace, and hopping a train to find a circus felt right."

"You're forgetting that Vincent has declined ever helping me unless I join his little fang-gang. Why would he help me now?"

Blythe's dimples shone as she said simply, "Because he likes me."

Yeah, join the club.

We descended upon the giant red and white tent, a lion in a too-small cage, and an elephant tied to a post by a flimsy rope. Blythe hardly noticed as she typed on her phone.

I leaned over her shoulder, only seeing his *what the fuck?* response.

"Let me guess, Mr. Kill-Joy is mad he didn't get an invite?"

Blythe quickly darkened her phone's screen. "He thinks we could have waited for him. But I explained that we were losing daylight and didn't want to miss the show. These circuses usually only stay in town for one or two days." She looked around, taking it all in. "This circus is like, stuck in nineteen-thirty. No one uses real animals anymore; it's inhumane. And there are … humans here?" She marveled as a little boy with a blue balloon ran past. "A circus run by a vampire coven … for humans?"

Wolf eyed the hotdog stand before replying. "Who else would come to these things? Humans love freaks. They just think they're, well, fake. Turns out, it's all real."

"Yeah, no shit," she whispered under her breath. Wolfgang disappeared in search of meat while Blythe and I watched a clown juggle pins.

I bumped her arm softly. "Don't worry about Ghost. He'll blame it all on me. He always does."

"Why do you say that?" she asked, not taking her gaze off the performer. Humans clapped as he added a fourth pin.

"It's The Halloween Boy way. Ames gets to call the shots when Judas isn't around, and Wolf and I follow their lead."

I almost jumped when I felt her small, warm hand take mine gently. "Maybe it's time you start calling your own shots."

Emotion clouded my senses. I couldn't decipher whether the feelings of compassion and care were moving from me to her or from her to me, but it was an unfamiliar experience. Outside of the guys, no one cared for me, and I cared for no one. It had been just the Halloween Boys for hundreds of years. Suddenly this little human, this little reaper, swung in like a wrecking ball. But for some reason, we were all obsessed with her.

My mate, our mate, the dragon's voice inside said. That voice, for the sake of our group and for the sake of me not doing something utterly reckless and dangerous, needed to take a back seat … *For now.*

My skin tingled and my fangs felt heavy as a group of vampires walked by in a gust of wind. Wolfgang was at my side, passing Blythe and me each a bag of popcorn.

"Vincent's here," he said. "I smell him."

We made our way under the big top, following Wolf, who was so large he parted the sea of patrons for us. I put my hand on the small of Blythe's back, and she stiffened. Whispering in her ear, I said, "Stay close to me."

The last thing I needed was a deadly incident involving vampires. And I knew what I'd do if anyone touched or threatened her. If she gave off the feeling of panic, the moment it hit my senses, the perpetrator would be dead. My usual restraint and diplomacy were smoldering in a pile of ash with the courthouse and the judge's bones.

"Where the hell is Vincent?" I asked Wolf as we took our seats.

Drums sounded before he could answer, and performers in tights and clown makeup cartwheeled into the big top. Two lions trotted in after them, and the crowd cheered. And then there he was.

Strutting into the center of the ring in a top hat and red lapel jacket, Vincent held a megaphone. "Welcome to the Phantom Circus! If you've found us, it's not by chance. You see, we don't advertise, and we operate under the veil of night and secrecy and magic." The lights dimmed, turning purple and blue. "So sit back and enjoy the show. But remember, everything is not as it seems at the Phantom Circus." Vincent turned with his usual flourish, fanning out his jacket and walking with a long, pointed cane.

Wolf leaned over Blythe and whispered, "He's so full of shit."

The crowd cheered at his exit and watched as acrobats climbed ladders to the top of the tent. As they swung and twirled, despite the lions lounging in the middle ring, a white horse trotted into the circle. The rider stood, her waist-length crimson hair flowing behind her as she balanced on the animal.

"Ezmerelda," Blythe gushed. "She's so beautiful, isn't she?"

"Not our type, I'm afraid," I answered for my friend and myself as I locked eyes with the Red Vampiress herself. She sneered, having heard me with her keen sense of hearing. I crossed my arms. It was good she knew we were here. Vincent would want an audience now.

She did a handstand atop her horse, and the crowd went wild. With a flip that was too high to be human, she landed on her feet and walked up the stadium stairs, the spotlight making her hair look like fire and her skin look like snow.

"For our next act, we'll need a volunteer from the audience," she crooned.

Stopping at our aisle, she reached out a hand to Blythe. "Darling, come with me." The patrons clapped their approval, but as Blythe stood and reached out her hand, Wolf and I stood with her.

"Absolutely not," I said lowly. "We're here to see Vincent."

Ezmerelda arched an eyebrow and disregarded us as she addressed Blythe. "Are the Halloween Boys your keepers now? I was under the assumption you were still your own person."

Blythe pushed past us and took her hand. "I am," she replied defiantly. "It's nice to see you again, Ezmerelda."

The Red Vampiress shot a lethal smile over her shoulder as she nosed Blythe's hair and inhaled. "It is, isn't it?"

I stepped forward, but Wolf took my arm. I argued, "We can't let her take her. There's no telling what she'll do."

"It's a public performance. If we make a scene and draw too much attention, we'll be in some deep shit. What do you think the coven would do if they found out a reaper was here?"

"Quiet," I shushed him and glanced around. No one could know what Blythe was. The ones who'd already discovered it had either tried to kill her or were actively hunting her. The fewer immortals on our tail, the better. I reluctantly settled back into my seat. "Fine, but if anything seems off, I'm stepping in."

Wolf nodded, and his jaw tensed as he looked to the stage. Ezmerelda held up a pink blindfold and tied it around Blythe's eyes before fastening her to a giant red and white wheel.

"What is she going to do, make her dizzy?" Wolf asked, grabbing a handful of popcorn. "See? This is harmless."

Once she was fastened, The Red Vampiress took the megaphone, shooting me a surly gaze. "For this trick, I'll need help from some friends. Please give a round of applause for The Phantoms!"

"The what?" Wolfgang asked.

Four men walked in with red and black coats and white face paint. I inhaled. They looked like men, but something was off. Reaching my senses out, I felt—

Ezmerelda gave the wheel a spin, and Blythe laughed as she wheeled upside down. Just then, three of the men walked the perimeter of the circle, performing small magic tricks to audience members. But my stare was fixed on the one who walked onto the stage. With a jester laugh, he opened his palm and blew. A cloud of glitter enveloped the big top in stars. The crowd *oohed* and *ahhed*. I was on my feet and racing toward the stage in an instant. But I was too late. When the sparkles cleared, he was gone. It was then, being close enough to feel and sense, I knew what they were—chaos magicians.

And Blythe had disappeared with them.

CHAPTER 12

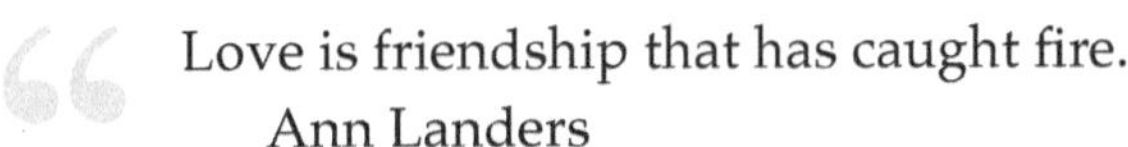

CHAOS MAGIC

> Love is friendship that has caught fire.
> Ann Landers

My lungs constricted at an influx of peppery smoke, and the air went cold and dry. The roar of the crowd faded as my spinning stopped, leaving me upright and blindfolded. I had the distinct feeling that I wasn't in the middle of the circus ring anymore. I coughed and struggled against the ropes around my wrists and ankles. "Hello?" My words were an echo into emptiness.

Suddenly soft fingers pulled the silk from around my eyes.

"Ezmerelda, what's going on? Where am I?"

The vampire let out an exhale of relief and tied back her long red hair. "It worked, thank hell."

I wiggled against the ropes. "Are you going to let me down?"

Just then, there was a movement across from us. A man with a painted white face and leather gloves walked in. "I told you I could do it. Pay up, vampire."

Ezmerelda hissed, "I'm The Red Vampiress to you, and you'll be lucky to leave here alive tonight. But if you do, I'll pay you later."

The man with the white face paint and black painted diamonds over his eyes walked over and regarded me from head to toe. He was tall and lean and seemed human but also … not. "She doesn't seem special to me."

"Is someone going to untie me and tell me why you kidnapped me?"

Ezmerelda shoved the magician out of the way and went to work on my bindings. "The phantoms said you were coming, but I didn't believe it until I saw you in the crowd. You disappeared after Halloween. Did the baphomet harm you?"

My chest constricted at the worry in her tone. I hadn't seen her, or anyone from Hallows Fest other than the witches, since Halloween night. Ghost said it would be better that way. That the fewer people who knew about me, the fewer targets I'd have on my back while I sorted through my new abilities.

"No, I'm okay. Where am I?"

Ezmerelda glanced over her shoulder to where the magician leaned against the wall, looking at me from under his top hat. The air was heavy with smoke, but as I searched, I didn't find a door or a window or any sort of escape.

The man answered. "Think of it like a waiting room, an in-between space. No one can find you here. Except phantoms like me."

Ezmerelda rolled her eyes. "This is Zyre. Zyre, this is Blythe Pearl."

I rubbed at my wrists. "Are you human?"

"I used to be."

Well, that was a disconcerting answer. Before I could ask more, the Red Vampiress held my shoulders. "I can hide you from them. Vincent and my coven can keep you safe. We leave tonight for a place where the Halloween Boys could never find you."

Confusion trembled through me at her earnest care. I held her elbows in response. "Why would you want to hide me? I'm safe with them."

"That's debatable. Aren't you their prisoner now?"

"What? No, of course not. We're friends."

Ezmerelda's ruby gaze searched mine before she looked over her shoulder to Zyre again.

He answered her silent question. "There's no glamor on her. The vampire-dragon she travels with hasn't altered her mental state. There is something … strange about her, though."

I swallowed, hoping he couldn't sense what I was. I needed to get out of here—this waiting room or whatever it was.

Ezmerelda looked up, sensing something I couldn't. "I had to make sure you were well. My offer always stands. If you ever need a reprieve from them, let me know. I couldn't imagine spending so much time with the Halloween Boys." She shuddered. "But suit yourself."

"I appreciate you checking on me, but they're going to lose their shit if I'm not back soon."

The vampiress sighed. "They already are. Dragon is so dramatic."

Zyre let out a low sound in his throat. "I'm dying to meet them."

I narrowed my eyes at the phantom, but he only smirked as he opened his palm and blew.

Glitter enveloped us again.

When it cleared, the dull roar of the crowd greeted me. They were on their feet cheering. Children pointed at me and clapped. I glanced around in confusion, the bright lights and sparkles blurring my vision.

A voice on a megaphone boomed. "She's back, safe and sound. Just a trick of the hand!" Vincent stood surrounded by green flames. Onyx's gaze reached mine in a panic, while Wolf exhaled and petted the lions that were next to him, poised to strike should the green flames allow them the opportunity. I hurried off the stage to their sides, hearing Vincent snap, "Bring them to my tent, you worthless fucking *magic men.*"

Zyre took rough hold of my arm as three other phantoms closed in on Onyx and Wolfgang.

Onyx's green eyes narrowed into slits as he addressed the magic man at my side. "Touch her, and you die."

Zyre scoffed as he let go and stepped away, gesturing for us to follow. Wolf and Onyx were at my side instantly, and I leaned into Wolf's warmth.

Onyx asked, "Did they hurt you?"

"I'm fine—"

"You're the hybrid, aren't you?" Zyre interrupted. "I've heard a lot about you."

Onyx's slitted eyes against his pale skin and darker features made him look wicked in the scariest of ways as he responded. "Not enough, apparently."

The phantom gave a nervous chuckle as he motioned for us to enter a large ivory tent on the outskirts of the circus. Inside was nothing less than what I'd expect from the coven leader. Ornate Turkish rugs, fine linen drapery, rich wooden chests, and plush velvet sofas. Vincent sat in a high-backed red leather chair and motioned for us to come forward.

Onyx laughed. "Some kind of circus king? Wow. With your arrogance, I expected more."

Vincent bristled at the comment, but his tone remained even. "Take a seat, friends. I heard you've been looking for me. Have you finally come to your senses and decided to pledge yourself to me, Onyx Hart?"

I took a seat on a long brown couch next to Wolf, but Onyx walked around the room with his hands in his pockets. He stopped by a golden drink cart and picked up a crystal decanter. Sniffing the liquid, he took a sip straight from the container.

"Help yourself," Vincent said, rubbing his temple. His long white hair was braided back, and he'd already changed out of his ringmaster attire and was wearing a white suit with a long ivory cloak. "You'd make a great addition to the show. The green fire really was a nice supplement to the act."

Wolfgang interrupted before Onyx could speak. "You know every vampire, correct?"

Vincent pulled his attention from Onyx and looked down his nose at Wolf. Until now, I'd felt neutral about the coven leader. The same hate the guys had toward him hadn't rubbed off on me. Until then. His arrogant regard made me want to slap him across his perfect porcelain face.

"I do, save for the new ones. But I do meet them once a year, as well."

Wolf put his elbows on his knees and nodded. He looked so wild in the pristine tent, his shoulder-length chestnut-colored hair falling in waves over the collar of his leather jacket. "We're looking for Onyx's father. Can you tell us where he is?"

Vincent leaned back, his gaze flicking from the werewolf to me. His red pupils dilated slightly, and I felt a jab of hesitation at his attention. Onyx casually stepped in front of me, then, taking another sip of the amber liquid. He held the crystal decanter lazily at his side.

"You've looked better, Onyx. I'd suspect consorting with demons and dogs would wear on one after a time. I take it you'll be offering yourself to me for this information on your father?"

Wolfgang lowly warned, "Don't taunt him, Vincent."

"A word of caution. I know her blood calls to you; we're all intrigued. Though knowing what she is, I wonder what it could do for one who's bitten her? How I might like to test that theory ..."

Vincent eyed me with a hungry gaze, and my limbs froze in place. Somewhere in my bones, I heard the caw of a bird. Raven hadn't come with us, but I had a pretty good idea where he'd gone instead, or rather, who he'd gone to find and bring here. With every bit of courage in me, I willed myself to stand, and Wolf stood with me. Each of the guys were pillars of deadly protection next to me.

"Let's go," I whispered, knowing we needed to get out of the tent quickly.

I turned on my heel when Vincent spoke again. Before I could register his words, he appeared in front of me. Would I ever get used to a vampire's speed?

"Perhaps I could be persuaded to divulge some *intel* in exchange for a bit of time with you, Blythe." His words were like a knife with a velvet handle. I couldn't be certain who moved first, but somehow, I was in Wolf's arms, and Onyx's hand was around Vincent's neck as they snarled at each other.

A roar rumbled through the tent, clinking the glassware.

"What the fuck?" Zyre said to the other three phantoms who ran to look for the source of the noise. They came back, pale even behind their face makeup. Onyx tossed Vincent to the side, and the vampire growled and rubbed his neck where a burn mark lingered. A shadow darkened the moon, and torchlight cast a looming figure over the white fabric.

Vincent hissed to the phantoms, "Don't just stand there. Get him out of here before he tears the place apart."

The men looked to Zyre, who replied, "If the stories are true, yeah, there's no fucking way I'm fighting a demon like him."

With a shaky exhale, I squirmed out of Wolf's hold. "Archdemon," I corrected, and walked past the trembling men. They startled as Raven jolted into the space, landing on my shoulder. I rubbed his chest. "You didn't have to bring him. I was okay," I said softly to my familiar as I walked outside. Behind me, Wolfgang put a protective hand on my back. I turned in time to see the calamity that happened next.

Zyre crossed his arms, and as Onyx walked by, the phantom whispered to his men, "All this for a pathetic human girl? She's not *that* hot."

Onyx chuckled darkly and opened his palm. "Oh, but you're about to be. Hey, can you show me that trick you did? I think I can do it, too. Does it go like ... this?" He blew before they could react, and an inferno of green and twisting flames erupted. The men shouted and ran, while Vincent swore and hastily began gathering the items he wanted to rescue. Zyre raised a chin through the flame, making steely eye contact with me—before I was lifted off the ground by the large hands and blue smoke of my archdemon.

I sat by a black fire near the train tracks as the guys argued in the woods next to me. I hadn't had a traditional upbringing, but I imagined this was how kids felt when Mom and Dad were fighting. Wandering away from their low tones as they discussed what just happened, *how dangerous it could have been* and *how Vincent would seek vengeance for Onyx's pyromania*, I grabbed a long stick to stoke the blaze. When I turned around, I was startled by a flash of red.

She stood as silent as a shadow, with her long finger over her lips. "I didn't mean to frighten you, and I'm sorry for the trouble I've caused this evening. But I think I can make it up to you."

I put my hands on my hips and looked over her shoulder to where the guys stood. "I'm listening, Ezmerelda."

"Onyx's father will be at the Bleeding Heart Ball on February the fourteenth."

I arched a skeptical brow. "How do you know that?"

"Because every vampire is required to attend. It's our once-yearly celebration with our king and a … census of sorts."

"Okay … that's great. Where is it?"

"It's impossible to get to without a coven leader. It would have been easier if you would have only gained Vincent's trust."

An exasperated sigh blew through me as I made to move past her. "I really don't have time for this."

"Listen." She stopped me, hurrying her speech. "There's another way. It's a little … unorthodox, and the crew is … rough around the edges. They'll take you, but you have to do exactly as I say."

CHAPTER 13

Ghost

FIGHT ME

 If you could be either God's worst enemy or nothing, which would you choose?
Chuck Palahniuk, Fight Club

Only a breed of immortals as flashy as the vampires would have a secret circus. One you can't use magic to get to. One you simply have to find. These circus freaks lured humans into seclusion and put on their little show, bathing in the applause. Sometimes the humans made it home, oftentimes they didn't. *It's their choice to stay*, Onyx would argue. Tempting a lesser being with sex and riches wasn't much of a choice, and it wasn't something most humans would turn down. But that wasn't my main concern. What sent me spiraling into a rage when I arrived at the heavily warded red and white big top was the realization that Vincent's coven had acquired chaos magicians, or phantoms, as they liked to call themselves.

I'd known of their circus activities for decades, but they'd managed to keep their new crew under the radar. They knew better than to bring their magic men to Hallows Fest or Ash Grove. And Onyx and Wolfgang should have known better than to endanger Blythe by bringing her around them.

"Nothing happened," Blythe cooed, rubbing my arm. "It was my idea; I was coming with or without them."

"Nothing happened?" I questioned her soulful gaze.

"We just watched the show and talked to Vincent. Everyone said I smelled like a human; no one noticed anything. In fact, I think they were happy to see me out and about after not knowing where I went after Halloween. If anything, this was smart because now they really don't suspect I'm anything special. We were unnoticeable. Well, you know, aside from the lighting Vincent's tent on fire thing."

Onyx shrugged and chewed a stalk of hay in the train car. "He called Wolf a dog, and that clown disrespected Blythe. It was only a mild inferno."

I rubbed my forehead, feeling a headache building behind my eyes. "And when the coven comes after her for what you did? What then?"

Wolf interjected. "They won't. I heard some vampires on the way out say they were packing up and leaving town. Sounds like there's some-place important they have to go."

"No harm, no foul." Onyx put his hands behind his head and lay back as the train puttered on. "Remember when we hopped on a train as boys? Ames, your mom was so pissed."

I did remember. It reminded me that my friend Onyx was always pushing the envelope of misconduct. He eagerly sought out trouble—forever plotting, scheming, and chasing mischief. It was acceptable as boys, or even for the Halloween Boys, but now that Blythe was involved, it rattled my core and made my blood boil. How could he so flippantly put her at risk?

"Yes, I recall," I said lowly, stroking Blythe's hair as she dozed in my lap. "But we aren't children anymore, and this is more than hopping trains. If you put her life at risk again, Onyx …"

Onyx opened a lazy green eye. "You'll what?" he challenged.

My hand balled into a fist at my side. "Find out."

Wolf sat up on his elbows. "Knock it off, guys. Can't we just enjoy the ride?"

Blythe spoke up sleepily. "I know how to find your father, Onyx. Ezmerelda told me."

She had our attention while she yawned above my knees. "We have to leave soon, though. Or we'll miss them."

Onyx sat up on his elbows. "Miss who?"

With another yawn, she murmured, "The pirates."

THE NEXT EVENING, our car sat packed with suitcases and food for travel. I stared at it, the implications hitting me one by one. I hadn't left Ash Grove in two hundred years. There had been times when it was all I wanted to do, all I thought about and seethed against. It was my mission for so many years to unravel the curse and find a hole through the invisible wall that bound me to the little town. Killing psychopaths only satiated my desire for more than what a traditional existence offered. And then Blythe stumbled into my office ... and I never wanted to leave. She was my home. I had no need to venture elsewhere.

But the boys did. And it seemed that she did, too. That fact scraped something rough against my black pit of a soul. Did I expect her to stay here with me forever? *Yes.* I couldn't chain her to Ash Grove. *Well, perhaps I could ... No, I'm not doing that.* We'd vowed to assist Dragon in finding his family. Though we never discussed what we'd do when we found them. Would Onyx stay to get to know his bloodline? If his father was alive, could it be that his mother was as well? Would he choose to explore his dragon heritage, or would he bow to his fate of joining a coven of his own?

As much as he was irritating me lately, a part of me fought against that thought. He wouldn't leave us, would he? Perhaps our bond was only as good as the curse. Now that he had the freedom, he wouldn't stay a Halloween Boy. Onyx would move on, like Wolfgang and I were nothing but a two-hundred-year-old distraction.

My gaze drifted out the window of his farmhouse to the tire swing. Neither of them was ever far from her. I watched as he pushed her on the swing. She giggled and spun, looking like an angel that none of us monsters deserved. He was falling for her. They both were. And as much as I wanted to lock her in a box for only my viewing, I couldn't blame them all for loving each other. I loved them all, too. But I loved her enough to protect her, and if I had to protect her at the cost of the Halloween Boys, I would. Onyx's smile dimmed as he helped her off the swing and caught sight of me stalking toward them. His hand lingered in hers for two moments too long, and I wanted to cut it off, detach it from his arm.

His jaw tensed like he felt my savagery and aggravation. Blythe rubbed my chest. "I'm going to go make dinner."

I kissed her forehead and let her go.

My friend took a step forward.

"Wait." I held up a hand, and Onyx shut his smug mouth. "Okay, she can't hear me tell you to *fuck off* now."

Onyx popped his neck and stretched his arm. He was dying to hit me, and honestly, I would have loved for him to throw the first punch. Something rustled in the brush, and I knew without looking that Wolf watched on in his shifted form. He was never far from her, stalking her as a wolf, like she was his own Little Red Riding Hood. At least he had the good sense to keep his fucking mouth shut—unlike our hybrid friend.

"I've been waiting, Ghost. How much longer are we going to do this? How much longer are you playing bodyguard, as if you have more claim over her than Wolf or I do?"

Anger rose in my chest, and I stuffed my fists in the pockets of my jacket. "Interesting word choice because she is *my Claimed*. But regardless, you want her now, all of a sudden, and it's really beginning to piss me off."

The vampire-dragon hybrid took a step closer, his eyes turning to narrow slits. He was easily rattled lately, on edge. I wondered how far I could push him before he exploded. Worse, I wondered how safe Blythe was when she was around him. After how unhinged he went the night prior, lighting Vincent's tent on fire along with a room full of chaos magicians, anything could have happened. What if he lost control with her? He'd come dangerously close to throwing her into harm's way at the circus. He'd be better off a damned soul in my cemetery compared to the havoc I would rain upon him for all eternity if she were ever harmed.

"You knew Wolfgang and I wanted her, but you broke our agreement and got to her first. *First*," he pushed a finger into my chest, "not last, demon."

I grabbed his wrist, and a black slash of fury blurred my vision at the contact. He jerked his arm away and stepped closer. "You want to fight me, Ghost? Come on," he challenged.

Wolf's warning growl rattled even my evil bones, and we both glanced at his shadowy canine form, towering tall, poised to pounce. I sucked in a deep breath and reminded myself that this asshole was my friend and more.

Meeting his green, reptilian stare, I said low and slow, "I'm too old to be married to the idea of monogamy. That's not what this is about. If she wants you, or any man or woman or monster, I'll chain it naked to a silver platter for her to fuck as she pleases."

His head tilted in predatory skepticism. The vampire in him was calculating how he could tear my throat with his teeth. Easy answer: he couldn't.

"Then what's the fucking problem?"

"You," I growled, pointing my own finger into his chest. "You're a goddamn loose cannon and a horny fucking vampire. She's not your plaything. You'll both wait." I flicked a glance to Wolf, who crouched in the brush. I didn't miss the gleam of his bare teeth behind his dark maw. "You'll wait until the time is right and until I say so. In the meantime, you're not allowed to be alone with her. I can't risk you harming her."

Onyx looked to the sky, and when his eyes met mine again, his smile was a sinister sneer, baring the points of his fangs. I'd admit, Wolf and I often underestimated Onyx's power. The hybrid had oceans of ability left to be discovered. He was much like Blythe in that respect. The abilities of both a vampire and a dragon were unprecedented.

I was sure I could take him in battle if it ever came to that, but it would be a long-fought war. Strong as he may have been, Dragon had deep fucking issues and trauma too thick to wade through ... and nothing to lose. And that made him dangerous, especially now that the want for a woman was involved. Onyx hadn't longed for a woman since Minnie, and it didn't take much of my training in psychology to piece together the fact that old feelings of loss and inadequacy were rising to the surface for him.

I knew he was sizing me up as well, wondering how he would kill me, blaming me for what had happened to Minnie. Our love for each other wasn't stronger than the evils inside. The bloodlust would win out every time. I waited for the blow. Would it be fangs or speed and strength? I was ready for either, even in my human body.

But instead of landing a blow, he brushed a piece of lint from his jacket and straightened his collar before calmly saying. "Okay."

I raised an eyebrow and glanced at Wolf, who, even in his wolf form, looked just as perplexed. "Okay?"

Onyx's eyes returned to their typical shamrock shade and round pupils. "You're the leader. What you say goes. You call the shots. Anything else?"

I searched his tone and tasted his emotions for any hint of anger or sarcasm and came up short. Perhaps Onyx Hart wasn't as petulant and immature as I'd thought. It was a step in the right direction.

"That's all," I replied, turning to find Blythe.

I needed to hold her, keep her safe. I'd promised to keep her safe from this world of monsters. I hadn't anticipated having two of the monsters living under our roof.

CHAPTER 14

Onyx

FOOL WITH PIRATES

I should have discouraged her. I should have told her the pirates would never let the Halloween Boys aboard their ship. An archdemon, a werewolf, a reaper-disguised-as-a-human, and me. Yeah, there was no fucking way. It would have been more virtuous to tell her that my hope of finding my family had dimmed considerably in the past few weeks. It had always been a faraway target, a goal to keep me living every mundane, unremarkable day of my pathetic existence.

Now that it was tangible, though, I didn't want it as desperately. That probably meant I was broken beyond repair. But she wanted it. She'd dragged us to the circus to find Vincent after Wolf suggested it. She'd lied to Ghost about having been in danger—and I applauded her for *that*. Her little hints of wickedness made my cock instantly harden. What else could I get her to lie to him about?

Now, on some asinine lead from the batshit crazy Red Vampiress, Blythe was determined to get us aboard a goddamn pirate ship. And not just any ship, but Captain Vex Beard's ship. The guy was the most famous pirate I'd ever heard of.

Legends about Vex and his crew were undoubtedly where all the well-known pirate stories originated. Okay, I'd admit, a tiny part of me hoped we really were about to embark on some swashbuckling maritime adventure. I recalled hanging a flag on my treehouse as a young boy and pretending to be a pirate … I didn't know why being around Blythe made me think of things like that. Memories I'd buried and burned long ago. That boy was dead, and now a fire-breathing monster wore his skin.

The moment our tires crossed the border, leaving Ash Grove, the guys and I exchanged glances. *Did we really just do that? The town let us leave?* The curse had truly been lifted. After two hundred years, we were free. A bittersweet chord progression of a song I'd never write flitted through my thoughts as we left Ash Grove behind. I'd packed my favorite guitar, a sapphire blue Fender.

At least when the pirates laughed us back into our car, I'd have something to keep my hands busy. I'd have something to think about other than the smell of Blythe's shampoo or the way her nose scrunched when she laughed at my jokes or the way her denim jacket pushed her breasts together and made her look like a sexy eighties mom in a White Snake music video. I kept unintentionally catching her gaze when I checked the rearview mirror to steal a peek at her. Did she have any idea how badly I wanted her? *Fuck me.*

But her power-tripping demon wouldn't let me get close. I'd sensed his urge to end me the day prior—felt his death stare as it bored into me. It both shattered my heart and enraged me. Even after all the nights and love Ames and I had shared. We'd shared love even before he was Ames —back when he was only James Cove, and we were passing drawings back and forth in church. He'd really throw it all away for her, wouldn't he? Would I? *Yes.*

But we didn't have to. We could live together as a happy little coven, her and us. So why didn't he trust me? Why'd he want to literally kill me? Well, fuck him. If Ghost thought I was about to give up, he didn't know me very well. Because I still had several tricks left up my sleeve. I was merely biding my time.

As we neared the coast, Blythe turned down the radio and asked, "Those circus magicians, were they really magic?"

Ames snorted, gripping the steering wheel. He was still cross at us for taking her. His anger pressed into me until I had to pull out my cassette player and headphones to block the burning sensation. "They call themselves phantoms, but we know them as chaos magicians. Formerly human, they came upon a demon or witch at some point and bargained or begged for power. They have magic, but it's a dark, restless sort. They're not so much powerful as they are crafty, worn down by the darkness that will someday fully consume them."

Blythe shuddered. "Creepy."

Wolfgang snorted, closing his book. "Not as creepy as what happened to our friend, Sloan. Anyway, these phantoms are weak. Their allegiance is for sale to the highest bidder. Which makes me wonder what they're doing following Vincent around. And what's the real deal with this Phantom Circus?"

Ames was quiet for a moment, considering. "I don't know. But whatever it is, he didn't want us to know about it."

We stopped in a sandy lot and approached a rickety pier. The air was salty, and gulls cried above us. Raven ruffled his feathers nervously. I got the impression he didn't like the beach. I wasn't sure I liked the coast either. It was so open, exposed, there were no mountains to hide in, no curves or interest to the land. Just flat, sandy earth and ocean. The ship was hard to miss and looked like a resurrected sunken vessel. I was suddenly thankful they were going to reject us. Blythe would get over it. That thing was barely staying afloat. Ames not so subtly got between Blythe and me and wrapped an arm possessively around her shoulder.

I turned up Led Zeppelin on my cassette tape, and my friends' mix of heavy emotions dulled. Anger, wariness, excitement ... loneliness. If only I could brush against Blythe and make her feel happiness, not that cloudy beat of forlorn she carried. If even for my own selfishness of wanting to feel her joy, however artificial the source may have been. But her bodyguard wasn't letting me near her, and my dragon was pacing in his cage, roaring to be let free. *Soon.*

"Throw me that rope, would ya?" a man's voice ordered from the side of the ship.

Wolf looked at us skeptically before tossing the thick rope to the man. "You got a good arm. Thanks," he replied before disappearing. The dock wobbled as the waves rocked. Were docks supposed to wobble?

Ames grumbled. "I don't like the look of this."

Ignoring him, I called up, "Hey, we're looking for Captain Vex Beard!"

The man shouted back. "Does he owe you money, or did he steal your woman?"

I stifled a chuckle. Blythe leaned back and tugged at my shirt. My breath caught in my ribs at just the tiniest of her touches. "Tell him we brought stories from The Red Vampiress."

We all stared at Blythe in surprise, and before Mr. Demon-In-Charge could stop me, I yelled up at the pirate. Ames shot me an icy glare, and I held his stare. *Come at me, asshole.* The pirate didn't speak, but moments later, a rope ladder clanked over the edge of the ship. Wolfgang held it steady and ushered us up. Ames stopped Blythe and said he'd go first.

"Wow, he's so brave," I sneered, which earned me an elbow in the side from Wolfgang as I took my turn. God, Blythe's ass looked good from that angle.

Once we were all aboard, the tall, bearded captain stalked toward us. "Well, would you look at that? The Halloween Boys got their leash snipped." He turned to Blythe with a wink, "Hello, Blythe Pearl, it's nice to see you again." Taking her hand, he kissed her knuckle. I think Ames almost exploded at the sight. The feeling of his raging jealousy made me chuckle.

He raised a dark eyebrow and asked under his breath, "Something funny, Dragon?"

I addressed Captain Vex instead. "We're looking for my father. Ezmerelda, The Red Vampiress—"

"I know who Ezmerelda is," he interrupted brusquely. *Okay, then.*

"Right," I continued. "She believes you can help us. But Blythe knows more, so why don't you tell him, Blythe?"

She looked to me, and a soft smile curved her cheeks. It was easy to be overpowered by us and our strong personalities. Blythe was quiet and observant, but she had things to say. She had a wealth of power and wisdom inside her. I was happy to make room for her whenever possible.

"It's nice to see you again, too, Captain Vex." She reached into the pocket of her high-rise jeans and handed him a folded note. "Ezmerelda said to give you this."

The pirate took the note as his parrot and Raven sized each other up, chirping intermittently and bobbing their heads. The pirate clicked his tongue before folding the note and pushing it into his breast pocket. His gaze lingered for a moment on Blythe's chest.

"Welcome aboard the Ship of the Story Keepers." He turned and bellowed for his men to drop sails and lift anchor.

Ames asked in a frenzy, "Wait, they're not actually taking us, are they?"

Wolfgang raced to the ship's edge, where the enormous barnacle-covered anchor cranked into its nook. Wind filled the tattered sails, and the ship jutted forward.

Wolf laughed heartily. "Holy shit, we're on a fucking pirate ship!"

I glanced at Ames, just as surprised. "I didn't expect it to work either."

Blythe put an arm around us both and pulled us in for a group hug. "We're doing it! We're finding your parents, Onyx. Aren't you excited?"

"Thrilled." I smiled at Ghost, baring my fangs. His jaw tensed, and I felt his anger simmering like hot coals. He didn't want her doing this. He only allowed her to come because he believed, as I did, that we'd be turned away. I occasionally underestimated Blythe, but he constantly did.

A woman with colorful braids looped her arm with Blythe's and introduced herself as Pasha. "I'll show you to your hammock," she said.

"We left our luggage in the car," Blythe whined.

Pasha only laughed merrily in response. "This here ship's got all you need."

As the shoreline faded farther and farther behind us, Ames stalked closer. I leaned casually against the ship's edge, watching the pirate crew pull ropes and mop the decks. "Yes, darling?"

"I don't like this. This is the furthest thing from keeping her safe."

"Well, then, tie her up in your hell smoke and fly back to shore. No one's forcing you to come with me. You've made it clear that you have no fucking interest in me anymore."

Ghost's simmering rage subsided, and something like care and guilt peppered the emotions I felt from him. "Of course I care about you, Onyx. How could you say that? But you're strong. She's ... she's been through a lot. And she needs us to protect her. Parading her through every immortal town and event is only going to draw attention to what she is."

"She's stronger than you give her credit for. Just because someone's lived through hell doesn't mean they need to be locked away. Hiding her won't help her."

"It'll keep her alive while we sort out her abilities. You're careless, Dragon. Like taking her to that circus. You don't think I know that something went down with those chaos magicians? I taste her fear when they're mentioned. You made her lie to me, didn't you?"

I rolled my eyes toward the pale stars poking out from the rosy sky. "Dude, you've always been sanctimonious, but now you're growing paranoid, too."

On cue, Wolfgang appeared between us, crossing his burly arms. "Guys, we're on a goddamn pirate ship. Like, on the ocean. You are not going to ruin this for me by bickering. Blythe's safer here than in Ash Grove. Nothing can reach her here. Not ghouls, witches, vampires, or a baphomet. Let's enjoy our first vacation in two hundred years and maybe find Onyx's fam while we're at it. Deal?"

Ames and I squared off for a few more moments. The guy was always looking to dick measure, I swear to god.

Finally, he backed down. "I'm going to go check on Blythe."

Something glowing neon in the corner of the ship drew my attention. It flashed and began playing, "Entrance Song" by the Black Angels.

My eyebrows rose with pleasant surprise. "These crazy sons of bitches have a goddamn jukebox. This might not be so bad after all." When Ames disappeared down the stairs, I looked up at my ridiculous friend, who nodded his head with the beat. "Who the hell gave you a pirate hat?"

CHAPTER 15
Blythe
WALK THE PLANK

The ladder creaked, and the ship rocked as I followed Pasha down to the sleeping quarters. Which was a generous name for a room of dangling hammocks between stalls made of barrels of alcohol.

"This hammock's free. It used to be Twilson's, but he went and ran off with a merman about a week ago."

I pulled at the dangling strings, suddenly rethinking every life decision I'd made that had led me to this point. I was on an actual pirate ship, sailing to some sort of festival of vampires.

"Any questions?" Pasha asked, amusement lighting her hazel eyes.

"How would someone run off with a merman? They don't have legs, right?"

Pasha rubbed her chin with her hook-for-a-hand. "You know what? That's a really good question. Anyhow, I'm the ship navigator. You know the captain, and Scully's the quartermaster. Food's always in the mess hall, which is the next floor down. Sailin's best when drunk, so help yourself to the rum. I've got chests of clothes over near my hammock. Feel free to take what you need, seein' as you didn't bring anything."

"I meant to. The ship took off before—"

Suddenly a bell rang out, and Pasha looked at the dusty ship's ceiling. "That'll be my cue to go chart our course. Make yourself at home. We should be at yer door in a couple of days. Hope you can swim."

With that chaotic introduction, she was gone.

"Wait, why do I need to know how to swim?" I called after her in a panic. I could have sworn I heard her chuckle as she disappeared above the boat.

What the hell had I gotten myself into? The idea of a pirate adventure was fun in theory, but what if Ezmerelda was lying? What if this wasn't the way to find Onyx's family? It was too late to question any of that now. We weren't going anywhere for a while. And while I trusted Captain Vex and the crew, it had also felt very easy to come aboard. I'd spent enough time with immortals by now to know that no one did anything for free or without their own motives, so I'd be watching the sea captain closely to see what those may be. The last thing the guys needed was someone else on their kill-lists. I liked the pirates and didn't want them, well, dead.

My thoughts drifted to Ash Grove, where Piper, the gentle witch, may have been dead because of me. Where my closest friend told me to leave. Ash Grove had been the only place that had ever felt like home. And now I was being kicked out. I'd wanted to help Onyx find his family, but guilt sat like a rock on my shoulders at the knowledge that my eagerness to get out of town wasn't entirely selfless. I was running again. Except this time, instead of running from my stepfather, I was running from home, running from myself. Maybe I'd find something on this journey that would help me know what to do. The story keeper's ship had a navigator, and I found myself wishing I had one, too.

It didn't help my confusion that something about Onyx was screaming at me for attention. I was attracted to him; it would be impossible not to be. There were witches claiming we were all mated, the Halloween Boys and me. And I'd been surprised to learn that what I'd perceived as possessiveness from Ghost was a bit more like protective-ness. He was okay with us being together, all of us, but he believed his friends to be immature and reckless. Maybe he was right.

But I couldn't help the pull of Onyx's emerald stare or the way my heart beat faster, just wondering what he'd say next. Onyx Hart was witty and beguiling … though there was something else. There was something else under his carefully crafted surface that I'd yet to uncover. And I really wanted to uncover it. But I'd never successfully navigated a long-term relationship, much less a polyamorous relation-ship with three men.

I didn't know where to start. I didn't know how to go about it in a way that honored them all the way they each deserved. For the time being, for this journey, I'd have to try to push those conflicting emotions aside and focus on the task at hand. Finding Onyx's family and finding a way back to Ash Grove that would allow me to stay.

How could I promise a town safety if I was the embodiment of death?

A steady knocking above me pulled my attention from my anxious thoughts. I inhaled an uneasy breath, worried the knocking was the guys fighting. They couldn't be thrilled about leaving our bags behind and being sequestered with pirates. There was a heavy chord of tension between them all right now. It was all my fault, too. I knew they each carried the weight of me being a reaper. The responsibility they felt to guard me from the beings who'd harm me, and maybe the chemistry that pulsed between us all created a heady mix, and we were all a little on edge. And I'd just thrown a crew of unruly pirates onto their thin patience. I climbed the ladder, ready to break up whatever argument or brawl was festering.

A blast of salty air greeted me as the rickety ship rocked against the purple hues of twilight. My mouth dropped at what took center stage against the backdrop of the vast ocean. The crew had assembled in a circle around a fire in a barrel, much like I'd found them in Ash Grove. Together they sang an upbeat medley that sounded like the beach on a sunny day.

Wolfgang clapped along as several pirates danced. Ames sat with arms crossed, tapping his foot in time with the beat. My gaze flicked from him to Onyx, who thrummed the tune on a faded black guitar. His stare followed me as I wove through the rambunctious dancers, Wolf included, and onto Ames's waiting lap. Ames gave me a squeeze, and I was silently thankful to be turned away from Onyx's gaze, though I could feel him still, somehow, watching me. I clapped along and cheered, watching Wolfgang swoop Pasha with a dip. Jealousy churned behind my ribs, but I tried to ignore it, along with the hypocrisy that I wanted all three of them while not wanting them to want any woman but me. Could I ever bring myself to ask that of them? That conversation seemed eons away from the present moment. I gladly accepted a goblet of rum when Scully offered it with a warm smile.

"It's good to see you again, Scully." I beamed, taking a sip.

I'd drunk half when Ames took it and downed the remainder in one gulp. I huffed in mock annoyance, but he only smirked.

"That stuff is enough to get a demon shitfaced. I did you a favor, little ghost."

Rolling my eyes, I kissed his stubbled cheek and settled into his hold as the merriment settled into something more somber. Thousands of stars sparkled above us, caught in the infinite beyond. For some reason, I thought of Maud back in Ash Grove. The ghost in the cemetery who'd rather chat with me and knit than move on. *Can you tell me what lies beyond?* she asked so innocently. I couldn't tell her. Death itself couldn't assure the dead.

Ames's low whisper interrupted my thoughts. "You taste like sadness. Why?"

His whisper sent chills of love and longing down my spine.

"What does my sadness taste like?" Ghost's ability to taste emotions was mystifying, and I found myself collecting my own flavors. Honey for arousal, something addictive for fear …

"Tell me why you're sad, and I'll tell you what it tastes like."

With a sigh, I leaned closer to his ear. The others had settled into the murmur of conversation as Onyx continued to play his own music then.

"It's not sadness, exactly … inadequacy, maybe."

He pulled back, as if offended. "How could you ever feel inadequate? You are perfection in every way, Blythe Pearl."

A breath left my lungs at his earnest care for me. What did I ever do to deserve an archdemon's love?

"I'm a reaper who can't reap. I'm death who knows nothing of dying or what comes after. There's so much I don't know and so much I'm failing at. If only I could learn, I could protect Ash Grove, and you guys wouldn't have to worry so much."

Ames hummed low in his throat, the night sky concealing most of his features. "Why are you worried about us and Ash Grove? Did something happen?"

Shit. I shouldn't have said that.

"No, nothing happened—"

"You're lying. I taste it, Blythe."

Panic seized me as I sat up. I was about to dig my hole deeper with another implausible lie when Onyx's loud voice cut across the crashing waves and pirates' laughter.

"Hey, Captain Vex, I'd like to trade for a story."

The laughter went silent. Even Ames stopped his questioning and looked at his friend. Captain Vex straightened from where he leaned on the side of the ship and walked over, looking more sinister in the light of the moon. He looked like a pirate you'd see sailing black seas in your nightmares, with his long beard tied with keys and trinkets.

"You best have a nice trade then, boy. Let's hear it."

The vampire-dragon hybrid gave me a sideways grin as he sat his guitar down gently. Had he interrupted to save me from my lie?

He walked over, tall and confident. "I want a story about where we're going. This vampire town, festival, and king."

Wide eyed, the pirates looked to their captain. The little I knew about the pirates included how they regarded their stories higher than anything else. Stories, and the keeping and sharing of stories, were their currency and leverage throughout this world. Apparently, Onyx had just had the nerve to ask for something huge. *He would.*

"You better have something worthy to trade for that kind of tale. For it's not one I've told before, and many died to bring me its chapters."

My hands went cold as Wolfgang made his way over, sitting at mine and Ames's feet to watch with us.

Onyx extended an upward fist, and when he opened his hand, it lit with green flame. "How about a fire that won't burn your ship? You'll have to keep it going, but it won't harm your boat."

Captain Vex's parrot whistled in appreciation. I glanced up to see my own bird perched on the bow, his black silhouette lit by a full moon. I missed his voice. When would Raven talk to me again?

When I looked back to the sea captain, he was shaking Onyx's hand. Onyx then lit a fire in an empty barrel. The pirates cheered around the flame and settled in, waiting for their leader to speak. Onyx went back to his seat, shooting me a wink as he did. My cheeks flushed. He *did* do it for me.

Captain Vex's voice was one with the ocean he commanded as he walked circles around his gifted flame. "Belladonia is where you're heading. And the only thing more frightening than the fact that every vampire in existence will be there is their king. Vladimir Drakon."

"Have you heard of him?" I whispered to Ames and Wolfgang. They both shook their heads, focusing on the captain's every word.

"King Vladimir Drakon is something of a legend. A terrible, cruel sort. Many say he's the original vampire. He's the one from all yer human stories," Captain Vex said to me, and I shivered. "The vampire king rules over every coven from his kingdom in the sky, Belladonia. Every year, all covens must appear before him at the Bleeding Heart Ball."

Wolfgang leaned back and murmured, "How are we supposed to get to a castle in the sky by boat?"

"Through the ocean, of course," Captain Vex answered, walking over. The werewolf crossed his arms, listening. "The doors are how the vampires get there. Each coven leader is given a skeleton key that opens a door to Belladonia. The doors are all over the world. However, since your lot couldn't find a coven nor leader who can tolerate ye, I'll be gettin' you there through another door of sorts."

Ames exhaled. "I'm not liking the sound of this."

"Gettin' there's the least of your worries, demon. Belladonia? It's as deadly as the plant it's named after. And from the stories I've gotten recently, some sort of darkness has crept in, lending itself to a strange sort of beast. As if the vampires weren't enough to scare ye, I reckon."

Ames shot Onyx an annoyed glance.

The hybrid shrugged, glowing by the firelight. "Any advice?"

The sea captain turned and faced him, the trinkets in his beard clinking together as he did.

"Yes." He nodded toward the side of the ship. "Walk the plank and let the mer and creatures of the deep have ye. You'd be better off with them than with King Vladimir and the blood-drunken likes of Belladonia."

CHAPTER 16

Onyx

BETRAY ME

Some people never go crazy. What truly horrible lives
they must lead.
Charles Bukowski

I often wondered if my skill of deceit led to my interest in law, or if my talent for the law made way for being an excellent liar. Regardless, it was an ability as useful as speed or strength. No one expected an immortal to be good at anything so *human*. Though that's why the Halloween Boys excelled. We didn't leave behind our mortality in totality.

We harvested what we desired from our humanity and hid it under the dark shadow of our monsters. Ames was perceptive, even without his need to feed on human fear. Wolfgang embodied a beast even as a man, using his kindness as a barometer to test the waters of people's discernment.

Unlike other vampires, werewolves, and demons, we hadn't had the luxury or hindrance of being coddled among our own. For hundreds of years, we lay trapped within the confines of a picture-perfect small town. Our inhuman wiles were next to useless there, which I assumed the devil that cursed us knew would be the case. We'd either have to tear each other, and the town, apart—again—or learn to suffer among the average man. The curse was crafted to drive us mad—and it had worked.

However, it likewise made me stronger.

Strong enough to form a brotherhood.

Strong enough to find my family, to risk a run-in with the king of the vampires.

Strong enough to pretend to be weak.

Strong enough to lie to my friends—to her.

One thing I hadn't learned to resist, however, in old age or enhanced supernatural ability, was the smell of her sex. The feel of her intense longing had my vampiric nature shrieking to be let out of his coffin. We were naturally sensuous creatures. What human myths perceived as bloodlust were only partly accurate.

We craved the blood of orgasm. The essence of all beings subsisted vibrating beneath their peel, like the rum beneath the oak barrels the pirates hoarded. We needed it, lusted for it. Sure, we could take it regardless, but it wasn't sweet like the offering freely given. Coerced or forced bites were bitter thievery with no payoff. What made our fangs ache to tear through paper-thin skin was arousal. And fuck me if Blythe wasn't always fucking aroused.

It wasn't all from Ghost, either. He tasted it, I felt it, Wolf smelled it, and she knew it. But we were all going to ignore it, right? For what? For the big sensitive baby archdemon? To spare his little temper. To assuage his need for control.

He didn't know I couldn't let him control this any longer. Not when she looked at me like *that*. Not when her doe eyes frantically searched for me when she was caught in a lie, like such a fucking good little girl. Yes, my pet, look for Daddy when you fib. I was the father of lies and deceit, and she fucking knew it.

I'll save you. I'll damn you. Just wait a little longer.

After a day of rocking among the waves of an ocean I never dreamed I'd see, I'd cornered Vex deep beneath the shadows of his piece of shit ship. He'd obey me, and he'd be paid handsomely for it. She'd hate me, of course. So would my lovers, my boys, but they needed this as much as I did, even if they didn't know it yet. Somewhere lurking behind the cobwebs of what could have formally been a soul, I might have felt a spasm of remorse for what I was about to do.

Until I heard her moan.

After watching Wolfgang live his boyhood dream of sailing a pirate ship and avoiding Ghost, who was, as usual, too focused on Blythe, I'd retreated to my bunk with my cassette player. AC/DC muffled the emotions of the boat well enough. Though the pirates' emotions were entertaining, to say the least. How one could feel deep and undying romantic love for rum was beyond me.

I felt it like a bolt of lightning through my dark heart. Her writhe of pleasure. My cock hardened at the feel of it, like a thick blanket of delectable sin. I shoved my music player into my jeans and stalked up the stairs—to find Wolfgang already watching. The deck was clear, the pirates all sleeping below, rocked gently by the easy push and pull of the tranquil sable ocean. It wouldn't stay that way, though, would it?

Wolf growled as I came to a stop next to him. The beast was awake and howling for her. His every ounce of canine was hinting at the heat that was inevitably coming, though he vehemently denied it. Ames had her laid out over the goddamn pirate plank as he thrust into her. Her whimpers rippled over the immense sea as she married her sounds of wetness with the water that splashed beneath her.

Blythe's naked body glowed pale under the bright moon, and I was no better than a goddamn werewolf at that moment. She was my full moon, and I was shifting into an animal for her.

He fucked her so casually. Like a man who'd been with the same woman hundreds of times. Like he knew her every curve and had stretched her pussy in all the ways that it conformed to his size. I'd never fuck her so flippantly, and if I ever did, I'd hope one of my boys would do to me what I was about to do to them. Ames claimed I didn't deserve her. As if he did. As if any of us ever could.

Our blood-stained hands marred her with every selfish stroke, but we'd never stop. Good men would stop, but we were neither good nor men. And she was in it way too deep to ever escape us. Vex was right. She'd be better off walking the plank than gripping a demon's cock with her immaculate pussy.

He looked over his shoulder and smirked as she came again, screaming the delight he craved. I felt her passion seep into my bones and beg for my fangs. *Oh, what her blood must taste like right now. How I'd roll it over my tongue to savor every tannin of its flavor …*

Wolfgang palmed his cock, his eyes turning amber and positively feral. "Her ass like that," he breathed. "How perfect it is."

My mouth dried to an uncomfortable rasp. I needed her so fucking bad that even Wolfgang's succulent length wouldn't suffice at that moment. Ames pulled out of her with maddening swiftness. Did he not relish the very feel of his ridges as she milked him with her aftershocks of pleasure? *I would.*

Blythe needed an exorcism of the demon inside her.

She needed something thirstier. She needed to be soaked and drained and bruised. How nice my fang marks would look as they turned shades of red, pink, and blue on her neck.

Sitting up on her elbows, cheeks rosy and mouth parted, she looked from Wolfgang to me and back to Ames, as if to ask permission. *Permission.* I'd wanted to beat my friend close to a second death countless times during our immortal relationship, but never as strongly as I did in that moment. Blythe Pearl, the Reaper, Death herself, should ask for nothing and should take everything she desired. Fuck him for making her believe otherwise.

"Your hedonists admire you on the sea tonight, little ghost," he said with velvet smoothness. He was sated and satisfied and ready to toy with us again, like he'd done in the church a few months prior. I'd accepted it then … would I do it again? My fangs yearned in defiance.

"She wants you. I can taste it. And I know you both want her." He gestured to her naked form. "So go ahead and taste her. Baptize yourselves in her holy waters."

"What?" she asked breathlessly, lying back like our own captured mermaid on a cursed ship. The line of her lush hips taunted me, asking me to come play.

He turned to her, running a hand through his dark wind-tousled hair. "Why are you surprised? I've said before that they may worship you. I'm merely the priest—the conduit between sinners and the divine. We worship you, Blythe. I'd never deny you what you wish. I only keep the sinners from you until they've earned your glory. And Onyx and Wolfgang have pleased me in their prayers to you, in their seeking of you. They aren't yet fully worthy, but as I said, they may have a taste. They may take part in your holy sacrament, should you allow it. You are our god, little ghost."

He was getting closer … but not close enough. Not quick enough for me to derail my plan.

Wolfgang's arm brushed mine as bright light from the haunted jukebox illuminated the dark boat, drenching Blythe in a sinful neon red. "I Get Off" by Halestorm thrummed through the speakers.

"Are we best friends now?" I asked it—and it blinked something like a wink in response. *Hell yeah.* I wondered if Wolfgang would help me steal it, when suddenly her emotions hit me like another bolt of electricity.

Me. She wanted *me.* My fangs pulsed as I watched Wolfgang drop to his knees before her. Every bit the worshipper that Ames wanted. "He's right about one thing. You really should act like the god you are. You look so beautiful. May I?"

"Please," she breathed.

I stalked closer, leaning on the side of the ship, meeting her eyes. She moaned and leaned her head back at the first stroke of Wolf's tongue. I'd had his mouth before, too. She was right to quake in pleasure. He finally got his handful of her ass that I knew he'd been longing for. His feelings of gratitude and heat were a dull ache alongside Blythe's heavy breathing as the wolf lapped the black that coated her pussy. Previously I would have asked the werewolf to save some of the demon cum for my enjoyment, but I didn't want it that night.

I ran my fingers through Wolf's wavy, salt-kissed hair. "Lick her clean. Get her ready for me, Wolf."

He nodded and growled, not pulling away from his feast. She writhed on the plank, and I looked over the edge, swearing I was met with a pair of glimmering eyes below. Did something from the depths secretly surface to enjoy the show?

Her knuckles brushed mine as she frantically pulled at his locks, bucking against his mouth as her release tore through her.

"Yes, that's it. Come in my mouth just like that," Wolf growled against her needy little cunt. "Ride my face, little one."

Ames looked on with arms crossed, the pleased and pompous priest. But I wasn't a member of his parish. I was my own god, and his church was about to be burned to hell. He just didn't know it yet.

Still perched on his knees, Wolfgang pushed his tongue into her again, only this time, I shoved him aside. "Move over, greedy bastard. It's my turn." My rasp was every bit the starving vampire the Halloween Boys and I often mocked. My pride was a dead rabbit drained of blood at this point, so I didn't give a fuck as I stood over her. She met my stare with hooded eyes as the ship rocked against a rogue wave. Her heart was beating out of her chest despite the pleasure Wolfgang had just wrung from her. I made her nervous. *Good.*

I didn't want to rush this, though the man inside me begged me to. I could be a mortal and push into her and pump away until I spilled, but that was cheap and easy. She was neither. Oh, what I wanted from her …

Ames snarled low in his throat behind me, no doubt sensing my unholy desire. I ignored him, letting my eyes roam all the places I'd suck her dry. The crook of her perfect neck, between her breasts, where the *oh-so-important* necklace rested. I let my eyes feast upon her silky-smooth ribs, working my way to the soft, lush center of her, the peaks and valleys of her flesh that screamed for bites and gashes of my fangs. How nicely she would bleed for me … And when my gaze hit its target of her plump ass pushing out beneath her dripping pussy, I dropped to my knees in what Father Ames Cove would call a prayer. He'd be right.

She whimpered before I'd even touched her, and my mouth curved. These over-eager friends of mine touched her too quickly and stopped too soon. They couldn't help themselves. To give them credit, it was fucking difficult not to just defile her like a monster's sex doll. Gently, I moved my hands under her ass, squeezing softly. She arched her back and bucked forward gently. She wanted me *so* badly.

"You are radiant like this, Blythe Pearl," I rasped, my throat dryer by the minute. Was the neon light from the jukebox making her red, or was it my bloodlust coating my vision? I'd never wanted a taste so badly. Ames took a step closer, his concern pushing against the wall of my cognizance. In one movement, I buried my nose in her cunt, inhaling her scent. My cock strained against my jeans, answering her siren's call as she groaned at the contact. Tilting my chin, I dipped in my tongue, tasting a faint remnant of Ames, more of Wolf, and then … *her.* Something snarled—was it me? And then my body jerked, my fangs bared as I jerked her forward by her hips. She screamed, I think, and I opened wide to bleed the space between her opening and her ass.

But before I could prick the skin, a large hand wrapped around my neck and pulled me away. *No!* My shoulder blades splintered the ship's edge, cracking the wood and sending streams of blood down my back. I stood with a primal snarl, facing the shifted archdemon with his sharp teeth bared.

This wasn't me—or it was me, but I wasn't in control. Blythe's fear rippled through my senses as I registered Ghost's roar as he charged forward. I dodged his advance and felt my skin burn, my fists and forearms igniting in fire. I faintly registered Wolfgang pulling Blythe off the plank and holding her like a naked damsel in destress. I wanted to go to her, but I needed to beat the ever-loving shit out of Ghost first. My fiery fist collided with his jaw, and I could have laughed at the enraged surprise that floated off him in that moment.

"You can't keep me from her," I growled with a voice that was no longer my own. My dragon blew fire inside me, begging me to shift, demanding to be let free. But if I accepted his request, my friends would be dead. This ship would sink in flame, and Blythe would see what an ugly creature I truly was. I couldn't release him, not yet.

"I'll take her to Hell if I have to. You won't fucking bite her." Ghost got in my face.

"Take her below deck," I ordered Wolfgang without pulling my stare from the icy gaze of the demon.

"No!" she protested. Suddenly I felt her hand push between Ghost and me, straining to push us apart. "Please, don't fight—"

With one easy burst of feeling, she closed her eyes. Suddenly tired, sleeping, dreaming of Halloween … and me. Wolfgang caught her before she fell and scooped her up, limp and naked in his burly arms.

"You two better work your shit out now," he demanded. "If I come back and either of you are dead, I'll fucking kill you both."

I rolled my eyes as he stalked away, feeling my head level slightly, though the wind began to howl, and rain sizzled against my flames.

I shoved Ghost hard, burning him, and he retreated a step. "I've stayed back. I've given you space. I've been respectful. Every goddamn day, watching her, feeling like my skin is on fire because I'm not touching her, scenting your fucking demon cum on her every night. Not telling her what we saw on Halloween—what we learned. She may be your Claimed, but she's ours, too. She's mine, too." My voice turned hoarse and ragged—and why did I feel the unfamiliar urge to cry?

Ghost straightened. "We aren't ruled by witch magic. Regardless, this proves how disturbingly unready for her you are, Dragon. You may be bound to her, but you don't deserve her."

My neck twitched as I evened my tone. "You're important to me, Ghost. You and Wolf are the closest thing I have to family. But if you think I won't lock you in Hell for keeping her from me, you don't know me very well. You have no idea what runs through my blood. What I'm capable of."

"My Claimed and I will see you to your father's house, and then we are going home to Ash Grove. Who knows? Maybe you'll want to stay and visit for a hundred years or so. Maybe I've already arranged for it."

My dragon roared inside me. *He won't keep her from us*, I assured the beast.

"We'll see about that. Let's see how long until the werewolf's primal desires kick in, and then you're truly fucked. Or, I don't know, maybe I slip, and the power of my touch puts you in a coma for a decade to let you cool off. Either way, your time of having her all to yourself is sand in an hourglass. So pull yourself together, you selfish piece of shit. I will *burn you* for her."

The archdemon smirked, dripping hate. "Try."

I would do more than try, and by the sudden shift of the wind, by what I'd caught a glimpse of in the water, I'd be doing it that night.

It was time to betray them all.

CHAPTER 17

Blythe

THE JUMP

> He who jumps into the void owes no explanation to those who stand and watch.
> *Jean-Luc Godard*

I saw him then, his eyes glowing as red as his crimson cape. His dark skin flickering in torchlight. Even the old Bible stories couldn't deny he was lovely to look at. We were alone on a dark, wet street. It had just rained, and the air was heavy with moisture. My breath puffed from my lips like smoke as he extended a hand to cup my jaw. I'd recognize him anywhere, most of all, in my nightmares.

"Devil," I breathed. "Judas."

His mouth quirked. "You've really gone and done it now, haven't you, My Death?"

"Where are we?"

He looked around, casually taking in the empty street. "You tell me. You brought me here."

"What? No, I would never."

He chuckled darkly. "Wouldn't you?" He glanced up at the sky. "I'll see you in Belladonia, Death."

. . .

I AWOKE in a puddle of sweat. It pulled against my corset, my dress. *My dress?* My hands floated down my ribs as I felt the fabric. The gown was similar to the 1800s garb I'd worn on Halloween. Though this was more casual. I racked my pounding head for memories of how I came to be wearing it. I was on the plank. I'd been with Ames, and then Wolf's mouth, the feel of Onyx's tongue before … oh god.

I tumbled out of my hammock and tripped, falling against a barrel of rum. The ground straightened, and I wobbled, lunging for the ladder. The ship rocked opposite now, and I screamed, feeling my feet lift and sway in the opposite direction. Just then, a hand bejeweled with gemstone rings reached down and grabbed my arm, pulling me up onto the deck. Water pierced my skin as if it were as solid as arrows. I rubbed my eyes and pulled against the man who held me. Through the pounding rain and flailing ship, he somehow stood steady and unaffected by the calamity that surrounded us. Captain Vex Beard.

"Come on, now. You don't want to miss yer exit. The storm's perfect. Beautiful, isn't she?"

I'd never thought too much of the ocean. I'd never considered it frightening until that moment. It thrashed like a living thing, like it was angry with us and raging against the ship. Lightning flashed white, and I made out a horrifying mountainous wave of black rising before us.

"Ghost! Wolf! Onyx!" I screamed.

"Ah, hush yer hollerin'. You'll anger the sirens." He pulled me toward the plank and threw me down. I gripped its side to keep from rolling across the deck. Where were the guys? Where was the crew? How were we all alone?

"What have you done to them?" I accused, shaking from the cold rain.

He chuckled and pointed. "Get on the plank."

Fear gripped my throat. And then he was there, like a vision in the rain.

"Onyx!" I yelled. "Help!"

His emerald eyes scanned me for the briefest moment as he walked over. Before I could grab on to him for balance and safety, he took hold of the back of my hair. With a quick yank that bit into my skin, he pulled my necklace from my chest. I dropped to the bobbing, slippery floor again as he sauntered back to the captain.

"Here you go. The necklace, as agreed upon."

The pirate captain turned the glittery obsidian stone over in his rough hand and nodded. "This'll do."

I gasped. "Onyx, what have you done?"

He only walked over and picked me up, looping an arm under my knees. I held on to his neck only because the ship was thrashing so wildly that I was afraid I'd fall. He stood firm as Captain Vex approached, a crackle of lightning striking behind him, making him look menacing and cruel as the rain poured from his pirate hat. "I'm cashing in my story with you, girl."

"What?" I said in a strained panic, watching with horror as another wave rose like a malevolent mountain in the sea.

"At Hallows Fest, you asked for a story about the Halloween Boys. About yer Ghost. And you agreed to a trade. Well, I'm callin' upon it. When you get there, find the mixologist and bring me his story."

Pain, confusion, and fury slapped against me with the rain. "When I get where?"

"Don't make it obvious. Watch him and let me know how it unfolds," Captain Vex shouted over the storm. "Been chasin' that bastard's tale for centuries."

Onyx stepped onto the plank, holding me tight. "Don't let go," he whispered, as if he were speaking to a lover, not a hostage.

"What are you doing? Put me down!"

The side of his mouth elevated in a wicked smile, revealing his prominent fangs. "As you wish."

And with one step over the edge, we plummeted into the furious ocean below.

WE HIT the waves and tumbled into silent darkness. The air pushed from my lungs on impact, and I lost my grip around Onyx's neck, but he didn't let go of me. Something grabbed hold of my ankle, and I screamed into a frenzy of bubbles and saltwater, but then a swift and sudden calm invaded my senses, and I relaxed. Closing my eyes, I nuzzled into Onyx's chest as someone, or something, pulled us lower and lower.

My lungs burned and constricted from lack of air, but I didn't—couldn't—panic. Damn his sex-touch changing my emotions. I faded out of consciousness and was surely one moment away from drowning when it felt as if a cyclone sucked us in, only to spit us out again. We slammed into fresh air. Water pooled around me as I tumbled down iron stairs and into a pile of dried leaves. My calm faded as I coughed, and horror and anger took its place. Drying my eyes, I looked up the staircase but couldn't make sense of what I was seeing.

We were in the middle of a forest. An ordinary looking forest, except for the harsh black bark of the twisted trees and the ruby red leaves that sparsely dotted their branches. I lay at the bottom of a wrought-iron staircase that led to an open door, revealing only the forest on the other side. It was a staircase to nowhere in the middle of nowhere. I spat out salt water and tried to stand on weak and wobbling knees. A hand took hold of my elbow, and I looked up at his smiling face.

"We made it," Onyx said with mirth. His jet-black hair slicked back, he'd removed his wet shirt, revealing his marble-pale six-pack abs and that stupid V above his low-slung, wet jeans. "Like what you see?"

I pushed him with all my might then, which wasn't a lot, but he didn't fight it. Only stepped back and put his hands in the air, as if I were the one acting crazy.

"What the hell is wrong with you?" I coughed out. "Are you trying to kill us?"

"Oh, on the contrary, my dear, I'm trying to save us. You're shivering. Let me warm you." He opened his arms and gestured me forward.

"You have some nerve, Onyx Hart. I'm not coming near you unless it's to punch your smug face. Where are we? Where—oh my god, where are the guys? Raven!" I called out, as if my familiar could hear me through whatever void we'd passed through. "Raven, I'm here!"

Onyx shrugged, shaking out his wet shirt before his hands glowed with green heat, drying it completely. "They're probably back on the boat. And you're right, I do have a lot of nerve, and you're lucky I do."

I wanted to hit him, and then strangle him, and then kill him. He quirked a grin. "You're cute when you're murderous. I can let you try to kill me if it'll make you feel better. That sounds like a tantalizing experiment, actually. But I fear it will only tire you out, and you need your energy."

"I hate you," I hissed, my teeth chattering on the words. "You— you've done something bad. Ghost will k-kill you if I don't do it first."

He nodded. "Uh-huh, come here." He stepped forward, and I stepped back.

"Don't come near me. I'm going back to Ames right now." Turning on my heel, I sloshed up the staircase, my shoes making a comical squishing sound as I did so. When I reached the random door at the top, I closed it, shut my eyes, and opened it again. *Nothing*. I tried again. *Nothing*.

Onyx loudly exhaled. "Are you done throwing your tantrum yet?"

"I'm going to end you," I threatened as I stomped down. "Why did you do that? Why'd you—what is happening? Did you kidnap me and abandon our friends?"

He shrugged, gesturing for a hug again. "Come closer and I'll tell you."

His tone was lighter and happier than I'd heard it in months. He was truly pleased with whatever it was he'd just done. "For fuck's sake, I can hear your teeth rattling from here." He eliminated the space between us in a breath of speed and wrapped me in his arms so tight I couldn't protest. I screamed in annoyance and wiggled as his heat enveloped me, drying my stupid pink dress and hair within moments. *Okay, the warmth was nice.*

I pulled out of his hold and glared up into his amused green eyes. "I love Ames" was the only thing I could think to say.

He didn't shirk from my declaration or tease me. He only replied. "I love Ames, too, and Wolfgang. They're my everything."

"Then why?"

Onyx spun with a flourish and plucked a rose from a nearby bush.

Doing a little dance that would have been wildly charming if I weren't furious with him, he imitated a ballroom waltz while trying to make me smile and humming a tune.

"I've been writing this damn song in my head for months; I just can't quite get the chorus right." With a bow, he offered me the rose, looking up at me through long, dark lashes, like a dark, mischievous god. "Forgive me for getting you wet? With the ocean, that is. Not the other way. The other way I quite enjoyed until we were so rudely interrupted."

"Are you seriously flirting with me right now? We've lost Ghost and Wolf and my familiar. And what the hell was that with Captain Vex?"

He sighed and batted his lashes like the saddest puppy dog I'd ever seen. Rolling my eyes, I jerked the rose from his hand, and he smiled in triumph.

"That was an old story keeper being extremely gullible. And the guys will catch up. I just beat them here and brought you along for the ride. Plus, this gives us a break. Room to breathe away from … everyone."

"I love him," I repeated, to both him and to myself. And he loved me. And he was okay with me exploring my connections with Onyx and Wolf, though he didn't think they were ready. Onyx seemed to be proving that to be true with his stupid stunt.

"Again, I love him, too. But tell me you didn't need space. That you weren't feeling a little suffocated under his holy fucking watch? They're only a couple of days behind us. I saw an opportunity to get us here a little sooner, and I took it. After two hundred years, can you blame me?"

I gritted my teeth together and surveyed the forest. Black trees and red roses for miles. It was eerie and haunting, even the sunlight had a cherry tint. When I realized Onyx was waiting for my answer, I exhaled heavily. "Fine, I won't kill you today. But they better be here soon. Now, where are we going?"

"Not sure. I'll figure it out, though."

I looked up through the snaked canopy and groaned.

He didn't have a plan.

Or did he?

CHAPTER 18

Onyx

FAMILIAR MONSTERS

 Excess is part of my nature. Dullness is a disease.
Freddie Mercury

My need to scheme had been severely hampered by Ash Grove's curse. Perhaps becoming an attorney scratched that itch—the reworking of words, the skating by on technicalities. They were all socially acceptable ways of creating mischief. Like anything, though, it had grown dull, and the Halloween Boys had settled into complacency. Ghost underestimated me. Judas likely didn't think of me at all. To them, I was a peculiar jokester, a shameless tease, and a restless musician. Brothers and lovers often trivialized the gifts of their counterparts.

Oh, he'd never do that to me. He's a good guy.

Always wrong.

And I'd been biding my time. I knew that my first betrayal should be swift and long-earned. My initial foray back into the world of monsters, released from my small-town prison cell, would have to be big. They'd have to never see it coming for it to work. And they didn't.

It was in my nature. I was an odd wretch of a creature. Part vampire, from my father, and part dragon, my mother. Vampires were sex, selfishness, and seduction. Dragons were elemental, earthly, and ethereal.

My breeding begged for chaos, my two parts in mortal opposition with one another. What a cruel and terrible thing my parents did when they created me. *Why?* I wanted to ask them. Or ask my father, because dragons disappeared a long time ago, and surely my mother along with them. What would possess such a union? To bear a hybrid offspring, only to erase its mind and stuff it into a human existence on a farm in the middle of nowhere. *Why?* Perhaps my parents were just as evil as I was. But now that I could know, I wanted to know, and fit the pieces of the cursed puzzle together.

And then there was Blythe. This darling little creature of death that came sulking into a diner with no money and only fear so strong it took my breath away. I couldn't ignore her, I couldn't get her out of my head, and I couldn't forget that she was mine. She was mine before Halloween, before the witches confirmed it, before our soulmate connection brought us together.

Ghost had stolen her away in October. He'd danced with her at Hallows Fest, stalked her through town, and fucked her on gravestones. The archdemon did those things knowing we wanted her, knowing *I* wanted her. Did he consider Wolfgang or me when he claimed her with his black demon cum? Ames hadn't considered my feelings when he sent her running through the woods, stumbling into my arms with his wretched seed dripping down her thighs. He'd allowed a legion to chase after her, and we were all supposed to forget that, weren't we? In Devil's absence, the leader of the Halloween Boys had deemed the werewolf and me too immature, not ready for her. We'd have to wait and be patient to have our turn with our beloved, to unite in the ways our blood demanded, to bond our group into something new, some- thing better, stronger.

As if Ghost hadn't placed her right into the hands of the baphomet— all while I was stealing demon letters and sleeping in her backyard to keep her safe. No, I hadn't forgotten. I'd buried my anger deep, collecting every bit of it like coins of gold for my dragon to build his nest. And then I waited. I heard her moan his name every evening, and instead of erupting in fire, I waited. She joined me at breakfast each morning feeling lonely, and I never mentioned it. I waited. Her innocent eyes betrayed her love as the flecks of golden brown called out to me, begging me to whisk her away. And so I waited.

What most don't understand about lies is that the best crafted deceit comes from weaving in forces outside your control. No one could trace it back to you. There were no strings to pull that would unravel the plan you were knitting in secret. They needed to want me to find my family, too. And it was Blythe who took up the charge. Vincent didn't need to help me, but he did need to know that I was looking for my father. I didn't know why, but I had a feeling that would be to my benefit later on.

I knew finding my family would give me the opportunity to get Blythe and the guys out of Ash Grove. And after two hundred years, they'd be gobsmacked by the wonders and horrors that sprang up like weeds in our hibernation. Ezmerelda was more than willing to help separate Blythe from the archdemon, and I used that to my advantage. After I spoke with her during the tent fire, she delivered word to Blythe. The Vampiress called upon Captain Vex, who agreed to take us to the doorway in the sea. For a price, of course. For something he'd wanted since Hallows Fest. For the very thing he came to Hallows Fest for—the Wandering Stone.

The necklace the Willow Spirit gifted a reaper was more valuable than treasure to a pirate. With it, he believed he'd always find the right path to the stories he sought. For the stone, he'd risk angering Hell itself. He'd risk the wrath of a demon and a werewolf.

He'd keep them occupied for a while and lead them in circles on a ship they couldn't escape before delivering them back to Ash Grove. Where Blythe and I would return, mated, happy, and ready to rejoin our lovers and form our family together. I wasn't harboring her indefinitely. Hell, I wasn't even keeping her all to myself. Ghost and Wolfgang were my loves as much as she was. But I needed time, and they needed time. And all would be set right when we returned. I couldn't have expected my plan to work so flawlessly, so perfectly. I thought surely the pirates would give us trouble, or Wolf would sniff out my deceit, but neither transpired. Blythe didn't suspect a thing. In fact, she felt a joyous mixture of intrigue, hope, and relief. And now that I'd had a small taste of her enchanting pussy, I knew I needed more. And I'd get it—soon.

The forest of Belladonia was incongruous and confounding. Though I wouldn't allow my hesitation to settle on Blythe, who stomped behind me with crossed arms and pouty lips. The trees were a wicked, unnatural sort, black as night, as if singed with fire but still living, as evidenced by the red leaves decorating their thin limbs. They curved at unnatural angles, as if frozen, trying to get a look at us. If that weren't eerie enough, in direct and unnerving contrast were the rose bushes interspersed between them. Some taller than I was, and I was six foot six. The scarlet blossoms seemed to watch us as we trekked through silence. Silence. No birds, no squirrels, no wind rustling vines—complete and dismal lifelessness.

I wanted to hold her hand, wanted to wrap her in an orb of fire to keep her safe, but I refrained. There was no need to alarm her. We'd head north toward the city. At least that's what Ezmerelda had instructed me to do when I'd cornered her at the Phantom Circus. Wolf and Ghost and the vampires and magicians were too distracted by the *erratic and impulsive* fire I'd started to notice me slip away to meet with the Red Vampiress. Ezmerelda was foul and self-serving, but somehow, separating Blythe from Ghost served her twisted purposes—so I leveraged it.

Onyx, you're unhinged. What were you thinking starting a fire like that? While they chastised me, Ezmerelda dangled the bait for Blythe to snatch. It was dull and predictable how easily they underestimated me. Truly, I would have had a more amusing time with it had someone caught on.

Blythe spoke softly. "This place feels different. I want to like it, the darkness and gorgeous colors ... something is wrong, though." She shook her head, as if clearing her mind.

"You should trust your instincts. You're a reaper, Blythe. It's possible the magic inside you is trying to tell you something with every strange feeling you have."

She moved to walk by my side then, looking up at me, her gorgeous magenta dress swishing along the ground as she walked. Wolfgang had dressed her well, though where he'd found a gown on a pirate ship, I had no idea. He loved pink, so the getup was clearly for his enjoyment, though I'd admire it in his absence.

"You're not going to brush me off and just tell me not to worry?"

A dark chuckle pushed from my throat. "You've been hanging around Ghost too long. You should always worry in this world. Nothing is ever as it seems, and the more comfortable you get with that fact, the better off you'll be."

"Even you?"

"Especially me."

Something moved in the corner of my vision, and I reached out an arm to halt her steps. Blythe opened her mouth to speak, but I moved and put a finger to her lips. Her arousal at the contact was … distracting, but I didn't alter her emotions. She needed to stay alert. The last thing I needed was her giggling and happy at some rogue vampire throwing her over his shoulder for feasting. *Ah fuck, vampires.* We were walking into a city of vampires. It would take every bit of skill I possessed to keep her safe, but I would. I had to.

The beat of her heart was all I heard as I surveyed the area. No smells, no sense of life …

Blythe whispered, "Maybe it was just a—"

Something screamed. No, shrieked. A woeful and preternatural reverberation that trembled the dry branches overhead. The source was somewhere far in the distance. It sounded again, only this time, something appeared in the foggy breadth. Blythe clutched my arm, gluing herself to my side as the creature came into view. In all my time in realms of the strange and horrible, I'd never beheld something as grotesque as what stood beyond the fog. Standing at least eight feet tall, its body resembled an upright werewolf whose fur had been scorched, leaving only pale purple flesh and strong muscle beneath. Its snout was scrunched, and its ears were wide and leathery atop its wide head. My assessing gaze landed on the beast's yellow eyes and jagged teeth. Blythe screamed, and it opened its maw with a high-pitched screech. Then it charged.

CHAPTER 19

Ghost

LOVE LIKE THE OCEAN

> Once, I saw a bee drown in honey, and I understood.
> Nikos Kazantzakis

Most never consider the willpower and mental energy it takes to withstand immortality. It's a sick and twisted curse, and once you decide you're done with living, there's no escape. Save for finding some fool strong enough—and willing—to end you. But even then, the soul lives on, and who knows what Hell would do with someone like me. For a hundred years, it was hate that kept me moving. Then hate morphed into revenge. And when revenge lost its delight, when the screams of killers who suffered in my grave-yard didn't excite me any longer, my only emotion was self-loathing. I'd dug this grave, I'd made a deal with the devil, the town I loved had suffered at my hand. And my penance was to suffer alongside them. My only solace was my friends, my lovers, my everything I'd found in Onyx Hart and Wolfgang Jack.

And then there was Blythe. Who'd been sucked into the black hole of our pathetic existences, only to shine a light in the dark and set us all free. Blythe was my savior. She was death—death fucking eternal—and the only thing my black heart could love with all its might. She was my milk and honey, my promised land. Like the one God had promised his people.

But then, I wasn't one of God's, was I? I played for the other team. My wretched soul didn't deserve the balm of death, of Blythe, of the reaper, my little ghost.

I awoke in a pool of lukewarm water in the hull of the ship. Only chicken bones and sand surrounded me and the rest of the crew. I pulled Wolfgang awake by the collar of his shirt. My archdemon's voice asked in panic and rage, "Where is Blythe?"

His amber eyes came alive, and he jolted. How were we all asleep in the moldy hull of the ship? How'd we get down there? Wolfgang's enraged gaze met mine in a flash of joint realization.

He snarled. "Where's Onyx?"

But we knew. Somewhere inside, we knew.

We climbed over pirates, stirring them from their deep slumbers, as the ship violently shook. A storm greeted us on deck, and thunder clapped as we searched for the pirate captain and our friend. Vex Beard stood at the helm, lazily gripping the ship's wheel. He raised a flask when he saw us. "Lovely night for sailing, isn't it?"

The only light was that of the moon and the out-of-place pink from the neon jukebox. Onyx would know the song that was playing. I didn't, and I didn't give a shit. A dark mass pulled my attention. Raven was cawing and circling the ship frantically. When he spotted me, he swooped down in a frenzy of dark feathers. "I ventured too high, too far. I was flying above the storm. I hate storms. I am a coward, and now she's gone," Raven cried out, forlorn, before taking flight again. He was as panicked as I was. "I'm going to find her. I'm going back. Wherever she went, I will go."

Wolfgang called after him. "Raven, no! You'll lose your way. There's nowhere for you to land when your wings get tired. We're too far out to sea!"

But Blythe's familiar had already disappeared into the darkness. I knew I liked that bird.

"Where are they?" I growled, feeling my body shift. I had allowed

Ghost to take control when Dragon had almost bitten her, and I would let him take control again to kill the story keeper if I had to.

Wolf paced the boat, searching, smelling. Even in the rain, no scent went dead to a werewolf. He howled, a sorrowful and desolate sound among the waves and rain. "They're gone. Blythe and Onyx are gone. Their scents end at the plank."

I took the captain in my grip before I even knew what happened. My growl was furious and ferocious. *No, she can't be gone.* My grip tightened as hell's blue smoke twisted around his neck and limbs.

He choked, pulling at my hand. "Would you let me speak, archdemon? Ghost, I'm yer friend."

It was an effort to let him go. I wanted him dead; I wanted his soul in my graveyard for eternity to punish for whatever part he played in this. He fell to the ground with a clammer of thunder.

"Where is she?" I demanded, and Wolf stood next to me. How he'd managed not to shift into the Wolf, I had no idea.

The captain rubbed his throat and straightened his hat. "The last I remember, I told Onyx where the door in the ocean was. We reached it in the middle of the night. I told him to fetch you, but when he returned, he only had her. He touched me with his magic. He touched my crew. We're helpless against such enchantments. And that's all I remember."

Wolf and I searched his hazy gaze for treachery before I roared into the night. I'd been asleep below the ship as well. Onyx had bewitched us all, exactly as he'd threatened.

"I should have killed him then and there." I paced the ship like a dog in a cage. "Take me to the door—take me *now!*"

Captain Vex Beard held on to his wheel. "I can do that, but you'll need not destroy my ship, or I can't get you anywhere but the mermaid's sandcastle or the kraken's abyss."

Whatever the fuck that meant.

Wolfgang put a hand on my shoulder. "They went through the door. They're in Belladonia. She's safe, he's safe."

My claws pricked my palms and blood trickled onto my knuckles. I wanted to tear the ship apart, tear them all apart limb by limb.

"You're wrong. Onyx is *not* safe. Not from me."

CHAPTER 20

Blythe

WELCOME TO BELLADONIA

Magic is really very simple, all you've got to do is want something and then let yourself have it.
Aggie Cromwell, Halloweentown

My collection of terrors and nightmares was ever-growing. My stepfather's dead body, puppetized by a legion of demons, had a starring role. The baphomet, with its burning chains and rectangular eyes, had a recurring role. But I was pretty sure the thing barreling toward us would soon become the star of the show.

"Shit," Onyx swore. "Can you climb a tree or something while I fight this thing?"

"Are you kidding me? No!" I screeched, my nails clawing into his bicep. He looked over his shoulder with a smirk just as a wall of green fire ignited around me like a flaming birdcage. "Onyx!" I pointed as the creature leapt. Instead of dodging and letting it slam into the protective blaze around me, he met it head-on.

I don't know what I expected. I hadn't watched many immortal battles. But watching the creature lift its massive claws, swing, and hit Onyx cracked a piece of me. Onyx slammed into a black tree with a shudder that shook my bones. I wanted to help. I needed to do something. I was a reaper, for god's sake. Surely I had something to offer. I tentatively held my hands against the wall of fire, finding that it didn't burn me, but it also didn't budge. The creature opened its huge mouth, revealing pointed, dripping teeth as it lunged for Onyx's neck.

At the last moment, he rolled, getting to his feet as his hands and forearms lit in flame. "If you broke my cassette player, I'm going to be pissed," he said, low and calm, as he and the creature walked a half circle around each other, sizing one another up. It reared back and jumped for him again. Only this time, Onyx's emerald flame twisted, and giant snakes unfurled from his wrists. The beast shrieked as two enormous cobras wrapped around its middle and its neck. Its flesh sizzled as it screamed, and the burned aroma of dying monster had me holding my breath to escape the disgusting smell. It twitched and writhed as the fire snakes constricted and constricted until … it broke into three pieces. Its head rolled into a rose bush while its torso and hips fell to the ground in separate pieces.

I shut my eyes. "Yep, that one's going into the nightmare lineup."

Onyx brushed the dirt off his black shirt and jeans before leisurely walking over. The bars of my birdcage dropped.

"I can keep you occupied while you sleep. I'm excellent at turning bad dreams into pleasurable ones," he said seductively, as if he hadn't just mutilated our attacker.

My heart sped up and my core warmed at his rugged, sexy, post-kill smile. "You pick the worst times to flirt."

"You pick the worst times to scream."

I huffed a small laugh. "Touché. What was that thing?"

"Hell if I know, but we should get out of here before its buddies come sniffing around. As powerful as I may be, the fire does need some time to regenerate. I don't think we're too far. The rose bushes are multiplying. That must mean something, right? Vampires love their decor."

I carefully stepped over a puddle of something gross and scurried away from the massacre. "Did you have to be so messy?"

He let out a laugh that lit something deep inside me. When was the last time I'd heard him laugh? He'd been so sullen for the last few months. I couldn't help my own giggle as he wiped away tears. He skipped in front of me and turned around, dropping to one knee and placing a hand on his heart. "Forgive me, my queen. Next time I slaughter beasts in your name, I shall take heed to not sully your loafers."

He was being a smart-ass, but stupid butterflies erupted in my heart nonetheless. And, of course, he gave me that stupid smirk, like he knew exactly what I was thinking.

"You said you can't read minds," I murmured, brushing past him as he made a show of kneeling.

In a flash of vampiric speed, he was by my side again. "I don't need to read minds when you wear your every thought on your face." I blushed, and he raised an eyebrow like, *See?* "But I do absorb the emotions of those around me."

I stopped mid-anxious scan of the woods, fearful of another creature like that finding us. "Wait, you can feel emotions? My emotions? You're an empath?"

"Yes. It's why I do the *sex-touch*, as you call it. It shuts people's big feelings off, or at least puts the emotions someplace else while I get away." He wiggled his fingers in emphasis. His tone was casual, but I noticed he was checking every tree, his gaze darting around us. It was unnerving. All I wanted to do was curl up and cry, but instead, I kept walking and talking to distract myself from the fact that more of those *things* could be chasing us right then.

"Ghost tastes emotions, and you feel them. Great. No wonder I can't get away with anything around you two."

He shrugged. "Emotions aren't black and white. They can be harder to decipher than you might think. There's a chance you haven't entirely lost your mystery."

I opened my mouth to respond when something glinted ahead of us. "There's something up there." We reached an impossibly high, ornate wrought-iron gate. Thorny rose vines twisted between the bars, emitting their sweet floral fragrance.

"This thing is at least two stories tall," Onyx mused, shaking the bars. "What're you trying to keep locked in there, Belladonia?"

"Or locked out," I added.

No sooner had I spoken than the screaming from earlier racked through the forest again. Hearing it again … it sounded like a woman. "That's the same scream we heard earlier …"

Onyx moved in front of me, blocking me with his body, as four silhouettes came into view. They stepped out of the shadows, every bit as massive and menacing as the one that had just been slain.

"Is your fire recharged?" I asked as the creatures snarled.

"More or less."

I hated his dumb nonanswers. "Don't waste fire on me. I don't need a cage. I'll … I'll try to climb the gate."

Before he could reply with what surely would have been a sarcastic, teasing remark, one of the beasts lunged. Onyx blasted it with flame just as another charged after me. I covered my head, bracing for impact, when I caught a peek of Onyx's fist colliding with its snout. It whimpered as the third launched itself at me.

Onyx grabbed my waist, pulling me out of the way as it hit the gate. "We're cornered. I need space to—"

The maw of a beast, open and ready to tear me to shreds, snapped inches from my face. Onyx pulled me behind him, pushing my back against the gate, ready to be eaten alive to protect me.

Suddenly, the creature jerked. Something sharp protruded from its chest, dripping with its muddy blood. Its yellow eyes went dim, and it fell over, clanging into the gate, pulling down red rose petals as it did. Its fellow beasts wailed and made to attack, but it was too late. Spikes shot into their backs, sending them tumbling forward in spurts of blood. Onyx still gripped my side as he pressed me into the gate.

A man appeared, gliding out of the forest on something like a wheelchair. The contraption had a high polished oak back and sat taller than typical wheelchairs. As he stopped in front of us, gaze level with Onyx's, he lifted his crossbow from his lap. Onyx pushed me farther behind him and straightened, again ready to take a death blow for me.

The man chuckled. "You, sir, are way too pretty to waste an arrow on." He lifted the weapon above his head, and it perfectly clicked into the back of his chair. With a tap of his wrist against the armrest, a dagger rose from the oak. "I might use this, though …" His hair was as white as snow and as wild as his clear blue eyes. He grinned. "Kidding."

Onyx relaxed slightly and stepped forward. "Nice ride. Does it have a sound system?"

"You can bet your ass it does."

"Right on. Well, thanks for your assistance. We'll be leaving now—"

The man clicked his tongue. "You'll be doing no such thing. Come on." He glided closer to the gate and pulled a skeleton key from around his neck. When he waved it in front of the gate, it opened with slow and steady precision.

"I'm Onyx, and this is my … wife, Blythe."

I shot him an incredulous stare, which he ignored.

"Nice to meet you both. I'm Elysium, the Vampire Hunter."

After Onyx's introduction, it was a wonder anything could shock me. A *vampire hunter?*

We stood at the entrance as Elysium spun around with a half smile. "Oh, and welcome to Belladonia, the City of Vampires."

CHAPTER 21
Blythe
NEEDLE AND THORN

What a pair we are, intrinsically broken but tied to one another by desire and death.
Sylvia Day

He looked so vulnerable, standing there, peering up at the huge gates and beyond at the castle spiking into the sky. Elysium went ahead as I rejoined Onyx, standing at his side and looking up with him.

His voice was low and gentle, without his usual hint of roguishness. "What if everything I've ever searched for is beyond this gate? Perhaps my father is here now, walking the streets. What if I meet him?"

I'd never seen him worried; he'd never revealed even a hint of insecurity to me before. But there he was, standing frozen, uncertain, and laying it bare for me. This was Onyx, naked on a pirate's plank, as I was for him, and he waited for what I'd do next. My knuckles brushed his, and he didn't pull away.

"If your dad is here somewhere, we'll say hello."

"That's it?"

"If you want to, yes. But if you change your mind, that's okay, too. We can leave."

He glanced down at me in disbelief. "Really?"

I nodded. "Why not?"

His lips parted, and my gaze dropped to the perfect carmine shade of them. When he didn't speak, I slid my hand into his and held it tight. My heart twinged with all the reasons I was continually falling for Onyx Hart.

"Thank you," he whispered, and I followed his lead as we crossed the threshold into Belladonia. The City of Vampires.

Elysium hid small, round glasses under the fringe of his snow-white hair. His chair kept him eye-level with Onyx and taller than me. It propelled him forward with air or magic, or maybe both. I kept wondering what else hid within its compartments if a crossbow, a dagger, and a sound system were commonplace items for him. "A vampire hunter?" I asked tentatively.

"Looks like you picked the right place," Onyx jeered. "I'm happy to make a few suggestions if you're looking for your next kill."

I elbowed him in the ribs, and he put his arm around my shoulder, tugging me close. The contact was comforting and casual, so at odds with the gothic city surrounding us.

Elysium chuckled. "I'll let you know when the chair adds a suggestion box. For now, it's not your breed of vampire I'm after. Though you seem … different from the others. You both do."

"Oh, I'm not a—"

Onyx cleared his throat. "It's our first time visiting Belladonia. My wife is a new vampire with a newly formed coven. We had a witch mute her scent to calm her nerves."

How did he lie so easily? So effortlessly? I went with it because it sounded like a lie that would benefit us. I hadn't even considered that I could be a point of interest in this city of the undead. I'd assumed my reaper gifts would shield me from prying eyes, as it always had, but I hadn't considered that even that fact would draw suspicion. Vampires were a nosy sort, I was learning. As I glanced at the torches and dark, stone shops, I half expected to see Raven tilt his head and caw to me. My heart clenched, missing him. Missing Ghost and Wolf. God, Ghost was probably tearing the ship apart. I shuddered, hoping I was wrong. Onyx glanced at me in concern, and I gently shook my head to tell him I was all right. He could sense my emotions … my every emotion. My cheeks heated in embarrassment at all he'd probably picked up on up until this point. The times he caught me staring at him, the untruths I'd told, the feelings I buried deep within——he'd felt it all with me.

"I take it your coven will be joining you soon? The Bleeding Heart Ball is fast approaching, and King Vladimir will want his offering from you all."

Offering?

"And it will be an honor to give it happily. There was a delay in receiving our key, so we had to find an unorthodox method here. Thus, wandering the forest."

That seemed to pacify the vampire hunter as he nodded in under-standing. "Well, you're welcome to stay with me while you wait for your coven to arrive. I own a little spot just around the corner."

As we walked, groups of vampires passed. Some in dark cloaks. Some were strikingly casual in jeans and sweaters. Others were wearing gowns similar to mine and resembling the renaissance era. The city was dark gray, with curving cobblestone paths snaking through quaint, jagged buildings, all the way up to the massive, looming castle on the hill. It seemed to stare down at us, watching our every move, reading our thoughts. I hoped I'd never have to go inside. Everything was black and charcoal gray, with highlights of cerise. Red roses were everywhere, painted delicately on roofs and lampposts and carved intricately into the street below our feet. Many women and men wore them in their hair. The only escape from the repeating hues was the doors. Brightly colored doors flanked us on either side and swirled with the city streets. Each door was unique, as if it were from a completely different place than Belladonia. I admired a bright yellow with a daisy planter under its window. Deep purple covered in ivy. Fluorescent pink with shimmering glitter paint beneath its archways. Something inside me wanted to explore each and every one to see what lay on the other side of its knob. As we passed more and more shop fronts, I asked, "What's with the doors?"

Elysium grinned, brushing back his shag. His hands were clad in fingerless leather gloves, and his shoulders were broad. He was the embodiment of a sexy steampunk monster hunter. "Remarkable, isn't it? I was amazed when I first came here as well. Of course, you know each door leads to a different coven's portal. However, the foyers between? Let's just say everyone's gotten very creative. I feel you'll enjoy exploring, so I won't spoil it for you by saying much more."

"My wife does love surprises," Onyx teased, squeezing me close. "Don't you, my little honey badger?"

Elysium snorted and moved ahead, giving me the perfect opportunity to elbow my pretend husband in the ribs. "Yes, and you're just full of them," I muttered through gritted teeth.

The vampire hunter stopped outside a bleached door with ornate gold trim and a giant garnet for a handle. "This is my cocktail bar, Needle and Thorn. I have a spare room upstairs you two lovebirds can have until your coven finds you."

The building looked so quaint on the outside. It was dark gray and lonely in all of its gothic charm. But when he opened his door, the inside didn't mirror the exterior. Not only in decor, but in sheer size. When we stepped inside, we were suddenly in an ultra-modern, posh lounge. Red velvet booths, leather chairs, and tall bookcases were expertly interspersed. There were dozens of vampires sipping from martini glasses, flipping through book pages, and smoking cigars—yet the space still felt massive. My shock must have been evident because Elysium chuckled. "Let me make you a drink before you go upstairs. You look like you need one."

"You're a bartender, too?" I asked, still dumbfounded, taking in the domed ceiling, complete with intricate artwork of flora and fauna. We followed him to the center of the room, an elevated area with sparkling vials of deep red liquid and various other amber bottles. It was then that

I remembered what Captain Vex had said before he'd taken my necklace and let Onyx pull me overboard. He'd wanted to collect what I owed him. His desired story. Could Elysium be …

He pulled up proudly behind his bar. "I'm known here as the Mixologist, and I'm dying to make you two a drink."

CHAPTER 22

Onyx

DO YOU WANT TO BITE ME?

> Love is something eternal ... The aspect may change but not the essence.
> *Vincent Van Gogh*

Vampires were weird as fuck. I knew that. Everyone knew that. Blythe did not yet know that. She was about to get a crash course and her first sip of vessense.

"Nice setup," I admired. "I'd love something smooth."

But Elysium wasn't a vampire. This *vampire hunter* was setting off hundreds of alarm bells in my mind. I'd heard of these hunters. Typically mortal men who had their girlfriends stolen by amorous coven leaders. The lovers scorned became privy to our immortality and decided to take it upon themselves to try to end us. Of course, other beings were more than happy to send their tender human foot soldiers after covens.

Supplying them with magic, weaponry, and anything they could. Vincent, as insufferable as he may have been, had at least been wise in not adding to his coven flippantly. I couldn't recall a time he shifted a human. Of course, there were others who hunted for their own reasons. But to have one walking among Belladonia, supplying the vessense? Unusual. But I had to ease in with him. I couldn't give too much away.

Questions revealed as much as answers, and I'd have to choose my words very carefully. Luckily, I was an exceptional wordsmith.

The man snapped his fingers, and his chair spun, lifting into the air and allowing him to grab a silver bottle. He lowered and pulled two small vials of red. Blythe and I watched in fascination as he stirred and mixed, finally topping off two coupe glasses with a single drop of red each. The one drop sank to the bottom of the glass and swirled as if it were alive. It was alive, I supposed, in its own way.

Blythe looked at me with a smile as her thumb fidgeted with the stem of her glass. She was nervous but trying so hard to play it cool. "Ready for your first taste of vessense, honey badger?"

She narrowed her eyes. "Sure am, cowpie."

I cleared my throat to hide my laugh.

Elysium removed his glasses and idly cleaned them as he said, "Vessense virgin, eh? Your coven didn't give you a taste after they turned you? That seems downright cruel."

"I wanted my first drink to be here in Belladonia." She lied perfectly.

He grinned, feeling only curiosity toward us. It was the only emotion I'd gotten from him since we met. "Well, I'm honored."

"Tiny sip," I instructed as we clinked our glasses together. "To us. May we always weather the storms of the afterlife together."

She shook her head slightly, and I could tell she wanted to roll her eyes. God, she was cute. Her dainty sip wrinkled her nose, and she coughed. I took a gulp, feeling the tingle and burn … before it hit.

Delirious and unnerving calm. I said smooth, but not this smooth. Not smooth enough to make me not think straight. And Blythe was having a hard enough time lying as it was. But that was exactly what Elysium had intended, wasn't it?

Blythe started giggling. "A vampire hunter and mixologist with a really cool haircut in the city of vampires." She took another sip, but I at least had enough mind to take her glass.

"Kind of ridiculous, isn't it? And Onyx, I'm sure you're wondering how I came to watch over the vessense supply."

"How did you?"

Elysium took Blythe's still-full drink and took a sip before admiring the red tint. "It's difficult to get genuine amusement from vessense. I imagine the one who gathered it was quite sure in themself. Nonetheless, I haven't mixed this particular blend in a while."

My mouth was moving, and *fuck*, I couldn't stop the words. "My first taste of vessense was … accidental. Her name was Minnie Smith. She was my first love. We'd scandalously had sex before marriage in my barn. She'd pricked her finger, and while she was … I sucked her finger. It was my first hint of who I was. She tasted like worry and rain. I avoid drinks like this because I'm afraid I'll taste her again and remember. Remember how she's dead because of me."

The drink had blurred my empathic abilities. Was Blythe feeling … sadness? It hadn't affected her long if it was already wearing off. She took my hand in hers as Elysium asked, "And who are you, Onyx Hart?"

"I don't know." But I did know I hadn't given him my last name. Though telling that story, saying her name, was exponentially more vulnerable.

The vampire hunter leaned his elbows on the counter, and I met his gaze. "Can't say I've ever met a vampire who didn't know who he was. I don't think you two are exiled. You? Maybe. Her? No. And she's with you because she wants to be." He scratched his chin. "And you're not diphylla."

"Are those what attacked us?" Blythe asked, still holding my hand. I liked holding her hand, and not because I was drunk on vessense. I just liked her.

"Sure are, and they're who I was brought here to hunt. Forgive me if I've been a bit … inquisitive." He gestured to the far end of the lounge. "I'll show you to your room."

The vessense faded with the elevator ride up to our room. Suite was more like it. I wouldn't kill the vampire hunter immediately, but I would kill him. Deceiving me for intel hadn't escaped my attention, and I'd slipped up in more ways than one. But for the moment, I had to play it cool. Luckily the only thing he'd accomplished was ripping out a shard of my shattered soul for Blythe to see. *Minnie.* How long had it been since I'd let myself think of her?

The mixologist showed Blythe an armoire of clothing and likewise for me. The suite was larger than my farmhouse and exponentially more luxurious. Vampires prided themselves on grandeur, and Belladonia was a testament to their culture. I eyed the large four-poster bed and its rich berry-colored canopy. Blythe would look so gorgeous sleeping there. I salivated at the thought of watching her all night, though the temptation for more would be very great.

"Should we worry about those … things … coming into the city?" Blythe asked the hunter, pulling me from my fantasies.

"No, they stay in the wicked woods, and you would do well to stay far from them. They've scented you now, so they'll be waiting, hoping to catch you again."

I rubbed my chin, peering out the window to the wet cobblestone below. A group of vampires in top hats and canes sat having their shoes polished. "You hunt them, then? The creatures?"

"I'm the best diphylla slayer there is. It's why I was invited here by King Vladimir himself." He straightened a vase of roses. "Food is in the pantry if you don't feel up for exploring tonight. Oh, and Blythe, everything you need for your cleansing is by the clawfoot tub."

Blythe gave me a panicked look. "Do I even want to know what that means?"

Elysium looked from her to me. Another test I'd failed, apparently. "All who identify as women must cleanse for fourteen days before the Bleeding Heart Ball. The king requires your purification for your offering."

She put her hand on her hip, and I felt the flutter of her indignation. I couldn't help the grin it brought me. "And the men? What cleansing do they have to do?"

Elysium shrugged. "I don't make the rules."

"I'm not dirty simply because I'm a woman. So you can tell King Vlad-Whatever he can shove it."

"You've got a fiery one there, Onyx," he said, smacking my shoulder. It was all the touch I needed to make his memory of serving us drinks very, very cloudy. He blinked a few times in confusion before shaking his head. "Anyway … I'll let you guys settle in. Ring if you need anything."

The moment the door closed, Blythe forcefully whispered, "What the hell just happened? What did I just drink? And why is this place so strange? Also, I am *not* your wife. Why would you even say that?"

I pulled my cassette player out of my pocket and fiddled with the tape. Miraculously, it looked dry, so I clicked it on, and "Space Oddity" by David Bowie trilled through the tiny speakers.

"Hell yeah, it still works," I said before meeting her glare.

"Honey badger?"

"So cute but so mean. *Cowpie*?"

"You're a farm boy. I thought you'd like it."

I chuckled. "You're good at reminding me that there's a man somewhere in me and not only the two half monsters that plague me."

"You're not a monster. Not a bad one, at least. But if you're going to have a pet name for me, it'll have to be something other than honey badger."

"Little ghost will be hard to beat, but I'm up for the challenge."

She smiled, the sight lovelier than anything Belladonia had to offer. "Good."

I fiddled with my cassette tape as I continued. "First of all, you don't need to whisper. Mr. Vampire Hunter Mixologist, as far as I can tell, is human, so he can't hear us. Second, you tried vessense for the first time and felt how fucked-up it can make you. *Why is this place so strange* is a layered question, but we'll get to it."

She hummed, taking in the area and noticing the singular bed. Nervous excitement surged through her—not fear or disgust. My cock twitched, and I cleared my burning throat. Her doe eyes met mine, and she sat on the side of the bed, her thick hips and thighs making that irresistible curved tulip shape again.

"I didn't feel anything from the drink. I only pretended because I didn't want him to suspect anything."

"Bullshit."

"Fine, don't believe me. It tasted bitter, and I had this random flash in my mind of someone I'd never seen before. Then it went away. But I can party with crows and pirates, too, so maybe my superpower is immortal alcohol tolerance."

"Interesting. See? You're already learning things about yourself on our solo outing." Thankfully, she didn't mention my vessense-induced confession.

"What is that stuff in the vials?"

I chuckled lightly. "Are you sure you want to know?"

She raised an eyebrow. "Yes."

"You know in old horror movies where the vampire bites the woman, and she screams? It's not from pain; it's ecstasy. Not just for her, but for the one who bites as well. The blood from sex … it's all we crave. Blood contains the essence of a person. *Vessense* is the blood extracted from sexual activity from different beings."

She coughed and rubbed her throat. "I just drank sex blood?"

"A very small amount, yes."

Blythe shook her head, absorbing the information. Would she draw her own conclusions about what I wanted from her so desperately? To taste her body dripping in red and weeping for me … to lick the blood as it trails down her inner thighs. My fangs ached and my body tingled in response.

"You forgot the last question." Her tone was a soft and teasing caress. "*Wife* is a bit much, don't you think?"

I strolled to stand in front of her and braced my arms on the overhead beams of the canopy. Her breath hitched. *Oh, you like me like that, do you?* I heard the uptick in the beat of her heart and felt her emotions come in a wave of arousal and desire.

I leaned forward, letting my breath blow through her hair. "I don't care whether you realize it now or a hundred years from now. If you never fall in love with me, fine. I don't care if Ghost thinks I'm not ready for you. You're his, but not only his. You are mine, Blythe Pearl. Accept it now or later, it makes no difference to me. I said you're my wife because *you are.*"

Her lips parted between her flushed, rosy cheeks.

My throat burned, and the fire in my ribs singed my insides. I wanted her so badly, and I could feel she wanted me, too.

Tilting my head back, I growled. "I can't have you walking around smelling like that."

"Like what?"

"Like you're just dying to be bent over and fucked hard. One whiff of you right now, and I'd be beating off hundreds of vampires wanting to bed you."

She sucked in a breath. "What should I do?"

"Lie back."

"Onyx," she whispered. "Do you want to bite me? Do you want to taste my ... vessense?"

"More than anything I've ever wanted."

"I don't know if I'm ready for ... that."

"You're in control, my dear. If you don't want it, it will not happen. But if you can trust me, I can make you feel good, and that will keep unwanted attention at bay. How does that sound?"

She leaned back on her elbows. "That sounds really nice."

My mouth quirked in a smile. "Having you like this, being the one to please you, is an honor." I dropped to my knees and gripped her ankles. She shivered as I moved my hands up her calves. Bringing fire to warm the surface of my palms, I asked, "Is this better?"

"Yes," she breathed. "Keep going."

I pushed her dress up over her stomach and pulled off her panties. I brought the fabric to my nose and inhaled deeply, salivating for her. My cock strained against my jeans, begging to slide into her and fuck her raw for days. But this wasn't about me right now ... this was about her. It had to be about her. I couldn't base our intimacy around vampiric sex, letting my vicious desires take control to fulfill some sick need of my breeding. Blythe was more to me than that. What she needed was release, so I'd give it to her, denying myself the bites of her I so desperately craved.

I continued my path up her thighs, relishing how soft her skin was, mapping where I may want to scar her later, when she was ready ... When I reached her center, I spread her folds and circled her glistening opening with my tongue. Her head lolled back with a long exhale.

"What a precious little toy you are…" She whimpered as I inserted a finger, feeling her pooling wetness for me. Her walls gripped me tight, and all I could imagine was how euphoric it would be to sink my cock into her delicious cunt. I could wait no longer. While pumping in and out, I let my tongue explore her clit, lapping up every taste of her. While blood contained the most concentrated essence, sexual fluids did, too. I moaned into her as her petite hands found my hair.

"I want to devour you for hours and hours. I'm going to make you come over and over again and wring every delectable drop from your perfect little cunt. What do you think about that?"

"Yes," she moaned, her hands moving from my hair to my forearms as I gripped her ass. "Yes, please."

I murmured into her pussy as I added a finger, stretching her slightly. Her delicate whimpers and the thrust of her hips were a melody and a dance—one for only us in this moment. "That's it, ride my mouth. Claw me so hard you make me bleed. I want those gorgeous little marks you leave on Ghost's arms."

"Fuck," she answered, pulling at me frantically. "I'm going to come."

"Yes, fuck yes. Let me taste your orgasm, Blythe. Give it to me."

I removed my fingers and covered her pussy with my mouth, pushing my tongue into her as she cried out. Her bliss hit me with a wall of exultation. I felt my throat rumble as I drank her in. It was stronger than any vessense I could have ever dreamed of. My mind floated to a far-off star as my mouth desperately sucked her clean, wanting it all.

I didn't know how much time passed, but we didn't stop. I didn't stop. The ability to feel her emotions seeped into me, and in turn, it radiated through my palms, enhancing her ecstasy and creating a continuous loop of unquenchable fervor. My lips remained slick with her, and my tongue plunged into her depths as I brought her to her peak again and again. Our combined euphoria hit me stronger and stronger with each uptick in the tempo of her hips. Every whimper was a song I'd fight to replicate on my guitar.

I was getting high off her, drunk off her body, and I hadn't even explored her blood yet. This was unlike anything I'd ever experienced, and I could have gone down on her for days. But I knew her body needed sustenance, and that was the only thing in the entire realm that could have pulled me off her delicious pussy. Her hips and thighs quivered, wet from my tasting, throbbing and sore and satiated. The joy and satisfaction that radiated from her was my own vessense cocktail. One I'd happily become drunk from every day for the rest of forever.

She leaned up on wobbly elbows, her knees still propped on the edge of the bed. "Onyx," she breathed.

"I'll draw you a bath," I rasped. "And you need to eat. It's been several hours now."

She looked out the window in surprise, where it had indeed grown dark with early morning haze.

"Wow. Well, um … thank you. I don't think you'll have to fight any horny vampires off me today."

"There's always tomorrow." I smiled.

After filling the clawfoot tub with hot water and lavender oil, I brought her a glass of water. When she was finished drinking, I cupped her jaw. "I'm going to go find you a warm meal. Take a bath and relax, all right?"

She stood, holding on to the bedpost, still shaking from our encounter. "Check for the guys, too, please? Maybe they're here early."

They wouldn't be. "Yes, of course."

They'd be halfway back to Ash Grove by now.

And I was here devouring her until I decided we were ready to go back. At that moment, I was certain it would be a very long time before I was ready to return.

CHAPTER 23

Blythe

SECRET KEEPERS

" I have told you, reader, that I have learned to love Mr. Rochester. I could not unlove him now.
Charlotte Brontë

I hissed as my sore muscles settled into the hot water. Onyx had left, because apparently the red wine and expensive looking chocolates weren't enough food after the night we'd had. I agreed and was thankful for the moment to clear my mind. My core still fluttered with aftershocks of Onyx's warm tongue and hot palms.

Soaking in the bath, I still felt the brush of his rough fingertips with their calluses from his guitar strings. The way his gaze met mine as he drank every release he coaxed free. I knew his fangs were hidden behind his lips, wanting to be unleashed, but he'd listened to me. He hadn't pressured me when I said I wasn't ready for … vampire sex. It only made me care for him more, and that made me want him more. The idea of pain mixing with pleasure—and blood becoming something sexual—was a new and taboo thought that sent quivers of excitement through me. But I needed a little time to adjust to everything that had happened.

Only twenty-four hours earlier, I was on a pirate ship … and had felt the mouth of Wolfgang. A soft shudder shook me in remembrance of the feel of his scruffy face against my delicate center. I wished we'd had more time. And then Onyx. He'd flown in like a whirlwind of passion and mischief. The last thing I remembered before I was on a plank, about to be plunged into the water, was Ghost's righteous anger. Had they gotten into a fight? I wouldn't know because Onyx had put me to sleep. His experience with vessense secretly made me happy that he'd finally gotten a taste of his own medicine. It's no fun having your emotions altered by someone else. Though my heart ached at his confession. I'd known by brief statements he'd made that he'd lost someone he had cared about. But now she had a name—Minnie. It was a pretty name. I wondered if I even held a candle next to her. I wondered if he'd ever love me like he loved her.

When I replayed it all in my head, I should have been screaming at him. I should have been fighting for a way back to the ship. Should have been sneaking out the moment he left and waiting for the guys to find me and take me back to Ash Grove. But I couldn't go back home, could I? My chest tightened. I also wasn't mad at Onyx. What he'd done was impulsive, but he'd been waiting for a chance to find his family for hundreds of years. Did we really expect him to wait and let the chance pass by? And what he'd said about me needing space wasn't wrong ... Ash Grove and Ghost and Halloween? It was all marvelous and a lot at the same time. It was only a couple of days apart. Maybe that wasn't such a terrible thing. The way he went about it was, but the outcome wasn't so awful, especially after what had just happened. He'd gone down on me for hours. Hours. The feel of his grip still lingered on my ass, the extra warmth he pushed into me, his groans against my flesh and the way he'd inhaled the scent of my panties. It all gave me delicious shivers and made me want him again. He called me his wife. I still couldn't get over that. Or even begin to sort out what it really meant. Was he serious or just messing around?

Pulling away from my jumbled thoughts, I assessed the tubes of rosy liquids by the tub. *Oil of Humility* and *Perfume of Poise* were among the oddest. Were these what King Vladimir had his femme subjects cleanse with? Yeah, he could go fuck himself. I may not have known the extent of my reaper powers or how to use them, but supernatural or not, I didn't need cleansing. As I was sniffing a tube of *Salts of Meekness*, I heard the front door close.

"I hope you found pizza," I called out. "I bet vampires eat fancy caviar and gold-flaked pizza. Wait, can vampires have garlic?"

No answer. I sat up, the water sloshing over the tub. Maybe I'd imagined the sound. The bathroom was lit by flickering candlelight, and the only sound through the cracked window was of horse hooves trotting along the street. "Onyx? Elysium?" I asked, though I knew it wasn't Onyx. He was never quiet. Not around me.

I sat back, thinking I must have imagined it or mistook a noise from outside, when the floorboard outside the washroom creaked. I sat up in a panic. A shadow blocked out the light from the crack under the door. I had nothing. No weapon, no known power to use against whoever—or whatever—this was.

I opened my mouth to speak again when the knob turned. Startling, I considered climbing out the window, but it was too high. All I could do was hope someone heard me scream—

A dark figure stepped into the room. I'd often heard his gravelly voice in my nightmares. "Hello, reaper." The greeting was a taunt, and him being here was a flippant and terrifying display of his power and omniscience.

I willed myself to pretend I wasn't scared out of my mind. He made me angry; he made me curious and skeptical, but something about me elicited those emotions from him as well—I could feel it somehow.

"Hello, Devil. If you don't mind, I'm taking a bath, and I don't remember inviting you."

He stood incredibly tall and broad, wearing a flowing cape. It reminded me of Vincent's cloak, only somehow, on Judas, it looked more menacing in how comfortable he seemed in it. He ran a black leather glove over the marble sink, and the candle flames grew taller in his presence, like kids sitting up straight for their professor.

"*Oil of Demure.* Now, I think this is one you could benefit from."

"I'll share it with you. I know exactly where you can shove it." I smiled, wrapping my arms around my breasts as the bubbles in my bath slowly disappeared.

He chuckled darkly and leaned against the counter, crossing his arms. "My subjects would never be subjected to such things as Vlad deems necessary."

"If you hate him, why are you here?"

"I have my reasons."

I sighed. "The water's getting cold. I need to get out—" I gasped as the water immediately heated to a comfortable but toasty level. My cheeks flushed, and I got the distinct impression that I'd probably never been around a being with as much power as Judas had. Had the Halloween Boys even spent much time with him?

He took a step closer and kneeled by the tub. I held my breath as he dipped a lazy finger along the remaining bubbles. I felt my nipples harden, and I tightened my arms and clenched my thighs. "What do you want?"

"Many things, but let's start with … getting to know you."

I scoffed a disbelieving laugh. That was just about the last thing I'd expected him to say. "Getting to know me?"

"I think we got off on the wrong foot."

"I'm kind of busy trying to keep myself from being a blood buffet while stranded in a weird vampire town."

"I can assist." His eyes glowed like deep garnets as the flame light illuminated his dark skin.

"How can you help me?"

He drew a circle in the bubbles, popping more and more until the folds of my bare stomach were visible through the water. "Anything you want. I can bring you your demon and wolf. I can get you out of this mess you've gotten yourself into in Ash Grove and lend a hand with Dragon's father. Give you advice." He huffed a small laugh. "You're going to need it."

My chest tightened at his tone that suggested he knew way more than I did about … everything. "Yeah, and what's the catch?"

"Again, you think so lowly of me. I'm a philanthropist helping sad little reapers."

He was taunting me again. Or was he serious? I felt like a mouse in the paw of a cat.

"Fine. Bring the guys here right now," I challenged.

"Ah, for a price."

I rolled my eyes. "There it is."

"You must agree to keep secrets. Secrets make things more interesting. I will see you ten times, Blythe. Ten times before my will is done. But you will speak nothing of our meetings to anyone, understood? In turn, I'll aid you here and there."

"That easy?"

"That easy." His glance lingered for half a moment on my body before meeting my stare. He extended his large hand.

"Why are you doing this?"

"I'm impatient. The faster we sort this out and you go through what the fuck ever with Dragon, and next Wolf, the sooner things that benefit me can transpire."

"Doesn't sound very philanthropic to me," I muttered. "But I guess I'm not really in a position to be turning away help, even if it means I have you sneaking up on me ten more times." I wasn't thrilled at the idea of keeping secrets from the guys, but I couldn't turn away an offer of help, especially from someone as powerful as Devil. Was this how he'd helped the Halloween Boys, too? What price did they have to pay for his generosity? My wet palm met his, and my heart fluttered as he shook my hand.

He smiled, and damn if it wasn't a gorgeous sight to behold. "We'll speak soon, Reaper."

Like he'd done months prior, he disappeared in a plume of black smoke. I coughed. "Really rude with the smoke." I could have sworn I heard his deep answering chuckle somewhere in the distance.

When the smoke settled, I stood and shrugged on a fluffy robe so soft I groaned. Vampires really did rock in the hospitality department. When I looked in the mirror, I was startled at the red, cursive scrawl.

Ten

AFTER DRYING OFF, I rummaged through the armoire. I slipped on a pair of black pants that hugged my curves and a black, long-sleeved top with a cinched waist. If only I had my makeup kit, I could have pulled the look together with a bold lip. Maybe I'd ask Elysium if one of the magical doors led to a makeup counter. Something told me that vampires had superb cosmetics to match their impeccable gothic style. I'd only just arrived at Belladonia, and I should have been terrified of being surrounded by vampires, but the city felt familiar in all its eerie darkness. In Ash Grove, the strange was hiding in plain sight. In Belladonia, the strange was decorated with stone gargoyles, horse-drawn carriages, and ornate magical doors. They highlighted all their oddities, and something about that made me feel at home. Though my heart still twisted at the thought of Ash Grove. How could I ever go back?

I surveyed myself in the mirror, twisting my brown hair into a messy French twist. Ames would have gone crazy for this outfit if he'd been here. He loved me in black. I missed him and Wolfgang and Raven. My heart ached for them to be near, and I hoped that Onyx would return with both dinner and the guys. We could all share this little room and continue what we'd started on the pirate ship …

Riding the elevator to the main level, I noted the intricate gold-flaked wallpaper and embellished rugs. It reminded me of Vincent's tent and the Phantom Circus. A circus and a coven I was itching to learn more about. And the way the phantom, or chaos magician, as Ames called him, looked at me through the flames? Did they suspect I was a reaper? Ames had led the charge in hiding my true nature from the world, and I appreciated the security while I sorted through this new world.

But I was slowly learning that I couldn't hide forever. At some point, I'd have to embrace whatever abilities I had and move through this realm as my own person, not just as someone belonging to the Halloween Boys. As long as I had the guys with me, it was impossible to need anything.

They'd always protect me fiercely. But what if a day came that I needed to protect myself—or them? The Moon Halo Coven thought me to be a liability, a danger to their home. But what if I could show them that I could be a protector of the town we all loved? Would they accept me then? The last thing I wanted was a war with the witches. Regardless of the Halloween Boys' past with them, they'd been kind to me. Yesenia had been my first friend when I found myself alone and afraid in October. I wondered if she hated me now for what I'd done to Piper. Whatever I'd somehow invited into her psychic circle only proved the witches' point. I was dangerous. At least I had time to figure out a plan while we searched for Onyx's family. And part of being a reaper meant immortals couldn't sense what I was. Maybe I was safer in the city of vampires than anywhere else in that moment.

I wandered into the lounge, passing two vampires playing chess and others drinking around sofas and bookshelves. The bar, with its hundreds of glittering red vials, sat empty, with Elysium nowhere to be found. I turned on my heel to return to my room for a nap while I waited for Onyx, when I was startled.

"You're new," a man with a tan complexion and long navy blue braids said. "And you're somewhat human, aren't you?"

I tried to sidestep him, but he stepped with me, cutting me off. A female vampire appeared beside him so fast that it was as if she'd appeared out of thin air.

"This is new, and she smells freshly sated. Who among us is bedding her, I wonder?" Her blond bob swayed as she turned to me with a sinister smile.

"My husband and I are here waiting for our coven," I lied, though not nearly as smoothly as Onyx.

The man raised his eyebrows. "Alone and covenless? Interesting … you don't smell like a vampire, but you're not wholly mortal either … what does she smell like?"

"Like a haunted attic," the blond vampire inhaled. "What a sensational and unique scent that tempts me to have a taste …"

The hair on my arms raised in discomfort at the way they were discussing me like I wasn't standing in front of them. I didn't think I'd ever get used to people examining me as if I were some exotic animal. I made to step aside again. "I really should be getting back to my room."

"I'm Via and this is Udelle," the woman said, putting her arm around my shoulders. "Come, sit, have a drink with us. We're terribly bored waiting for the festivities to begin. Though we aren't eager for the offering, it is certainly fun to watch the infamous King Vlad the Impaler do his bit. Who will survive and who won't?"

Vlad the Impaler sounded ominous. They ushered me to a dark corner, where I took a hesitant seat on a cold Chesterfield sofa. My gaze stayed fixed on the door, willing Onyx to appear and get me out of my awkward encounter.

Udelle groaned. "I believe we've visited one hundred doors today already. Some years I wonder if we've seen them all. If I've worn all the fabulous clothes there are to wear to the Bleeding Heart Ball. It feels as if nothing is new and exciting anymore." He put his nose in my hair. "Perhaps that is what is so intriguing about you. Something different for once."

"Indeed," Via agreed, perching on the other side of me. "No wonder your husband has kept you hidden away from us. Does he not like to share?"

I cleared my throat, my heart rate accelerating with anxiety. *Where was Onyx? Where were the guys?*

"He's just fetching breakfast. He will be back any moment."

"Oh, for good food, he'd have gone to the Cocina District. It's in the heart of Belladonia, so I imagine it will take him some time to return ..."

I should have had Onyx teach me how to lie during our many late nights around the breakfast table in his cottage in Ash Grove.

Via twirled a stray piece of my hair, and I shuddered, scooting away and right into Udelle, who moved in closer. I strained to keep the fear out of my voice and change the subject from *food*.

"I'm looking for a cosmetic shop to buy some lipstick for the ball. Do either of you know of any?"

Via smiled, eyeing my exposed neck. Why did I think wearing my hair up was a good idea? "Yes, dear. Visit Lady Rouge near the castle. She'll find your perfect shade ... Oh, your mouth is nice. Wouldn't you like to come a little closer?"

I made to stand when Via grabbed my wrist and pulled me back down. "Don't be frightened, dear. The blood doesn't taste right mixed with fear. This will be such fun."

Udelle handed me a martini glass filled to the brim with red. "Here, have a sip. It will calm your nerves and excite … other areas."

Via giggled, her pointed nails digging into my wrist. If I struggled, they could easily overpower me.

Knowing it had no effect on me, I took a sip of the vessense cocktail to appease them and tried again to pry myself away. A vision of a glimmering turquoise mermaid fluttered through my mind. I shook the invasive image away and tried again to lie. "I think I see my coven outside. I should go let them know I'm here." I stood, but the vampires moved so quickly I could only briefly take in what happened next.

Via pinned me against the sofa while Udelle brought my wrist to his mouth. "The vessense will have her nice and calm. Don't worry, this will feel so enjoyable for us all." Via's giggle mixed with my scream as the male bit down on my wrist. Surprisingly, it didn't hurt. It was more of a tingling pressure. Another scream pushed from my throat as Via bit down on my shoulder, through my sweater. If there were other vampires in the room, none came to my aid. No one responded to my screams as I thrashed. This was it; I was going to die from vampire assault. I thought of my Halloween Boys, Ghost, Dragon, Wolf, and—

Suddenly the door burst open. A dark figure flew to my side, and two feathery, leather-gloved hands grabbed the vampires by the hair and pulled them off me, tossing them to the ground. They each growled, my blood coating their chins as I shook. Then I recognized my savior. The curved beak and the black feathers protruding from his vest. Raven helped me to a shaky stand as tears flooded my vision. "How—how?"

My familiar in his humanoid form tilted his head, just like he did when he was a bird. "I'll always find you, Blythe. I promise."

I made to wrap him in a hug when my assailants stood. "Another strange new creature to sample. How lucky for us—"

The same shrieking scream from the forest tore through my awareness, and I covered my ears. It sounded like a woman screaming, though no one else looked concerned, and I couldn't locate the source. Was she in the building?

Udelle stepped forward, and Raven tucked me behind his back, his long feathers falling from his arms like wings. But on the vampire's second step, he collapsed.

Via looked down at him in horror and then back up to me with wide red eyes. "What *are* you?"

Realizing what was happening, a small smile curved my lip. "Death."

Fear flashed across her awareness before she fell to the floor, joining her friend. A relieved laugh pushed from my throat as Raven frantically turned me around to look at me. "You're bloodied. We need to get these wounds clean. Though I am very happy to know your blood kills vampires."

"How did you get here? Are the guys with you?"

Raven shook his beak. "I flew straight from the ship after you left. I was escorted by seagulls to the spot you went under the waves, and a very kind kelpie pulled me to the door. Then I flew straight into town. But Blythe, you shouldn't go into these woods. I saw some very strange things."

"Wait," my brain finally caught up to the moment, "my blood kills vampires?"

My familiar nodded patiently.

My head raced with the times Onyx had nearly bitten me. And blood was so important to his sexuality. If we crossed that line, he would die. I looked to the fallen vampires in horror, and I wasn't the only one. Two tall, cloaked figures stood over the bodies. I hadn't seen them come in or noticed them being there. In fact, I hadn't seen anything like them at all in Belladonia.

"You will come with us," one spoke in a voice I knew belonged to the spirit realm. "Now."

Raven took my hand and whispered, "I'm weary from the flight. I don't believe I can get us out."

"It's okay," I whispered back. The cloaked figures didn't move, didn't sway, only stood, frozen and menacing. This wasn't something I was going to get out of. If I were in some sort of trouble and thrown in vampire jail, the worst I'd get was teased mercilessly by Onyx when he bailed me out later. At least I had Raven, and my attackers were dead. Both of those things brought me peace. "Where are we going?"

The hunched figures floated toward the door, and it opened for them. A long, bony finger gestured for us to follow. As we passed it by, one rumbled, and my blood iced over with fresh fear.

"To the king."

CHAPTER 24

Onyx

TELL ME LIES

> Everybody is equally weak on the inside, just that some present their ruins as new castles and become kings.
> *Simona Panova*

I considered killing him right there. What would anyone do about it? The only thing that kept me from setting the entire wretched bar ablaze was knowing that Blythe was upstairs. But when Elysium so intrusively insisted he show me the way to the Cocina District, I thought I'd rather end him then and there than endure more small talk with the vampire hunter. He'd crossed the line with the vessense.

Not that I could entirely blame him. I'd used my abilities to alter emotions to my advantage more often than not. What bothered me about Elysium was that he was *lying*. Lies were sometimes blatant, sometimes crafted with skill, and sometimes they were the embodiment of an individual. Everything about this guy's carefully crafted nice guy persona screamed deceit. If I were bored enough, I would have toyed with him awhile and unraveled the yarn ball of lies. But as it was, boredom wasn't my trouble at present.

Not when Blythe had allowed my mouth between her thighs. I should have kept going. She was a little immortal, right? She could have gone for another day or two without stopping. I vowed to test that theory when I got back to our room. For the moment, I was drowning out Elysium's chatter.

"We just passed the gaming district. The clothing district is closer to the castle, and right around this corner is Cocina. The best food in all the realms, if you ask me."

I didn't ask you. I stole small glances at his chair. I'd gathered that it ran on some sort of magic, though the way he petted it and treated it made it seem more like its own entity, or perhaps an extension of him.

"You can ask about Airwen. It's fine by me."

I raised my eyebrows, suddenly interested, as we wove through the gloomy streets. Somehow, we'd passed both horse-drawn carriages and a futuristic Porsche. Each coven had their own ideas of what was superior, and seeing them all together was a comical clash of luxury. "Honestly, I wouldn't know where to start. Why don't you just share the story?" In that moment, for the first time since I jumped ship, I missed the guys. How long had it been since I'd spent so much time away from them? I wanted Blythe lying back on Wolfgang's broad, muscular body as I took her. I wanted to watch his hands explore her breasts as my tongue worked. Then Ghost … I wanted him to be the spectator for once. To get hard watching us take her before unleashing him and letting him fuck her until she screamed in that darling way he enjoyed.

I wanted all of that. But I wanted them here, exploring the city with me, too. There was something I was missing, and it was gnawing at me like a rat. Wolf could smell it and tell me more than I could have deduced in a week. Ghost could have killed everyone here with a look, and that would have been to our advantage, because as it stood, I didn't know entirely what I was up against in Belladonia. Then Judas, if he ever deigned to come around, would be a game ender. They'd all fall to revere him, even their lofty king.

We were stronger together; that was indisputable. And fuck if I didn't love the bastards, too. Something like guilt furrowed into my gut, whispering about how they hated me now. Elysium spoke as we turned a corner, a wave of salty aromas enticing me forward. Meats, herbs, and pastries smoked from open doors. I couldn't stop, though, because I was after one meal in particular.

"An old friend gifted me this. It's one of the most powerful items of machinery in existence."

Not a lie. Interesting, but why would he tell me that?

"And is that why King What's-His-Name invited you here? A vampire hunter in a town full of vampires, invited by the ruler himself. I feel like I'm missing some information here."

"Why have you never come to Belladonia before? It's required for all of your kind. I don't expect King Vladimir will be pleased once he senses you've been ignoring the law." he said, taking me off guard.

"I was cursed by witches to stay in one place. Though, thankfully, the witches died, and here I am. I found Blythe through a coven that took me in, and our first order of business was paying our dues here."

He nodded, seemingly satisfied, yet doubtful of me at the same time. "Witches are a tricky sort. Belladonia will soon host the Bleeding Heart Ball, which I'm sure you've heard of. You and your wife will be required to mask yourselves beyond recognition and arrive separately. When you find each other, you must dance. This is part of the offering that pleases the king."

That sounded familiar, and an awful lot like Hallows Fest.

"Seems a little random," I said before stopping outside a vendor selling trays of duck and parsnips. "But I'm always down for a party. Will there be music?"

Elysium chuckled as he tapped his chair, bringing forth two cigars through the wood. He passed me one, and we lit up. Rum cigars were my favorite, and he won a few points for that. "It's to honor both the history of the Lovers of Belladonia, and to honor the king in his quest to find the lost queen. I think it's disgustingly romantic, personally."

Unfortunately, I'd have to wait to ask him more about that, because it was my turn in line. "I'm looking for waffles. Got any?"

The vampire with an impressive handlebar mustache looked offended. "Excuse me? You won't find food for children from me or any other of the esteemed chefs in Belladonia."

"Give me a break, man. I've got a wife at home. New vampire, and it's all she wants. You know how the cravings for your human comforts come and go at first, right?"

He stroked his mustache, and I felt a shot of compassion radiating over the smells of butter and rosemary. *Got him.* "I suppose I have flour and egg. I shall whip something up, but only in the spirit of finding a *belladonna* like yours someday."

"Thanks, man," I smiled.

Elysium and I stood to the side, watching others walk by. The clash of 1800s garb and modern leather and mohawks made me chuckle. "This place is like none other."

"Vampires are like none other—but more like humans than they'd like to acknowledge. Your *Belladonna* is their *Valentine.* Your *Bleeding Heart Ball* is their *Valentine's Day.* The story goes that a vampire lived his entire lonely existence in hate and sorrow until meeting his mate. She was gorgeous and she loved him, too—"

The chef cut in. "She didn't truly love him, or she wouldn't have done what she did." Batter sizzled as he poured it into a waffle press.

Elysium smiled at him and shrugged. "Everyone views it differently. But the fact is, she was the belladonna flower. Deadly nightshade, aconite, or wolfsbane, it's often called."

"Doesn't sound like a cheerful tale. Why celebrate?" I asked, feeling a twinge in my heart, thinking of Blythe.

The chef twirled his mustache again. "Because the wicked man chose her, chose death, rather than be without her. It is the tale of love, is it not? Love is the death of self. To ask someone to be your belladonna isn't just for the party and festivities. It's a symbol that you would give your life for theirs."

Elysium removed his round spectacles and dried them with his shirt. "Damn, Bastien. You're making me choke up over here, you old romantic."

He nodded. "That I am. Though the story of the Bleeding Heart Ball may be my favorite, even over that one. The king himself may be more romantic than us all. Collecting offerings to gift her upon her return ..." The chef took a spatula and removed the waffle, putting it into a Styrofoam container with strawberries and honey on the side. "May your belladonna be comforted by my cooking."

"Thank you, Bastien," I replied, taking the meal and palming my jeans for cash. It would be soggy, but I never went anywhere without money.

He lifted his palm. "Everything in Belladonia is free. We all have currency through whatever doors we call home. Here, we are all the same and want for nothing. We don't reduce ourselves to human capitalism."

Elysium put an arm around my shoulder as I thanked the chef again. "I appreciate you showing me the way. I believe I can make it back on my own."

I felt a stab of hurt from the vampire hunter, and I wasn't sure why he'd be feeling that way. "Sure, yeah. I'll see you back at the bar."

He wove through vampires and disappeared into the crowd, leaving me feeling like an asshole. I was about to jog to catch up to him when a snickering group of vampires passed me. "I heard they grabbed a bird man and a human. How the hell do you think they made it in?"

I stopped and whirled around, grabbing the woman's arm. She looked up at me in disgust, and I let go. "Excuse me, what did you say?"

"Eavesdrop much?" She looked me up and down, not impressed by what she saw. I wasn't sure how that was possible, but I ignored it. "A couple of weirdos were taken by the Hoods. Though I wish they'd let us have a taste first. Imagine the vessense we won't get now that they'll be property of the king."

"Maybe we have time to intercept them. I heard they're on Lone Street," a man with her replied.

"You'll do no such fucking thing. Where is Lone Street?"

"God, you're truly insufferable." The woman rolled her eyes. "It's four blocks south."

I ran, irritated by my new surroundings. I knew Ash Grove better than anyone, but I didn't have that luxury in Belladonia. There were too many vampires and too much new information. I was constantly playing catch-up, and now I'd apparently lost Blythe and Raven. Blythe and Raven? Were Ghost and Wolf around? No, they couldn't be, or she wouldn't have been taken.

The soles of my worn Converse hit the cobblestone of Lone Street in time to see a crowd parting. Three hooded figures led the way, and the crowd gaped and whispered. I stepped out into the center of the street. "I'm going to need you three to find someone else to fuck with today."

The crowd gasped and gloved hands went to mouths as the three figures floated toward me. They were bigger than I'd anticipated, but I'd taken on bigger. … Though I had no clue what they were, exactly, they didn't look strong. I turned my hands, and my blaze lit my palms. The chatter of the crowd rose, but the beings didn't stop. When one dared to get too close, I sent out a serpent of twisted flame, and it … *went right through it*. As if air. What the hell?

But I had no time to regroup when it extended a long bony finger from its robe and pointed at me.

Something hit my head, and my vision blurred as I faded into oblivion.

CHAPTER 25

Ghost

MARITIME MADNESS

> So we beat on, boats against the current, borne back ceaselessly into the past.
> *F. Scott Fitzgerald, The Great Gatsby*

Captain Vex shouted from the wheel as his crew and Wolf scurried about with their orders. "We should be reaching the doorway in a matter of minutes."

After a moment, Wolf joined me, still wearing a goddamn pirate hat. I snatched it off his head. "How can you be calm? Do you not care for her?"

Wolf rubbed his jaw. "I care for her more than you know, Ames. Likewise, I care for Onyx and for you. This kind of thing happens. They're safe. Onyx is likely wining and dining her in his fancy vampire city while they find his dad. By the time we get there, they'll probably be ready to come home."

I snorted. "Such an optimist."

"Doesn't hurt to not be miserable all the time. You should try it out sometime. Remember our pirate ship tree house as boys? We had those little wooden swords your dad made us. This is like that, only real. Tell me you don't think it's cool."

"No, Wolfgang, I don't think it's cool that my Claimed was just stolen away by someone who I thought was my closest friend."

"He still is. He's just going through some stuff, and she's his mate, too. You've been hard on him lately, but I seem to remember that, before Blythe, you were crawling out of your skin for a kill, for anything to do to take your mind off our curse, our plight. You have her now, and Ash Grove and everything you've ever wanted. I have Fenrir and my pack. What does Onyx have? His human family wasn't his real family, his first love was taken by demons, and the curse being lifted for him leaves him with the option of finding the family that seemingly never came looking for him in two hundred years. And all the while, he's had to watch you parade Blythe around like your shiny new plaything."

That elicited a growl from my throat. "Watch it."

"You know I'm right. Now, if you don't mind, I have to practice my reef knot if I'm going to be allowed to steer the ship later." He snatched his hat back and wore it proudly. "Maybe try pulling the stick out of your ass and having a tiny bit of fun for once in two hundred years. Our girl is safe. Onyx needs this solo adventure, and we'll see them tomorrow."

My sickeningly positive companion went back to his newfound pirate friends, who patted him on the back and tossed him rope. Something inside me knew he was right. I'd been too hard on my friend in favor of keeping Blythe all to myself. The sun began to set, and I put my elbows on the edge of the ship and watched the waves all the way to the horizon. I'd never been so far away from home before, aside from Hell. This had considerably better views. As much as I wanted to rage and kill them all, to hunt down Onyx and tear his head from his body, that probably wasn't the right answer.

After several moments, or hours, I didn't know, the sun sank, casting the sky in oranges and purples. The smell of rum and saltwater invaded my senses as a parrot chirped from a man's shoulder next to me. "I know the look of a sailor missin' his woman. I am sorry for what happened. And if it's any consolation, I'm not taking you boys back to Ash Grove like he asked. You'll be seein' Blythe soon."

I met his stare. "Onyx asked you to take us back to Ash Grove?"

The captain shrugged. "We're all fools in love."

"Some more than others."

He positioned his elbows next to mine and looked out over the ocean. "Can I give you some advice, son?"

Son. As if I wasn't an archdemon created by Hell itself. But, as Blythe had so often reminded me, I was a man, too. Somewhere. With a sigh, I nodded. "Sure."

"I believed this boat to be the greatest love of my life. Thought I'd live and die here, seein' her down to the shipwrecked shores below. That is, until I met her. Met a woman, well, a vampiress, so fierce, so true that I knew I'd sell all my stories and capsize my ship if it were ever to her benefit."

I raised an eyebrow. That seemed like a lot of effort for the Red Vampiress, but I supposed that was how she liked to leave her men. Needy, anxious, and utterly obsessed. I kept my mouth shut on that one. "And?"

"And the truth of it is, if I did that, she wouldn't want me. I wouldn't deserve her either."

"Care to make it make sense, Vex? I have a migraine."

He chuckled. "Women are like the ocean, especially women like Ez and Blythe. They're as deep and mystical and mysterious as the all-knowing waves. Any pirate is a fool if he tries to control it, to own it, or keep it in a jar fer only himself. You'd be killin' yourself tryin' and disrespecting the sea herself."

"I know that I do not own her, and I don't want to. There are others for her. Wolfgang and Onyx. But I do want to keep her safe. That is my job, Vex."

"Yer self-appointed one. The ocean don't need chains, boy. She needs skilled sailors. Respect and love make a captain. Tryin' to control it is the fastest way to lose yourself and lose the woman you love; I guarantee you that. Demon or not, love's the same for all creatures, powerful and weak." His bird repeated his last words, and the jukebox lit up with yellow light and emitted a slow ballad.

The captain continued. "I know she's special. I've felt power like hers before, long ago. Lots of those wanting to use it. More of those hopin' she never sees it and realizes what she's capable of. Are you one of them? Cause the ocean has a way of reminding us of who's in charge."

I exhaled, searching for a reply that would shake him off, that I could use to convince myself he was wrong. Thankfully, I didn't need to say anything, because Wolfgang bounded over and slapped the pirate on the back. "I'm ready to show you my knots. Also, what's with the haunted jukebox? Can I request a song?"

Vex chuckled. "You can ask. Not sure if she'll oblige. The music drowns out the sirens. Keeps my crew safe from all manner of temptresses of the deep."

I didn't even want to know.

"How much farther until we're at the door?" I asked as they strolled away.

The captain said over his shoulder. "We're already here. This very spot. Just waiting."

"Waiting for what?"

"A storm, of course."

AFTER OUR LITTLE CHAT, I'd assumed the pirate meant a metaphorical storm, but as the ship bobbed in place and the night sky grew muddy with gray, I knew a storm was coming. Though how he knew it, I had no idea. Pirates, especially these story keeper variety, were much wiser than people assumed. I stood on the outskirts of their tales around the fire. Onyx's fire. I watched it pensively, as if I could look through it and see where he and Blythe were at that moment. Were they even thinking of me? Or were they both happy to have a break from the hurricane that was Ghost? Wolf turned, as if sensing my gloom, and waved me over, patting the barrel next to him. I begrudgingly obliged. and after a sip from his goblet of rum, I sighed. "I pushed him too far."

Wolf wrapped an arm around my shoulder. "He'll forgive you."

The sea captain, drunk, no doubt, wobbled over and chuckled as his men sang, and someone played the fiddle.

"Something you want to say, captain, better fucking say it." I growled. I'd really had enough of the damn pirates.

"Your friend is a vampire and a dragon. An unholy combination that never should have happened." A few eavesdropping pirates grumbled their agreements before he continued. "You know how many stories I've collected about vampires? The powerful ones almost always steal their mate away—same with dragons. You've never heard of villages offering a maiden to their fire-breathing beast? What do you think happens after the dragon takes her? I'd say this day was always coming. I'd even say he'd planned it. It's in his nature. You're both fools for not seeing it coming."

Wolfgang stood and tightened his ponytail. "You said we're hovering over the door now? We just jump in and swim for it?"

"You can't go until it's stormin'. Even then, you should pray a guide is around to grab you and lead you there before you drown."

I raised my eyebrows at Wolf. "Oh, now you're in a hurry?"

He shrugged. "I don't like the idea that Onyx has been plotting a betrayal for centuries. It's probably not true, but ... I'm protective of Blythe, too. She shouldn't be in a situation she didn't consent to."

"I agree."

Just then, a raindrop pelted my jaw. *Finally.*

The werewolf and I walked to the plank, staring the very long way down into the dark and torrid waters below. Fear wasn't an emotion I had the capacity to feel, not as an archdemon. But as a man ... that moment was fucking terrifying.

Thunder clapped overheard as Wolf joined his hand with mine. "I guess we're—"

The ship shook violently then. Pirates shouted before pops of guns blew behind us. The floor was rumbling again as we turned, holding on to the side of the boat to see ... another ship. A larger, less dilapidated ship towered over the story keepers' ramshackle vessel. Captain Vex yelled orders just as a cannonball whirled by him, breezing into the deck with a crash. Scully, the tongueless first mate, ran by us frantically, only firelight lighting his worn face. We met stares for the briefest of moments before he tossed Wolf and me each something. We caught them by the handles as he raised his own sword over his head. Wolfgang joined him. "Come on, man. It's a real-life pirate battle!" The werewolf's canines glimmered in torchlight; he couldn't contain his broad smile. "The storm will last; we've got time. What do you say?"

The boat quaked from another blow as hooked ropes tore onto the deck. The enemy ship's crew began zip lining over with war cries. I looked over the plank, knowing my doorway to Blythe only existed for this storm. Though somewhere inside me, I knew Onyx would keep her safe, and beyond that, I had to trust that Blythe could handle herself. She had to learn how to move through this world on her own terms somehow. And sometimes I wouldn't be around. She was the ocean, and I was but a humble raft adrift on her tides forever. And the pirates, as uncouth as they may have been, had helped us when we needed them. Wolfgang elbowed me, waggling his eyebrows.

I raised my sword. "Let's kill some bad guys."

CHAPTER 26

Blythe

KING OF NOTHING

> O! for a muse of fire, that would ascend the brightest heaven of invention
> *William Shakespeare*

If I ran, it was possible I could escape through the crowd, but Raven couldn't. And I was guessing that if these hooded figures worked for the king, they were powerful. The casual, slow way they moved with my familiar and me at their backs suggested that they weren't worried we'd flee or try to harm them. That made me think that neither was a possibility. And regardless, I wouldn't risk my friend. "You should turn into your bird form and fly away," I whispered, still holding on to one of his long black feathered arms.

"I don't have the strength to shift after flying here, and I would not leave you, regardless. This is where I'm supposed to be."

I gave him a small squeeze as we walked up the dreary, winding steps to the castle. It was enormous and jagged in all its overcast glum. The closer we got to the top, the heavier my feet felt. The weight of tremendous despair pushed down on my shoulders until I was unsure that I could take another breath. Raven stopped next to me, looking anxiously to the hovering figures as they moved ahead. "I'll carry you," he offered.

"I've got it. I'm okay. It feels so sad up here. Do you feel it?"

His gaze held mine, and I remembered when I first met him at Hallows Fest. Raven was my first real friend. "Trust yourself, Blythe, and whatever you are feeling. I'm right here with you. Though this place is very odd. There are no birds here; only bats."

I fought to swallow down the overwhelming feeling of melancholy as we walked through the enormous front doors of the castle. I wondered if this was how Onyx felt all the time, feeling others' emotions. Was that what I was doing? How could that be?

We made our way down a long corridor lit by dripping red taper candles. New wax pooled over old, creating gigantic mismatched shapes and shadows. When it felt as if we'd walked miles, and maybe we had, we reached another ornate set of double doors. The three hooded beings stopped before passing straight through the iron and wood. I caught Raven's gaze as he said, "They are some sort of dark spirits that come in threes. I believe I saw three in the woods of Ash Grove once, a very long time ago."

"As soon as you can shift, do it and fly away. Do you understand?"

"I'm not leaving—"

"I'm commanding it. You have to listen if I do that, right?"

He didn't have time to answer before the doors swung inward and a cold, musty wind invaded my senses. We stepped forward, following a crimson carpet into a vast, hollow throne room. The dark spirits were nowhere to be seen, and I would have thought we were alone if it weren't for the voice that echoed from across the room. "It was a dreadfully dull day before you two. I may thank you for allowing me to kill you to ease my boredom."

His voice was hollow and primordial, and that was how I would have described his appearance as well. A tall figure stepped out of the shadows near a looming black throne and casually strolled toward us. The flecks of dust in the candlelight made him look misty and misshapen, but as he approached, I realized he was anything but weak. Shoulder-length black hair grazed the broad shoulders of his white poet shirt. The material was nearly the same shade as his lily pale skin. His garnet stare met mine, and I cut short a gasp in my chest. Something about him was horrifying, powerful and *familiar*. Had I met him before? Maybe at Hallows Fest?

Raven moved to step in front of me, but I stopped him, instead positioning myself in front. I forced my voice through my dry throat. "You won't be killing either of us today."

He sauntered closer. There was something I recognized in the way he walked, but it didn't ease the fear that bloomed in my belly as his lip curved, exposing a long fang.

"You must be new to Belladonia. I am King Vladimir Drakon, and I do what I please. No vampire's whore or beast man will deny my urges." The king stepped closer, and I fought to control my trembling. I hoped Raven would be able to shift soon. I hoped he'd fly fast enough that he wouldn't hear this lethal king of vampires break my bones and drain my blood.

But my blood had not favored his kind so far … I reached out my wrist. "Please, my king, have a taste."

His eyes widened, and I felt Raven tense as the man stopped in front of me. His ice-cold fingers wrapped around my forearm, and I was certain he was about to break me in half.

Bringing my wrist to his nose, he inhaled. "I haven't tasted a woman since my bride, and I won't be doing so today. Though the prospect of a swift death, as you gave the two odious souls earlier, presents a mouth-watering appeal …" His tongue licked my palm, and I shuddered, resisting the urge to pull back. I opened my mouth to respond when there was a commotion behind me.

The heavy doors rattled on their hinges, and hope fluttered within me. It probably wasn't normal that the thought of monsters tearing down buildings excited me. But they were my monsters, and I loved each of them. The king's crimson stare looked on in shock as his doors blasted open with flame. Onyx stumbled forward, looking wild and crazed, as if he'd run the whole way up the winding stairs and through the castle.

"You'll let go of my wife, or you'll become a pile of ash. I don't give a fuck if you're some king of nothing."

The king let go of my hand and took a step back. I grabbed Raven and ran to Onyx, flinging myself into his arms.

He held me close, pressing his nose into my hair. "I got you waffles, but I'm afraid they're cold now."

A warm tear of relief streaked my cheek. "Luckily I know a guy who's basically a portable microwave."

The corner of his mouth curved, and I gasped, spinning around. The king had approached us so swiftly, so silently, that I hadn't felt him inches behind me. Onyx moved me behind him as they stood toe to toe. Holding on to Raven, I inched backward. The two vampires stood at the exact same height, and I could only make out the king's wide, red eyes as he assessed Onyx. The blue tint of their black hair shone in the firelight, the pale gauntness of their skin ... The king reached out and cupped Onyx's face in his palms, his chin quivering.

"My son ... Onyx Hart Drakon, Prince of Belladonia."

CHAPTER 27

Onyx

PRINCE OF NOTHING

There is something at work in my soul, which I do not understand.

Mary Shelley, Frankenstein

"You're my … are you sure?" The king looked like me. Even sounded like me, in a way. "How could this be?"

I was still reeling from my trip here. How I'd woken up being carried by some sort of magic by those hooded creeps. Powerful dark lords or not, their cloaks eventually caught fire, the same as anything else. They'd dropped me at the base of the castle, and I'd sprinted the rest of the way, burning down door after door, searching for Blythe. She was okay. No one had harmed her, though they could have. The thought still had my blood boiling. And now there was King Vladimir, my … father?

His grip dropped to my shoulders, pulling me from my trance. "Do you know where your mother is?"

It was like being smacked in the face with a sheet of ice. I shook my head.

"You don't know where she is?" I felt the subtle squeeze as his long nails pressed through my shirt.

"There is much to discuss, of course. The rapturous truth remains, the prince … *of nothing* … has returned," the king said wryly.

Blythe appeared beside me, lacing her fingers with mine. God, how long had I longed to hold her hand like that? Though she was likely only doing it out of pity. The lonely, forgotten son meets his strange and royal father … or perhaps she was maintaining our farce of matrimony.

Regardless, I held her tight. "There is much to discuss indeed. For now, may I trouble you for a place my wife can rest?"

King Vladimir shook his head, remembering himself, and snapped a finger. "Of course. Someone will show you to your room. I understand this may be a shock. It seems as if you are not aware of your grand heritage, my son. It has been several hundred years, but I never gave up hope that your mother … and you … would be returned to me."

I didn't know what to say. My mother was the lost queen from Belladonia's stories, and my father was the king of vampires. It didn't seem real. Part of me was skeptical, and part of me wanted to explode with joy. Standing in front of me was the first tangible piece of my family, of where I'd come from. King Vladimir held the answer to every question that had plagued me for centuries.

And now I stood before him, a peasant in front of a king, and all I could do was shrug and paste on my mask of casual indifference. "Yeah, well … let's talk soon."

"Of course. I shall meet with you both after you have had time to adjust. This castle is yours. Use of it as you wish. Though I do prefer the point of the sky we occupy at present."

Blythe must have looked more bewildered than I did, because he smiled slightly as he addressed her.

"I do apologize for my previous behavior. I could not have known who you belonged to. And to answer the question so clearly upon your face, you stand upon Castle Drakon of Belladonia. We are a city of the heavens."

Raven spoke for the first time. "This is a castle in the sky?" The pirates had mentioned a castle in the clouds, but one could never be sure if they were serious, poetic, or drunk, at any given moment.

The king nodded. "The entire city floats in the sky. We are the safest place in all the realms. My son, did your coven fail you so that you know not of Belladonia?"

I cleared my throat. "Everything's a bit hazy right now. But I do want to hear more about … all of this. I appreciate you allowing us to stay. I'll try not to break anything … else."

Every word I uttered rang like clashing gongs next to harmonious flutes. King Vladimir, my father, was poised and eloquent, while I was severely altered by my time spent in a small human town, with only my chosen family of the Halloween Boys to confide in. I had denied joining Vincent's coven for all these years, not wanting to serve an arrogant prick like him. It turned out I was the arrogant prick all along. A Prince. Fuck. My father held my shoulders and surveyed me from head to toe. "I see too much of me, but blessed glimpses of your mother, too. The prince has indeed returned," he declared with a proud, emotion-filled tone. I didn't know how to act. Was I supposed to hug him? Bow?

"I'm in shock that this is happening right now" was all I could muster.

Soon after, the king pulled his attention from me as a frail, gangly woman with long, stringy black hair ushered us out of the throne room. A dull sort of resignation was the only emotion I could gather from her, though her scent was abnormal.

Blythe broke the silence as we pattered down the hall, following the quiet woman and her lantern. "I'm Blythe," she said and startled when Raven suddenly shifted into his crow form. The wind from his wings flickered the flames as he rose above and in front of us, seeing our way. "That's Raven, and this is Onyx. What's your name?"

After a few more turns and up a set of narrow stairs, the woman finally replied. "I am Lolth." She turned a bronze knob and pushed open a heavy door.

We stepped in, and I was pleasantly surprised to find that the furnishings seemed comfortable. The canopy bed was large and draped with red silk, and a fire roared in the hearth. Blythe would sleep well here, … and I would watch and savor every slumberous breath. By the time we'd uttered our thanks, Lolth was gone.

"She seems cheery," I said.

"What a clusterfuck," Blythe breathed, slumping down at a small breakfast table filled with smoked meats and cheeses. She bit into a block of cheese, and I joined her, uncorking the bottle of red wine. "Are you okay?" she asked.

"Why wouldn't I be?"

She raised a skeptical eyebrow and accepted the crystal stemmed glass. "I don't know, *Prince*. Why wouldn't you be? Onyx, we found your dad, and he's, like, a famous ruler."

"Was there ever a doubt I had royalty in my blood? Look at this handsome face."

She giggled, the sound tugging at the chorus of the song I was always writing in my head when she was around. "Seriously, what's the plan?"

I stretched my hands over my head, catching her gaze lingering on my biceps. Heat from her attraction hit me in the chest, and it was all I could do to contain my growl of longing. Something about having her alone in a castle, sprawled out on a red four-poster bed ... My fangs ached. I should have been thinking of anything but sex. Like how I'd just found my father, and he was a king. Of how my mother was dead, missing, or both. I should have been finding a way to contact Devil and beg him to help me find Ghost and Wolf.

But no, my errant attention lingered on her breasts in that black top. I wondered what her blood would taste like dripping down her nipples for me ... I cleared my burning throat and took a sip of wine, pretending the black currant tannins were comparable to blood.

"The plan is to get to know my father and get some questions answered." I downed my glass. "And then inevitably disappoint him, become an outcast again. The chapter is closed, the book is done, we go home."

Blythe regarded me with kinder eyes than I deserved as her hand grazed my knuckles. "You could never be a disappointment, Onyx. This is a weird situation. It's okay to feel unsure."

"You sound like Dr. Ames Cove."

"He's rubbed off on me a bit."

"I'd like to rub off on you."

Her cheeks flushed a gorgeous shade of pink before she recovered. "Speaking of Ames, any idea when the guys will be here?" Raven squawked at me from a nearby window. I quickly made my way over and opened it, gesturing for him to make his exit. I'd be damned if a bird sold me out or cock blocked me.

I let out an exhale. "I'm not sure." Silence settled into the room as the fire crackled and Blythe finished her food. Finally, I asked, "How'd you even get here? I heard the hooded assholes had a girl and a birdman. Found a few hooded spirits that weren't yours, I guess, and they snatched me for throwing flames. But how'd they get you, and where the hell did Raven come from?" She patted her lips with a napkin before gently folding it and setting it aside. Hesitation seeped from her to me. "What don't you want to tell me?"

"Stop reading my feelings, creep."

"Stop feeling them so loudly then."

She reached for the wine and wiggled her fingers. I pulled it back, just slightly out of reach. "Tell me."

Resting her chin on her fist, she bit her lip. "I killed two vampires."

No emotions of merriment or teasing accompanied her declaration, and I fought to calm the dragon inside. "You were threatened, then?"

"Yes, they … they pinned me down and bit me. Raven flew all the way here from wherever the ship was. Somehow, he found the door. He got them off me long enough for them to stand and—"

"And what?" I felt the fire in my palms warming the wine bottle as I clutched it too tightly.

"They dropped dead. My blood. It … killed them."

"Good," I growled, trying to steady my breathing. "Can you use your reaper magic to bring them back to life so I can kill them again?"

She let out a nervous snicker. "I'm okay, but you know what that means for … us."

My rage remained a steady simmer as I pieced together her implications. If biting her brought on death, then her blood … My thoughts drifted to the times I'd almost bitten her. In the church at Halloween. Watching Ghost take her. All I'd wanted to do was bite her as she came on his cock. In the forest after I'd burned down the courthouse. I'd considered just doing it then, just to see her reaction, to taste her surprise … And then on the pirate deck. I had fully intended to bite her thigh when Ghost pulled me off. We'd fought over it, but I guessed he'd saved my life. But not biting her *ever*, how could I endure that?

"Is that too scary for you?" she asked timidly.

I refilled her glass with wine before taking a long sip from the bottle. What could I say? It would be like never touching a lover, never beholding them with my sight again, it would be like eons of a crescendo that builds and builds and never releases, the musical number left unfinished.

To love Blythe was to die. To love Death herself was to embrace her inevitability. Death took my first love, and now Death was my last love …

"No," I rasped. "I'm not afraid, my sweet belladonna."

***

HOURS LATER, I leaned against the window that overlooked the city below. Blythe had bathed and had found a lace nightgown, then she'd fallen fast asleep. I told myself I was standing by the window to watch and keep her safe, but it was more to keep her safe from me. I wanted her so badly it hurt. The thought of her blood killing me dead should have been a deterrent, but it was the opposite. Now it was a nagging question mark, a risk I wanted to take. Her blood was daring me to taste it, and I wanted to rise to meet its challenge. But I couldn't risk it now. Not at the risk of leaving her alone in Belladonia without protection.

I wondered how much the king knew about her or if he even cared. The man seemed more ancient and eccentric than Vincent. King Vladimir was the oldest vampire I'd ever met. The elder vampires were strange and temperamental. I knew not to trust him; I knew not to let sentimentality or desperation cloud my thinking. Though my stupid heart wanted to believe he could be a good father somehow. Was it possible he'd been waiting and searching for me? I supposed I'd find out when I spoke with him next. Gazing upon him was like seeing myself in another dimension, another life. A life where I was older, wiser, and fully vampire. But I was none of those things, was I? I was young in comparison to many immortals. I was brash and irrational, as Ghost so often reminded me. And I wasn't fully anything. A half-breed: a dragon and a vampire. Who was my mother, and what had she seen behind the ruby eyes of the King of Belladonia?

Ghost and Wolf would have known what to do, what to tell me to do in that moment. But because of my impulses, they weren't here, and Blythe had been bitten. If I had bitten her as I'd gone down on her the day before, I may not have been alive to protect her. Ghost was right—I wasn't ready for her. But that didn't mean I was giving her up. I would fight for her, to be what she deserved. I'd become better for her. To do that, I'd need to begin by setting things right. I'd find a way to bring the Halloween Boys back together while treading lightly with my newfound kin.

But I was going to need help. I was going to have to trust someone I didn't want to trust. As Raven glided to a stop on the windowsill, I gave him a nod, silently passing the torch of guardianship as I slipped out the door in search of the vampire hunter.

CHAPTER 28

Onyx

GUARD YOUR HEART

> Bitterness is like cancer. It eats upon the host. But anger is like fire. It burns it all clean.
> *Maya Angelou*

Elysium was sitting outside Needle and Thorn, smoking a long wooden pipe. The streets were quiet, with only a few men walking by and tipping their hats to me. It was like the early nineteen hundreds on one block, and on the next, it was the eighties with mohawks and acid wash jeans. This town was wild.

The vampire hunter noticed my approach, and his chair whirled and clicked before gliding forward. "I heard about what happened. Is your wife okay?"

"She's fine. We need to talk."

"How can I help you, Onyx Hart?" he asked, blowing a smoke ring into the night.

I raised an eyebrow, and his glance flicked to mine. My eyes were probably glowing green. "I suppose it's Onyx Hart Drakon, but you probably already knew that, didn't you?"

He didn't look surprised, and his emotions didn't change. "I had my suspicions. You look just like the king, though your eyes are distinctly your mother's."

Air left my lungs in a dry puff. "Did you know my mother?"

"Maybe, or maybe I've only seen the painting in Queen Cassiopeia's music room, the one of her and you as a baby and her dragon. He's been searching for her, you know, for hundreds of years."

"What happened?"

"No one knows for certain. Only that she disappeared one day after a diphylla attack. I was employed here shortly after to hunt the beasts. Unfortunately, there are no more dragons to help aid in the search. But something tells me you didn't seek me out at this hour for a history lesson."

"Why didn't you take me straight to the king when you suspected who I was?"

Another puff of smoke before a compartment in the arm of his chair opened, and he tucked the pipe inside. "That's a good question."

I wasn't entirely sure if Elysium was someone I could trust. But he hadn't lost my trust yet. If he'd handed Blythe and me directly over to the king, he surely would have been rewarded, so why didn't he? Unless keeping us to himself would have allowed him to gain something greater. I couldn't be sure, but I had no other allies in Belladonia, so I was going to have to take a chance on him. "I'm looking for a witch."

"What witch?"

"Any witch. Know any?"

"The only witches allowed here are the ones used to assist the king in his search." He straightened his glasses. "Why do you ask?"

"You know, I'm an attorney, and you're really good at not answering questions. How about this? I tell you everything you want to know about me in exchange for getting me to a witch who can help me communicate with someone."

"How do I know you'll be truthful?"

"Give me more of the vessense cocktail you tricked me with earlier. That should do it, don't you think?"

He swallowed and brushed his shaggy white hair from his eyes. "Curiosity got the better of me. I apologize for the intrusion." I'd done the same thing to people for centuries; I couldn't hold it against him.

"Okay, but no one can know I'm helping you, got it? Meet me at the front gate seven nights from tonight, on the full moon. I'll take you to what you seek."

"Deal." I turned to leave, when his voice said lowly behind me, knowing I could hear even the smallest of whispers.

"Guard your heart around the king … all is not what it seems here … Prince."

THE VAMPIRE HUNTER'S warning was only confirmation what I'd suspected, but I appreciated it all the same. The following days were immersed in vampiric castle life. Blythe and I would have breakfast while the strange woman, Lolth, would watch on and then show us around the castle. I wasn't sure what I expected when I found my father, but it wasn't that we'd be reunited after hundreds of years, and then I'd have to schedule an appointment to speak with him again. Clearly vampire fathers were not the sentimental sort, though his search for my mother would suggest otherwise. I sought her in every painting. At every cracked door, I wondered if it was her room, but there were no hints of who she was or had been. On the third day, when Blythe had left for bed, I walked by Lolth as she slithered down the hall and asked, "Did you know the queen? My mother?"

After a moment, standing stone-still in the low light, she responded. "That is a question for His Majesty. He will see you tomorrow."

My mother was some sort of secret hiding in plain sight. Another secret in plain sight was the growing attraction between Blythe and me. Now that I thought I couldn't have her blood, I only wanted it more. My thirst for her was burning me alive, and I knew I'd break soon. She'd sleep all curled up in the bed as I watched from the window, gripping the stone wall to keep from ravishing her as she dreamed. And after several days with no word from the guys, I was only worrying further about the bomb that seemed to be ticking.

It was one week until the Bleeding Heart Ball, when the grand masquerade would take place. Blythe and I would be separated, having to find each other beyond the masks and crowds. Leaving her unattended again made my skin crawl, though at least there would be Raven. The bird humanoid who hadn't shifted or so much as spoken one word to me since we arrived at the castle. He was likely sore with me, too. He could join the list of those who despised me at present. I was certain Ghost was seething and fantasizing over the ways he'd torture my sinful, deceptive soul. I couldn't blame him. I deserved it. And Wolf, my other love … I left without a goodbye or an explanation, leaving him to cool the rage of the archdemon. He probably hated me. If they were back in Ash Grove, though, I could probably reach them when I spoke to the witch. I just hoped they'd answer my call.

The gangly creature with flat, eerie emotions led me to the king's library the following day. It was vast and ornate, with deep woods, leathers, and velvets. And the largest collection of books I'd ever seen. He stood in the corner, thumbing a hardback, when he gestured me forward without lifting his eyes from the page. As I approached, he flipped the book closed and tucked it back into its place on the shelf. As he did so, the shelf rumbled and slowly slid open.

With a half grin, he said, "Welcome to my secret lair."

Beyond the bookshelf was a cavernous room, burning with lanterns and covered with portraits. It was hard to take my eyes off the king. It was as if he wasn't real. Like he was some illusion I'd dreamed up. But when I did look away, my breath lodged in my throat. The same woman adorned each of the hundreds of portraits. Her hair was long and golden blond. She had a cheerfulness about her that oddly reminded me of the light I'd found in Wolfgang.

From the look in her twinkling eyes, it seemed as if she'd say something uplifting and kind. In one photo, Vladimir stood behind her as she wore a burgundy dress and held a rose. Emotion clouded my eyes, and I sniffled back the surge of feeling.

A palm landed on my shoulder. "She named you Onyx Hart. I would have called you *Dracul*, but she insisted." Something like a smile etched his hard features. "Your mother was the most beautiful creature the world ever beheld. I made her happy, but I believe you made her happier." I couldn't speak. I could only stare in awe at the image I'd seen in my dreams. The woman I'd assaulted my mind for hundreds of years searching for, begging for some sort of memory. "Come, sit with me, son."

When I composed myself, I sat across from a fireplace in an armchair, though I noticed something strange in the corner of the room. My father poured a glass of amber liquid and passed it to me before taking his seat across from me. He put an ankle on his knee as he assessed me with deep, red eyes. He looked nothing like a king in that moment.

He looked startlingly like me. Like a better, older version of me. "I hope you and your wife have found the castle and Belladonia to your liking. Thank you for your patience with me and my absence. It does not reflect my desire to see or to know you both. There are things that … require my undivided attention at present."

I lifted a finger toward the corner of the room. "A coffin? Is this your room?" I'd heard of very ancient vampires sleeping in coffins, but I'd never met one who actually did.

He tilted his chin. "I do not eat or sleep, as seems to be the recent trend of our people. Though sleep, I imagine, is much like dying, and death may be the closest I come to being reunited with Cassiopeia. Imagining my end and seeing her again brings me peace."

It was romantic in a Shakespearean tragedy sort of way, I supposed. I ran a nervous hand through my hair. This was it—the moment I'd thought of, worked for. It was sitting right in front of me, drinking million-year-old scotch. Now that I'd found him, I didn't know where to begin. I asked the first thing that came to mind. "What kind of music do you like?"

He chuckled, a crude grumble of a sound. "I've never been musically inclined. Your mother was, though. She played the harp. Curious, being she had no voice. She communicated through her spirit and through touch, you see. Her touch could play images in the mind, and her spirit could speak directly into your thoughts. It was extraordinary. She was extraordinary."

"What happened to her?"

His expression went dark for a moment before he took another sip of his drink. "She was stolen by a creature that should not exist. Something Hell would not even accept into its fold when petitioned. You were tied to her in a wrap, and she protected you with her life."

"But you're looking for her, so … you believe her to be alive?"

"I have hope to at least find her soul. Hope is something you never lose for your mate."

"Did you have hope for me to return?"

He leaned forward, putting his elbows on his knees in the same way I did at times. His long hair hid his features. "When you're as old as I, you stop believing in miracles. I don't know why she, or perhaps the evil that took her, would have hidden you from my vision. I have searched every day with a fervent hope for you. Strange as it may have been, you burning down my doors was certainly the first miracle I've witnessed in my long life. It deeply reminded me of your mother."

I huffed a laugh. "Sorry about that."

"Your very existence is remarkable. Born of fire and blood. I always wondered how your breeding would manifest. You carry the blood of an original vampire and of a dragon. You were not bitten and made, nor even forged in Hell. You were grown like any child. Truly, your existence is fascinating. It is clear you have access to fire. Are there any other abilities your mother imparted to you? Can you shift into a dragon? She could, if you did not know."

"No, only occasional fire," I lied. Why did I lie? "I did inherit the vampiric love of law. I'm an attorney in my human life. And my friends do say I have a flair for bravado, but I think they're just jealous."

"And your coven? Why have they never brought you to me for your offering? You should have been discovered ages ago."

"My coven is … unconventional. And for the past two hundred years, I have been under a curse, unable to leave my town."

"What is the name of your town?"

"Ash Grove."

He nodded. "Well, you're here now. There is much to learn about the running of Belladonia, the magic of the castle, the guarding of the doors. Being a prince will not be easy, but I believe we can get you ready to introduce to the people at the Bleeding Heart Ball."

"Oh, I don't think we'll be staying long-term—"

"You're the long-lost prince. The peoples' only blood connection to their beloved queen. They will want you ruling alongside me. Is this not why you've come to Belladonia? To claim your birthright?"

A shard of pain shot through my heart. "No, I just wanted to … know you. To see where I came from. I didn't even know you were a king."

Vladimir tilted his head slightly, but I couldn't sense any emotions that I could articulate. There was something like surprise there, and something else I couldn't name, but it wasn't a particularly friendly feeling.

He stood when he finally said, "Perhaps you can stay awhile and get to know the place before making your final decision? This is your home, Onyx. More than any Ash Grove, or whatever the insignificant place you ended up is called. Come, I will show you your mother's favorite room."

I followed him out of his cave and rubbed the back of my neck, feeling like a kid somehow. "You must have really loved her."

"Mates are one flesh. Their essence tied together as the same. The blood of mates even tastes complimentary. Like spices in a dish. Mates' bloods together, combined … are powerful." He trailed off, his pale gauntness looking monstrous in the dim castle light. "You're never fully whole again if you lose them. Without one's mate, you go mad."

CHAPTER 29

Blythe

MAYBE WITCH

> I oscillate between thinking I am crazy, and thinking that I
> am not crazy enough.
> *Joyce Carol Oates*

I was giving Onyx his space. Or maybe he was giving me space. Ever since coming to the castle, meeting his dad, and learning that my blood was lethal, things had been weird between us. Maybe he was rethinking his feelings for me. Maybe now that he had his father —and was a prince—he wanted someone grander, someone better than me. A beautiful vampiress with blood he could freely drink. The thought made me want to curl up and cry. And my heart was heavy. I missed the guys. Something was wrong. They were taking too long to get here, yet every time I expressed my concerns to Onyx, he brushed me off or changed the subject. Suspicion was creeping in, making me wonder if he was lying … if maybe I was falling victim to his charm, as I so often did. I was getting swept away in him and in Belladonia. I needed to regain my focus. Onyx was preoccupied with the king so often that I would be asleep when he slipped in at night. He didn't even join me in bed. It was as if the thought of me was now repulsive. I couldn't give him what he needed, and now he was moving on. So much for being his *wife*. The hurt was heavy on my heart as I changed into black knee-high stockings and a purple sweater dress. I wasn't sure where the modern wardrobe had come from, but I opened my armoire to several skittering spiders atop the folded clothing. Maybe Raven had gotten it for me one night as I slept. My familiar had been tasked by me to patrol the city in search of any sign of Ghost or Wolf. So far, there had been nothing. And something felt really wrong.

I walked out the door and was startled by the long, gaunt female. Her stringy hair hung in her face as a product of always looking down at her feet. I'd never seen her eyes, and there was something unnatural about her, but I'd always been attracted to the strange. In fact, she reminded me of a ghost in the cemetery of Ash Grove. Though that didn't make any sense at all because she was clearly living. I made a point of being kind to her and seeking her out, though she rarely spoke more than one word. "Hi, Lolth, I was just," *sneaking out of the castle to do something dangerous,* "going to explore the city a little. I'm getting cabin fever."

"I will come watch you," she replied evenly.

"You don't need to do that. Really, I'll be fine."

I quickly scooted by her and stopped at the sight of a hooded figure at the end of the hall. It lingered before passing through a wall, its two counterparts following behind it. A shudder shook through me. Ghosts and spirits were some of my favorite beings, but those things felt different.

Lolth appeared next to me, looking up slightly through her blunt lashes. "*Genii Cucullati,* they're called. I don't like them either."

It was the most she'd ever said to me, and it even held a personal opinion. Maybe Lolth was warming up to me. "Do you want to come shopping with me?" I wasn't sure how I could fit her into my plan, but I didn't want to leave her in the drab, creepy castle if she didn't want to be there.

She followed me wordlessly down the halls, which I took as her way of saying yes.

We finally made it out the front doors and into the crisp air of Belladonia. Bats screeched overhead as they darted beneath the heavy rain clouds. It was hard to fathom that this city was floating in the sky.

Lolth lifted her chin and looked down the staircase to the city below. I took in her worn beige linen dress and tattered shoes.

"How did you come to work for the king?" I asked, not expecting an answer. We made it about halfway down the stone walkway when I said, "I was thinking of visiting someone I heard of, Lady Rouge, for some makeup for the ball. Maybe we could find you something nice, too?"

At the bottom of the stairs, as we made our way through the streets, she replied, "I am bound to the king, and I do not dress for the ball."

"Why not? Dressing up is fun. If you want, I can help you find something."

"Lady Rouge is one block west." She pointed a frail finger. "I will look with you."

I'd take that as a win. We spent an hour sorting through gowns. I pulled a lavender dress for Lolth, and to my joy and delight, she actually put it on. Then I found her a new pair of shoes before I moved on to finding my perfect shade of red lipstick. The outing made me miss Yesenia. I missed listening as she talked, going on and on. I snorted at the irony that, to her, I was Lolth, and to Lolth, I may have seemed like Yesenia. There was more freedom in my spirit now that I'd found Ash Grove and the Halloween Boys. They'd loved me when I was frightened and fragile and distrustful. Maybe that was why I was emboldened to show compassion to my strange acquaintance. When I rejoined Lolth outside, she was looking at herself through the reflection in the shop window. "That color lavender is lovely on you. Lady Rouge said she'll send my makeup up to the castle. Do you want to—"

A shriek tore through the street. I strained to look over the top hats and horse carriages to find its origin. "Did you hear a lady scream? I've heard her a few times since I came here."

The scream pierced through the atmosphere again, but no vampires even looked over their shoulders.

Lolth only followed behind me silently. Though I could have sworn there was more of a spring in her step than there was before. "I hear it. It is the banshee. She screams before death."

Nothing surprised me anymore, but this was a being I'd never heard of. "Is the banshee like ... a witch?" She had to be clairvoyant to know if someone was about to die. "I heard her in the forest once. Is that where she lives?"

I made my way through the streets and vampire couples to the gates of the city. Shaking the heavy bars, I groaned when they wouldn't budge.

Lolth placed a cold hand on my arm. "I cannot let you leave."

"I'm not leaving, Lolth. But I need ... I need to find a witch. Someone to tell me where my ... family is. They should have been here by now. Unless you know of another witch, finding the banshee is my only shot."

"Would your family help you if they came here?"

All of Lolth's questions were strange. This was no different, and I didn't have the time or mental energy to sort through what she meant, so I nodded. "Yes, they'd help me."

She tapped the toe of her new shoe to the bottom of the gate, and it slowly swung open. I hesitated, remembering the creatures that greeted us when we arrived. But Onyx was hiding something. This whole city was hiding something, it seemed. My boys weren't here, and it was driving me crazy. Something had to have gone wrong for them to take so long to arrive. What if Onyx was losing himself in this lavish world of vampire royalty? I would need Ghost and Wolf's help to pull him back to us. They'd risked everything for me. I'd risk it all to find them, too. So I took a step forward, into the wicked woods.

THE FOREST WAS silent in a way that forests should never be. An unnatural hush where there should be life and movement. Lolth trailed wordlessly behind me. "Are we getting close?" I whispered, noticing the sun was setting. We'd been walking for hours past twisted trees and rose bushes.

"I do not know if she will be there, but her scrying stone is over this hill."

As we walked, whispering helped to keep me calm. I tried to map out where we were, but every rose and tree looked the same in the twilight haze. "We came through a door with stairs somewhere around here," I said. "Then we were attacked by those werewolf things."

I glanced over my shoulder to see Lolth still looking down at her feet. She tilted her head slightly. "There are no werewolves in Belladonia. We are a city in the sky."

That was something I'd yet to ponder. Somehow, being dragged through the ocean lead to a doorway to a floating castle community. "You must, because they definitely tried to eat us."

Maybe that's what Lolth was trying to do. Maybe she'd led me all the way out into the woods so she could drink my blood or something equally disturbing. Then there was a whooshing sound and a flurry of leaves. We stopped, and I was afraid to breathe. What would I do if one of those diphylla creatures found us? I didn't have so much as a knife. Something sharp grabbed my shoulder, and I shrieked.

There was a flurry of black when he strained a low voice, still in his bird form. "I'm going to try to zap you out of here. I warned you not to go into these woods." Raven flapped wildly as Lolth tilted her chin slightly to watch us. I'd still never seen her eyes, only the black hair veiling her face.

"No, I'm almost to the place where the maybe-witch might be."

"Do you hear yourself, Blythe? This is ludicrous, and it's getting dark."

"Let me just see if she's there. If she's not, you can teleport us back to Belladonia, okay?"

My familiar's throat vibrated in disagreement, but he took his spot on my shoulder. As I climbed the hill, dodging thorns, Lolth said, "You speak as equals with a bird. Only powerful beings own familiars."

"I don't *own* Raven, and we *are* equals," I replied, exasperated. "I'm no better than anyone else. He's my friend."

We crested the hill, and Raven outstretched his wings and dropped them in what looked like a very human shrug of annoyance. There was what looked to be a large stone birdbath, but no one else was there. I walked to the center of the small clearing and looked around. Hoping the banshee would appear. "Okay, fine. Let's just go back—"

A piercing cry ripped through the night air. I covered my ears, and Raven squawked. "Hold on," he said.

"No, that's the banshee. She's who I need to talk, too."

Lolth spoke, calm and low. "She screams before death. Diphylla are nearby. I am sensing their vibrations."

No sooner had she spoken than I saw it across the clearing. Only this one was twice the size of the last one. It stole the breath from my lungs as its beady gaze met mine and it bared its pointed yellow teeth. "Okay, maybe teleporting is a good idea," I said, putting a hand over my bird's talons.

"Hold on—"

"Wait," I took Lolth's icy, frail hand. "Lolth, too."

Raven flapped his wings. "I can only do one at a time—"

The creature broke out into a sprint, propelling itself forward with its massive arms. "I'm not leaving her," I said to my familiar. The creature lunged, and I jumped out of the way, but Lolth didn't move.

"Lolth!" I screamed.

But she only stood, holding its attention. Raven flapped frantically in my face. "Blythe, we have to go."

I looked over his wing to see the diphylla raise its massive claws, ready to destroy her feebleness with one blow, but before it could strike, she disappeared. The creature looked around in confusion before setting its attention on me. It snarled and made to step forward when it stopped.

What I saw next was another log for my nightmare playlist. Four giant, hairy legs appeared over the creature's back. It shook and reached around, but it was too late. Two more legs and giant pincher fangs appeared before sinking into its neck. The diphylla convulsed before hitting the ground with the force of a falling tree. The giant spider then clicked at me, as if I knew what it was saying, before spinning the body over and over, wrapping it up like a mummy. I sat on the wet ground and watching in morbid fascination. Even Raven went silent, though his talons were digging into my shoulder so tightly I may have bled. He was ready to disappear with me at any moment. The enormous spider's several eyes glanced over my shoulder, and when I turned to look, the trees were shuddering.

A man holding a crossbow glided out of the forest, along with the glow of familiar green eyes. I didn't care if he didn't like me anymore. I ran into Onyx's arms. "What the hell are you doing out here?" He pointed behind me. "You. Did you bring her here?"

When I turned, I saw Lolth standing next to the body, looking at her feet as if nothing had happened. As if Lolth wasn't a *massive freaking spider*.

I choked on my words, but managed, "No, it was my idea. I wanted to find the banshee because I think she's a witch, and I need a witch to try to find the guys."

Elysium chuckled and brought his crossbow over his head, clicking it into place on his chair. "You two were made for each other. But I hate to break it to you—the banshee isn't a witch." He whirled by the freshly wrapped diphylla and looked to Lolth before stopping by the elevated stone dish. "The banshee is a very old spirit with no form. She could be standing right beside you and you wouldn't know it. Though if you've heard her often, perhaps she's taken a liking to you and is following you around, Blythe."

I shuddered. So much for that plan. "Why are you out here?" I asked, tugging out of Onyx's hold.

He rubbed the back of his neck. "Midnight stroll through the woods?" I shoved him, and he rolled his eyes with a sigh. "I'm looking for a witch, too. Likely for the same reason you are. Though I should have anticipated you doing the dumbest thing possible and made you sleep before I left."

"Yeah, well, you'd have to actually see me and talk to me to do that, and you're avoiding me again."

"I'm not avoiding you."

Elysium cleared his throat. "I hate to interrupt a lovers' quarrel, but the full moon only stays in this station for so long. We're running out of time to reach your friends."

I pulled my hand away as Onyx tried to hold it and walked over to stand between Lolth and Elysium. Ignoring the hurt on Onyx's face, I whispered to Lolth, "That was really cool. Thanks."

It was dark, and her hair hid all of her features, but I thought I may have noticed a small smile. The vampire hunter took my hand and instructed us all to make a circle around the stone. "What the hell is this?" Onyx asked, looking into the dark, shallow water.

"It's a scrying stone. It helps with communicating over long distances."

"Where's the witch?" Onyx asked.

Elysium shrugged. "You're looking at him."

"Oh, come on," Onyx protested. "Vampire hunter, mixologist, and a witch? Save some sex appeal for the rest of us, would you?"

Despite wanting to be annoyed with him, I couldn't help my giggle. He met my glance with an accomplished smirk, as if he'd hoped to make me laugh and had succeeded. Before Elysium could continue, Onyx and I spoke in unison. "*I need to say something first.*"

Everyone looked between us in surprise. "What?" I asked Onyx.

He exhaled. "I haven't been completely honest. I orchestrated the thing back on the ship. I paid Vex off with your necklace to get us here, and … to take the guys back to Ash Grove."

My mouth dropped open. "You—they're back home right now? Why would you do that?"

"A stroke of madness and pure selfishness, but it was stupid, and I was wrong. I'm sorry, Blythe."

I shook my head, trying to quiet my emotions so he wouldn't feel them. I wanted to shuffle through them myself, without him sensing each one. I changed the subject quickly. "Ash Grove kicked me out. The witches said I had to leave, that I was a liability being a—" I glanced at the vampire hunter. "What I am."

"Oh, so you're allowed to initiate trips with ulterior motives, but I'm not?"

I rolled my eyes and continued. "When I fought the witches on it, they did this thing where we all held hands. One witch said she could find your dad by looking into minds. But when we did …"

Elysium shifted in his seat. "Someone died, didn't they?"

"I don't know. I hope not. She blacked out. Maybe I should sit this one out and let you all try without me."

"You both have a strong connection with these guys. Our odds are better if you're both in the circle. Don't worry about me. I always have tricks up my sleeve."

"Clearly," Onyx grumbled. "Fine, let's get on with it."

I nuzzled my bird's velvety feathers and whispered, "Why don't you keep watch overhead? Let us know if you see anything trying to kill us."

He cawed before leaping into the sky and disappearing into the night.

I was the last to close my eyes, and before I did, I noticed the water trembling.

And when my eyes shut, I found myself someplace else, somewhere dark and lonesome, before a hand took hold of mine in the darkness, and a female voice echoed.

"Blythe, what have you done?"

CHAPTER 30

Blythe

DANCING IN FIRE

> You said I killed you — haunt me, then! The murdered do haunt their murderers. I believe — I know that ghosts have wandered on earth. Be with me always — take any form — drive me mad!
>
> *Wuthering Heights*

Onyx was at my side, but I didn't see the others.

"This is like one of the in-between rooms. Like where the phantoms took me at the circus." The voice spoke again, lower, like she was talking to someone else I couldn't see. "Who's there?" I asked.

"I'm here with Yesenia," she said, and I recognized Cat's voice.

Yesenia spoke, her words echoing through the room. "What's going on? We've been trying to reach you for so long. Things are going haywire in Ash Grove …"

Onyx snapped back. "You kicked her out, and now you blame her for the trouble your coven let in? That's disappointing coming from you, Yesenia. I thought you were her friend."

My friend's voice was pained as she responded. "I am her friend, and I've been in divination every day trying to reach her, or you, or any of your godforsaken Halloween Boys. Something's not right with our crones—"

"You're just now figuring that out?" Onyx scoffed. I elbowed him in the ribs and gave him a stern look.

"I'll help any way that I can, but why don't you ask Ghost or Wolf? Can you get them for us? We need to talk to them."

Cat's typical surly tone hushed as she answered. "Blythe, Ghost isn't here. Nor is Wolfgang. You've all been gone for two years."

"What?" Onyx protested. "It's been a few weeks, Cat. Are you sure Ghost isn't there? Who's watching the damned?"

Cat hissed. "Yes, I'm sure, I've been caring for the cemetery and the damned all alone for two years now without any help from the Halloween Boys or their reaper. The curse lifted, and you all abandoned us, and now Ash Grove is falling to shit."

Yesenia whispered a firm warning as my chest seized. Two years? How could that be? "What's going on in Ash Grove? And, oh my god, Piper. Is she okay?"

It was quiet for a moment before she said again, sounding farther away now, "We don't have much time. He will be listening soon. The blood is the way, Blythe. Do you hear me? It will unite you all in your bond and with your powers. Do you not see that a reaper has mated with a demon, a hybrid king, and an alpha wolf? You're capable of great power. You four can set things right in not only Ash Grove but Belladonia and every other place unbalanced. This ritual will solidify your bond and show you what needs to be done to set things right. A blood ritual is the way …"

The room shrouded in fog, and Onyx wrapped me in his arms, holding me tight as the witch's voice faded. When I opened my eyes again, I was holding hands with Elysium and Lolth in the clearing, as if nothing had happened. Onyx's green stare met mine, and he nodded slightly, as if to say, *I saw it, too.*

The vampire hunter opened one squinted eye. "Did you find what you were after?"

I opened my mouth to respond, but Onyx spoke first. "No, I guess that means you should stick to making cocktails."

Elysium ran a hand through his shaggy white hair. "I don't understand. I felt three beings on the other side. You heard or saw no one?"

A chill slithered down my spine, and I met Onyx's furrowed brow before he recovered. *Three* beings? "Maybe you should have installed cell service in that glorious contraption."

Elysium huffed. "Yeah, I'll add that in with the next upgrade."

Raven pulled our attention as he squawked overhead, swooping to land on my shoulder. "He's seen something," I said. "We need to go."

"Diphylla are strongest at night. We must hurry. The underground is right this way," the vampire hunter said, leading us around the side of the bank. It was then that I realized that Lolth hadn't let go of my hand. I held hers back, leading her along with us. Onyx passed me a quizzical look but didn't comment.

"You guys came here through an underground tunnel? That would have been nice to know about."

"Next time fill me in on your idiotic plans, and I can help you out." Onyx put a hand on my lower back, sending a thrill of heat to my center.

"I'm not done being mad at you. What you did was messed up."

"I know, and I know we've been gone … longer than we anticipated."

That was an understatement. The bucket door shut above us, and we climbed—and Elysium's chair hovered—down into the cave that would lead us back to the castle. Pebbles and dirt shook free from the ceiling as the diphylla trampled overhead, growling and sniffing in their search. Fear rippled through me, and, sensing my distress, Onyx wrapped his arm around me as I held Lolth's cold hand. What was happening in Ash Grove, and why hadn't the Moon Halo Coven been enough to stop it? If we'd truly somehow been gone for years, where the hell were Ghost and Wolfgang?

We said goodbye to Elysium while Lolth let us into a side entrance to the castle before disappearing to wherever it was she went. After what I'd just witnessed, I wondered if she had a web or spider den somewhere. I shuddered at the thought. Onyx laced his fingers through mine as we crept quietly down the hollow corridors, passing grotesque statues and dripping candles. "Two years?" I whispered. "Something's really wrong. I'm worried about the guys. I'm worried about Ash Grove."

"I'm working on a plan. Just bear with me."

"Trust you, even though you've done nothing but lie?"

His pace slowed as he cast me a sideways glance of his green eyes. My gaze caught on the line of his jaw and his broad shoulders. "You've done some lying yourself. You're just not as good at it as I am."

I made to jerk my hand away, but he didn't let go. He only squeezed harder. I grabbed his wrist, but he grabbed both of mine in a flash of speed and power he often hid from me. The wind knocked from my lungs as he pushed me against the wall of the corridor. He held my wrists above my head in the grip of his large hand as his knuckle lightly grazed my cheek.

"Let me go. I hate you," I breathed in a weak, half-hearted plea.

He smirked, exposing his fangs and looking like the dark prince he was. The dark prince I'd always somehow known he was. "There it is. Another lie. You don't want to be let go, and you *really* don't hate me, my sweet belladonna."

"Stop." I pulled at his hold in a feeble attempt to break free. But only excitement trilled through me when he didn't budge. He smiled again. "Stop reading my emotions."

"Would you rather me fuck them out of you, my little liar?" I squirmed again, breathless, my mind racing with heat and desire. "Yes, move your hips just like that when I'm inside you. I want to feel it when you're screaming for me to stop. Because, Blythe, I won't want to stop. Not ever." His fang lightly brushed my ear, and my head tilted back, my body betraying my need. "I want to fuck you until you're drenched in me and begging for reprieve."

"Onyx," I panted as he took the lobe of my ear between his lips. "We can't."

"I've spoken to Ghost," he said gruffly. "He's okay with us … as long as I act right, and I plan to be so, so good to you," he purred. "Wolf is on board, too. I promise we will find them, and we will all be together like this. Doesn't that sound nice?"

God, it sounded more than nice. I wanted him. I wanted Ghost and him and Wolf. My brain was hazy with adrenaline and yearning. To be with my Halloween Boys, body and soul. For us all to be united as one. Even Yesenia had said something about us needing to unite, something about blood … blood. I arched my back, trying to push Onyx off, but it only made him press in closer. The weight of him pushing me into the wall was so freaking hot. I liked feeling trapped by him. But I couldn't give in. It was too risky. "Onyx, stop. If you slip up and bite me, if I bleed, and you … you could die. I can't lose you; I won't lose you."

"I would deny myself air and sunlight and fire and music for you, Blythe. I can live without blood. But I cannot exist another moment without my cock buried inside you." He pushed his erection into my stomach, letting me feel the anguish of how hard he was.

"Maybe if you're very careful," I whispered, closing my eyes as his kiss trailed down my neck. His touch heated as it eased over my ribs, feeling like a candle was pressing against me. I twisted in his hold and let out a breath. He brought my arms down and held my knuckles so my palms were facing up.

"Do you trust me?"

"Theoretically."

He chuckled darkly. "Stay very still," he purred. Black fire illuminated in my hands as he cradled them.

He smiled triumphantly. "If you can hold my flame and not be burned, I believe I can taste your death and not be killed."

I watched in awe as the blaze sparked and twisted in my grasp. Onyx leaned forward, unburned by its lashes, and I stood on my tiptoes to meet him. Our kiss was warmed by the flames and heated by our desire. He let go of my knuckles and wrapped me in his embrace. As our kiss deepened, a sigh left my lips as he shoved me back against the wall. I wrapped my legs around his hips and bucked forward, searching for any part of him to grind against.

Breaking our kiss, he tilted his chin to the left. "Your flame wants to watch."

Unsure of what he meant, I turned to see we'd been encircled by black fire. It twisted and bobbed around us, not burning the carpet or the walls. It was simply cocooning us.

"Smart fire," I breathed, pulling him back to my lips. His kiss was so soft and full, yet claiming and fierce. The two parts of Onyx thrashed within him: his fire and his ice. Yet in that moment, I felt they both wanted me. And I wanted both of them, too. The duality of Onyx Hart would probably always perplex me. The cold and icy killer and the fiery god of mischief—I loved them both. And something deep within me recognized a sameness between us. I was the reaper, a dead and ominous thing, while also being a girl who slept with a stuffed bat and kept lip gloss in my pocket. The darkness drew me in, and I loved it, but not for the evil perception it had garnered. I loved it for all its dreary, all of its misunderstood and eerie. I was the dark, but I loved it from a place of light. My dichotomy wasn't too different from his, and something inside us knew that long before we were kissing in the corridor. Our hearts had always recognized the counterparts we found in each other.

Onyx tugged off my dress, and I lifted my arms to help him. When he'd removed his clothing and I'd kicked off my stockings, we stood—naked, surrounded, protected by wisps of black fire.

He tilted his head. "What's that emotion you're feeling?"

"Tell me yours first."

He smiled as he took a step closer. I sucked in a breath as his ice-cold skin pressed against me. His hard length pushed against my stomach again.

"The same as I always feel around you, Blythe." He kissed my forehead gently. "Awe, gratitude, love."

When our lips met, his body warmed, and he picked me up, pushing me against the wall. Hooking a hand under my knee, he wrapped my legs around him again. I reached between us, finding his girth and panting. I brushed the hair from his eyes, and he smiled before ignoring my grip and plunging forward. I cried out, feeling him stretch and fill me with abrupt precision. When I pulled my hand free, allowing him to sink further, we both groaned.

"You're so perfect, belladonna," he murmured as he nibbled my ear.

I writhed against him, angling my hips so that every thrust allowed his girth to stroke my center. The build in my core was an inferno that could turn a forest to ash. Taking his hand from my waist, I held his palm by my head against the wall. Our breathing turned frenzied as I bit his lip and asked. "More fire, please?"

Surprise flashed across his gaze before he smirked and whispered against my lips. "If you turn me on even more, you'll be nailed to this wall for a week."

I gasped when I felt my hand warm. When I looked over, black fire enveloped us as one. He picked up his pace as I rode him in time with his thrusts. Our wetness where we joined pooled down my ass. The black fire from our hands moved, snaking down our arms, and then our chests, wrapping us head to toe in prickly warmth and a thin veil of black. He pushed his fiery hand between us and found my clit. I gasped, feeling the warmth from the fire that still encircled his fingers. It raged and flickered like its own entity, along with his caress.

The mixture of ice and fire and the blaze that encompassed us, along with his glorious stretch of my pussy, ignited my bliss like a bomb. I detonated and shattered, screaming the echoes of ecstasy down the hall of the vampire's castle. Onyx dropped his lips to my neck, taking the skin between his teeth but not biting down like I knew he wanted to. Instead, he pushed into me, thrusting so hard it took my breath away as he roared his release against my neck. I felt him fill me, and it was both cold and hot, just like him. The sensation inside me tore another moan from my throat and barreled into another orgasm as his cum filled me to the brim and dripped between us.

I collapsed into his arms as he carried me back to our room. Our fire followed us the whole way, shielding any of my worries that someone could happen upon us. It stayed outside the door as he closed it and laid me tenderly on the bed. "I think my fire likes you more than it likes me."

I giggled, bundling up under a sheet. He joined me when I pulled at his arm, and I sat on my elbow, stroking his chest. We lay there for several minutes, basking in the afterglow of our lovemaking. Fire sex was … fun.

After a moment, I broke the silence. "Can I ask you something?"

"Anything."

"What happened to Minnie? You spoke about her after our first drink here."

His somber gaze found mine, and his brows furrowed. "She was a victim of the tragedy that chases me." He sighed. "I believed I was human. Believed we could marry and have children. And then she was taken, and I was revealed to be a monster worse than the ones who'd killed her."

"Onyx," I whispered, sadness crippling my tone.

He shook his head. "She deserved better than me."

I caressed his soft obsidian hair and kissed his jaw. "I'm sorry that happened to you both. But she wouldn't want you to blame yourself."

He shrugged. "Her death was the perfect sequence of being entirely my fault. If I had known what I was sooner, I could have protected her. Instead, I learned it afterward, and I most likely burned all of Ash Grove to the ground."

"You don't know that for sure."

He took my hand and kissed my wrist. "You are too kind to me. Too forgiving."

I snuggled into his embrace, listening to the crackle of the hearth. After a few tender moments, he sat up and tugged playfully at a lock of my hair.

"Do you want to see my mom's favorite room in the castle?"

I bit my lip and nodded before slipping on a red silk robe.

We held hands and snuck quietly down the corridor like naughty teenagers. I even had to contain my giggle a few times at the absurdity of it all. "I think it's past these windows," Onyx said. "This place is a maze of gargoyles and creep-factor."

"You must feel right at home, then," I joked as we passed under the moonlight filtering in through the tall, aged glass. "Let's be quiet. I don't want those hooded things to pop out and scare me—" I stopped, tugging on Onyx's hand.

"What?"

I shushed him and moved against the cold stone, peeking over just enough to see the courtyard below. "Is that your dad?"

Onyx furrowed his brow and looked over. King Vladimir was standing and looking out over the city, his hands moving. "He's saying something. I'm not sure who he's talking to, though. No one's there."

"What is he saying?"

Onyx's eyes narrowed, glowing green. "He says the plan is coming together ... he will get the offering at the Bleeding Heart Ball, and it will all be over then."

"What does that mean?"

"I don't know."

Suddenly, the king turned, his wide, crimson eyes glowing as his cape flared out. Onyx pulled me to the ground, breaking my fall with his body. He held me tight, placing one finger on my lips. We lay there a moment before crawling past the windows and pacing down the hall. "Did he see us?" I whispered, my heart still racing.

"I don't think so. The room is just up here, and we're safe."

We slipped inside the dark room, and Onyx made his way to the fireplace, setting it ablaze with a flick of his wrist. As soon as my eyes adjusted to the light, a figure in the corner made me yelp. I was pressed into the door by Onyx's back before I even realized he'd moved to shield me. A dark chuckle sounded. "I can appreciate your quick reflexes, my son. Though I did not mean to frighten you. I do prefer the dark."

Onyx cleared his throat, and I moved from behind him. "I was showing Blythe this room. I hope that's okay."

"This castle is both of yours now," King Vladimir said, looking only at me. "You may go wherever you please. It is a glorious night for a stroll under the stars, is it not?"

"We appreciate your hospitality."

"What is she?" the king asked abruptly, still looking at me. "A hybrid? Human and witch, perhaps?"

Onyx bristled and held my hand tighter. Something about the king made me feel afraid. I had the distinct feeling that he wasn't as kind as he was portraying. The small things I'd gleaned from the way the other vampires talked about him. The way Lolth cowered next to him. His treatment of me before he knew who I was. None if it was quite right, but I couldn't place my finger on what my opinion of him was. I wanted to be supportive of Onyx, and I wanted to be happy for him. Happy that he'd found this link to his lineage and family. Though the way Vladimir Drakon stared at me like a viper poised to strike stabbed me with unease.

"She is my wife, and the newest member of my coven, whom you'll meet soon," Onyx replied with a hint of an edge. "If this is a bad time? We can view this room later."

The king slowly walked by a piano, tapping a few odd keys. "Cassiopeia only allowed her closest loved ones in here. Sharing this room was a sign of great trust ..." He sighed, seemingly remembering we were standing there. "I look forward to your coven's offering at the Bleeding Heart Ball next week." He paused as he passed me. I stood stone still, as if any quick movement would provoke him to pounce. "*All* of your coven's offerings."

Onyx turned, moving between the king and me. "What is the offering I keep hearing about? Gifts or gold? Like a tax of sorts?"

Vladimir paused in the doorway. "Dear prince, we do not care for such trivial things in Belladonia. The offering is of the only thing we vampires do care for. The thing we crave and seek." Onyx's hand tightened around my wrist as the king looked me up and down and exposed his fangs. "Blood."

CHAPTER 31

Onyx

SWEET NIGHTMARES

> There are bad dreams for those who sleep unwisely.
> *Bram Stoker*

Perhaps I wasn't too bad a guy. Sure, I'd killed people. Just a few weeks ago, I'd relished the feeling of the blood of someone's throat dripping down my chin and setting a courtroom on fire. They deserved it, though.

My father, King Vladimir, wasn't too bad of a guy, either, I thought. Though he also had centuries of blood on his chin and looked at my wife a little too hungrily. Secrets were a part of who I was. Tricks and mischief kept me living from one day to the next. I now assumed that flair for mayhem came from my father. Though he'd been nothing but kind to us. He'd embraced me as his child, though less affectionately than I would have liked. And he'd been more than willing to share his kingdom. I chalked his oddities up to being ancient and living so long without my mother. Though Blythe seemed more skeptical than me.

She thrummed an out of tune harp. "Why was he in here, and how'd he get here so fast?"

I shrugged. "He's fast. All vampires are." Uncertainty vibrated off her next out-of-tune thrum. "Look, I know he's eccentric, but we expected no less from the man that sired a bastard like me."

I kneeled next to the harp to tune its old and withered strings, expecting one to snap at any moment.

Blythe took a seat on the piano stool. "And the blood offering? How will we avoid that? He wants my blood, and my blood isn't … good." Skepticism and unease trickled through her.

"I've been sorting through his emotions since we arrived here. All I've gathered is that the guy misses his wife and has gone a little nuts over time without her. I'm sure the blood offering is just a symbolic show of loyalty. A pricking of thumbs, a show of solidarity. We'll figure it out. I'll keep you safe, always." I plucked the chord and felt satisfied when it made a perfect F note.

"I'm not worried about me, Onyx. I'm worried about you. What if …" She sighed. "Forget it. Show me the room."

I tuned the G chord, marveling that this harp was my mother's. I was holding my mother's favorite instrument. "This was my mom's music room."

"It's beautiful. She was beautiful." Blythe nodded over my shoulder, and I turned to see a large painting of the queen. My mother was sitting in a grassy meadow in a glaucous gown, with a large earth-toned dragon flying overhead. She was holding a dark-haired baby—me—and the dragon resembled the one I frequently crafted out of fire. My heart ached, wishing I could have met her. This must have been the painting Elysium was referring to. But if he'd seen it …

"Can you shift into a dragon?" Blythe asked quietly, pulling me from my thoughts. "I'm sorry if that's too personal."

It was, but I'd share with her anyway. I'd already told her about Minnie; I thought I may as well show her everything. Opening up to her was … helping me, somehow. "I can, but I don't like to. I've only done it a handful of times. Unlike Ghost and Wolf, I don't much care for myself as a beast. Who I feel I am disappears, and this thing takes over. We aren't the same. The dragon's consciousness takes over, but we're one, too. It's ugly, monstrous. It's everything I am on the inside, in plain sight, for stares and gawking and running in fear. Perhaps I'll make friends with him someday, but for now, I keep him locked away. I only took on the name Dragon to separate myself from Vincent's pompous cult and to remind myself of how hideous I truly am."

"I'd like to meet your dragon someday and make friends with him, too." She tilted her head, but I focused on the next chord of my mother's instrument, not wanting to meet Blythe's pitying gaze. "I rarely show who I am either, you know. People say I'm mysterious, but I'm only mysterious because I hate sharing about myself. I'm afraid that the more people know, the less they'll love me."

I paused on the D string and glanced up as she kicked her feet under her seat. "I only love you more the more I know," I said without pause.

Her cheeks heated. "I only love you more the more I know, too. And I believe I'd love your dragon, too. You have all this rich backstory. While I… I have a mom who's dead and an absent dad. And I'm apparently a reaper—like the plastic version that hangs in shop windows in Ash Grove and goes *wah, ha, ha*. Because that's about as much as anyone knows about them."

I chuckled, surprised I could talk about any of this and smile. Somehow, she made my darkness more bearable.

"I can relate. While my vampire heritage is full of drama, it's only half of me. I can relate to enjoying rules, but only so far as I know how and when to break them. I like posh things, but only until I'm bored with them. The other half of me is much like you—unknown. Dragons died out a long time ago. I know nothing of my mother or these dragon abilities I possess. We're similar, you and me."

She stood and walked over to me. I scooped my arm around the back of her knees and pulled her hips to my chest. Rubbing a hand through my hair, she smiled. "Immortal mutts."

A hearty laugh escaped my throat, despite my previous desire to sulk in self-deprecation. "Immortal mutts with fantastic taste in music and breakfast meats."

After showing Blythe around the music room, I felt I'd gotten to know my mother on a more intimate level than I'd imagined possible. Queen Cassiopeia was a musician who preferred strings, like I did. Her harps were worn and well played, along with her standing cellos and several violins.

She also owned numerous guitars, a piano, and drums. I slung a guitar over my back as I walked Blythe back to our room and tucked her into bed. By the light of the moon, I leaned in my corner, thrumming the song I'd desperately been trying to write for her as she slept. Anything to keep my mind off that dip her hip made under the sheets when she lay on her side. I jotted down a note and gave it to Raven to deliver to Elysium. I swear the crow rolled his eyes at me as a bird. He must have learned that move from Blythe.

After an hour, she yawned and sleepily asked, "Why don't you ever lie with me?"

My fingers stopped over the melody. "You don't want to know."

"Yes, I do." She sat up on an elbow. "And I can't sleep, anyway. Every time I close my eyes, I see the diphylla or the baphomet, the legion, the hooded things ..."

"My sweet belladonna is haunted," I purred. "But the answer to your question would only add to your nightmares and keep you further from sleep."

"Please?"

I sighed and set the instrument on the armchair, taking a seat on the corner of the bed. "Absorbing the emotions of others is taxing. It's why I alter people's feelings so often. It's not out of any goodness in me or desire to ease their suffering. It's to make it stop so I don't have to feel it." Blythe didn't grimace at my confession. She simply put a hand atop my knuckles, so I continued. "The only time I don't feel emotions, the only time I get to be around someone without an assault of feeling, is when they are asleep."

"That makes sense," she replied. "Why wouldn't you want to tell me that?"

I ran a hand through my hair. "It turns me on, Blythe. Sleep— watching you sleep. It drives me wild."

Her cheeks reddened, and I felt blessed arousal radiate off her. Astonishingly, she felt no alarm or repulsion.

"You ... want to have sex with me while I'm sleeping?"

"Yes, but only if you wanted me to. Please don't be afraid that I'd do ... anything without your consent."

"I'm not afraid. Have you ever done it before?"

"I do it with Wolfgang fairly regularly."

She raised her eyebrows, her arousal only intensifying. "And he doesn't wake up?"

"No. We've been doing it for long enough now that he's trained himself to stay asleep. Though I don't take advantage of him. He enjoys it, and I only initiate after we've connected on a personal level."

Humming, she nodded. "I want to try it."

Surprise took my breath away. "Are you certain?"

"It sounds fun. It definitely sounds better than nightmares. Most nights, I'm just counting down the hours until morning. This could help me enjoy sleep a little more. Though it might take some practice to not wake up. I want to try … if you do."

My cock strained against my pants in zealous desire. "I can help you stay asleep, with my touch, if you'd like."

She swallowed, biting her lip. "Okay."

"I'll tell you beforehand for now, and once you're accustomed to it, if you still like it, we make it a more surprise occurrence. What do you think?"

"I think I'm ready to try to go back to sleep."

I smirked and held out my palm. "One touch, my sweet belladonna, and I can make that wish come true …" She lay back, and my gaze fell to her breasts.

"I'll wait for you in my dreams, my prince."

My heart pattered in my chest as she closed her eyes with a sigh. "You are truly remarkable," I murmured, sliding my hand from her ankle to her knee, sending her straight into a blissful slumber. I wouldn't knock her out cold. She'd be able to wake up if she desired, and if I felt any hint of tension or reluctance, I'd stop immediately.

I left her momentarily to rummage through the armoire until I found what I needed. When I returned, I removed the blankets, dropping them to the wood floor. Slowly tugging off her robe, I slid it down her voluptuous form until she was naked and breathing deeply in rest. The moonlight fell upon her, making her look like a goddess carved in stone. I wished I were an artist; I would have painted her then and there. Instead, I etched her beauty into my mind as I tied a silk scarf to her ankle, attaching the other end to the bedpost. I repeated the process, binding her to the four corners, spreading her bare for me.

Truly, I was a despicable creature. I was no better than the lowest of the demons in Hell. Kneeling between her open legs, I felt my hardness throb behind my zipper, begging me to bite her. Tonight wasn't for that sort of tasting. Though I wasn't sorry for it when I dipped my head between her thighs to sample her wet pussy.

My balls tightened, and while I licked her, I allowed my palms to roam her ass, squeezing her supple flesh. Her hips jostled, and she let out a sleepy whimper as her walls fluttered her orgasm around my two fingers. That was another thing I loved about sex with a sleeping partner. Their readiness. The wishes of their body were granted willingly, with no preamble to fully formed thoughts or feelings. This was Blythe in her purest, most vulnerable form. And she was all mine.

With a gratified growl, I jerked off my pants and pulled off my shirt. I climbed up her tempting form, licking her ribs, tasting the underside of her breasts, and sucking her nipples for as long as I pleased. My dick pressed into her thigh, slicking her with my want for her. "You're perfect like this, my belladonna," I hummed into her ear. "All tied up, open, helpless. You're mine to play with as I like, aren't you?" Her lips parted, and I claimed them with a kiss, flicking my tongue into her mouth. "See how good you taste?"

I untied her ankles and held her legs, carefully draping them over my shoulders as I kneeled before her again. This angle tilted her ass up and lined her perfectly with my cock. I was still reeling from our encounter in the corridor, but it had only intensified my desire for more of her. Gripping her soft hips, I allowed my tip to stretch her lightly. Even that smallest motion coaxed a groan from my throat.

"God, your sweet cunt was made for me." I sank into her halfway, noticing her eyelids flicker as she wiggled, lost in a dream where I was fucking her. The gate was open for her to wake up, but she didn't, so with another groan, I pushed in deep. "Fuck, Blythe," I sighed. Somehow, in that moment, I was worse than a demon. I was a human man, unable to control my need. I'd meant to go soft and slow, I really had, but when she tightened around my cock, just begging to milk me, it unleashed my inner beast.

I thrust into her hard, bucking her hips, feeling her slickness pool down her ass. Kissing the inside of her knee, I moaned into her flesh, denying my fangs the bite I craved. All my pent-up frustration channeled into my cock as I slammed into her over and over again. Her breasts bounced erotically with each plunge, and I had full view of them with her arms tied to the bedposts.

She let out a strained whimper and constricted around my cock like she had done with my fingers, and my release peaked. Burying myself to the hilt, I let all of me pour into her as she clasped her perfect, sleepy little cunt. "So good for me, belladonna. I love you limp and powerless like this," I said breathlessly as I gently lowered her legs to the bed. I lay next to her then, letting my fingers roam where I'd just been and feeling my seed gathered there. Her hips jerked, and her chin tilted toward me. "Yes," she sighed.

"You like that? Me touching you with my cum …"

"Mm-hmm …" she answered sleepily. No emotions clawed at my senses; she was still in the daze of a dream.

I drove three fingers into her, gathering our combined nectars and bringing them up to her clit. She moaned gently, bucking forward. "I'm ready to have you again, but I think I'll take you with my cum first."

Sliding three fingers back in, I pumped into her, the wetness resounding along with the crackling fireplace as my thumb flicked at her bundle of nerves. "That's it. Let my release claim you again."

Her back arched softly as she whined again with ecstasy and a gush of her orgasm.

Blythe blinked and tugged weakly at her bindings. "I love this. Don't stop," she whispered drowsily before closing her eyes and nuzzling back into the pillow. My shock and awe rippled through me as my cock throbbed with the need to have her again. She liked it, and goddamn, was she doing beautifully. Sleeping, dreaming, and letting her unconscious body respond to my every whim. I intended to fuck her all night this way.

And I did.

AFTER PULLING a blanket over her shoulder and kissing her cheek, I left my belladonna in a trance, slumbering serenely. She'd have good dreams that morning as I made her rest off the sleep I'd disrupted for hours and hours. Blythe would have blissful dreams every night for as long as I roamed the earth. I'd never let another nightmare near her. I made it swiftly from the castle to the mixologist's bar, where Elysium buffed his countertop with a wet rag.

"Neat trick with the bird," he said, not looking up. "Want a drink? Espresso vessense martini, perhaps?"

"I want to try again to contact our friends. Can you help?"

The vampire hunter rested his chin on his knuckle. "Tell me about your coven. You told me if I helped you find a witch, you'd tell me whatever I wanted to know."

"Well, your witchy adventure didn't work so—"

"You lie a lot, Onyx. Tell me about them. Why aren't they here, and what's this going on between you and them?"

I looked to the bar's ceiling and exhaled. "My coven consists of an archdemon, a werewolf, and a rogue devil, though he's only around when he wants to be. You know how devils are. And Blythe, of course, our girl, has her own … gifts. That's my coven. We're a merry band of villainous misfits."

"You're lying again …"

"If you see them in the woods, best not fire any shots. The demon gets cranky easily."

He went white as a sheet. "I spoke to one of them. They're almost here."

"What? How? Who did you talk to?"

"I was in the woods. Knew the moon was shit but tried again and got someone's voice. Said his name was Wolf, and that they'd see you soon."

I prayed that *soon* didn't equal a few years like Yesenia and Cat had implied …

"Did he seem … mad?" I dared to ask.

"Not particularly. Why would he be mad?"

Only because I split with no word, stole our mate, betrayed them, and left them stranded with a ship full of drunk pirates while I fucked Blythe endlessly in her sleep.

"No reason."

IN THE DAYS THAT PASSED, I grew more and more anxious for their arrival. A large part of me missed them and wanted them near. Another part knew that if something happened, if they were lost in time and space, Blythe would never forgive me. The Bleeding Heart Ball was fast approaching, and the king had requested I join him in the throne room. When I arrived, another throne sat next to his. He gestured to it as he took his seat. "This is yours. Whether you decide to stay or not, you'll forever be the Prince of Belladonia." I still wasn't used to that. The king's face grew cold as the room chilled and the three hooded figures floated to a stop before him. "What word?" he asked, full of authority.

The middle dark figure responded. "We have found no new realms and no new doors this day. Our search for Queen Cassiopeia's body and soul continues."

Tension tightened my jaw. "How many days have you been searching?" I impulsively asked the hoods.

"Ninety-one thousand, two hundred and fifty-five days we have scoured the realms—"

"Enough," the king cut them off, his anger hitting me like a door in the face. His eyes were ferocious and his knuckles white as he turned to me. "I speak. You listen."

The spirits left, and my father didn't say a word or spare me a glance before a vampire sashayed in. She was wearing a poodle skirt with her hair in a bun. An American fifties themed coven, apparently. "Preparations are finalized for the Bleeding Heart Ball tomorrow, Your Highness. All covens are accounted for, and wardrobes for your guests," she flicked me a curious glance, "have been delivered to their room."

The king didn't speak, only tapped a finger in dismissal. A group of six vampires entered the throne room then, herded by the hooded spirits. I repositioned in my seat, feeling like an arrogant prick looking down on people. Wolfgang would be laughing his ass off if he saw me like this. A wave of agony burned into my chest so heavy it labored my breathing. Five male vampires stood around the source of the pain—a sobbing female.

"Speak," the king demanded, his tone firm but disinterested.

A male vampire pushed up his spiky blond hair before he spoke. "This one, her name is Renaia." He grabbed on to the teary vampire. I fought my urge to gut him then and there. "She's no good to us. None of us have mated with her. She has no useful skills, and she frequently tries to run away. It's a shame because as we reported last year, we ... lost ... two other members of our coven right after the Bleeding Heart Ball." He cleared his throat, nervousness flitting from his shoulders. What wasn't he saying? "We're seeking your permission, Your Highness, to kill her. Better that than to let her live and become ... well, you know."

"What?" I asked my father.

To my surprise, he replied lowly, ignoring the group's want for an answer. "I have a count of every vampire in existence. If one is killed or ... goes missing, I must know how and why. Vampires must never die at the hand of another of our kind without my approval."

I couldn't speak, only sat back in my silly throne.

"Go ahead. Next," the king called.

I sat up as the woman began to shake with grief, dropping to her knees. "No, there must be another way. How do we know they haven't mistreated her? Clearly she's distressed."

My father responded evenly. "The only way for her to live is if another coven will take her. And I do not see one here to claim her as their own."

The men snickered as she buried her head in her hands. "Please," she looked up, meeting my gaze, "please, Lost Prince, help me."

One of the males corrected her. "There is no prince. What are you going on about?"

"I know a coven that will take her," I answered.

"Who?" my father asked, unamused.

"Vincent Albescu will take her. He is a coven leader and a friend of mine." It was a stretch, but I was sure I could convince him to do it, if only my father would allow it.

"Vincent ..." The king huffed an amused sound. "I'll allow it. Though Vincent will need to announce her as his own during the offering tomorrow."

Relief sagged my shoulders. Shock and gratitude swelled through the woman as the men stared daggers at me. *Try me, motherfuckers.* Something in my eyes must have conveyed that message because they stepped back with bows to the king. Renaia blew me tearful kisses as she stumbled out. I wanted to go after her, ease her pain, and help her find Vincent. He must have been somewhere in this labyrinth of vampires. The king didn't seem too cross with me for my intervention as more of his servants and advisors filtered through.

Next came reports on the town, the number of doors, last year's count of vampires ... a lot of numbers.

But then a tall male vampire stalked in with information that perked my attention. "Your Highness, there was a minor incident involving the diphylla at the south gate. Three beasts have been eliminated."

Despite the king's warning, I asked, "Were they brought down by the vampire hunter?"

The man and my father stared at me as if I'd just said something very, very wrong. The tall vampire looked to the ground as the king leaned in and spoke slowly, unable to conceal the rage in his tone. A temper I hadn't witnessed before today, not fully. "You dare speak of such a thing in my presence? A slayer is the most forbidden creature in Belladonia, and you say the name so flippantly. One took your mother, you fool." He growled.

I swallowed my nerves. Even with my excellent debate skills, I hadn't been prepared for that reaction, for that declaration. *My mother had allegedly been stolen away by a slayer.* Vampire hunters were forbidden and, apparently, made the king mad with fury. So what the fuck was Elysium doing here and why had he been lying to me? I could have sold him out right then and there. And when I first came to Belladonia, I would have without hesitation. I'd wanted to kill the man myself when I'd first met him. But something had changed. Maybe I had changed in my time here.

"Bad joke. I apologize."

"My companion was robbed of an education by vampires," the king explained, turning back to the tall man. "He does not understand our customs, our history, or what is and isn't appropriate. You did not hear him mention such, do you understand?"

The man nodded, pale and trembling. "Yes, Your Highness."

The king flicked his wrist in dismissal, and I was apprehensive about being alone with my father for the first time since I'd met him. "The Bleeding Heart Ball will reveal much to you about our way of life here." He stood. "Leave me. Lolth will instruct you on your duties at the ball tomorrow. You will join me here on the throne after the first dance, and I will crown you prince."

The words were cordial, friendly even, but his tone was anything but. I nodded and made my way out, hearing things slamming behind me as the king growled and raged.

I'd gleaned three vital bits of information during that meeting, even at the risk of having my head ripped from my shoulders.

King Vladimir Drakon was *not* good.

Elysium was a liar.

And my father had never been searching for me.

CHAPTER 32

Blythe

DOORS

A woman being never at a loss... the devil always sticks
by them.

George Gordon Byron, Lord Byron

Lolth sulked into my room carrying a fresh stack of clothing and a gown bag. She dispersed the items in the armoire as I ate fruit and granola, listening as she blandly explained the rules of the Bleeding Heart Ball. It was one day away, and Onyx was sitting with his father in the throne room like the regal prince he was. Royalty suited him, though I remained skeptical of the king. I supposed it didn't matter. He'd told me that the guys sent word, somehow, through Elysium, that they would be here at any moment. My heart thrummed in excitement at seeing Ghost and Wolf again. I'd missed them so, even if it hadn't been that long. It felt like years had passed. And according to Cat and Yesenia, they had.

My mind was still puzzled over that encounter as Lolth droned on. Onyx and I would arrive separately, like all couples, polyamorous groups, and covens did. Fully masked, we would find each other through the crowd and dance. That all sounded nice, if it weren't for the blood offering that immediately followed. It was the only matter Lolth wouldn't elaborate on. My hope was that Onyx was gleaning the information he sought from his father, that he'd found some sort of peace here, after spending time with him. But would he want to stay? My heart sank at the idea. He wouldn't leave us, would he? Admittedly, Belladonia was a lot fancier than Ash Grove. And it was hard to compete with a floating town in the sky. Belladonia seemed to be made for him … so where did that leave him and me?

I ate my evening meal all alone in a grand dining hall, with Lolth creepily standing in the entryway. The varieties of food were always hot when I arrived at my seat, though I never saw it being prepared or brought to the table.

"Lolth, where are all the staff? I only ever see you or the hoods."

Lolth angled her head toward the ground, her stringy black hair dangling, and I saw hints of the spider within. It made me wonder how a spider shifter had come to serve the king of vampires. "There are no servants here," she replied.

"Then where does the food come from? Or how are the fireplaces always lit at night, the beds made, and candles tended to?" It was impossible that there was no one behind the scenes when the castle was as well stocked and attended to as it was.

The spider shifter lifted a shoulder. "How does the castle fly?"

It was one of the more human responses I'd gotten from her, and it startled me in both tone and eerie implications. I jumped and almost choked on my potato soup as a pair of hands dropped onto my shoulders. Onyx sliced an uncertain glance at Lolth and grabbed my palm. "Let's hit the town and have some fun. It's been a long day."

I didn't need any convincing as I followed him, leaving the heaviness of the castle behind. "How was throne time with your dad?" I asked. "Did you judge lots of unruly vampires?" I teased lightly, hoping to ease the obvious tension from his face and shoulders.

He tugged at one of my braids as we arrived in town. "I'd rather focus on these darling little pigtails. Wear them to bed?"

My pussy clenched in anticipation. I was really growing to like sleeping-sex. "Maybe if you're good," I teased. I couldn't help but look through the crowd for any sign of the guys.

"They're coming. I promise … and they'll likely both kick my ass when they do." He squeezed my hand. The blue glint of his black hair shone in the pale sunlight, making his green eyes glow that lovely bright green shade.

"You deserve it." I smiled.

He chuckled darkly, pulling me closer to him. "Fair enough, belladonna."

"I do like that pet name. A belladonna is like a vampire's valentine, right?"

"Something like that." He pulled back. "Let's play a game."

My eyebrows rose with surprise. "Yes, let's."

His smile was pure mischief. I loved seeing him smile again.

"Whoever finds the most outlandish door wins. Meet back here." He knocked on the eggplant-colored door nearest. "Try not to become fang-food this time."

I rolled my eyes at his bantering. "Loser has to catch a frog for Raven," I wagered.

Onyx raised an eyebrow, and we shook hands.

We ran in opposite directions, opening, peeking in, and closing doors. I thought it would be a struggle to find the weirdest passageway. These odd little holding areas that lead to different parts of the world, different realms maybe, too. I wondered if one lead to Ash Grove and wished I'd happen upon it, though each door I opened was stranger than the next. Behind an arched ivory door were vampires dressed in full renaissance garb. They were ballroom dancing, men bowing to their partners as classical music played.

No one noticed above the noise as I closed it again. The next two doors made me giggle. One was a comic book store with vampires with bright neon pink hair flipping through pages. The next door made me duck, as a big rubber ball flew over my head. Eighties music played as a vampire shouted, taking off his sweatband. "Hey, toss it back, would ya?"

I left the door ajar, letting the thumping base and skittering of sneakers filter into the gothic street. He caught the ball on a bounce as I threw it back, yelling his thanks as I closed the door.

"Okay, dodgeball eighties vampires have to be the weirdest."

This game was fun, but I missed Onyx already, so I strolled down the street back toward our meeting place. On my way, an unassuming splintered wooden door caught my eye. It wasn't decorated or freshly painted, and it was both inconspicuous and an eyesore all at once. If any door led back to a small town like Ash Grove, it would likely be that one. I stopped and clicked its metal handle and pushed forward. A record sputtered in the corner of a small, modern room lit by red light. "I'll Be Seeing You," by Billie Holiday drew me inside, despite the warning red usually implied. The door clacked behind me when I noticed a string of papers hanging from the ceiling. A man was standing, his back to me, as he dipped something in water and turned, grabbing a clothespin.

"We meet again," Judas's deep timbre rumbled.

Warmth tingled in my lower belly at the sound of his voice. It shouldn't have, and I most certainly shouldn't have walked closer, but I did. "What are you doing here?"

He took a clip and pinned up a dripping page. My gaze lingered on the devil's rolled-up shirt sleeves and his thick, dark forearms. "Developing some photographs while I wait for you to sort it all out."

I crossed my arms, stopping at the edge of the table, close enough to touch him if I wanted.

"Waiting on me to sort things out? If you're so almighty, why don't you do it?"

"Where's the lesson in that? And you need many, many lessons, reaper."

That quiver in my belly intensified at that statement, but I brushed it off.

"Teach me then."

He paused, the water dripping from the photo between his thick fingers. It was then that I got a good look at him in the crimson light. Judas was tall and broad, maybe even larger than Wolfgang. But it was the intensity in his downturned stare that almost rendered me speechless every time. The legends about his beauty were all wrong, I decided then. He was much more handsome than they portrayed. The side of his mouth curved slightly, and I hoped with everything in me that he couldn't read minds.

"My time to school you is coming but is not here yet. There is much for you to learn before you're ready for me."

I sighed. "I know I'm a bad reaper. I hide from scary things; I don't know what happens after death. Are we even sure that's what I am? I'm truly death?"

"You are, though there are steps that need to be taken for your power to be fully realized."

I mulled over his answer as he attended to his photographs. Suddenly, I remembered what Yesenia had said. "A blood ritual? Is that what you mean by steps I need to take?"

"It would be a start," he rumbled. "Or I could snap my fingers, and you'd know everything, here and now." He dried his hands on his pants and walked around the table to me. My knees felt weak and my palms slick.

My voice was a rasp when I replied in his looming shadow. If I took too deep a breath, my breasts would have touched him with how close he stood.

"You could fix everything, reveal it all, and help me and the Halloween Boys, but you don't?"

I craned my neck to look up at him as he answered. I'd gotten so lost in his domineering presence that I hadn't even stolen a glance at the photos he was developing. What did the devil photograph?

"Solving problems is relative. Solving the mouse's problem leaves the snake to starve. It is meant to be this way, reaper." He gently tucked a lock of hair behind my ear, and a gasp fled my throat at the electricity in the small brush of our skin. "Though I am tempted to intervene if only to … speed the process along."

My mind went hazy, and I was thankful the red light hid my flush. All I could think to reply was, "I don't like the name reaper."

"Then make your own."

In a blur of smoke that smelled like vanilla and leather, he was gone, and I squinted at the bright light of the sun. I was standing on the street in front of a stone wall peppered with a bundle of roses arranged in the shape of a *nine*. The splintered door was gone, as if it had never existed. Judas *would* want to be the most memorable door I encountered. He was watching me closely. The thought sent anger and fear through me a few months ago, but now, a strange sort of comfort settled in my chest instead. The devil was watching me … and for some reason, I liked it.

Onyx leaned against the purple door, looking pleased with himself. "Find anything thrilling?" he drawled.

"Like you wouldn't believe," I answered honestly. Though it was starting to feel uncomfortable not telling him about my interactions with Judas. Keeping secrets was harder than I'd thought. "What about you?"

He put his arm around me and pulled open the purple door. "Shall we have a drink and discuss the many batshit crazy doors of Belladonia?"

When we walked in, I expected a normal bar. But I was quickly learning that nothing in Belladonia was normal. It was more of a night-club, with neon lights and plush booths surrounded by oddly shaped furniture and chains with cuffs hanging from the wall and—my cheeks flushed as a topless woman walked by. "Can I get you two a seat or did you come to … participate?"

"A booth, please," Onyx replied, his palm finding the small of my back. We followed the vampire, passing a woman bent over a stool, being spanked with a wooden paddle. I quickly averted my gaze.

"Is this a sex club?" I asked, sliding into the booth, wanting to hide under it instead.

Onyx chuckled darkly. "Yes, one of many. Vampires are an amorous sort. But I'm not here to do that with you. Unless you really want to. I'm looking for someone."

The topless woman returned, and I looked at the table to keep from admiring her perky breasts. Vampires were all so breathtaking; it was hard not to gawk when they were fully clothed. When they were naked, it was close to impossible. Thankfully, Onyx smoothly ordered our drinks, and a blessed flute of pale liquid soon appeared in front of me.

"Prosecco, no sex blood." Onyx winked. I downed my glass eagerly, hoping it would ease my awkwardness.

"Who are we looking for?"

"Just keep sitting there looking ravishing, and I promise they'll find us." He took a sip of his red wine. "They can't help themselves—"

"Well, look who finally made it to Belladonia," Vincent purred, tossing his long platinum blond hair over his shoulder. "And where are your other friends? I hope they are aware that only vampires are allowed beyond the gates."

"Nice to see you so *uncharred*—unlike your tent," Onyx said. "Have a seat."

"Yes, despite your best efforts. Thank you for ensuring my men make my accommodations fireproof from now on," Vincent mocked. I wondered if the vampire knew who Onyx was, who his father was.

A red-haired vision joined Vincent in a flash. She smiled, her fangs glowing in the neon light. "Hi, Blythe, I'm glad you made it. Feel free to ignore the vampire dick measuring. I always do."

"Thanks for your help getting here." I smiled. "And I'll try."

Onyx laid his palms on the table. "I have a gift for you. Congratulations, you've gained a new coven member. Her name is Renaia, and you'll claim her at the call tomorrow."

Ezmerelda leaned back in her seat, biting her lip as Vincent fumed. "You have the audacity to make demands of me after burning my tent to the ground and refusing to join my coven? What gives you the right?"

I glanced at Onyx; his smirk was gorgeous in all its rogue impertinence. "I found my father, and he's the temperamental sort. You know, royals typically are. If you do these things for me, I won't let him know that you've kept me out of the Belladonia loop for so long."

Vincent went still in that unnatural way that made me want to squirm in my seat. "I take it you've been introduced to His Majesty, then?"

"You knew this whole time and didn't tell me? I thought we were friends, Vince." Onyx leaned back, taking a sip from his wine. I had no idea what he was playing at, but I refrained from asking questions.

"You were better off not knowing. Believe me." Vincent plucked a piece of lint from his coat. "There are rumors, you know, that he's gone mad. Rumors that his search for his lost bride and the grotesque offerings are a farce." He leaned in. "*Vlad The Impaler* they're calling him. If Belladonia is as safe and sacred as some claim, then where are the beasts in the forbidden forest coming from, hmm? Riddle me that, *Prince.* Though no one seems to mention a royal baby going missing; only the queen. Curious, don't you think?"

Onyx thrummed his fingers against the table, ignoring Vincent's baiting. I marveled at how many times he'd probably done the same thing in court. "Do you have a key, a door, whatever is needed, to get back to Ash Grove?"

Vincent smiled and glanced at Ezmerelda, who watched on with an indiscernible stare. "He only comes to me when he needs something. It hurts me. Truly it does. We could be so great together. A powerful team, the three of us." Glancing at me, he tilted his head. "Possibly four. It depends ..."

With a labored sigh, Onyx interrupted. "Will you make a way for us to return, or does the king need you brought to his attention?"

Vincent scoffed. "You know nothing of Vladimir. I'm nearly as old as he is. He wasn't always what he is now; know that."

"Did you know my mother?"

The vampire's throat bobbed, and I knew if I caught the movement, so did Onyx. "If you're here when we depart, you may join. But my patience in handing out free favors is wearing thin. There will come a time very soon, little *Dracul,* that I will call in what you owe me." Vincent stood, smoothing his trousers as Ezmerelda slid from her seat. I hadn't expected to find so much passion and opinion buried beneath the velvet finery that was Vincent. I resisted the urge to question him about the strange name and his history with the king and queen of Belladonia.

I asked instead, before they could leave, "What can you tell us about time here? If I contacted someone in Ash Grove, would they be in a different time period than us?"

Vincent crossed his arms. "That I do not know. I have never attempted to communicate with anyone while in Belladonia. All vampires are here, and they are the most important company I keep. Though I have heard," he leaned in and spoke softly, "that the doors are fewer. Some disappearing, perhaps, but no new ones appearing as they should. The creatures in the woods were not always there. This city feels different each year. Doesn't it, Ezmerelda?"

She nodded, her usual sass vacant from her expression. "Something is happening here, though I'm not sure what. Please exercise an abundance of caution, especially tomorrow," she warned.

"That was surprisingly helpful." Onyx shrugged. "Thanks."

Ezmerelda shot me a wink on our way out. "See you in another realm, Blythe."

CHAPTER 33

Onyx

THE BOYS ARE BACK IN TOWN

*When you love someone, you love the whole person as he
or she is, and not as you would like them to be.*
  Leo Tolstoy

The morning of the Bleeding Heart Ball, I found the slayer trimming a rose bush along the city gates. "You know, you take hiding in plain sight to a whole new level. Introducing yourself as a vampire hunter is one thing, but running the town's vessense supply while slaughtering diphylla on your off-time ..." I clapped slowly. "Bravo. Your excellence at deceit surpasses even my own."

"I'm hunting diphylla because no one else is," he answered, casually snipping a branch. "And I don't care for the vampires, but if the diphylla accessed the countless doors here, they could wreak havoc on manifold territories, killing innocent people. And King Vladimir is doing nothing to stop it. I slay twenty, and fifty more appear shortly after the offering."

"Why isn't he doing anything to stop them?" I felt like a fool that I hadn't even thought of that. The potential for evil to utilize Belladonia's resources was astronomical.

"Because he's checked out, Onyx. He's been checked out for

centuries. His mind is deteriorating, and his mad obsession with finding the queen has driven him insane. It's all he cares about. I'm doing the best I can, but vampires won't help. They all pretend that nothing is going wrong, that they aren't dissipating in number." He shook his head.

"How old are you? I thought you a mortal man by your smell."

He lifted an eyebrow. "Old."

"Did you know the queen was taken by someone like you? A slayer? Cheers, by the way, because according to the king, not even Hell will have you."

Elysium snorted before looking through the bars of the gate and into the foggy distance. "I know that tale. That the beautiful bride of Drakon was stolen away by a slayer. I don't believe those stories to be true, though. At least not in the way he tells them."

"I could have sold you out."

"But you didn't, and you won't. And while you're here, I need your help."

"Sorry, I'm no good at gardening, and I kind of have a party to be at later."

He rolled his eyes. "I've planted sensors in the tunnels beneath these wicked woods. I track the diphylla's movement through vibrations in their migration." A keypad appeared on the palm rest of his chair and illuminated a holographic diagram. "There's new significant movement near the center of the woods, not too far off from where I first sensed you and Blythe. Though whatever this is, it's big. I could use some dragon fire if you don't mind. It's highly effective against these beasts."

"You know about dragons? I didn't know the fire was anything special."

"More precious than you know. Whereas demons and other creatures rely on hellfire, a dragon's flame is from the sun itself. It's a life-giving sort of magic all its own."

I stretched, knowing I'd missed expending my blaze. It had been weeks of castle drudgery and vampire politics. An inferno raged inside me like a wild beast begging to spread its wings and scorch the earth. I agreed to go with him, and we sleuthed past the gate and into the dark and dreary red and black forest.

"Where do these things come from?" I asked as we crunched through the leaves. Well, I crunched the leaves; Elysium's chair hovered above the ground. He was silent and deadly. After typing something on his pin pad, the holographic map lit up, and a dot flashed at our destination.

"Where indeed? Rabid and deranged beasts appearing in a floating city in the sky …"

"I feel like you're asking me to solve a riddle, Elysium, and I much prefer crosswords with the answers upside down at the bottom of the page."

He chuckled. "If you don't already see it, you will. Their blood is fascinating. It's why I play with the vessense. It allows me ample time around blood and allows me to study it. Vampires' fascination with blood is for recreation and sexual pleasure, but what immortal blood is capable of goes much further."

I played with a ball of fire in my palm. "I'm impressed. A vampire hunter and blood witch studying them all like little test rats, right under their noses. No vamp has ever come sniffing around, wondering what you are?"

Elysium shrugged. "Vampires are way more concerned with them-selves. They don't look too closely at anyone else, unless it's to turn their noses up at them. You were different, though. Unpretentious, gracious. You know, I was hoping you had grown into a good man. I'm glad to find that you have. You know, you'd probably make a pretty decent king."

"Absolutely I would, but it seems like such a drag of a gig." I smirked, eliciting another chuckle from my friend. "We're getting clos-er," I noted as we came upon the dot.

"This pack of diphylla is large, and for some reason, they aren't moving. Diphylla are always in motion. They don't sleep, they don't nest, and they're always searching for their next kill."

"There's something up ahead." I passed him, curiosity pulling me forward and my inferno raging in my veins. The space grew quiet, the kind of tomblike calm that only came before a predator attack. I surveyed the blackened trees and disorienting crimson flowers. Nothing seemed amiss, and yet everything was all wrong. I'd just turned to glance over my shoulder to say something to Elysium when my back was struck.

A shadowy mass pummeled me to the ground. My brain registered sharp teeth and a bone-chilling snarl. The beast's claws dug into my shoulders, piercing into skin as it roared. I didn't fight back, only gripped its fur-covered paws as they pressed the air from my lungs. The whirling of the vampire hunter's chair kicked in, and I called out, "Don't fire! It's all right!"

"Are you insane!?" Elysium answered. "Oh, my god. Holy fuck—"

I looked up and met the glowing yellow eyes of my friend, my love, and emotion clouded my throat. "It's good to see you, Wolfgang."

His glowing glare narrowed before he released me. By the time I sat up, he'd shifted back into the man I knew. Rippled muscle and thick, broad shoulders—bare and showing his tattoos. His jaw tensed, and I felt his conflicted emotions. Elysium mewled, trembling with his crossbow, though it wasn't pointed at us. "Onyx … I don't fuck with demons this big …"

"It's fine. He's nice … sort of," I answered, not taking my eyes off my friend.

Wolf kneeled, placing his hands on his knees. "You left us. You left *me*."

My cold, stone heart cracked through the middle, and I swallowed, rising to kneel in front of him, but not daring to reach out and touch him yet. "I'm so sorry, Wolf."

Something huge stomped near us, and I could feel his presence as he shifted into a man. Even in human form, he was menacing, maybe more so, the judgmental priest. Ames crossed his arms, peering down at me.

I looked to the ground between Wolf and me, knowing I had no excuse, knowing I didn't deserve to even speak with them. Ames demanded, "Tell me Blythe is safe." An order, one that if I could not fulfill, I had no doubt he would kill me then and there. I'd want him to.

"She's safe." I inhaled deeply. "There's no excuse for what I did—"

My words muffled as Wolf grabbed my shoulders and pulled me to his hard trunk. His arm squeezed me close as his hand held tight to the back of my head. My emotion unleashed then as I wetted his chest with hot tears. I felt Ames's palm on my shoulder, then, before he dropped to his knees next to us, taking us both in an embrace.

I pulled back, stunned at their reactions. "You're not going to kill me?"

"Maybe later," Ames rumbled.

Wolfgang took my face in his large hands as emotion filled his expressive and kind eyes. "Never, *ever* do that again."

"I don't know what I was thinking," I answered.

Ames squeezed my shoulder, his blue gaze softening. "I do. You were thinking you needed to be free from my scathing over-possession of our mate. My treatment of you has not been justified, Onyx. For that, I am sorry."

If I hadn't already been on my knees, I would have fallen over. Ghost was apologizing to me. "Thank you, friend."

He hugged me then, and we stood.

"Come here," Wolf said gruffly, grabbing the back of my neck. He pulled my face to his, and his warm lips were on me. God, I'd missed him. Springtime, a rushing creek, and warm wind through the trees hit my senses at the taste of him. After our moment, I wiped my eyes with my wrist and remembered my companion.

Elysium had his crossbow slung over his knees and a palm over his heart. "That's just the most goddamn beautiful thing I've ever seen." He sniffled. With a small wave, he said, "Hi, I'm Elysium. We spoke briefly, telepathically."

"This is my friend, the vampire hunter and blood witch."

Elysium grinned. "Don't forget bartender. That one's my favorite."

Wolf raised a quizzical eyebrow at me. "Not even out of the woods, and Belladonia is weird as fuck."

I glanced to the wet stairs and the opened door in the middle of the clearing. "Where've you guys been?"

A twig snapped in the distance, and we all froze, each of our keen senses picking up on something unique. Wolf sniffed the air and recoiled. "What the hell is that?"

"Not a demon," Ames replied lowly. "Or from Hell."

Elysium picked up his crossbow slowly. "They're surrounding us."

I whispered to the vampire hunter, calling flame to my palms as we all moved until we were back to back. "Can I make a request?"

He raised a questioning eyebrow over his round glasses.

A creature growled low and slow from its hiding spot behind a tree.

"Play 'The Boys are Back in Town,' by Thin Lizzy."

"Are you fucking kidding me?" Ames grumbled. "Obviously Metallica is the correct choice for a fight like this."

Wolfgang interjected. "If your new buddy is also a DJ, then I humbly disagree and request 'Back in Black' by AC/DC."

Elysium shook his head while grinning from ear to ear. "This is going to be fun," he said as his fingers tapped his chair.

And then the first creature struck him from the side.

CHAPTER 34

Blythe

IN HIS WEB

> So comes snow after fire, and even dragons have their endings.
>
> J. R. R. Tolkien, *The Hobbit*

My corset binding cut into my ribs as Lolth tugged and laced the strings. The dress was old but made of finer material than I'd ever worn. The deep emerald green matched my prince's eyes, and the gold threading glimmered under the flickering candlelight. Lolth said I'd stand out among the vampires who always wore red, black, or white, but I didn't mind. My heart fluttered at the thought of Onyx finding me wearing it. I colored my lips with crimson lipstick from Lady Rouge and secured my lacy mask.

"It's Hallows Fest, Valentine's Day edition," I joked to Raven, who bobbed his head as he peered out the window, watching carriages and sports cars alike arrive with partygoers. I hadn't seen Onyx all day, which was the custom of the event, apparently. It was the first whole day I'd spent without him, and without Ames or Wolf since … I couldn't recall. I could hardly remember a time before the Halloween Boys. My heart ached, missing them, needing them all to be together with me again. Onyx had promised soon. When was soon?

Lolth assessed me through the hair that hung in front of her face. I wanted to pin it back for her. She'd gone back to wearing her same beige frock, but she'd continued wearing the new leather shoes we'd gotten on our trip into town. "You didn't cleanse. His Majesty the King will not be pleased."

"It doesn't seem like much pleases the king at all. What is he after? Do you like working for him?" I asked candidly, taking a bobby pin from between my teeth and pinning back a stray curl. "I think Belladonia could use a little girl power, personally."

I watched as the spider shifter slipped away, pausing in the doorway. "Go straight to the ballroom to begin the ritual. Do not wander down an extra two stairwells."

By the time I'd spun around, she was gone. "What did she mean by that?" I asked as Raven squawked, landing on my shoulder. "Do you think she was giving me some sort of clue?"

I gathered my dress as we wove through the corridors of the castle. Stone gargoyles and dripping candles were the only markers of where I was. When I ascended the spiral staircase, I paused, looking toward the door that led to the ballroom and then down the remaining stairs. Raven made a vibrating noise in his throat. "Maybe I'll just have a quick peek at what's down there. What's Onyx's dad hiding?"

My familiar ruffled his feathers in disapproval, but I was already halfway down. "Onyx has kept me safe; it's my turn to keep him safe. There's something off about the king, this place, all of it."

Two floors down, the atmosphere changed dramatically. It was as cold as an icebox. I rubbed my arms as I walked over the creaking wooden floors. The space wasn't decorated; there were no lavish furnishings or candles. Only a dull light in the distance. When I reached it, the area opened into a rounded sort of cave. Lined against the wall were tiny corked glasses. "A wine cellar?" I whispered to Raven, whose head sank down his shoulders. I made my way closer to the wall and plucked one of the tiny bottles. It was half the size of my hand, and in cursive scrawl, it read *Nymph*. I put it back and inspected another. *Merman*. I took two more: *Werewolf* and *Fairy*. Swirling the dark liquid, it dawned on me what I was holding.

A woman's voice echoed behind me. "Blood. It is all he wants, all he cares for."

Almost dropping the bottles, I turned to see Lolth. She was crawling down the wall, her elbows turned inward, and her knees outward at the ghastliest angles. I swallowed my fear, setting the vials gently back in their places.

"There must be hundreds of thousands of these. What does he want with them?"

Lolth paused on the wall and wiggled a finger over a glass. "Why do you play dead?"

Her question caught me off guard. "What?"

"You pretend to be weak. I cannot understand it."

"I'm not pretending. There's a lot I don't know about what I am."

Her head lolled to the side, and then I saw what her hair hid. Eyes, several rows of beady eyes. My mouth went dry as Raven's talons dug into my shoulder.

"Spiders aren't taught web patterns. We just create. You create, too. You're like a spider, like me." She crawled down the side of the wall, wobbling on two feet. As she stalked forward, I resisted the urge to run or scream. I could do this. I had to do this. She was helping me. At least I thought she was. "You must abandon the prince and leave through any door. The first door you reach." Lolth stopped, looking down at her feet, hiding behind her stringy black hair again.

"I'm not leaving him."

She took my wrist then and pressed something into my palm. "Then you are flying into his web tonight, and I cannot help you. I am sorry."

Lolth dropped to the ground, her limbs contorting as she slinked back up the wall, disappearing deeper into the darkness of the cavernous space.

When I opened my trembling palm, a fresh wave of dread washed over me. I held five small, empty vials, labeled *Ghost, Dragon, Wolf, Devil* ... and *Reaper*.

CHAPTER 35

Blythe

SWEET POISON

> I love her, and that's the beginning and end of everything.
> *F. Scott Fitzgerald*

The masquerade's grandeur transformed into a sinister gloom after what I'd just discovered. My previous plan of having Raven shift into a humanoid and escort me seemed too risky, and I wouldn't put him in the line of fire if something nefarious was brewing. My luck with grand parties wasn't great. Memories of the baphomet ramming me into time and space to torture for its master played through my mind. Its hollow voice repeating *my master will be pleased* haunted me each night.

It was a solemn reminder that I was being hunted, and like the witches told me during our fitful hand-holding session, something was watching me. And now my suspicions toward the Vampire King were at an all-time high. I'd stuffed the vials into the pockets of my dress. How could Vladimir have known about the Halloween Boys, and possibly me, and not say anything? Nothing made sense, but I knew I had to find Onyx before the offering began.

I wove through vampires dressed in their elegant fashions, my bare shoulders brushing against soft feather boas and fur shawls. But even on my tiptoes, I couldn't see above the long masks and piled high hairstyles. The dais sat empty. Only two dark thrones watched beneath iron flame-lit chandeliers. What if I didn't find him in time?

I passed by a couple who'd just found each other. The beautiful vampire kissed her mate's cheeks and admired her yellow gown. My anxiety accelerated. What if Onyx had been captured, what if something had gone wrong—

A large hand landed on my shoulder, and I startled. My dress swished and flared as I spun to look up at the man wearing a red leather mask over his eyes and a sanguine velvet suit, complete with a top hat. It would have looked ridiculous on anyone but Judas, but of course, he made it look like the sexiest outfit a man could ever hope to wear. He bowed and offered me a leather-gloved hand. "Care to dance with the devil?"

Something fluttered in my chest as I took his hand. "Do you enjoy being so mysterious?" I asked as he gently placed my palm on his shoulder.

The side of his mouth lifted slightly as he guided me into step in perfect time with the music that had only begun playing with the first move of his feet. "Perhaps I'm only mysterious because I hate sharing about myself."

Shock reverberated in my chest when I heard my very private words repeated back to me so casually. "You—how did you—"

"I'm wherever the fire is, darling." He leaned in close to my ear. "Whatever happens this night, remember that what you are is whatever you want to be. You've always had everything you need inside you."

Before I could question him, he pulled me in, my back to his chest, and spun me out again, releasing his hold. A flamboyant vampire wearing a white pants suit with the black number *8* sown into the fabric squeezed past me. "Show-off," I muttered under my breath as I stood alone. Though I wasn't without a man's arms for long, as strong arms curved around my waist and took my hand. I was about to pull away when I looked up and saw the dark blue glint of a wolf mask. I knew his broad shoulders and the rough feel of his palms. It felt like home. Wolf-gang always felt like home. "Hey, beautiful. You smell nice." He smiled as I buckled into his chest. He held me tight as we swayed to the symphony.

"You're here," I sniffled, drying my eyes. "I missed you so much."

Taking my chin between his fingers, he tilted my face up and leaned forward, kissing the tip of my nose softly. "I'm never letting anyone steal you away again."

My heart raced at the small, tender contact. Wolf had been slow but steady in his affections toward me, but with each step closer, I only fell for him more. "Good." I hugged him tight. "Wait, does that mean …"

Wolf grinned and nodded over my shoulder. I turned on my heel and almost lost my breath at the sight of him. He wore a white gold skull mask to hide his face and a black and silver threaded suit. He bowed when he saw me and extended a hand. A hand which I ignored and flung myself into his embrace. Ames's dark chuckle lit my soul on fire as my throat tightened with emotion.

"My little ghost," he rumbled. "I love you."

"I love you," I repeated. "You're here. You're all here."

Ames brought my hand to his mouth and kissed it, his blue eyes scanning me from neck to ankles. "You're so lovely and … unbitten."

A mischievous voice sounded beside me. "For now," Onyx replied, with Wolfgang at his side. God, they were all so stunning together in their formal wear. Onyx wore deep green and black, with a serpentine gold mask to match his emerald eyes.

"No, not for now. Forever," I replied. "If he bites me, he could die. My blood … isn't good."

Onyx tilted his head and took my hand, tugging me close, though Ames didn't let me go. I nestled between the two of them. "Everything about you is good."

"That's true," Ames agreed, smelling my hair. He didn't seem to mind Onyx's public affection. "Onyx has kept you safe through my overprotective errors. He's put your needs above his own. And not that you need my approval, but I do believe him worthy of sharing you with me. I'm happy you and the prince have connected."

Wolf interjected, holding on to the fabric of my dress. "Though I believe we could all connect a little more. What do you think, princess?"

Onyx smirked. "The royalty jokes will never end, so just get used to it now." He tugged me closer as his lips dropped to my ear. I relished the feeling of Ames's arms around my waist, Wolf holding on to me, and Onyx's lips nibbling at my pearl earring. "And I *will* be biting you. The boys are here now. You're safe. I'm not waiting any longer to taste my sweet belladonna's blood."

I pulled away, reminded of blood. "Something strange is happening. I think your father hasn't been completely honest with you."

Wolf chuckled darkly, smelling my hair. "A dishonest vampire. Imagine that."

The temperature in the room felt warmer, and a dull ache was pulsing between my thighs. Ames planted small kisses along my jaw as he pulled me closer.

Onyx brought my wrist to his lips and smiled, revealing his pointed fangs. "Shall I taste you here? Or perhaps I'll start with a thigh ..."

I glanced up at Ames, whose jaw tightened. "If you want it, I won't stop you. But I will stop him if he gets carried away."

"Get carried away with us," Onyx countered toward his friend.

I giggled. "Have you guys forgotten that we're in the middle of a crowded dance floor right now?" Vampires were flicking their glances from us to their mates, no doubt sensing our desires and hoping to view, or take part in, the passion we emanated.

Wolf purred against the back of my neck. "We've got a surprise for you. Something to make up for the Halloween fiasco. But we've got to go set up." He pulled away reluctantly, and I immediately missed his towering warmth. "I hope the king of vampires likes rock 'n' roll."

Ames kissed my temple just as I caught the multi-eyed stare of Lolth. She was slinking behind a column, watching me. If I could only get her to talk to the guys. To explain the blood vials and what she knew about the king.

"I think Lolth can explain it better than me. I'm going to go get her, and we can talk after." I slipped out of the grasp of my men.

My skeleton man tugged my wrist and gave me one last kiss before whispering, "We're going to do a lot more than just talk after this, little ghost."

Excitement pricked my exposed skin, and I wished I could fast forward the night to when I could be alone with them. For the immediate moment, however, I had to keep them all safe, and Lolth could be the key to doing just that. Not wanting to let her out of my sight, I pushed through vampires who were dancing and kissing and drinking vessense to find her. I caught a glimpse of the back of her head as she slipped out the front entrance. When I arrived outside, however, only dark gray clouds and lightning in the distance greeted me.

I swore under my breath, turning to look up at the looming castle, wondering if she'd crawled up the side of it in her spider form. Onyx's voice drawled in the distance. "Trying to run away? I think it's a little too late for that. You've got three monsters hooked."

He'd removed his mask, showcasing his handsome and pronounced face. His eyes flashed a predatory gleam in the low light of the oncoming storm. "I'd like to drink you now, belladonna. Just you and me. Now that all the trouble is behind us, and we're all together again."

"Onyx," I warned, backing down a step. "I'm not willing to risk your life. You mean too much to me."

He took a casual step forward. "And you are my life, Blythe. Fuck my immortality."

My heel caught on my dress, and I stumbled back. Arms were around me in an instant, catching my fall. He gripped the back of my hair, eyeing my neck with parted lips. His incisors were so sharp and pronounced, and his eyes held a feral tint of lust. "No," I protested, squirming, but he wouldn't let me budge.

"Kiss me," he demanded, his voice sensual and low. He gently untied my mask, and it fell to the ground. "I can feel you want me. You long for the prick of my fangs."

"We can't do this; I can't risk hurting you."

"Yes, you can, and you will."

The force of his hold was too strong, the determination in his stare too fierce. I wasn't physically able to stop him from risking everything for a taste of me. The vampire inside him was too strong. "You'll die," my voice cracked.

He chuckled, making me flinch as his lips grazed my sensitive skin and he inhaled deeply. "You don't think I know that? Don't you see the tragic irony is perfect? I couldn't have written a better lyric myself."

"What are you talking about?"

"I finally, after more than two hundred years, find something that makes me want to live. And she is Death, and tasting her will kill me. In finding my life, I have found my death, and I have never been more sure, Blythe. You are the verse, the bridge, and the chorus. You are the melody of every song I've ever tried to write, and this time, I'm going to get the chords right. I know how this one ends. Now let me sing it. This is my choice, the most glorious risk I've ever been afforded. You don't scare me. Let me taste you, my belladonna."

Thunder clapped, and a woman wailed a high-pitched shriek. The banshee. She screamed before death. "You're going to die for my blood. This is madness," I protested. A hot tear rolled down my cheek as his teeth slowly brushed my jaw and down. I gripped the back of his hair, relishing the softness of his obsidian locks. He was so handsome, so perfect. And I was about to lose him. I was about to kill him.

He bared his fangs, and I interrupted. "Kiss me first."

Without a hint of hesitation, he obliged, meeting my lips with his ferocious kiss. I moaned into his mouth as his tongue mingled with mine. His taste was rich and unexpected, like him. I pulled back and opened my mouth to speak, to say anything with the time I'd bought, when he struck.

His mouth was on my neck. I pushed at his chest, but his hold on the back of my head and my hip tightened. And with preternatural speed, the tips of his fangs sank into the side of my neck. I cried out, and a flash of lightning shot across the sky.

"Stop," I begged weakly, my eyes closing in ecstasy. It was as if my entire body was vibrating with pleasure. Orgasmic resolve spread across my body, just like the electricity in the stormy sky. It snaked through my arms, over my breasts, down my stomach, and shocked against my center. My senses heightened. The press of his fingertips, his body flush against mine, and his teeth … the burning bliss was like a thousand orgasms at once. My back arched as I writhed, screaming again as shocks of pleasure zapped against me with no warning. He moaned, gulping at my neck.

I felt his tongue lapping against me as he went into a frenzy of need. His hand snaked up my front and palmed my breast, his grip hooking into my top and pulling it forward, leaving me exposed. Pulling off my neck with a deep suck, he wrapped his lips around my nipple.

"Oh my god," I tilted my head back, feeling my knees weaken. He caught me and laid me gently against the stone steps. I didn't care that they were hard and cold or that frigid rain began to fall above the chorus of the storm. I needed him, needed his bite all over me. "More," I whimpered.

I jolted as fire erupted in a circle around us. The stones and puddles warmed and heated my skin. He was in a blood craze, risking death for me, and he still had enough consideration to keep me warm. His gaze roamed my body hungrily for a moment before showcasing a red smile, my blood darkening his chin as fire lashed behind him. He was evil embodied as a mind-blowingly sexy man. A vampire, a dragon, *mine*.

"Yes, my belladonna. More and more and more …"

How long did we have before he fell over? Before my blood took effect and killed him like it did the other vampires that had bitten me? I should have been sobbing and shouting for help, but instead I was wrapping my legs around his hips as his bite gripped around my nipple. Sinking in a single, sharp fang, he circled the spot with his tongue, drawing out droplets of blood. Again, the voltage from the bite wrecked me, and my hips bucked wildly against him as I screamed in blissful agony. He groaned and mumbled against my breast, "Your blood has bewitched me. I'm afraid I'll suck you dry."

In my vampire-induced love haze, that sounded wonderful, and I wanted it. "Yes, please. I'm yours," I agreed. Delirium was pulsing into me with each prick of rain and each tinge of throbbing pain from my punctures. He could drain me of everything I had, and I'd use my last breath to thank him. As he drank, his hand felt its way up from my knee to my thigh. He jerked my panties aside and thrust two blood covered fingers inside my wanting opening. I cried out, bounding my hips to meet him and grinding against his wrist. But I didn't want to waste time on his fingers. I needed him. I pulled frantically against his pants, and he unbuttoned and yanked them down. The storm picked up, raging above us as the fire hissed around us, but it did nothing to slow our passion. He pulled off my breast, showing me his glistening crimson lips. "Kiss me again," I asked. "If my blood is going to kill you, I may as well taste it, too, and beg for it to take me with you."

He growled low in his throat, and his slick lips met mine. My blood tasted bitter and tangy as I explored his mouth with my tongue. He pulled his hand away then, and my hips surged forward, feeling empty. His tip pushed at my entrance as he broke our kiss. His mouth fell back to my neck, and just as he took another bite, his cock sank into me with one hard thrust, filling me with more bliss than I could have imagined possible. All I could do was claw at his back like a rabid animal. Pulling at the rain-soaked fabric of his shirt, I stared up at him as he drank from me, willing the thrumming pleasure inside me to allow me a glimpse of my dark, blood-stained prince of vampires. He was pure wicked evil, and wholly beautiful at the same time. The pleasure and pain intensified as he moved in and out at a maddening pace, building my release slowly and in his own time. "Onyx," I whimpered. "Please, don't leave me."

He vibrated against my red-soaked neck. "I love you, my belladonna. My wretched soul is tied to yours. Your blood is mine now. It runs through my veins, down my throat, haunting me. Now come on my cock while I indulge in your delicious blood."

I didn't know the exact mechanisms of vampire bites, but they seemed to compound and escalate in intensity with each puncture. My mind and body became disconnected with overwhelming elation. Onyx was feeling it, too, from the intensity of his sucks and moans. He kept one hand under my head, and the other under my hip. Water rushed down the stairs, adding to the drenched feel of blood and sex. Each thrust brought me past the height I thought I would explode at. Until finally his tongue licked around the sensitive flesh of the fresh wounds on my neck, sending quivers of sensation straight to my core. My orgasm tore through me, and my moan joined the thunder as Onyx hurried his cock inside me with force, lightning illuminating our blood-soaked wetness as he braced himself on his palms. He came with a roar as his fire exploded, hissing at the rain gathered in puddles around us on the stone steps of the castle. Holding me there, he used his body as a shield from the storm as I caught my breath. I reached up, cupping his jaw and kissing his lips. The aftershocks from his fangs still rang through me.

"You're still here," I whispered hoarsely, feeling my neck and breast pulse from his bites.

His eyes shut as he rested his forehead to mine. "Perhaps even death is not strong enough to tear me away from you." Standing, he scooped me into his arms. "Though I'd like to try again … and again …"

I shook my head, grinning. "I'd like that, too."

He'd cheated death, somehow, and I was so eternally grateful. His mouth was mine. His blissful bites and his piercing fangs were all mine forever and ever.

WE REENTERED the castle to the merriment and melodies of festivity. Suddenly my skin and clothing heated, and all the water that clung to me evaporated. My hair was a mess, falling in loose waves. I moved it, draping it over my neck to hide any evidence of what we'd just done. I'd ease Ghost into the scars slowly. For now, I was happy to have Onyx clutching my hand, alive and well. Dried and as put together as we could manage, we reentered the ball. This time, I met the stare of King Vladimir, who clapped once, signaling a halt to the music. I looked around for the guys and found them standing on the music podium, Ames with his guitar and Wolf on the drums. "They started without me," Onyx grumbled. "The acoustics in here are sublime."

"This is feeling a lot like Halloween night," I whispered unsurely, not enjoying the way the king's eyes lingered on me.

He stood and outstretched a hand. "Come, my son, and my daughter in marriage. Join me so we may begin the offerings."

Onyx's hand tensed around mine as we stalked forward. I looked over in a panic to see Ames set down his guitar and Wolf stand from behind the drums. They were ready to strike, though I hoped they wouldn't need to. This was Onyx's father, his only real family, the man he'd searched for his entire life. If he was indeed planning something terrible, what would we do? Any move we made threatened to break Onyx's heart, and I knew that none of us wanted to do that. I knew it was the only thing that held Ghost inside of Ames in that moment. His love for Onyx was strong, and that made me so incredibly happy. I just wanted us to all be together and in love, but first I had this ominous offering to attend to …

We reached the throne, and thousands of eyes landed on the king while hundreds more scanned us with circumspect curiosity.

"Welcome, my beloved vampires. I have a special introduction to make," the king boomed as he circled us on the dais. I felt like a bleeding seal being circled by a shark, but I held on to Onyx's hand as I scanned the crowd. Was Judas out there watching me? What did his last warning mean? I needed to piece things together and somehow stay one step ahead of ancient, unholy beings. *Don't trust anyone*, Onyx had told me when we first arrived. *Least of all me*, he'd said. My skin prickled with fear.

"Your prince, the son of mine and your beloved Queen Cassiopeia, has returned. Prince Onyx Hart Drakon." He said Onyx's name like a growl, and the crowd cheered and whistled. "Before a thrilling surprise from the prince, I'd like to invite Vincent Albescu to give the first offering."

Vampires turned, and the crowd parted as Vincent strode forward, looking paler than normal, his long white hair cascading down the back of his red cloak. He kneeled and said lowly, "Your Majesty, it would be an honor."

"Ah, my kin. Onyx, this is your uncle, Vincent Albescu Drakon. I believe you are in each other's acquaintance."

"Vincent is your brother?" Onyx asked lowly.

"A hundred years removed, which is still exceedingly old, though not nearly as powerful and wise. He is a Drakon, nonetheless. An original vampire. Though he cannot give an offering himself, someone from his coven may."

My throat gripped, and it was an effort to control my gaze as Vincent glanced at Onyx, judging his reaction. His father's brother had taunted him for a century, passing him at Hallows Fest, attempting to lure him into his coven. He knew they were related. Had he been reporting to Vladimir the entire time? I squeezed Onyx's hand in support. He stood stone-faced, not giving anyone the satisfaction of catching him off guard. It was then I realized why the Halloween Boys hated Vincent, and now I agreed. The king interrupted my revelations. "And you're taking on a new coven member, is that correct?"

Vincent looked to the side and slowly gestured a woman forward. "I claim Renaia as a member of the Phantom Coven."

"Wonderful." The king clapped his hands together a little too happily. "Now, show the new prince how we make our offerings here."

The Coven leader's jaw tensed as he walked forward. It was then I noticed an ornate table of glass vials. It looked like a prayer table of candles, only the prayers wouldn't be going to a god; they'd be offerings to the vampire king. Renaia trembled as Vincent approached her. Something passed between them as she nodded, squinting her eyes shut. "What's happening?" I whispered to Onyx, whose gaze held forward on the scene.

"For the king," Vincent declared in a hollow tone, lifting something long and silver in the air. "For the king," the crowd repeated.

With preternatural immortal speed, he was behind Renaia then. With his hand over her throat, he plunged the silver into her chest. I gasped, leaning into Onyx. The female vampire grimaced and fell to her knees as Vincent removed the thin blade and inserted the blood into a vial. The silver item was a needle, and it had taken blood from her heart. Kneeling, Vincent placed the vial back on the table.

King Vladimir met my horrified gaze and smiled. "Welcome to the Bleeding Heart Ball."

CHAPTER 36

Onyx

VLAD THE IMPALER

If I cannot inspire love, I will cause fear; and chiefly towards you my arch-enemy, because my creator, do I swear inextinguishable hatred.

Mary Shelley, Frankenstein

Vampires had a flair for dramatics. Even in the delirium of Blythe's blood on my tongue, I'd expected no less than a spectacle at the ball we were all required to attend. Though the literal nature of bleeding hearts was shocking, even to me. What was more surprising was the king's desire to throw me off. He believed me to have an emotional attachment to Vincent, which couldn't be further from the truth.

And now, in learning that he was my uncle? It only made me want to kill him more. The lying, opportunistic bastard would burn the moment the guys and I got a hold of him. Vladimir also assumed I'd cared for Renaia, which I didn't, other than I preferred not to watch her die at the hands of an asshole coven. I knew Vincent would take her in. But to use her as an example of the offerings to come was as intentional as it was cruel. It was also crafty. My father had somehow sorted out my soft spots and had waited for this moment to prod them.

Though the *why* still confounded me. As Blythe stiffened next to me,

I flicked a glance to the stage of instruments, and the guys were nowhere to be seen. They'd moved somewhere closer and hidden, no doubt ready to kill. But if it came to blows, could the Halloween Boys take on thousands of vampires willing to die for their king and protect Belladonia and all its portals to pleasure?

This wasn't merely fighting monsters in the forest; this was worse and by far more dangerous. This was politics. The crowd cheered as Vincent helped the girl off her feet, ushering her back into the crowd and hopefully far, far from Belladonia. And he'd be wise to get equally far away from me.

"The next offering comes from our prince himself." I glanced over, unable to hide the ferocity in my features. My father smirked, noting my anger, but continued. "The prince has not been idle in his time away, and I am sorry, dear children, for keeping him a secret from so many of you." He circled us again. "You see, he has been assisting me the entire time, serving me diligently. And tonight, he will be the reason that *Queen Cassiopeia returns to us.*"

The crowd gasped and murmured. I moved between him and Blythe and snapped. "What the fuck are you playing at?"

Ignoring me, he raised his hands to silence the multitude as he addressed them. "My dear son, Belladonia's prince, has wooed, procured, and mated with a reaper. He is immune to her blood, my friends, and with his offering of her, we shall bring back our queen. He has just drunk from her, mixing their blood together as mates. I shall now take offerings from them both."

The crowd gasped and applauded. *A reaper. She's a reaper* they collectively murmured. Blythe let go of my arm and stepped away. "Did you plan this?" she asked in confusion. "Is this why you stole me away ..."

"No," I replied, fire burning in my throat. "And you'll step away from her, Vladimir." He'd joined her side and wrapped an arm around her shoulder. If I killed him here and now, how would we escape? I could feel the Halloween Boys' stares on my back. They were waiting for my lead. They'd back up whatever I did. If I wanted to slay my father, the vampire king, here and now in front of thousands who'd descend upon me, they'd be here fighting with me until the end. But Blythe … how could we get her away?

My belladonna scanned the crowd and the ceiling in a panic. She'd gotten better about planning ahead, about not trusting us. It was good, but not good enough.

My father noted her concern and chuckled. "Oh, are you looking for your bird?" He gestured behind his throne, where Raven bobbed and bit at the bars of his cage. "He cannot escape nor do magic inside a bewitched cage. I have plenty of them. You see, I have a familiar, too."

She looked to him with wide eyes and then to me as we both realized far too late. Lolth was his familiar.

Taking her hand, my father spun Blythe, and her gown flared out. I moved to attack then, but found myself frozen. He smirked, glancing over my shoulder at the three hooded spirits who'd appeared. They held me steady, as if I were merely standing there by choice. No strain or effort showed, and I sensed Blythe's confusion and fear. She thought I'd betrayed her; she thought I was handing her over and standing there to watch it transpire. *Never*, I wanted to scream. But it was no use. I felt her heart breaking inside me and could do nothing to stop it. Even my fire froze in my palms.

"The reaper wears the queen's gown. And with my blood, and the blood of my son, Cassiopeia shall be brought back to us." A gangly arm reached around me, and something sharp pierced through my chest. I wouldn't shout, wouldn't give anyone the satisfaction. Blythe cried out. I wished to touch her and ease her pain as she watched the needle impale my heart. Though something strange happened when it reappeared. The golden needle pulled from my chest was dry, with no blood to be seen. My father met my eyes in bewilderment but shook it off and pivoted back to Blythe.

There was screaming then, and I already knew why. Ghost, in all his demon might, with our werewolf trailing behind, prowled forward. Even the king revealed a hint of fright before nine hoods appeared, chanting. A glowing circle appeared around my friends then, and they were silenced inside as they raged against its walls. Vampires dodged out of the way, giving it space, while several cried in terror at what was happening. They were forced to watch as the king destroyed us all. The people here were as much his prisoners as I was now.

When I looked back to Blythe, she was lying on the ground, the king tipping a drink into her mouth. "Your mother's vessense," he explained, as if I were a part of this monstrosity. I fought against my invisible hold, hearing Ghost's and Wolf's roars of rage through their magical entrapment. My arms didn't budge. There was no fighting my way out, no sweet talk, no trick or hidden plan. There was nothing my vampire abilities could do to save us from the king of vampires himself. *Vlad the Impaler*, I'd heard the covens whisper. Impaling vampires, bleeding their hearts to add to his collection of blood and aid his obsession with his lost bride. What happened to a vampire after being drained of life-force for hundreds or thousands of years? What sort of beast would that create—

"Son," the king said calmly as Blythe's eyes shut. I heard her heart beating. She was okay for now. Though I raged inside, needing to be near her. What if she died thinking I'd betrayed her and used her for this? "Tell me. If I offered you a trade … If I said I'd let her live if you let this city of vampires, and your friends, die. Would you accept?"

I swallowed my burning fury and answered lowly. "Yes."

He chuckled darkly and strode toward me. "Then you are my son. You are *the Dracul*, as I would have called you. And we are more alike than you realize. Though you lie to me, my child, and this displeases me. Your ability to sense emotions doesn't only come from your mother's line, you know. You see, I have gifts as well. The moment I meet someone, I see their weakness as clear as the brightest night. Yours, Onyx Hart, is love. Your weakness is for acceptance, women, those in need, the pathetic among us. So very un-vampiric of you. Though very much like your mother." He smiled fondly, though the smile looked mad. The fucker had been playing me, playing Blythe … leveraging my weakness, my want for a father. Now all I wanted was to rip out his throat. I *would* rip out his throat.

He continued, "I know of Ash Grove, the little town that held you. You see," he glanced over at Ghost as blue smoke enveloped their cage, "I had demons, too. Though not quite as strong as your friend. They took females from wherever witches said they sensed your mother. The Halloween Boys, that's what you call yourselves, right? Charming. You and your friends killed most of the demons and some of them got away with girls. The witches told me they were unsuccessful. Though I did receive one gift from the demons as an apology for their failure. A baphomet. Something I sent roaming the earth in search of a reaper. A fool's errand. Finding Cassiopeia was all I cared about."

Pain and anguish twisted in my chest. "You don't care that those innocent girls died." My… Minnie. Ames's sisters. Others taken and god knows what done to them like Ellie May. "You don't care that Blythe could have been hurt on Halloween by that creature …"

"Your shortcomings and limitations are not mine. The only thing that concerns me is getting your mother back. The demons must have mistakenly sensed you instead, because you have so much of your mother in you. I would apologize for the confusion, but it seems my meddling did something to lift your personal enchantment and restore the memories your mother erased. Though somehow you picked up another curse, which bound you to Ash Grove for hundreds of years. A trade, it sounds like. Likely the work of a devil. They love trades. You know a devil, do you not?"

My mouth went dry, and I wished I could fall to my knees and burn the castle to the ground. But I had to ask, if even just to buy Blythe more time to recover. "Did you curse the town and the Halloween Boys for killing the demons? Did you slaughter the town or … did we?"

"I do not know what you speak of. Curses are not within my capability or desire. I could not have cursed you or your town, and I have no qualms with the mortals there, nor would I waste my resources. That was something else. Someone else. Though I perhaps regret not retrieving you sooner. Believe it or not, Onyx, I do care for you. We could still rule Belladonia together. Me, your mother, and you. A family of Drakons together at last. But first, I've been dying to bleed the hearts of your friends. An archdemon and an alpha werewolf? How divine."

The banshee shrieked. *She was here?* Maybe she was everywhere. Maybe the banshee was Belladonia herself, calling out from beyond and warning us all. Vampires screamed, and the sound of creatures gargling and snarling echoed through the mighty ballroom. I didn't look to see them flood inside, but I watched on as darkness surrounded Blythe, and she vanished. I hoped it was a reaper trick for her to escape and not ... something else. I met my father's stare then, feeling my vision glow. My father had set it all in motion by plaguing my town. He'd killed my first love, and now he'd taken my last. He looked at me with wonder and watched as I lifted higher off the ground, my body growing, changing. And the king's gaze transformed into true terror.

I'd relied heavily on my vampire strengths. I'd feared the power and carnal, uncontrollable ugliness of my beast. Though he'd been gnawing at his chains, begging to be set free. My pride and denial of who I was went too deep to let him loose. But here and now, in my mother's castle, I knew what she must have known at some point before she fled. Something she must have known when she named me, giving me a clue and reminder of who I was. She let me know that the blade would run clean and the reaper's kiss would not destroy my *onyx heart*. The bleeding heart would not be mine this day.

There was nothing I could do as a vampire. But there was plenty to be done as a dragon.

CHAPTER 37

Blythe

KNIGHTS AND DRAGONS

I love you because the entire universe conspired to help me find you.
Paulo Coelho

The Vampire King's face never looked happier than when he poured vessense down my throat. At least it tasted sweet this time. Sweet and familiar. And as my nightmares rose to greet me as darkness claimed me, I saw the legion and the baphomet and remembered the baphomet concocting a drink for me as well. Was it vessense? These were questions I thought I may never get to ask. Onyx could not have betrayed me so deeply, could he? He wouldn't have lured me to his father and sold me out. Unless he'd seen an opportunity to gain his favor and had taken it … no, I couldn't ruminate on that as my body faded out. But the way he just stood there watching haunted me. Cold, hard cement greeted me as I sat up in a familiar, dark room. It was the same room I'd disappeared to at the Phantom Circus. The same room my first sip of vessense brought to my mind. It was the room Onyx and I had been in when we'd contacted Ash Grove with Elysium in the forbidden forest.

"Well, this will be a boring room to die in," I muttered to myself before noticing a sliver of light. A door. I'd never seen a door in this place before. But I'd always assumed someone else brought me here—a phantom, a drink, a witch. Could it be I found this place on my own? Ezmerelda and the phantom had called it a holding place. An in-between.

I peeked through the door before pushing it open. Something grim, gray, and horrible wouldn't have been a shock. But a field of dandelions was. Birds chirped as I walked forward, shielding my eyes from the bright sun. There were no birds or bright sunshine in Belladonia, and my skin warmed and soaked in the rays of light. In the distance, a woman's back was turned to me. Her long blond hair grazed the grass around her ankles as she hung clothes on a line. I lifted my gown and strode nearer. "Excuse me," I shouted. "Can you help me?"

She took a pin from between her lips and secured a wet white shirt before turning.

"Hello." Her sing-song voice rang in my mind, though her mouth didn't move. She was stunning up close, with glittering green eyes and glowing, tanned skin. My mind fought to remember where I'd seen her before.

"You brought me here, Mortala. You tell me." She reached a hand to her chest. "Dear, your neck."

I touched my collarbone, feeling a trickle of blood. "Oh, yeah. Vampires."

Her expression turned apprehensive, and tension furrowed her blond brows. "What of vampires? Did one send you here?"

"I don't know," I answered honestly. Had King Vladimir sent me to this place?

She assessed me more quickly then and took a step back. Her head bumped into the clothesline. "Your dress … I know that gown. It was mine."

Understanding dawned, and I gasped. "Oh my … are you Queen Cassiopeia?"

There was a whooshing sound overhead, and the sun went dark for a moment before something enormous crashed to the ground. I dropped to my knees in fear, clutching the soft grass as if it would save me from what I was seeing. A gigantic winged creature—no, a dragon. A serpentine dragon with evergreen scales and jagged teeth hanging over its massive maw—stood behind the Queen and snarled at me, smoke rising from its nostrils. Each of its breaths sounded like waves crashing ashore. I couldn't speak. I could only stare at the mythical being I'd only heard of in fairy tales.

Queen Cassiopeia pulled me from my panic, her voice ringing in my mind. "Did he send you after me? I'm not coming back to him; you cannot force me."

"Yes, King Vladimir gave me a drink. I think it may have been your blood. It brought me, I think, but I don't mean you any harm. I-I know your son, Onyx Hart."

Her dragon's smoke ceased, and it straightened, widening its eyes and looking down at Cassiopeia.

She took a step forward, hands over her heart. Her long, flowy white gown shimmered in the sunlight. "You … you know my little prince? How … how is he?"

"He's … magnificent. Handsome, thoughtful, and kind. And so funny and smart." I looked up at her, feeling tears build behind my eyes. That man who gave me a rolled up vintage shirt to make me smile, who paid for my breakfast when I had nothing, who threw his body in front of mine when any monsters plagued us … he could have never betrayed me, I decided in that moment. King Vladimir was a liar, and he wouldn't steal an ounce of love I had for Onyx.

The queen took a seat in the grass in front of me, stroking a yellow dandelion. "It was the hardest thing I ever had to do, leaving my baby. But I had to escape Vladimir. I loved the king. I still love him, if I'm honest. But what he is, what he's become, is not good. Is he using you to bring me to him?"

"Yes, he's trying. Are you … dead?"

Her giggle echoed like a wind chime in my mind, making me smile. "Some would call it that, I suppose, in your realm. Here, to me, I've just moved on to this place."

"Is this Heaven?"

"Heaven is wherever your soul finds rest with those you love. So yes, I suppose this is my heaven. Vlad did well in laying claim to the magic of the city in the sky and its doorways to portions of utopias like mine. Vampires are remarkable when they want to be. However, I wish they'd share their ingenuity with others outside of their own kind."

I ran my fingers through a lush bed of clover, not brave enough to meet her kind gaze. "I'm sorry for the intrusion and for the questions. I don't really know what I'm doing. I feel this compulsion to bring you back, to give the man I love his mother again, to give the people back their gracious queen, but I won't if you don't want to."

Cassiopeia let out a breath. "I don't believe *Mortala* is one to give choices. We would call you that instead of *grim reaper*."

I actually liked that name, and something inside me resonated with it immediately, though I had no idea what it meant. "I guess I'm doing this my own way. I've been going crazy trying to figure out how I should or shouldn't be what I am, but I can't do that anymore. I have to go about this in a manner that honors the dead and the living and me, too."

I met her emerald gaze then, Onyx's emerald gaze, and it glowed like his. She smiled warmly. "I respect that. My son chose his mate well. Though he could stand to not mark you so painfully."

"Want to come back and scold him yourself?"

"I would have to face Vlad. What I did in leaving … his evil has only expanded in its search for me, and that is my burden to bear. I see it when I look upon him." She gestured to a scrying stone, the same as the one in the forbidden forest. "Instead of facing it, I have run, and it has cost many lives. Such a tragedy that space and time and death have not relieved me of my affections toward him. Nor him for me, it seems." She reached out and cupped my cheek tenderly. "And this is where our paths lead, dear. Always back to them. They will lay waste to everything in their paths to keep us. And that onus is likewise ours to bear, I suppose. We could have chosen the knight, but we prefer the dragon. We gave them a taste, and now they are slaves to their cravings." She reached up and ran a palm along the underside of her dragon's chin as it nuzzled into her touch like it was nothing but a kitten being petted.

She stood then and offered me her hand and said, "We are the women who fell in love with monsters."

CHAPTER 38

Dragon

DARK HEARTS

'There are darknesses in life and there are lights, and you are one of the lights, the light of all lights.
Bram Stoker, Dracula

At long last, my small flesh cave released me, allowing me to bathe this wretched and hate-filled place in warm, life-giving flame. The dark beings that attacked with ruthless gore, ripping heads of bloodsuckers and feasting on the dead, needed the light of my dragon fire. I flew overheard, scorching them, releasing souls from torment. Something reached me, a floating human in a chair. I felt he was my friend, somehow. The man with disheveled white-hair put down his bow when he saw me and shouted over the screams. "Hello, Dragon, I am Elysium. Help us with the diphylla. Leave the vampires and all others, okay?"

I appreciated the introduction and instruction. Onyx had kept me far away from his life, from the honor of having his friends be my own, but I still knew them. I heard them from the other room as I was locked inside. The archdemon and the werewolf found they could escape from their cages as men. They shifted back into men, and their human bodies were impressively strong as they fought. I would have been proud to have them ride my back in flight any time. I nodded toward the flying man, Elysium, and he dropped back into the crowd, firing his bow and slaying three of the diphylla at once. My keen vision spotted a new group entering the castle, and I swooped low, enjoying their frightened screeches as my fire released them.

Pleasant, blistering, avenging fire.

I remembered then, who else needed avenging. Her, our love, our heart's song, Blythe. Landing in a thud of power, I searched for her, smelling every inch of space. She'd disappeared, but I'd find her for us. I'd burn the one who took her. The wolf man ran up to me then, and I enjoyed finally being much taller than he was. "Hey, Dragon. Way to be the star of the show, as usual."

I didn't comprehend his meaning. Dragons were always the greatest fighters in any battle. The one with the bright blue eyes walked forward, gallantly covered in the burgundy blood of enemies. "We saved the king for you. If you want him, he's yours." The demon man pointed his sword toward the throne, where the king stood, surveying the carnage as his people fought and died needlessly. "Elysium says Blythe is in another realm. She's okay."

Onyx would want the king, his sire, to die. I wanted him to die.

The white haired one with the crossbow slashed through a group of five diphylla as they squealed and writhed their slow deaths. The three men cleared a path for me, and I stalked toward the king. He didn't balk or run. Only sat on his throne, scrutinizing my approach. Vampires bowed and kneeled, honoring my grandeur, as I walked past. As we reached the podium, our sire spoke to Elysium with a sneer. "You found your way back in, I see. You took my wife and have come back to challenge me, I presume?"

Elysium tapped his fingers consideringly along his crossbow. "I helped her because she asked me to. Your hate and fixation created this. It turned your people into these creatures. Do you feel no remorse for what your evil has wrought upon this place? Did you not love her as I did?"

"I care *only* for her," he rumbled. "And no one could ever love Cassiopeia more than me."

Vampires screamed and fought as diphylla continued to lunge in ruthless attacks. I knew they smelled similar. The creatures were vampires gone mad. I knew they were trapped; I knew I was freeing them with holy blaze. My companions made to rejoin the battles when the hooded figures encircled us, reaching out their bone hands. The king lifted a finger, halting them, and looked up to me finally.

"You are as glorious as she was." There was great sadness behind his eyes, not the bloodlust of a captain of war. "Go ahead and kill me, son. I drove her away, and I could not find her, could not bring her back to fix all I've destroyed. My failure has seeped into Belladonia and spread sickness, turning vampires to monsters nearly as ruthless as I am. There is nothing left for me in this realm. Send me to Hell for my punishment. For no hellfire could be worse than living this life without my bride."

The men looked to me as my fire collected in my throat. One burst seemed too quick, but it would have to do. I reared back, and the king closed his eyes. My fire rippled over my tongue and heated my maw, but then darkness overtook the ballroom. Something thumped onto the marble floor, and then another, and then dozens more. When I turned, vampires marred in grime and blood stood over the twitching creatures who'd dropped dead. The darkness had released the creatures, some-how. When I looked again, there she was, the most beautiful being, looking up at me. Blythe. Oh, how we loved her. My fire dissolved in my mouth as I lowered my head before her. She reached out slowly and pet my snout. "Nice to meet you, Dragon. I'm Blythe."

A purr rattled my chest, and she giggled. Somewhere inside me, Onyx said, *I love that sound.* Over her shoulder stood another woman. One I recognized from long ago. She placed both hands on her chest, and her voice swam through my mind. "Onyx, my sweet baby boy, my little prince."

ONYX

I lowered and lowered, until two feet, not four, touched the ground. Taking Blythe into my arms, I kissed her hair. "I'd never—"

"I know." She kissed my shoulder and pulled away, looking to the blond woman. My mother. Emotion gripped my throat as she opened her arms, pulling me in for a hug. Her smell rushed back to me then, the smell I'd fought to remember and chased for two hundred years. Grass, firewood, and flowers. Rushing waters and sunshine. "I left you, but I will never leave you again. I'm back now." Her voice, like a harp, sang in my mind as tears flowed down my face. When we turned, my father, the king, was on his knees, looking to the ground. I moved to stand in front of my mother, to protect her from him, to keep him from ever hurting her again. She moved a hand to my chest and tilted her chin, moving me out of the way. Blythe and my friends surrounded me then. I held my wife in my arms as Ames and Wolf put their arms around my back. They'd witnessed my dragon, and they were still here. They still loved me, somehow.

My attention returned to my mother, who was even more ethereal than the paintings conveyed. My father's stained black soul didn't deserve her. My mother was ten times the king he could ever be. I felt it in my soul as her righteousness enveloped the throne room. Vampires looked on with gasps of awe. The lowly ruler of Belladonia trembled before her, not a king in that moment, but something pathetic and tired. She tilted his chin, and he sighed at her touch while her voice echoed for us all to hear. "My love, what have you done?"

He wrapped his hands around her wrist and looked up into her eyes, pleading. "I had to find you, Cassiopeia."

"You chased after my soul."

"Yes."

She glanced around at the destruction, at the bloodied vampires who'd stayed to watch on, and the dead diphylla. "You bled their hearts, and after many years, they devolved into those beasts. All to find an answer in their blood to find me."

"I did, and I would do it again to have you."

The queen shook her head softly and sighed. "You should die for what you've done, for prying me from my peace, for tormenting our kingdom and using our son."

The king reached into his cloak and pulled out a dagger. I made to step forward, but Elysium, who I hadn't noticed at my side, reached out an arm to stop me. The king flipped it, gripping the blade, and handed my mother the handle. "Kill me then, for I was already dead without you. At least now I can die at the hand of my love, knowing I lived for one more moment because I was able to feel you once more."

Blythe held her heart, and I felt her tear slide down my arm.

My mother took the jeweled dagger and pointed it between his eyes, but instead of going for his neck or chest, she nudged off his crown. It fell to the marble with a clank. "You will hand over Belladonia to me. I will be queen, and you will serve under me as I set things right, as I rebuild what you have destroyed. We will work to earn our son and his family's trust in whatever way they deem necessary. Do you agree to this?"

The king let out a breath, and I was sure he'd scoff and turn her away, but instead, he only nodded. "You can have it all. The kingdom, my castle, my servitude. Every door, every key, is yours. I would rather be a peasant for you than a king for thousands."

Even my own heart gave way at that. Maybe somewhere inside him, my father did love my mother as more than an obsession. Her face softened then, and she pulled him to stand. He towered over her and reached out, cupping her small face in his hands. Tears streaked his proud cheeks as he said, "My love, my bride, my queen. Please, stay with me now."

He'd burned the world for her. He'd torn through realms, killed hundreds of thousands, made deals with Hell, and collected so much blood he'd created horrors. All for my mother. All to get her back. He'd asked me earlier if I would do the same for Blythe.

The honest understanding dawned on me, watching this proud, ancient, evil man quiver before his love. I would indeed do the same for Blythe, or for Ames or Wolfgang. They were the loves of my life, and like my father, I was no good man. The earth could burn into cinders of ash if only I could have them. Like my mother said, they were my family. The family I'd searched for clutched me now. They'd had me all along. They were each bloodied and bruised for me. And I knew then, looking at each of them, that I was just as crazed as my father. I'd be their Dracul and their Dragon. I would become a beast to keep them safe. I'd roam the realms for all my days chasing their love.

I would bleed my heart dry for them.

CHAPTER 39

Blythe

SCARIER THAN NIGHTMARES

> The minute I heard my first love story, I started looking for you, not knowing how blind that was. Lovers don't finally meet somewhere. They're in each other all along.
> *Rumi*

Raven stretched his wings after I unlatched his cage. I stroked his chest as my thoughts tried to catch up with everything that had happened. Somehow, I'd communed with the dead in the beyond and brought back Onyx's mom. And I'd done it in my own way, on my own terms. I'd only ever considered the death within me and never the power of life I held. Something inside me felt proud as Raven nudged his cool beak to my cheek. Maybe I was growing into my abilities at my own speed and becoming the kind of reaper—or *Mortala*, as Cassiopeia said—that I wanted to be. And then there was the complicated love I'd witnessed between the king and his lost queen. I felt it would take years to unravel my feelings about that. But for now, they seemed contented as they held hands and excused themselves, leaving the Halloween Boys and Elysium and me standing among the wreckage of the Bleeding Heart Ball.

Ames hugged me from behind and nuzzled into my neck. "I'm killing him for marking you."

"No, you're not." I slapped his arm playfully. "I'm fine, and you're covered in blood, too."

Wolfgang stretched as he sauntered over from where he was speaking with Onyx and the vampire hunter. "Well, looks like we've thoroughly wrecked another party. But wait, let me get this straight. The king was responsible for taking girls in Ash Grove and sending demons because he was looking for his wife. And he's been collecting blood for experiments and to use blood magic to bring her back, turning vampires into diphylla in the process?"

Onyx appeared next to me and crossed his arms. "Yes."

"And he made Blythe drink vessense to bring Queen Cassiopeia back from the dead after attempting to bleed his own son's heart?"

"Yes," Onyx answered.

Wolf turned to me. "And you brought her back?"

I bit my lip. "Well, yes, but I gave her the choice, and she wanted to return."

Wolf ran a hand through his beard. "So, King Vladimir's evil master plan worked … and we're supposed to be happy about that?"

"The bad guys win again, I guess." Onyx shrugged. "Obviously my birth family is a bit complicated, but if my mother feels that my father can change, I support her. Maybe I got one good parent out of the deal."

Ames gave me a squeeze. "Okay then. Let's get cleaned up."

I asked hesitantly, "And then back home … to Ash Grove?" I met Onyx's eyes then, and we all turned to him. He'd come so far, been through so much—would he be coming back with us?

He only smiled and put an arm around Wolf. "Yeah, let's go home."

Elysium interrupted after looking after the queen with longing eyes. My heart twisted for him as I wondered what his story with her entailed. His chair whirled and clicked as he hovered next to us. I'd wished I could have seen him fight. He was covered in more blood than Ames and Wolf combined.

"Sorry to interrupt, but there have been changes in Ash Grove since you left. I'm not certain what's going on, but when you mentioned two years had passed, I investigated it. Something is going haywire with the magic there. It's similar to how it was thrown off kilter here in Belladonia, making way for the creation of diphylla."

I looked to the guys before asking, "So how do we fix it? Yesenia mentioned a blood ritual." *So did the devil, but they weren't allowed to know that ...*

"You four have tremendous power together. I don't believe chance is what brought you into each other's lives. A blood ritual is necessary to unite you all together, to combine your souls' purpose."

"How do we do that?" Ames questioned.

"I will contact your friend, the witch, Yesenia, and we will weave a spell tomorrow night. You will need to combine your vessense for the spell to take hold."

Wolf gave Raven a gentle stroke before saying, "Combine our vessense? You mean orgasmic blood? Blood during sex?"

"You sound like Blythe," Onyx teased, and I was happy to hear his usual mirth returning to his voice after this whole ordeal.

"Yes, it would be the only way the spell would grab hold of you all as a unit. I'm a blood witch. Blood is the essence of life, or vessense, as the vampires call it. It has more magical properties than we could ever discover. King Vladimir was not wrong in that belief. Blood holds the power to build and destroy worlds, the ability to unite beings and to destroy them. Vampires use blood for sex or recreation, while some, like me, believe that is only scratching the surface of what blood magic is capable of. And I believe blood magic is the key to helping you fully become what you are, Blythe."

I sighed, overwhelmed by the influx of information. Ames scooped me into his arms and kissed my cheek. "Let's get you a bath and some food. We'll sort this all out after that." I was so thankful for my demon in that moment, always sensing what I needed.

I asked him to stop, and he paused on down the dais stairs. "Elysium, do you mind if we stay at your place? I've had enough creepy castles to last a lifetime."

He chuckled. "I don't blame you. And of course, your suite is just as you left it. It may work better that way if I'm closer. I'll be downstairs performing the ritual. We'll begin tomorrow night."

I tried not to think about my first-time having sex with all three of my men happening right above Elysium.

*T*HEIR BLOOD. *The blood of the Halloween Boys holds your purpose, your fate, and maybe even the key to fixing your home.* The words rang through my ears as I rested my head on Ames's shoulder. I felt the cool post-storm air invade my lungs as the guys all spoke softly, carrying me down the castle steps and back into the city of vampires. As my eyes drifted shut at the overwhelming relief of having my men around me, I wondered if all of Belladonia knew they'd just lost their vampire king to a dragon.

***

O*NYX MUST HAVE KEPT* me in my dreams because I vaguely perceived being bathed by three pairs of gentle hands. They didn't want to wake me as they cared for me, and I sighed into the feeling of warm water over my naked flesh. And then I was dry and warmed and laid on a bed under the soft murmur of their mingled voices. My favorite sound in the world was them all together, whole, and content. Listening to them as I slept was like overhearing a conversation from another room and feeling comforted by the presence of others. It made me wonder if the rooms I went to when I disappeared were like that, if perhaps death was just another room away. Maybe death was just a door we all walked through eventually, inside the same house as our loved ones. Those thoughts fell like raindrops in my dream. But even Onyx's induced slumber couldn't keep the nightmares away forever. I attracted evil, and darkness clung to me wherever I went. There was no rest to be found behind my eyelids as his touch wore off faster and faster now, for some reason.

I was alone in a forest that was half Ash Grove and half Belladonia. My stepfather stumbled forward, slurring curses as the legion sprayed out of his chest. I thrashed, feeling them descend upon me. Then suddenly, it wasn't the legion's claws and hate piercing me anymore. Their touch transformed into something else. A featherlight embrace that beckoned to me from somewhere beyond my consciousness. I was still in the forest, but I was lying down as the legion of shrieking demons turned to ash and floated away.

Something large took me into his hold, and I reclined back into a large chest. His palms brushed up my ribs and under my breasts, holding them firmly. And then what felt like a snake's tongue pinched at my nipple. I jerked beneath my firm protector, who smelled like maple trees and honeysuckle. My awareness answered my dizzy thoughts, and I knew I was lying atop Wolfgang.

The tongue that explored my nipples and lapped between my cleavage was long and dripping with desire. My archdemon was somewhere above me, his tongue exploring and teasing before finally lapping gently at the punctures on my neck, the spot where Onyx drank so fiercely. A sigh shocked through me, and I was surprised to find the area tender yet still releasing reverberations of pleasure as Ghost's tongue pressed and licked.

The licking pulled back then, and I reached out for it again as Wolf softly massaged my breasts, rolling his rough thumbs along the sensitivity of my hard nipples. My eyes opened slightly to see a blurry, pale light-drenched room. It was morning, and my men were gifting me with pleasure as I dozed in and out of lucidity. I made out the lazy smirk of my vampire-dragon prince as someone pulled me down, my head resting between Wolf's thighs. It was then that I really wanted to be awake. I forced my sleepy eyes open as someone straddled above me, and I felt Onyx's slippery tip prod at my lips. When I looked up, I caught his kiss colliding into Wolf's, as the werewolf's palms continued to roam my breasts. Opening my mouth greedily, already feeling my slickness dripping down my slit, I licked at him, letting my tongue explore Onyx's cock as Ghost's tongue had just explored me.

Gentle hands spread my legs wide as they hung over the side of the bed. As I wrapped my lips around Onyx, Ghost pushed into my wanting, ravenous cunt. I cried out, and taking advantage of my scream, Onyx thrust in, hitting the back of my throat. I gagged on his cock as Ghost plunged into me again, forcing me to adjust to his massive demon size, the feel of his stretch burning and filling me. Each thrust out and back in was blissful agony. I pulled off Onyx, not sure if, in my just-woken-up haze, I could focus on him while Ghost increased his speed between my thighs.

"You can take them both, little one," Wolfgang rumbled as he inserted three rough fingers between my lips, hooking them on my bottom teeth and opening my mouth wide. He gripped Onyx's hips then and eased him into my mouth. We all groaned as I choked around Wolf's digits and Onyx's shaft.

The vampire's hand then wrapped around Wolf's sizable length that was erect next to my cheek. He pumped him in time with us, his knuckles brushing against my face. I joined him, reaching my palm up and gripping at Wolf's massive girth. Wolf pushed his hips forward, which gave way to better access for my mouth as I sucked Onyx's cock with sloppy wetness dripping down my chin and the sides of my cheeks. I wanted to feel all of their cum all over me, filling me to my brink and dripping down my every opening.

My peak grew quickly with voracious pressure as Ghost slammed into me in time with Onyx's guided thrusts. I moaned around his cock, feeling his grip reach feverishly into my hair. I came, letting my orgasm shred through me as my walls clenched around my archdemon. He groaned his release in time with Onyx, who plunged forward, spilling himself down my throat with hot and salty bitterness. Ghost's black release pooled inside my pussy, warming my lower belly and making my cunt pulse and throb in sensitive acceptance of all he'd give. Wolf-gang came then, in ribbons of warm ecstasy, painting my face. I pulled off Onyx, swallowing what was left of him in my mouth, and licked my lips, taking my hand and pulling Wolf's flavor onto my tongue. I grabbed Onyx's hand then and licked him clean from Wolf's release, both men watching with pure adoration in their gaze.

"You're extraordinary," the werewolf breathed.

Ghost then shoved Onyx off and took me in his arms, forcing Wolf to move so he could lie beside me like we always did. The guys made their mock grumbles but obliged while getting dressed.

They left with promises of breakfast and coffee while my archdemon shifted into his human form and stroked my hair. I kissed his jaw and took him between my arms and legs. I couldn't get close enough as I nuzzled into his chest.

He chuckled darkly. "Good morning, little ghost. How'd you sleep?"

"I preferred the waking up part."

He nibbled at my ear while his thumb drew idle circles on my hip. "Onyx has good ideas occasionally."

I giggled softly, trailing my finger down the line of his hard abdomen. "I'm glad you've forgiven him and we're all together."

Ames gave me a squeeze. "I understand why he did what he did, though I won't tolerate you being taken away like that by anyone ever again."

"I don't think you have to worry. Who would even try?"

A slash of red and fire and a graveled chuckle flashed through my mind at that moment. Leaving my body warmed again and wondering if I was imagining things. I was probably still sorting through my nightmares, because being taken by a certain devilish someone in red would certainly be a nightmare of hellish proportions. I settled back into my lover's embrace and into the security my men offered. I knew I was safe … for now.

CHAPTER 40

Onyx

BEAUTIFUL DEATH

> I would die for her. I would kill for her. Either way, what
> bliss.
>> *Gomez, The Addams Family*

I met my mother in the rose garden in the courtyard of Vladimir's gloomy castle. She looked like a ray of sunshine piercing through a storm cloud as she sat on the stone bench waiting for me. When I hugged her, I felt all the motherly warmth I'd been searching for, and at last I finally felt like my quest was worth it.

"Where is Vladimir?" I asked after we said hello.

She sighed, and her voice sang through my mind. "With the aid of my touch, he is indulging in sleep for a while."

In his coffin, I presumed. "I'd support you if you wanted to make that a permanent sleep."

I felt her amusement ring like bells behind my ribs, and my dragon stirred, feeling comforted by the nurturing sound. "Your father is one of the oldest and original vampires, and his line of vampires, my love, comes from dragons. We are not so different from each other."

Shock tensed my shoulders as I surveyed her serene face and formal posture. "How can that be?"

"The Drakons had fangs and abilities relating to emotions, the ability to transform into beasts, and of course, your onyx stone hearts that cannot bleed. I am a dragon, from a line of long-gone dragons. Our dragons live inside us until we move on from this realm and we are reunited as two separate beings, though we will still always be one with them. Your father and I had no idea if we would be blessed with a child, but I suppose with his lineage, we should have suspected that it was possible. I loved him dearly. He was much different back then. And he loved you, too, incredibly so. Who he became, who he is now, I do not know that man. His obsession was in possession of me, hoarding me away like gold, which, of course, is another Drakon family proclivity he inherited. He became obsessed with blood; it was his treasure trove. Collecting it in vials, experimenting, using it to control. He wanted your blood, wanted to test you, to infuse you with other bloods to make you stronger. I couldn't allow it; I wouldn't subject you to his infatuation. So, with Elysium's help, I escaped. I had every intention of staying with you in Ash Grove, but I heard the drag-on's call. I knew you'd be safest there, so I left you with a kind mortal family and erased your memory of your father and me. It was the hardest thing I've ever done." My mother looked at me then with watery eyes. "I'm not sure I did the right thing, but I am back from the beyond, thanks to your mate, to try to make amends. With you, with the people here."

"You don't need to make amends with me … Mother." It felt nice calling someone that for once. "You did what you had to do."

With her hand on my chest, her voice reverberated through me like a symbol crash. "Dragon, thank you for protecting my son. You are good. You are both so *good*."

My throat tightened with emotion. "I'm anything but good."

"Your family, your mates, the way they look at you, tells me that you are. Your dragon tells me that you are. I hope that you come to see that in yourself, as the ones who love you do. Though you should let Dragon out more often. He needs the sunlight and socialization."

I dried my eyes and exhaled. "I can't believe you gave up whatever paradise is beyond to come back to this hellhole."

"It's just a visit for a while." She smiled. "I do miss my dragon, though. She is inside me now, as yours is." She pawed at a rose and grimaced. "I will admit, however, that I find roses a horrid flower."

I chuckled. "Well, now I know what *not* to send you for Mother's Day. Are you going to be all right here? I'm sure I can convince my crew to stay if you need us."

"I'm fine. It will be a lot of work to restore what has been damaged, but we'll survive. And I have Elysium to help as well. Though our feelings for each other are complicated, I believe we'll manage."

"What a con that his most impressive and hidden title was not only immortal, but a queen rescuer."

"Elysium has many secrets. If Vlad weren't so possessive, perhaps things could have been different." She exhaled and shook her head before standing, her blond hair brushing the ground. She outstretched her hand. "Would you like to play music with me?"

And so we did. Outstretching a melody over the city of vampires that had just been claimed by a mighty dragon queen.

MY FAMILY AWAITED me that evening, telling me tales of their explorations of the city and its many doors. Many covens had retreated back to their homes or through their respective doors after the attack at the Bleeding Heart Ball. But some still lingered in the aftermath. Honestly, they seemed excited about the changes to come to Belladonia. I still worried about my mother, but she gifted me a key so that I could return at any time. I added it to the silver chain around my neck, and the room hushed as I entered.

Wolfgang stood from the table covered in smoked meats. "Everything go okay?"

I nodded. "My father's in his coffin for now, and my mother seems shockingly normal to have spawned something like me."

"Hush." Blythe rolled her eyes, taking a sip of wine. "You are *good*, Onyx Hart."

Something bloomed in my chest when she unknowingly repeated my mother's words, grasping that they'd both been saying them to me for a long time. Maybe someday I'd believe them. Perhaps I was closer to believing them now than I ever was before.

Ames assessed me and thankfully changed the subject. "Something *not* good seems to be whatever has happened in Ash Grove in our absence. It would appear more time has passed there than it has here."

"What's happening?" Blythe asked.

"Elysium said that Yesenia and Cat were vague, which doesn't surprise me. I'm assuming the Damned have reeked some havoc, and the witches have likely made a mess of everything. I'm sure it's nothing we can't remedy when we return. Though I am concerned. There seems to be a correlation between the potency of the energy in Belladonia and in Ash Grove. Like two very magical places in the universe." He refilled Blythe's wineglass and sliced Wolf and me a glance as she focused on her drink. A glance we knew meant there was more he wasn't saying. A glance that said something was wrong.

Blythe took a small sip, her golden-brown hair cascading down her shoulder. I could get used to seeing her in dresses. They were so flowy and provided such easy access for all my wicked desires. "I guess tonight is the night we do the … blood thing."

"Only if you want to," Ames answered with authority. Wolf and I nodded our agreement.

Wolfgang ran a hand through his hair. "There seems to be some magical benefit to us uniting with blood bonds. Werewolves have similar practices reserved for the strongest of mates within the pack. At most, it rallies our abilities to help Ash Grove and face any future threats. At the least, it's …"

"Hot as hell," I interjected.

They all chuckled as Wolf punched my arm. "Says the vampire."

"Dragon-vampire," I added.

His answering smile was too damn sweet as he wrapped an arm around me and squeezed. "Dragon-vampire who missed out on a pirate battle."

"What?" I asked, looking to Ames.

He leaned back in his seat casually. "Swords, cannons. Captain Vex's parrot was almost eaten by a shark …"

"Lies," I hissed. "Those are like the games we played as boys."

Wolfgang said, "Exactly the same, and you missed out, bud."

My friends continued jeering me as Blythe laughed. I'd traveled so far to find what I already had in front of me, and they'd supported the journey. Blythe was my raging fire, Wolf was my warming flame, and Ames my smoldering coal. Perhaps I would never be a good man, but I would always be their villain, doing anything for them. It was in my blood as a vampire, and it was in my soul as a dragon.

As the moon grew higher in the sky, the flames and heat in the room intensified, along with our hungry glances at our mate. Ames and Wolfgang pulled themselves away to go downstairs and talk with Elysium. They played like it was to get the details on the blood ritual, but I knew them, and I knew they were assessing his trustworthiness. For good reason. Apparently the guy had been in love with my mom forever, which was … something to unpack another day. Blythe was looking out the window, her emotions hard to read. I knew that face, that lonesome current pulling me under her waves. Her melody played in my mind again then. The one I couldn't ever catch, but I was so, so close. I'd heard my mother's song on her harp, and it had my fingers aching for a guitar or a piano. But at that moment, looking at Blythe, I ached most for her. Leaning on the windowpane, I reached into my pocket and took out the silver trinket.

When I placed it in her palm, she eyed me with that skeptical glance I'd loved from the first moment she flashed it at me in the diner where we met. "When we were exploring doors, I found one full of gumball machines, and as expensive as my personal tastes may be, I felt you'd prefer something like this."

She turned it over in her hand as a radiant smile touched her perfect lips. Slipping it on her finger, she giggled. "You got me a mood ring?"

I tugged at a lock of her hair. It would always be worth it, making a fool of myself for her, just for that smile alone. "I'm waiting for the joke about how I'm moody or because I read your moods or change your moods … go on."

She twisted herself under my arm and lay her head on my chest, letting me inhale her sweet scent. "Too easy," she teased. Reaching out her hand, she admired the ring. "It's perfect … and I guess my mood is black. I love it."

I kissed her head, daring to ask the question that had plagued me since we met and especially after. Her prevailing emotion, the under-woven fabric of every feeling I picked up on from her—it was the beat to every laugh and every fear just the same. "Why are you so lonely, even when the guys and I are near?"

Her big brown eyes met mine in wonder. Glancing back to the misty street, she laced her fingers with mine. "Melancholy is in everything I do. It's the feeling I'm most at home with."

I tilted my head to inspect her, intrigued. "You enjoy being sad?"

"I like the dark and storms and monsters, and maybe I like life tinged with a bit of sorrow. It makes the good moments more beautiful, more potent, I think." She shrugged. "Do you think I'm crazy?"

"I think you're exquisite."

Her answer was a kiss, honeyed and dark, just like her. I gripped the back of her neck, feeling my fangs ache to taste her like this. I heard the guys' footsteps and the creak of the door as they returned. Reluctantly I pulled back, taking her hand and leading her to the fireplace. A giant bearskin rug and various blankets and pillows were dispersed around it, just below the foot of the grand canopy bed. "As good a place as any for an evil, demonic blood ritual, huh?"

"Works for us," Wolf answered, tugging off his shirt. My cock jolted as I watched Blythe's eyes roam his form. I thought then that I'd love to watch them together. To see him fuck her in that meditative and rapt way of his. Ames enclosed his arms around her from behind, pushing her dress strap over her shoulder.

"How are you, little ghost?" he purred, kissing her neck in the place I'd like to be.

She met his glance and kissed his lips before turning to us. "A little nervous, honestly. How do we do this? The ritual part, I mean."

Ames answered, "We combine our blood during sex, all of us. I'm sure Onyx will take the lead in that department."

"Gladly." Moving to stand in front of her, I pulled on the other strap, and her gown floated down her cleavage, stopping on the fullest part of her breasts. "My bite looks lovely there."

Ames growled in disapproval but didn't argue. I was sure I'd hear about it later. For now, blood was the most important thing on the menu. It was my time to shine, to sample each of them and create a cocktail of us all. My mouth watered, and my cock strained against my pants in response. "My belladonna," I whispered, dropping to my knees and tugging her gown to the floor. I wrapped my arms around her thighs, pulling her hips to my face, relishing the hair that awaited me there. I took Ames's hand and pulled it to my mouth, grinning before biting his palm. His eyelids grew heavy as blood dripped down our girl's side. He pulled his hand to her breasts, and she reclined into his embrace as he continued to drip, streaking her in red. I pressed my nose into her cunt, inhaling before pushing my hands between her soft thighs. Letting my tongue explore, I lapped at her taste, detecting notes of Ghost's cum from earlier. They tasted nice together. Like nectar and spice.

She looked to Wolf, who'd moved to sit in front of the fire. He'd already removed his clothes and was slowly stroking his length. I'd always thought he looked most at home naked. His physique was too glorious for clothing. "Can I have you?" she asked him.

I felt his adoration and excitement at her request as he responded. "Always. Come here."

She made her way over, and Wolf took her palms and led her to the adjacent bed. He lay back over the bed with his feet on the ground and helped her straddle his wide frame, placing her knees on the edge of the bed. She lowered atop his lap, his thick cock resting between the folds of her cunt. Her hands roamed the hair on his chest, down to his biceps and back up to his jaw, before she bent forward and kissed him. He grunted into her kiss, revealing just how badly he'd been wanting it, just how long the wait to have her had been for him. He'd snap eventually. Maybe even worse than I did. His alpha sol tendencies were a ticking bomb, and Blythe would have been wise to prepare for him. I hoped this night would go far in taming his beast, holding him off for a little longer.

She reached her hand down and gripped him, rubbing him from shaft to tip, slicking him with her arousal. He put his hands on his head, as if he were restraining himself. I smirked. "Fuck her, Wolf. She can take it. Isn't that right, Ghost?"

Ames and I removed our shirts and kicked off our jeans and boxers, then stood next to them. "If she can take me, I'm sure she can handle you," Ames replied. It wasn't a taunt. He was right; Ghost was fucking huge.

Wolf's resolve snapped then, and he grabbed her hips, picking her up and slamming her onto his cock. She cried out, shocked and elated, as he growled a feral, primal sound. I moved behind her and bent to kiss her neck. Leaning her head back, she groaned and tensed, antici-pating what I'd do next. But her neck would only be kissed by me for now. I kneeled behind her, rubbing her perfect ass as Wolf thrust into her. She was on all fours, the way he liked it, her perfect ass bouncing as she rode him. I shot Ames a glance as he leaned against the bedpost, blood dripping down his forearm. He shook his head. "Go ahead. I don't blame you. I've considered it myself, and I'm not even a vampire."

"Considered what?" Blythe asked with a breathy whimper until Wolf raised his hips and released a moan, penetrating her deeper.

"This," I answered, moving fast and sinking my aching fangs into her ass cheek.

She screamed in ecstasy, riding her first orgasm atop the werewolf as her blood streamed down the back of her leg and down Wolf's hip.

I moved behind her then, my cock unable to wait any longer, as Ames climbed onto the bed, knees on either side of Wolf's head. He positioned his dick near her face, and she immediately took him in her hand and guided him into her mouth. He hissed and grabbed her hair. "You're perfect, little ghost. Look how well you're taking each of us."

She moaned against him as I prodded against her ass, teasing her opening with my thumb, pressing it in and out to ready her for me. With each thrust Wolf made, I pushed my cock closer until she had no escape. I nudged my tip inside, and as she cried out; I wrapped my hand around her hair, bringing her neckline to my mouth. The angle tensed my cock in the best way possible as she stretched from Wolf and from me. I bit down as she moaned, heightening her pleasure and drinking in her pain. Another shredding of bliss racked through her as her screams were muffled by Ames's standing and returning his cock to her mouth.

His blood dripped down her cheek and mingled in her hair while her blood flowed down her neck and ass while she rode Wolf. She was a wicked blood painting and an evil gathering's plaything.

"Our slaughtered, bleeding lamb. An offering," Ames murmured lowly.

Wolfgang sat up, yanking her close with a rumble. "Drink me, too," he ordered me.

As he stilled inside her, I thrust in another inch, and she whimpered. "Good girl," I assured her. "You're taking three cocks so good. We knew you would."

She resumed her position on all fours as I pressed into her, leaning forward and finding Wolf's bulging neck. I licked at his sweat and savored the salty taste before tearing into his flesh. He groaned, gripping the back of my head and thrusting hard into Blythe. She screamed, which elicited a hiss from Ames as he made her gag on his girth. I continued my rhythm, too, as did Ames between her lips, as I drank from my werewolf. I was messy with it, just to get the blood coating us all. I didn't have to be gentle with him like I did with Blythe. I knew my friend liked it rough. Wolf's blood flowed down his chest, coating Blythe's breasts in red, mixing with Ghost's. All that was left was me. I pushed my arm toward Wolf, and he knew instantly what I was asking. His canines were thick and painful, made for killing, not for tasting, but he bit down on my forearm, spilling my blood between us all.

Our sighs and moans mingled together as our thrusts intensified. We thrust and rode fervently, my front pressed to Blythe's back, Wolf pressed against her breasts, and Ames with one hand in Wolfgang's hair and another wrapped around the back of Blythe's neck as she sucked him. Our hands collectively roamed her flesh as she writhed and dipped between us. We etched her in red and black, the same hues of the the wicked woods, she was our enchanted land. Ours to mark, to claim, to get lost in.

Ames grunted his release into Blythe's mouth. It was so much, so heavy, so influenced by his demon, that it spilled black from the sides of her lips and dripped down her chin and onto Wolf's throat, adding inky black to the red canvas we'd made of her. Wolf's release came with a roar as it shot inside. His cock knotted, holding his seed in place in the deepest parts of her. I was jealous of that werewolf feature; I would love to be able to do such a thing. When I came, my bliss shattered me as I poured into her, pooling from her ass. The taste of her blood was on my tongue, mixed with Wolf's and Ames's, the three of us filling her and marring her with red and black, tying her to our bodies as one.

A euphoric haze fogged the room like smoke. Or was it actual smoke?

Still connected to us each, Blythe struggled to catch her breath as she looked around, unable to pull from Wolf if she tried. "What's happening?"

"I'm not sure." I heard Ames say somewhere in the distance, but when I looked to him, he was gone. And so were Wolf and Blythe. And dusk a deep shade of the blackest garnet enveloped me, pulling me under its bloody expanse.

If love was death, then I was dead. My onyx heart ripped from my chest and bleeding at my beloved's feet. Every unholy offering from me, half beast, half monster, belonged to my belladonna. Ghost's deadly nightshade, Wolf's Bane, Devil's cherry, Beautiful Death, Sweet poison — all ancient names of the flower of death, and they were all talking about her, and us: a gruesome and wicked prophecy.

A garden of deadly flowers. And it was there in the comforting shadow of unconsciousness that the riff clicked into place. The crescendo built and exploded with perfect harmony. The lyrics joined together. Death was my love, and I'd spend eternity dying for her. I would title it "Death's Love Song."

CHAPTER 41

Blythe

BELLADONNA

> And so being young and dipped in folly I fell in love with melancholy.
>
> *Edgar Allan Poe*

My knees were braced on silk. My inner thighs still felt the stretch his hips forced, my body still aching and covered in the blood of my lovers. But instead of waking in a pile of blankets and draped in their strong arms, my cheek pressed into soft grass. I sat up slowly as my head spun. *The blood ritual.* Around me, moss-covered stones appeared in the glow of a bright, full moon. I knew this place, recognized the smell of hollow earth. I brushed off my gown as I stood, saying a silent thanks to whatever force clothed me before sending me here. Rough and crumbling stone scratched my palm as I walked by the grave of James Cove, my ghost. Wandering through Ash Grove Cemetery, I searched for my Halloween Boys. Surely they were transported here, too.

Something translucent floated past me, and I turned to see Maud, one of my ghostly friends. "You're back," she said plainly, knitting something with her see-through fingers. "I'm glad. The feline is terribly bossy."

"Hi, Maud. Have you seen Ghost or Raven or any of the guys?"

She didn't answer, fixed intently on her wool. My heart cracked, wondering how long she'd been working on her knitting. How the hundreds of years of time had warped her spirit. Maud was one of only a few old Ash Grove spirits who'd refused to move forward. I recalled her asking me what lay beyond, and I couldn't respond then.

Walking up to her, I placed a gentle palm over her knitting needles. "Do you still want to know what death is like when you move on?"

Her misty gray eyes shot to mine. "Yes, can you tell me now, reaper?"

I inhaled deeply, realizing it wasn't February's chill that greeted me. Sweet, cool night air with a promise of warmth invaded my lungs. *Spring.*

Closing my eyes, I ran my thumb along her bony knuckles as I clutched her fists. My smiled bloomed when the visions flashed through my mind, and I spoke as they appeared. "I see a shop full of ribbons. Blues, purples, and greens. There's a man and a woman behind the counter waiting for you with a tray of," I giggled softly, "chocolate fudge, it looks like. The man with the white mustache says he's been waiting for you to come home. Waiting for you to work the shop with him."

My fingers dampened, and when I opened my eyes, I watched Maud's tears fall like rain. I didn't know that ghosts could cry. "That's not like the Heaven I read about in church."

"I know, but I believe it's yours if you want it."

With a sniffle, she nodded, and I saw her real face then. The face of a young woman with ringlet curls all tied in bows and lace. "I think I'm ready now. Thank you, reaper."

"Mortala," I corrected, opening my arms.

With a smile, she repeated my newfound title, the one I'd learned from the Dragon Queen. "It suits you. You're growing," she said proudly before hugging me tight. "But something is watching you closely. Be careful, Mortala, my friend."

With my next breath, my arms closed into my chest. Maud was gone. Despite the unease that pricked my skin at her last words, I wiped a tear from my cheek as I picked up her knitted blanket that had fallen to the ground. When I closed my eyes, I heard the bells of the shop jingle as the shop owners laughed and cheered. Maud was accepted into her paradise of ribbons and fudge and love. The smell of sugar and cocoa tickled my nose and warmed my chest. It was perfect for her.

I exhaled a shaky breath and looked around the cemetery surrounded by the opaque woods of Ash Grove, my home. This was my town, and no witch, monster, or threat would keep me away from it. I was back where I belonged, and nothing would scare me away ever again. But where were my men?

Strolling closer to the tree line, I peered into the darkness, making out images of brush and branches through the disappearing fog. A twig snapped, and another. Something huge rumbled the ground with its steps. My heel snagged on a tree root, and I stumbled backward. Regardless of what it was, whatever monster or darkness, I was a bigger monster, a greater dark, and I could handle it. I would always find a way. There were countless keys inside me, just waiting for their doors to be revealed.

A growl reverberated through the forest, shaking the trees and sending birds fleeing in a frenzy. I felt it in my bones, the ferocity and carnal urge behind the low, guttural sound. My heart jolted as a beast's amber eyes glowed like fireflies in the shadows. It stalked forward on powerful smoky claws. Ears laid back, it sniffed and bared its sharp teeth. I reached out a trembling palm as it stalked forward, staring me down. I knew those eyes and that terrifying maw as I looked up at his enormous and powerful shifted form.

"Wolf?" I asked on an unsteady breath.

He didn't stop, didn't show any flash of recognition in his primal gaze. Stopping at the base of a giant oak, he tilted his snout to the sky. My body startled in shock as he howled, deep and forlorn, before fixing his gaze to me again. I would have fared better against a legion of demons or a baphomet, because a plan of escape evaded me. His gaze was possessive and hungry … oh, so hungry.

My blood chilled at the lack of warmth and kindness I'd come to admire. I didn't know who this beast was. The Wolfgang I knew would never try to frighten me. I crawled backward, palms slipping on damp soil. He snarled, and I realized I shouldn't have done that, shouldn't have tried to flee a predator. Ghost had warned me once before, in this very cemetery, to never try to run from a monster. Queen Cassiopeia's words haunted through my thoughts. *We gave them a taste, and now they are slaves to their cravings.* If that was true, then I would forever be theirs to take, giving in and giving them whatever piece of me they desired. And Wolf was no different. I stopped crawling and took a deep breath. With a menacing growl, the werewolf leaped, and his black shadowy mass blocked my vision as he made his claiming attack.

Should I have expected any less?

Would you?

WE ARE the women who fell in love with monsters …

Afterword

Ready to howl at the moon after that ending? I understand. As a balm, I have some offerings. Wolf's primal and wild story releases on June 14th of 2023. Preorder here.

Sparks fly when Count Drakon meets Cassiopeia. Catch a glimpse of the first vampires and the heat between Onyx's parents from years past. Read the short story, *Stay for a Bite* for FREE by signing up for my newsletter at katblackthorne.com.

If you loved The Halloween Boys, I'd so appreciate a review on your favorite platform. And join my coven on Facebook to chat all things spooky and spoilers. You can also see updates and top secret first looks on my Patreon.

Acknowledgments

To everyone who loves my fire and my ice. Who shows up when I burn everything down and when I freeze everyone out. You're my family.

For my coven on Facebook, my patrons, every booktoker, bookstagrammer, and ARC reader. Your passion keeps me writing when I want to delete it all and become a bunny breeder in the woods. I don't think I'd be good at giving the bunnies away so this is probably the safer bet for me career wise.

To my team, that includes everyone from baristas to editors. I cherish every bit of kindness and support the world gives me.

AND TO YOU, READER. *THANK YOU FOR MAKING MY SWEET NIGHTMARES COME TRUE.*

- Sign up for my newsletter to be the first to know about new book releases
- Join my patreon for NSFW art, early chapters of The Halloween Boys, secret projects, and more.
- Join me on #spicybooktok TikTok:
- See fan edits on Instagram:
- Follow for updates and quotes on Twitter:
- Follow me on Amazon for upcoming books:
- Join my reader coven on FB

Business or press inquires please email
katblackthorneauthor@gmail.com

Also by Kat Blackthorne

The Halloween Boys

Ghost

Dragon

Wolf

Devil

Wicked Ecstasy

The other villains of Ash Grove

Come For A Spell

Familiar Taste

Hot Queens

Contemporary polyamory

Hotwife

Hot Life

Let it Snow Queen

Browse by Trope for more

at katblackthorne.com